GIN BLANCO HAS CRITICS SNARED IN HER WEB!

More praise for Jennifer Estep's thrilling Elemental Assassin series
SPIDER'S BITE

"Bodies litter the pages of this first entry in Estep's engrossing Elemental Assassin series. . . . Urban Fantasy fans will love it."

—*Publishers Weekly*

"When it comes to work, Estep's newest heroine is brutally efficient and very pragmatic, which gives the new Elemental Assassin series plenty of bite. Shades of gray rule in this world where magic and murder are all too commonplace. The gritty tone of this series gives Estep a chance to walk on the darker side. Kudos to her for the knife-edged suspense!"

—*Romantic Times*

"The fast pace, clever dialogue, and intriguing heroine help make this new series launch by the author of the Bigtime paranormal romance series one to watch."

—*Library Journal*

"Loaded with action and intrigue, the story is strong and exciting. . . . With a knock-out, climactic ending and a surprising twist that I didn't see coming, I was definitely impressed. This dark, urban fantasy series has a promising start."

—*SciFiChick.com*

"Electrifying! Jennifer Estep really knows how to weave a fantasy tale that will keep you reading way past your bedtime."

—*ReadingwithMonie.com*

The Elemental Assassin titles are also available as eBooks

"*Spider's Bite* is a raw, gritty, and compelling walk on the wild side, one that had me hooked from the first page. Jennifer Estep has created a fascinating heroine in the morally ambiguous Gin Blanco—I can't wait to read the next chapter of Gin's story."

—Nalini Singh, *New York Times* bestselling author
of *Archangel's Kiss*

"Watch out world, here comes Gin Blanco. Funny, smart, and dead sexy."

—Lilith Saintcrow, author of *Flesh Circus*

"I love rooting for the bad guy—especially when she's also the heroine. *Spider's Bite* is a sizzling combination of mystery, magic, and murder. Kudos to Jennifer Estep!"

—Jackie Kessler, author of *Shades of Gray*

"Jennifer Estep is a dark, lyrical, and fresh voice in urban fantasy. Brimming with high-octane–fueled action, labyrinthine conspiracies, and characters who will steal your heart, *Spider's Bite* is an original, fast-paced, tense, and sexy read. Gin is an assassin to die for."

—Adrian Phoenix, author of *Black Dust Mambo*

"A sexy and edgy thriller that keeps you turning the pages. In *Spider's Bite,* Jennifer Estep turns up the heat and suspense with Gin Blanco, an assassin whose wit is as sharp as her silverstone knives. . . . She'll leave no stone unturned and no enemy breathing in her quest for revenge. *Spider's Bite* leaves you dying for more."

—Lisa Shearin, national bestselling author
of *Bewitched and Betrayed*

KARMA GIRL

"Chick lit meets comics lit in Estep's fresh debut. . . . A zippy prose style helps lift this zany caper far above the usual run of paranormal romances."

—*Publishers Weekly*

Venom

AN ELEMENTAL ASSASSIN BOOK

JENNIFER ESTEP

POCKET BOOKS

New York   London   Toronto   Sydney

Pocket Books
A Division of Simon & Schuster, Inc.
1230 Avenue of the Americas
New York, NY 10020

This book is a work of fiction. Names, characters, places, and incidents either are products of the author's imagination or are used fictitiously. Any resemblance to actual events or locales or persons, living or dead, is entirely coincidental.

First Pocket Books paperback edition October 2010

POCKET and colophon are registered trademarks of Simon & Schuster, Inc.

For information about special discounts for bulk purchases, please contact Simon & Schuster Special Sales at 1-866-506-1949 or business@simonandschuster.com.

The Simon & Schuster Speakers Bureau can bring authors to your live event. For more information or to book an event contact the Simon & Schuster Speakers Bureau at 1-866-248-3049 or visit our website at www.simonspeakers.com.

Cover design and illustration by Tony Mauro

Manufactured in the United States of America

10   9   8   7   6   5   4   3   2   1

ISBN 978-1-4391-4801-3
ISBN 978-1-4391-5545-5 (ebook)

As always, this book is dedicated to my mom, grandma, and Andre. Your love and support make me a better person.

Acknowledgments

Once again, my heartfelt thanks go out to all the folks who help turn my crazy words into a real book.

Thanks to my super agent, Annelise Robey, and to my equally super editors, Megan McKeever and Lauren McKenna, for all their editorial advice, input, and encouragement. Writing about Gin wouldn't be nearly as much fun without your support.

Thanks to everyone who read the rough draft of *Venom* and helped me with a plot point. Your comments were insightful and greatly appreciated.

And finally, to all the readers out there. It's been a pleasure sharing Gin and her adventures with you.

Happy reading!

✳ 1 ✳

The bastards never even would have gotten close to me if I hadn't had the flu.

Coughing, sneezing, aching, wheezing. That was me. Gin Blanco. Restaurant owner. Stone and Ice elemental. Former assassin. And all-around badass. Laid low by a microbe.

It had started as a small, ominous tickle in my throat three days ago. And now, well, it wasn't pretty. Watery eyes. Pale face. And a nose so red and bright even Rudolph would have been jealous. Ugh.

The only reason I'd even crawled out of bed this evening was to come down to Ashland Community College and take the final for the classic literature class I was auditing. I'd finished my essay on symbolism in *The Odyssey* ten minutes ago. Now I plodded across one of the grassy campus quads and feverishly dreamed of sinking back into my bed and not getting out of it for a week.

Just after seven on a cold, clear December night. This was the last day of finals for the semester, and the campus was largely deserted. Only a few lights burned in the windows of the kudzu-covered brick buildings that rose above my head. The stones whispered of formulas, theories, and knowledge. An old, sonorous, slightly pretentious sound that was decidedly at odds with the sinister shadows that blackened most of the quad. No one else was within sight. Which is probably why they decided to jump me here. Well, that and the fact that kidnapping me would be such a *bother*.

One second I had my face buried in a tissue blowing my sore, drippy nose for the hundredth time today. The next, I looked up to find myself surrounded by three giants.

Oh, fuck.

I stopped, and they immediately closed ranks, forming a loose triangle of trouble around me. The giants were all around seven feet tall, with oversize, buglike eyes and fists almost as big as my head. One of them grinned at me and cracked his knuckles. Someone was anxious to get down to the business of beating me.

My gray eyes flicked to the leader of the group, who had taken up a position in front of me—Elliot Slater. Slater was the tallest of the three giants, his enormous figure making even his flunkies seem small in comparison. He was almost as wide as he was tall, with a solid, muscled frame. Granite would be easier to break than his ribs. Slater's complexion was pale, bordering on albino, and almost seemed to glow in the faint light. His hazel eyes provided a bit of color in his chalky skin, although his thin, tousled thatch of blond hair did little to cover his large skull. A diamond in his pinkie ring sparkled like a star in the dark night.

Up until my retirement a few months ago, I'd moon-lighted as an assassin known as the Spider. Over the years, I'd had plenty of dealings in the shady side of life, so I knew Slater by sight and reputation. On paper, Elliot Slater was a highly respected security consultant with his own platoon of giant bodyguards. In reality, Slater was the number-one enforcer for Mab Monroe, the Fire el-emental who ran the Southern metropolis of Ashland like it was her own personal fiefdom. Slater stepped in and ei-ther cut off, took care of, or permanently disposed of any pesky problems Mab didn't feel like dealing with herself.

And tonight it looked like that problem was me.

Not surprising. A couple of weeks ago, I'd stiffed some-one during a party at Mab Monroe's mansion. Needless to say, the Fire elemental hadn't been too thrilled about one of her guests being murdered in her own home when she'd been entertaining a few hundred of her closest busi-ness associates. I'd gotten away with it so far, but I knew Mab was doing everything in her power to find the killer. To find *me*.

I sniffled into my tissue. I wondered if Mab had fig-ured out who I really was. If that was why Slater was here tonight—

Elliot Slater looked over his broad shoulder. "Is this her?"

Slater slid to one side so another man, a much shorter human, could join the circle of giants surrounding me. Underneath his classic trench coat, the man wore a perfect black suit, and his polished wingtips gleamed like wet ink in the semidarkness. His thick mane of gunmetal gray hair resembled a heavy mantle of silver that had somehow been swirled and sculpted around his head. Too bad hate made his brown eyes look like congealed lumps of blood in his smooth, tight face.

I recognized him too. Jonah McAllister. On paper, McAllister was the city's premiere attorney, a charming, bellicose defense lawyer capable of getting the most vicious killer off scot-free—for the right price. In reality, the slick attorney was another one of Mab Monroe's top goons, just like Elliot Slater was. Jonah McAllister was Mab's personal lawyer, responsible for burying her enemies in legal red tape instead of in the ground like Slater did.

McAllister's son, Jake, was the one I'd murdered at Mab's party. The twentysomething, beefy frat boy had threatened to rape and murder me, among other things. I'd considered killing him pest extermination more than anything else.

Elliot Slater and Jonah McAllister tag-teaming me. This night just kept getting better and better. I sniffled again. Really should have stayed home in bed.

Jonah McAllister regarded me with cold eyes. "Oh, yes. That's her. The lovely Ms. Gin Blanco. The bitch who was giving my boy a hard time."

A hard time? I supposed so, if you thought turning him in to the cops for attempted robbery, breaking a plate full of food in his face, and ultimately stabbing Jake McAllister to death was a hard time. But I noticed that Jonah McAllister didn't say anything about me actually *killing* his son. Hmm. Looked like this was some sort of fishing expedition. I decided to play along—for now.

"What is this meeting all about?" My voice came out somewhere between a whiny wheeze and a phlegmy rasp. "Are you taking up Jake's bad habit of assaulting innocent people?"

Jonah McAllister's face hardened at my insult. As much as it could, anyway. Despite his sixty-some years, McAllister's features were as smooth as polished marble, thanks to a vigorous regimen of expensive Air elemental facial treatments. "I would hardly consider you innocent, Ms. Blanco. And you're the one who assaulted my precious boy first."

"Your *precious boy* came into my restaurant, tried to rob me, and almost killed two of my customers with his Fire elemental magic." I spat out the words, along with some phlegm. "All I did was defend myself. What does it matter now anyway? Your boy is dead because of some weird heart condition. At least, that's what was in the newspaper."

Jonah McAllister stared at me, trying to see if I knew more than I was letting on about his son's untimely demise. I used the lull to blow my nose—again. Fucking microbes.

McAllister's mouth twisted with disgust at the sight and sound of my sniffles. Admittedly, it wasn't my most attractive moment. He jerked his head at Elliot Slater, who nodded back.

"Now, Ms. Blanco," Slater drawled. "The reason for this meeting is that Mr. McAllister thought you might have some information about his son's death. Jake did have a bit of a heart condition, but there were also some suspicious circumstances surrounding his passing. Happened a couple of weeks ago."

Suspicious circumstances? I assumed that was polite talk for a sucking stab wound to the chest. But I kept my face blank and ignorant.

"Why would I know anything about Jake's death?" I asked. "The last time I saw the little punk was the day he brought his old man there down to the Pork Pit to threaten me into dropping the charges against him."

Lies, of course. I'd run into Jake McAllister one more time after that—at Mab Monroe's party. Even though I'd been gussied up as a hooker, he'd still recognized me. Since I'd been there to kill someone else, I'd lured sweet little Jakie into a bathroom, stabbed him to death, left his body in the bathtub, and washed the blood off my dress before going back out to the party. Nothing I hadn't done a hundred times before as the assassin the Spider. I certainly hadn't lost any sleep over it.

But right now, it looked like I might lose a whole lot more.

"See, that's the problem. My good friend Jonah doesn't believe you. So he asked me and some of my boys to come down here and see if perhaps we could jog something free from your memory." Slater smiled. His lips drew back, giving me a glimpse of his pale pink gums. The giant's grin reminded me of a jack-o'-lantern's gaping maw—completely hollow. "We're going to pay these sorts of visits to anyone Jake might have had a problem with. And your name was at the top of the list."

Of course it was. I was probably the only person in

Ashland who'd ever dared to stand up to Jake McAllister. Now his daddy was going to make me pay for it.

Slater took off his suit jacket, handed it to Jonah McAllister, and started rolling up his shirtsleeves.

I sniffled, blew my nose again, and considered the situation. Four-on-one odds were never terrific, especially since three of the four men were giants. The oversize goons could be hard to bring down, even for a former assassin like me. None of the giants showed any obvious elemental abilities, like letting flames flicker on their clenched fists or forming Ice daggers with their bare hands. But that didn't mean they didn't have magic. Which would make them doubly hard to get rid of.

Still, if I hadn't had the flu, I might have considered killing them—or at least cutting down a couple so I could run away. Although I'd dragged myself out of bed this evening, I'd grabbed my silverstone knives on the way out the door. Five of them. Two tucked up my sleeves. One nestled in the small of my back. Two more in the sides of my boots. Never left home without them.

Of course, being an elemental myself I didn't really need my knives to kill. I could just use my magic to take down the giants. My Stone power was so strong that I could do practically anything I wanted to with the element. Like make bricks fly out of the wall of one of the surrounding buildings and use them to brain the giants in their melon-size heads. *Splat, splat, splat.* It'd be easier than using an Uzi. Hell, if I really wanted to show off, I could just crumble all four of the buildings that ringed the quad down on top of them.

I was also one of the rare elementals who could control more than one element. Stone and Ice, in my case. Until recently, my Ice magic had been far weaker than my Stone power. But thanks to a series of traumatic events, I could do much more with it now. Like create a wall of Ice knives to fling at the men. I'd sliced through a dwarf's skin doing just that. Giants weren't quite as tough as dwarves, at least when it came to cutting into them. Even if they did have more blood to spare than their shorter compatriots.

But the odds or how to go about killing the giants wasn't what was holding me back. Not really. It was the consequences; what would happen afterward when their boss, Mab Monroe, got involved.

Seventeen years ago, Mab Monroe had used her elemental Fire magic to kill my mother and older sister, a fact I'd only recently learned. She'd also tortured me, using her magic to superheat and burn a spider rune medallion into my palms. I was planning to deal with Mab myself after I figured out a few things, like why she'd murdered my family in the first place and where my long-lost baby sister, Bria, was now.

Taking care of Jonah McAllister and the rest of his hired help tonight would definitely tip my hand and draw even more of Mab's attention my way. I didn't want Mab and her minions to realize that I had any elemental magic. To suspect that I was anything more than the simple restaurant owner Jonah McAllister wanted dead for tattling on his son to the cops. At least, not before I killed her for what she'd done to me.

All that left me with only one option tonight—I was going to have to let the giants hurt me, beat me. That was the only way I could keep my cover identity as Gin Blanco safe, along with who I really was, Genevieve Snow.

Fuck. This was going to hurt.

Elliot Slater finished rolling up his sleeves. "Are you sure you don't have anything to tell us, Ms. Blanco?"

I sighed and shook my head. "I told you before. I don't know anything about Jake McAllister's death except what I read in the newspaper."

"I'm sorry to hear that," Slater murmured.

The giant stepped forward and flexed his fingers, ready to get on with things. Time for me to put on a little show. I widened my eyes, as though it had just sunk into my flu-addled brain what Elliot Slater was planning to do to me. I let out a phlegmy scream and turned to run, as though I'd forgotten all about the two giants standing behind me. I ran right into them, of course, and they reached for me. Even though I had no real intention of trying to break free, I still struggled to keep up appearances. Yelling, flailing, kicking out with my legs.

While I fought with the bigger, heavier men, I managed to discreetly slip the two silverstone knives that I had up my sleeves into the pockets of my jacket. I didn't want the giants to feel the weapons when they finally latched onto me. Most innocent women didn't go around wearing five knives on them, and my being so heavily armed would be the final nail in my coffin as far as Jonah McAllister was concerned about my involvement in his son's death.

The two giants laughed at me and my weak, exaggerated blows. After a minute of struggling, they seized my upper arms and turned me around to face Elliot Slater once more.

And that's when the fun really started.

Slater snapped his hand up and slammed his fist into my face. Bastard was quick, I'd give him that. I hadn't braced myself for the blow, and I jerked back in the giants' arms. The force almost tore me out of their grasp. Pain exploded like dynamite in my jaw.

But Slater didn't stop there. He spent the next two minutes beating me. One punch broke my drippy nose. Another cracked two of my ribs. And I didn't even want to think about the internal bleeding or what my face looked like at this point. *Thud, thud, thud.* I might as well have been a piece of meat the giant was tenderizing for dinner. Every part of me hurt and burned and throbbed and pulsed with pain.

And he laughed the whole time. Low, soft, chuckling laughs that made my skin crawl. Elliot Slater enjoyed hurting people. Really enjoyed it. His hard-on bulged against the zipper on his black pants.

Slater hit me again and stepped back. By this point, I hung limp between the two giants, all pretense of being tough and strong long gone. I just wanted this to be over with.

A hand grabbed my chin and forced my face up. I stared into Slater's hazel eyes. At least, I tried to. White starbursts kept exploding over and over in my field of vision, making it hard to focus. The light show was better than fireworks on the Fourth of July.

"Now," Elliot rumbled. "Do you want to reconsider what you know about Jake McAllister's death? Maybe you have something new to add?"

"I don't know anything about Jake's death," I mumbled

through a mouthful of loose teeth. Blood spewed out of my split lips and cascaded down my navy fleece jacket. "I swear." I made my voice as low, weak, and whipped as I could.

Jonah McAllister stepped forward and peered at me. Malicious glee shimmered in his brown gaze. "Keep hitting her. I want the bitch to suffer."

Elliot Slater nodded and stepped back.

The giant spent another two minutes hitting me. More pain, more blood, more cracked ribs. As I coughed up another mouthful of coppery blood, it dawned on me that Slater just might beat me to death, right here in the middle of the campus quad. Jonah McAllister certainly wouldn't have any objections to that. Damn. Looked like I was going to have to go for my knives, blast them with my elemental magic, and blow my cover after all, if I still had the strength to do that—

"Enough."

A low voice floated out from somewhere deeper in the shadows. A soft, breathy sound that reminded me of pieces of silk wisping together. I knew that tone, that sultry cadence, knew exactly whom it belonged to. So did my inner psyche. *Enemy, enemy, enemy,* a little voice muttered in the back of my head. A strange, primal, elemental urge flooded my body, the desire to use my Stone and Ice magic to lash out and kill whoever and whatever was within striking distance.

Elliot Slater ignored the command and hit me again, adding to the pain that racked my body.

"I said *enough.*" The voice dropped to a low hiss that crackled with power, menace, and the promise of death.

Elliot froze, his hand pulled halfway back to hit me again.

"Let her go. Now."

The two giants who'd had their hands clamped around my upper arms dropped me like I had the plague. I lay on the ground, my blood soaking into the frosty grass. Despite the pain, I managed to roll over onto my side. I also slid one of my silverstone knives out of my jacket pocket and palmed it. The weapon felt cold and comforting against the thick scar embedded in my palm.

Something rustled, and Mab Monroe stepped out of the shadows to my left.

The Fire elemental wore a long wool coat done in a dark forest green. Her red hair gleamed like polished copper, but her eyes were even blacker than the night sky. A bit of gold flashed around her pale throat in between the folds of her expensive coat.

I couldn't see that well, given the stars still exploding in my vision, but I knew what the gold flash was. Mab Monroe never went anywhere without wearing her signature rune necklace. A large, circular ruby surrounded by several dozen wavy rays. From previous sightings, I knew the intricate diamond cutting on the gold would catch the meager light and make it seem as though the rays were actually flickering. Or perhaps my vision was just that screwed up at the moment.

Still, I knew what the rune was. A sunburst. The symbol for fire. Mab Monroe's personal rune, used by her alone.

At the sight, the silverstone scars on my own palms started to itch and burn. Mab wasn't the only one here with a rune. I had one too. A small circle surrounded by eight thin rays. A spider rune. The symbol for patience. The rune had once been a medallion I'd worn on a chain around my neck, until Mab had used her Fire elemental magic to superheat and burn the silverstone metal into my palms like it was a cattle brand. That's how she'd tortured me the night she'd murdered my family. I was looking forward to returning the favor—someday soon.

Enemy, enemy, enemy; the little voice in the back of my head kept up its muttered chorus.

Mab Monroe walked over and stood beside Elliot Slater and Jonah McAllister. She glanced down at me with all the interest she might give a cockroach before she crushed it under the toe of her boot. Her dark eyes swallowed up the available light, the way a black hole might. I lay very, very still and tried to look like I was a mere inch away from death. Not much of a stretch tonight.

"I said enough, Jonah," Mab said. "Or have you forgotten that you and Elliot work for me?"

After a moment, Elliot Slater stepped back and bowed his head in deference. The other two giants did the same. But Jonah McAllister was too angry to heed the hard edge in Mab's breathy tone.

"This bitch made problems for my son, and I think she knows something about his death," McAllister barked. "I want her to pay for that. I want her to *die* for that."

Mab stared down at me again. "You're letting your emotions cloud your judgment, Jonah. Ignoring the facts. It's most unbecoming."

"And what would those *facts* be?" McAllister demanded.

"That Ms. Blanco is just a woman, a mere, weak woman with no elemental magic or other notable strength or skills. Otherwise, I'm sure she would have used everything at her disposal to keep from being so viciously beaten tonight. She's not the person you're looking for, Jonah. More importantly, she's not the woman *I'm* looking for."

McAllister's brown eyes glittered. "You and your obsession with that blond whore. Why can't you accept the fact that she's dead? Buried somewhere in that coal mine, just like Tobias Dawson and his two men were?"

Mab's eyes grew even blacker. She reached for her Fire elemental magic, holding the power close to her like she might a lover. As an elemental myself, I could feel her magic, especially since she was consciously embracing it. Just the way Mab might have been able to sense my Stone and Ice magic, if I'd been stupid enough to actually reach for any of it.

Of course, I would have felt Mab's magic anyway, since she was one of the elementals who constantly gave off waves of power. The Fire elemental literally leaked magic, the way water would drip from a faucet. Unlike me. As long as I didn't draw upon my own elemental strength, didn't use it in any offensive way, others couldn't sense my power. A trait that had saved me more than once over the years.

Mab's magic pricked my skin like hot, invisible needles, adding to my misery, but I stayed still, giving no indication I could sense it—or that I knew what they were talking about.

"I doubt that hooker was a real hooker, and they never

found her body in the rubble of the collapsed mine," Mab replied in a cold voice. "Until I see her body, she's not dead. I'm going to find her, Jonah, and then we can both have our revenge. She killed Dawson, and she's the one who killed your son. Not Ms. Blanco."

They were talking about the night of Mab's party, when I'd dressed up as a hooker to get close to Tobias Dawson, a greedy mine owner who was threatening some innocent people. Dawson was the one I was supposed to kill that night, but Jake McAllister had spotted me before I'd had a chance to do the hit. Mab had caught me in the bathroom a few minutes after I'd stabbed Jake to death. Evidently, the Fire elemental had put two and two together and realized that I'd stiffed Jake, then done the same to Tobias Dawson later on in his own mine. Not good.

"I agreed to this little test with the understanding that Ms. Blanco would live through it, should she prove herself to be innocent of your son's murder," Mab continued. "She's done so, at least to my satisfaction. Nobody would willingly let herself be beaten the way she has."

So Mab didn't understand the concept of self-sacrifice. Not surprising. I might have laughed, if it wouldn't have hurt so much. Still, I was doubly glad that I'd let Elliot Slater hit me. Otherwise, I would have been dead by now, ambushed from the sidelines by Mab and her elemental Fire magic.

"Who cares if the bitch lives or dies?" Jonah McAllister scoffed. "She's nobody."

"That might be true, but unfortunately, Ms. Blanco is not without friends," Mab replied. "Most notably the Deveraux sisters."

"I don't care about those two dwarves," Jonah snapped. "You could easily kill both of them."

Mab gave a delicate shrug of her shoulders. "Perhaps. But Jo-Jo Deveraux is quite popular. It might be entertaining, but killing her wouldn't win me any favors. Besides, I have other concerns at the moment, most notably Coolidge."

My dazed mind latched onto the unfamiliar name. Coolidge? Who was Coolidge? And what had he done to piss off Mab Monroe?

"You've had your fun, Jonah. Face it, Ms. Blanco isn't the one who killed Jake. And she's suffered plenty tonight for whatever insults she laid on him previously. Now, are you going to come quietly so we can talk business? Or should I start looking for a new attorney?" Malice dripped from Mab's voice like acid rain.

Jonah McAllister finally realized he wasn't going to win this one. And that if he kept arguing with his boss, she was likely to use her Fire magic to fry him where he stood. So the lawyer clamped his lips together and nodded his head, acquiescing to his boss's wishes. At least for tonight.

Then the silver-haired bastard turned and kicked me in the stomach as hard as he could.

The blow wasn't entirely unexpected, but it still made me retch up even more blood. Something hot and hard twisted in my stomach. I needed to get to Jo-Jo Deveraux soon so the dwarven Air elemental could heal me. Otherwise, I wouldn't be breathing much longer.

"Fine. We'll move on to the next person, then." Jonah McAllister leaned down and grabbed my brown ponytail, pulling my face up to his. "You talk to the cops about this, bitch, and you will die. Understand me?"

Cops? Oh, I had no intention of going to the cops. No siree. I was going to handle this matter all by my lonesome. But to keep up the act, I let out a low groan and nodded my head. Satisfied that I was suitably cowed this time, McAllister let go. I flopped back onto the ground.

"Let's get out of here," the lawyer growled. "The bitch dripped blood all over my coat."

Jonah McAllister stepped over my prone body and disappeared into the darkness. Elliot Slater and the other two giants followed him. But Mab Monroe stayed where she was and studied me with her dark gaze. Her power washed over me again, the invisible, fiery needles pricking my bloody skin. I bit back another groan.

"I do hope you've learned your lesson this time, Ms. Blanco," Mab said in a pleasant voice. "Because Jonah's right. Next time you cross one of us—any of us—you will die. And I promise you that it will be far more excruciating than what you've experienced here tonight."

A bit of black fire flashed in her eyes, backing up her deadly promise. Mab Monroe smiled at me a moment longer, then turned on her boot heel and vanished into the cold night.

☼ 2 ☼

After Mab left, I must have passed out from the pain. Because the next thing I knew, a pair of scuffed black boots were planted on the ground in front of me. Whether they belonged to friend or foe, well, I didn't much care at the moment. I just lay there, too beaten, bloody, and bruised to move. The cold blades of grass dug into my throbbing cheek like miniature icicles. The frosty chill felt good against my feverish skin.

A walkie-talkie squawked above my head, and someone started speaking. It took me a moment to focus on the clipped words.

". . . a body on the southwest quad between the English and history buildings . . ."

A body? Didn't he realize I wasn't dead yet? He probably hadn't even checked for a pulse. Probably hadn't wanted to touch me, given all the blood. Couldn't blame him for that. Besides, this quad was close to Southtown, the part of Ashland where the homeless bums, junkies, vampire prostitutes, and other rough types lived. Mine wouldn't have been the first body to bleed out on the community college campus. Still, if I'd felt like it, I would have rolled my eyes. I wasn't dead-dead. Just halfway there.

I craned up my neck so I could see my would-be rescuer. One of the community college's rent-a-cops stood above me, a black walkie-talkie clipped to his shoulder like he was a real officer. He let go of a red button on the device, and another squawk sounded. I couldn't make out the first few garbled words, but I caught the gist of the conversation.

". . . cops on their way . . ."

Jonah McAllister had warned me not to call the police, and I'd been planning on following his wishes. Not because I was afraid of the lawyer and what he might do to me, but because I intended to take care of McAllister myself—with no help and no outside interference. But it looked like the po-po were coming whether I wanted them to or not. Nothing I could do about it now.

So I put my head back down on the grass and closed my eyes. I already looked the part. Might as well play dead and rest up until the cops got here.

I wasn't sure how long I lay there on the ground, drifting in and out of consciousness, but the lights pulled me up out of the soft blackness I was swimming in. Red and blue lights swirled around and around far above my head. I squinted into the glare. Someone had parked a dark SUV on the grass a few feet away from me. The vehicle doors opened, and two pairs of boots hit the ground. One set definitely belonged to a man, a giant judging from the size. The shoes were almost as long as my arm. The other pair of boots were decidedly feminine, smaller and smartly cut with a low, sensible heel.

The boots crunched on the frosty grass and headed in my direction, joining the ones of the security guard. I got the sense the three of them were staring down at me.

"Is this how you found her? Just lying there like that?" The woman spoke in a voice that was as light and high and delicate as a set of wind chimes. It would have been a pure, lovely sound if not for the cold, flat resignation in her tone. Mine wasn't the first body she'd seen. Maybe not even the first one today.

"Yes, ma'am," the security guard replied. "I was making my usual rounds and called you guys right away."

Well, now that I had a proper audience, it was time for Gin Blanco to come back from the dead, so to speak. I pulled in a breath and rolled over onto my back. The dull wave of pain I'd been surfing on surged into a tidal wave that threatened to drown me. A low groan escaped my lips, and white starbursts filled my vision again.

Silence.

"You idiot! She's not dead. Didn't you check her pulse before you called us?" the woman snapped. "Call the paramedics, Xavier. Right now before she bleeds out."

Xavier? I knew him. He was the giant who worked as a bouncer at a nightclub called Northern Aggression. Xavier also moonlighted for the Ashland police force on occasion. He wasn't what I would call a close friend, but he'd probably help me if I asked him nicely enough. And slipped him some money later. C-notes would buy you all the friends you wanted in Ashland.

When I'd pushed the pain back down to a bearable level, I opened my eyes. The swirling police lights on the SUV made it hard to see the three figures, but I still recognized the giant. At around seven feet tall, Xavier was hard to miss with his shaved head and jet-colored skin and eyes.

"Xavier?" I mumbled, trying to move my broken jaw as little as possible.

More silence.

Then the three figures turned to stare at me once more. Probably shocked I could form a coherent sentence, much less actually speak, given the way my face looked right now.

"Do you know her, Xavier?" the woman asked.

A large knee flattened the grass beside me, and a shadow fell over my face, blocking the bright lights. I stared up into Xavier's dark eyes. The giant's gaze flicked over my features, trying to see through the blood, bruises, and swelling. Finally, comprehension filled his face.

"Gin?" he asked.

"In the flesh," I mumbled.

"Do you know her?" the woman asked again.

Xavier nodded his massive head. "Yeah, I know her. Name's Gin Blanco. She owns the Pork Pit. It's a barbecue restaurant a few blocks away. Geez, Gin, they really did a number on you, didn't they?"

"You're talking to her like she can actually understand you," the woman said somewhere above my head.

"That's because she can, detective," Xavier replied.

"Gin's the toughest gal I know. Takes a licking and keeps on ticking, just like a Timex. Isn't that right, Gin?"

"Right," I croaked. "Now, do me a favor."

"Name it."

"Call Finn."

Xavier nodded, pulled his cell phone off the holder on his belt, and flipped open the device. "What's his number?"

I forced out the numbers, which Xavier punched into his phone.

A few seconds later, the giant smiled. "My man, Finn. It's Xavier. Listen, I need to talk to you about Gin . . ."

I let myself drift as Xavier explained the situation to Finnegan Lane. After a brief conversation, Xavier snapped his phone shut.

"The man's on his way. Should be here in about five minutes. He said to tell you that he's calling Jo-Jo right now, whatever that means."

I nodded. Jo-Jo was Jo-Jo Deveraux, the dwarven Air elemental who always healed me whenever I got into a rough scrape. Like the one tonight.

"Good," I croaked. "Now, help me sit up. Please."

"You really shouldn't move her—" the female detective started.

Too late. I wrapped my hand around Xavier's massive forearm, and the giant eased me up into a sitting position. It took me several moments to get my breath back and blink the white spots out of my vision. Once I did, I realized I was the center of attention. While I'd been unconscious, someone had strung yellow crime scene tape around the spot where I'd been lying. A small crowd of late-night students had gathered around the tape like vultures flocking to a fresh corpse. Several of them had their cell phones out, snapping pictures of my battered face to post on the local campus gossip websites.

I squinted against the glare, trying to see if I recognized anyone. I spotted a couple of other coeds from my classic literature class, but that was it. Hardly worth the effort of sitting up. The pain washed over me again, and I would have toppled over from the force of it if Xavier hadn't been propping me up. Right now, all I wanted to do was lie on a soft mattress somewhere, whimper, and plot my revenge against Mab Monroe, Elliot Slater, and most especially Jonah McAllister. Because the three of them were going to die. By my hand. Sooner, rather than later.

"Xavier, put her back down," the female detective snapped. "She needs medical attention. Immediately."

My eyes flicked up, but all I could see of the cop was her navy coat, the longish shag of her blond hair, and the three small rings she wore on her left index finger, which tapped out a quick pattern on her thigh. I would have tilted my head up so I could get a look at her face, if I hadn't thought the movement would make me vomit blood all over the detective's boots. Still, despite my limited view, something about the woman seemed familiar. Strangely so. Then again, the way my eyes were ping-ponging back and forth in their sockets, anything that didn't spin around felt familiar.

"You want her to asphyxiate on her own blood? Trust me. She needs to sit up," Xavier replied. "Besides, her friend will be here in a few minutes. Gin can hold her own until then. Can't you, Gin?"

"Oh yeah," I mumbled. "This is nothing. You should see me on a bad day."

The detective snorted. "Snappy comeback for a woman covered in her own blood."

"Oh, that's me," I said, staring at her jeans. "Snappy to the bitter, bitter end."

Against my side, I felt Xavier's wide chest quiver with contained laughter. At least I was amusing someone tonight.

The detective hitched up her jeans and crouched down in front of me, so we were eye level with each other. I blinked away another round of white starbursts and got my first good look at her.

And my heart stopped.

Longish, wavy, honey blond hair that curled under at the ends. Cornflower blue eyes. Perfect, rosy skin. A full, lush mouth. The detective was a breathtaking woman. But her beauty wasn't what made my raspy breath catch in my throat and my heart twist in my bruised chest. It was what was on the silver chain she wore around her neck.

A primrose.

A small silverstone rune shaped like a delicate primrose rested in the hollow of the detective's smooth throat. A primrose. The symbol for beauty. The same rune, the same necklace my baby sister, Bria, had worn as a child.

Bria.

She looked exactly the same as she did in a photo I had of her and exactly like my memories of our mother, Eira Snow. The only real differences were the hard glint in Bria's blue eyes and her tight, remote features. Both were more pronounced in person than they'd been in the picture. Bria's beauty was a cold, guarded one. An elemental Ice queen come to life in every sense of the word.

For a moment, I wondered if I was losing my mind. If I was already dead, and this was just some sort of bizarre dream or final wish fulfillment before the powers that be shipped me off to Hades. A brief, tantalizing glimpse of what I wanted to see most, only to be taken away as quickly as it had appeared.

I drew in a ragged breath and had to spit out another mouthful of warm, slick, coppery blood before it choked me. No, not a dream. A dream wouldn't hurt this much.

Bria, my baby sister, the one I'd thought was dead for the past seventeen years, the one I'd thought I'd inadvertently killed with my Ice and Stone magic, was here, crouching right in front of me. And all I could do was just stare at her.

Bria's blue eyes met mine. She frowned, as though puzzled by the wonderment in my gaze. "Ma'am, I understand you have a friend on the way. Personally, I'd suggest you wait for the paramedics to get here. You've got some serious, nasty injuries. You need to be stabilized before you go anywhere."

I kept staring at her. A pressure gathered in my chest, an icy fist squeezing my heart so tight and hard I thought it would explode right then and there. Shatter into a million icicles that would impale what was left of my body. An odd, cold wetness ran down my face. Tears this time, instead of blood. Big, fat, salty tears.

Crying. I was crying. I hadn't expected to cry when I saw Bria again. Hadn't expected to feel this icy tightness, this cavernous ache, this intense longing that made me want to scream and wail and weep all at the same time.

"Ma'am?" Bria asked again. "Can you hear me?"

I snapped out of my daze. Now was not the time to be thunderstruck. Now was the time to think, to piece the facts together. Bria was here in Ashland. A detective working for the po-po. I was in no position to talk to her tonight, in no position to do anything but gawk at her. But underneath the blood and bruises, I was still Gin Blanco. Restaurant owner. Stone and Ice elemental. Former assassin. And all-around badass. I could track down my sister easily enough when I was well. When I'd had some time to process her sudden reappearance in my life—and figure out what I was going to do about it.

I wet my split lips to say something, anything, to her. Anything to keep her right where she was—

"Gin! Gin!"

A male voice shouted my name. A moment later, Finnegan Lane stepped underneath the yellow crime scene tape and hurried over to me. Finn wore his usual uniform of a perfectly fitted, impeccable suit. A navy one today, with a powder blue shirt underneath. Even in the semidarkness, the light color further brightened his green eyes, which always reminded me of the smooth, polished glass of a soda pop bottle. His walnut-colored hair just curled over the collar of his suit jacket in an artful array of thick, sexy locks.

In addition to being my best friend, Finn was the son of my mentor, Fletcher Lane, the old man who'd taken me in off the streets years ago. An assassin himself, Fletcher had taught me everything I knew about my former profession. Finn was like a brother to me and one of the few people I trusted since the old man's murder a couple of months ago. Even though I'd retired from being the assassin the Spider, Finn was also my handler now, for lack of a better word. I might not be dealing in the shady side of life anymore, but Finn kept me informed of any goings-on that might impact me—as well as his own lucrative schemes in the corporate world of investment banking that he inhabited.

Finnegan Lane squatted down beside me and stared into my face. His green eyes swept over my bloody features, analyzing and assessing the damage just like his father, Fletcher, would have done once upon a time.

"Geez," Finn said. "I thought you looked bad yesterday. You look like shit tonight."

"Great to see you too, Finn," I replied in a dry tone. "Yesterday I just had the flu. As you can see, it's turned into something a bit more serious."

"Indeed," Finn murmured. "Indeed. And you can tell me all about it later. Right now, we need to get you out of here. Xavier, if you would be so kind?"

The giant nodded, put his free hand under my legs, and scooped me up into the air the way a child might pick up a wayward puppy. Finn held out his arms, and Xavier passed me over to him. They were being as easy and gentle as they could, but the movements hurt. Pain tightened my chest again, making it hard to breathe. Felt like one of my cracked ribs was scraping against my lungs. More blood also pooled in my mouth, but I swallowed it down. I was in enough agony already. I didn't want to have to listen to Finn bitch about me spewing blood all over his precious suit too. At this point, my ears were just about the only part of me that didn't burn with pain.

Finn turned toward the crime scene tape, but Bria got to her feet and stepped in front of him.

"Hold it," she snapped. "She's not going anywhere. The paramedics aren't here yet, and she needs medical attention."

Finn did what he always did when confronted by an angry woman—he checked out her boobs. His green eyes landed on Bria's breasts, analyzing and assessing them just the way he had my injuries a moment before. His lips curled back into a wolfish grin at the sight. If I'd felt stronger, I would have punched him for ogling my sister.

Once Finn got his fill of Bria's breasts, his green gaze drifted up to her face to check out the rest of the perky package. He'd seen the same photograph of Bria that I had. It took him a second to recognize her, but when he did, Finn's smile cracked, then flaked off his face like old paint. He blinked a couple of times, trying to make sure he was seeing exactly what he thought he was. When he realized that it really was Bria, Finn immediately looked down at me to see if I'd noticed her, if I'd recognized her. I nodded the tiniest bit to him.

"She's not going anywhere. The paramedics aren't here yet," Bria repeated and stabbed her finger into Finn's shoulder for emphasis.

That got Finn's attention. He didn't like anyone messing with his clothes, unless they were female and taking them off him. "I'm taking her to an Air elemental healer, and she's going to get the best medical attention there is in Ashland as soon as I get her out of here," Finn snapped. "Gin is my sister, and she's coming with me. So back off, copper."

Back off, copper? Geez. Finn had been watching too many old crime movies with Sophia Deveraux.

Bria's blue eyes narrowed. "Why don't we leave it up to Gin? See what she wants to do?"

Finn narrowed his own eyes in response. "Fine. She'll tell you herself that she's coming with me, detective."

The two of them glared at each other another moment, before staring at me. Finn, his features pinched tight. Bria, looking just as serious as he did. The man I considered my brother and my long-lost baby sister. Emotions welled up in my chest, making it hard to breathe. Or maybe the sensation was just from all the internal bleeding I was suffering from tonight. Either way, it *hurt*.

But I really only had one choice in the end. Finn was my foster brother, my closest confidant, my best friend, the one person I trusted above all others. Bria was a mercurial ghost from my past, a stranger with an angel's cold face. Gotta dance with the one who brung ya.

"Finn. I want . . . to go with Finn." For more reasons than one, it pained me to force out the words through my broken jaw, but I did it anyway. Pain and I were old, old friends.

Bria frowned and looked at Finn, who gave her a haughty, smug, I-told-you-so smirk. She turned her attention back to me.

"All right. That's your choice, ma'am. But before you go, can you tell me who did this to you? Who beat you?" Eyes hard, lips tight. Grim, determined features, but not unkind ones.

Detective Bria was just trying to do her job like an honest cop would. She seemed so . . . *good*. So protective of others. So willing to help. For some reason, all that made me proud of her. That she seemed to have grown up so strong. Right now, she still thought I was an innocent victim, instead of someone who'd brought all this on herself.

The absurd thought made me smile, but I don't think it came off very well because Bria blanched at the expression.

"I . . . fell," I rasped.

Against my side, Finn's chest twitched with laughter just the way Xavier's had a few minutes ago. Finn was trying to stifle a chuckle. He recognized sarcasm when he heard it, even if I was merely mumbling the words, instead of delivering them with my usual dose of dry, sardonic acid.

Bria's blond eyebrows shot up. "You fell? Onto what? Somebody's fists?"

"I fell," I repeated again.

Xavier stepped closer to Bria. "Let it go, detective. Just for tonight. Gin needs to get some help. I'll vouch for her and Finn."

Bria glanced at the giant, then at Finn, and finally back at me. She realized we were all aligned together, but she didn't rage and rail against us the way I thought she might. Instead, she gave a curt nod of her head. "All right, Ms. Blanco. You fell—for now. But don't think this is over. I'll have some questions for you in a few days when you're feeling better."

"Does that mean we can go now?" Finn drawled.

Bria's eyes narrowed. "Yeah, you can go now. And if I

find out your sister hasn't gotten the best medical treatment in Ashland, I'll be charging you with abuse. Got it, pal?"

Finn flashed her a wide, toothy grin. "Oh, I've definitely got your number, detective."

Bria snorted and turned on her heel, much the same way Mab Monroe had done earlier in the evening. She moved off and started talking to the security guard who'd found my supposedly dead body. I couldn't hear what she was saying to him, but the guy didn't seem pleased by Bria's short, clipped words. He scrunched his neck down into his jacket, a turtle pulling its head back into its shell. Looked like my sister was all grown up now—and something of a badass herself.

I wasn't sure if that was good or bad—or what I was going to do about the whole situation. Too many questions, not enough answers. Not to mention the relentless pain pounding through my body like a red-hot sledgehammer.

"Xavier, you have our thanks," Finn murmured to the giant. "I'll take good care of you the next time I'm at Northern Aggression. Promise."

Xavier nodded. "No problem. I helped you with your situation tonight, you can help me with mine tomorrow."

The two men exchanged a long look that was just a little too meaningful for my liking. What was that about? What kind of problem did Xavier have that he couldn't take care of himself? That he needed Finn's help with? The giant didn't strike me as the kind to hide money from the IRS, which was one of Finn's specialties. But I was in too much pain to puzzle it out tonight.

Finn nodded and carried me toward the yellow crime scene tape. Xavier lifted up the flimsy barrier for him, and we left the bloody, frosty grass of the quad behind.

"It's okay, Gin," Finn whispered in my ear. "I'm taking you to Jo-Jo's. She'll heal you up, and then we can figure out what to do about Bria being in Ashland. You can relax now. Everything's going to be okay."

Even though it felt like my own bones were stabbing me, I turned my neck, looked over Finn's shoulder, and stared at Bria. She was still busy berating the security guard, so she didn't see my pained gaze. My eyes landed on the primrose rune she wore around her neck. The blue and red lights made the silverstone metal gleam like a small moon in the semidarkness.

I never thought I'd see that rune again—much less my baby sister. But seventeen years later, seventeen years after the brutal, fiery murder of our mother and older sister, Bria was back in my life. The tightness in my chest swelled up again, stronger, colder, and harder than before.

The delicate primrose was the last thing I remembered seeing before the world went black.

❋ 3 ❋

I felt like I was on fire—from the inside out.

Hot needles stabbed up and down my body in a slow, relentless, agonizing path. My raw face, my broken jaw, my cracked ribs. The needles swept over everything, like I was some sort of warped voodoo doll come to life. The hot tingles made everything hurt even worse than it had before.

I whimpered and thrashed, trying to get away from the horrible, burning sensation.

"Hold her still, Sophia," a voice commanded. "Or her nose is going to look like something from a Halloween shop. You too, Finn."

A pair of iron hands tightened around my shoulders, immobilizing me. A larger but lighter set of hands clamped around my ankles.

"Hmph," someone grunted.

For some reason, it sounded like she was saying *go ahead*.

The burning continued a moment longer, then abruptly ceased. The sour stench of my own sweat filled my nose, and I panted with relief. A gentle hand smoothed back my damp, bloody hair, then cupped my cheek.

"Go to sleep now, darling." This time the voice was low, warm, sweet, soothing. "Just sleep, Gin."

So I did.

The next time I woke up, I was stretched out in an over-size salon chair that had been laid back like a recliner. Much better than lying on the cold grass of the college quad—or on a steel slab at the morgue.

My eyes drifted over the white and blue, cloudlike fresco painted on the high ceiling. Familiar as always. I knew where I was, of course. Jolene "Jo-Jo" Deveraux's beauty salon. This wasn't the first time I'd woken up in one of the cherry red chairs staring up at the cloud painting after being healed. I didn't think it would be the last time either.

Something rough and wet and warm scraped against my right hand. I craned my neck to one side. Rosco, Jo-Jo's pudgy basset hound, had dragged his fat, lazy ass out of his wicker basket in the corner long enough to come over and lick my hand.

"Good boy," I murmured and rubbed one of his long, floppy ears between my blood-spattered fingers.

Rosco grunted out a huff of pleasure and collapsed in a brown and black furry heap next to the chair. Walking the thirty feet across the room to me had plumb tuckered him out. I smiled and rubbed the hound dog's other ear.

"About time you came out of it," a feminine voice drawled off to my left.

A pair of bare feet strolled into view next to Rosco's inert form. Bright fuchsia nail polish covered her toes. Only one person I knew still padded around without socks in early December. I looked up to find Jo-Jo Deveraux looming over me. Well, as much as a dwarf who topped out at five feet could loom. Then again, Jo-Jo was rather tall for a dwarf.

Although she was two hundred fifty-seven and counting, Jo-Jo didn't look a day over one ninety-nine. She always reminded me of a Southern magnolia, aging ever so gracefully. Tonight the dwarf wore a long, fuzzy, pink flannel robe, topped off with a string of gravel-size pearls. Jo-Jo never went anywhere without her pearls. To her, they were the ultimate symbol that she was a true Southern lady. Even though it was getting late, Jo-Jo's bleached-blond-white hair still stood tall, teased, and proud in its usual helmet of curls, and her eye makeup looked as fresh as if she'd just applied it. Gloss covered her pursed lips. Strawberry, from the smell of it.

Most people would have thought Jo-Jo was just another aging debutante, still trying to be the belle of the ball and clinging to her youth despite the laugh lines around her mouth and eyes. They would have been wrong.

Everybody knew Jo-Jo Deveraux was an Air elemental who used her beauty salon and magic to help folks stave off the ravages of time on their faces, breasts, legs, and asses. Pure oxygen facials could do wonders for even the most stubborn crows' feet. But few people knew the dwarf was also the best healer in Ashland, capable of curing everything short of death. Even then, you had a better chance of Jo-Jo finding some way to bring you back to life than with anyone else.

Jo-Jo Deveraux had been fast friends with my mentor, Fletcher Lane. When I'd started doing the assassinating instead of the old man, Jo-Jo had transferred her healing services over to me. Of course, I always paid for her time, expertise, and magic, but the dwarf was family to me now. So was her younger sister, Sophia, who was a cook down at the Pork Pit, the barbecue restaurant Fletcher had left me upon his death. Sophia was also rather handy at disposing of the many bodies I left in my wake.

"How are you feeling?" Jo-Jo asked in her low, easy voice that oozed like warm honey.

"Like I got beaten by a giant."

Concern flashed in her pale gaze. Except for the pin-prick of black at their center, the dwarf's eyes were almost colorless, like two cloudy pieces of quartz set into her middle-aged face.

"Sit me up, please," I asked.

Jo-Jo nodded. She moved behind me and hit a lever on the chair. The back tilted up, moving me into an upright, seated position. I shifted around, wiggling my fingers, toes, and jaw. I felt tired, but that was to be expected. The body could handle only so much trauma, and going from being well to being severely injured to being well again in the space of a few hours always left me feeling drained and lethargic. It took my brain a while to catch up to the fact that I was still breathing and not six feet under like I should have been.

Dried blood still covered my clothes and hands, but everything else was in pain-free, working order once more. I sniffed. Jo-Jo had even fixed my drippy nose and purged the flu from my system. Humpty-Dumpty had been put back together again. Despite all of Mab Monroe's men.

My eyes scanned over the salon, which took up the back half of Jo-Jo's massive, antebellum house. It looked the same as it always did. Lots of padded swivel chairs. Several old-fashioned hair dryers. Counters cluttered with hairspray, scissors, pink sponge rollers, nail polish, makeup, and gap-toothed combs. Pictures and posters of models with various hairstyles taped to the walls. Piles and piles of beauty and fashion magazines everywhere. I drew in a breath. The air smelled the same too—chemicals mixed with coconut oil from the tanning beds in the next room.

Jo-Jo plopped down in the chair to my right. On the floor between us, Rosco actually expended enough energy to roll over, so the dwarf could rub his pudgy stomach with her bare foot.

"You want to talk about it?" Jo-Jo asked.

I shrugged. "Not much to talk about. Jonah McAllister got Elliot Slater and two of his giant goons to jump me at the community college. McAllister thought I might have info on his son Jake's murder. Since I didn't want to blow my cover, I had to let them beat me. End of story."

Jo-Jo stared at me, a reproachful look in her pale eyes. The dwarf had known me long enough to realize when I was fudging the truth.

I sighed. "And Mab Monroe was there too."

Jo-Jo opened her mouth to ask a question, but Finn chose that moment to pop his head into the salon.

"Is she finally awake?" he asked.

"Finally?" I groused, looking up at the cloud-shaped clock on the wall. "It's barely after ten. I only got the shit beat out of me a couple of hours ago. I'd say I was recovering nicely, all things considered."

"That's what you think," Finn said.

He leaned against the door frame, a mug of chicory coffee in his hand. Finn drank the stuff at all hours of the night and day, but the caffeine seemed to have little effect on him. Or perhaps he'd just become immune to it. Fletcher Lane had drunk the same kind of coffee.

I breathed in again, this time tasting the caffeine fumes in the air. The warm, comforting scent always reminded me of the old man. I wished Fletcher had been here tonight, to talk to me about the attack and seeing Bria again. I wished a lot of things about the old man that were never going to come to pass.

Heavy, plodding footsteps sounded, and another person entered the salon. Sophia Deveraux, Jo-Jo's younger sister. Where Jo-Jo was all sweet pink sunshine, Sophia was the heart of darkness—as in Goth. Sophia wore her usual black jeans and shit-kicker boots. Her T-shirt was actually a girly pink tonight, although images of decapitated doll heads dotted the light fabric. A black leather collar studded with plastic pink hearts ringed Sophia's neck. A bright pink gloss covered her lips, but her cropped hair was as black as black could be. It stood out in stark contrast to her pale skin.

Sophia was an inch or so taller than Jo-Jo and had a much more muscular figure than her big sister did. At a hundred and thirteen, the younger Deveraux sister was in her prime, instead of firmly entrenched in middle age like Jo-Jo was. Sophia plopped down in the chair to my left and nodded at me. I nodded back.

And then the three of them stared at me. Finn, Jo-Jo, Sophia. Hell, even Rosco turned his head back in my direction. All of them looking steadily at me, expectation shining in their eyes. Oh, fuck. They actually expected me to *talk* about what had happened tonight. To share my *feelings*. I sighed again. I'd much rather have hacked and slashed my way through a platoon of Mab Monroe's giants than explain how I was dealing with my emotions.

But they were my family, for better or worse. They deserved to know what had happened tonight—and how it could affect them tomorrow.

"All right," I said. "Here's the short version."

I recapped the events of the evening, starting with Jonah McAllister and Elliot Slater bracing me, Slater beating me, and Mab Monroe stepping in and leading her goons off into the dark night. And then there was the biggie—my unexpected meeting with Bria, my long-lost younger sister.

"So Bria's a detective? Working in Ashland?" Jo-Jo asked. "Why didn't we know this before?"

"Because she's a new transfer, only started a week ago," Finn said, taking another sip of his chicory coffee. "I did some checking while you were healing Gin."

In addition to (mis)handling other people's money, Finn was also something of an information trader. If you wanted dirt on someone, Finnegan Lane could get it for you—in a hurry.

"Bria has been working down in Savannah, Georgia,

ever since she graduated from the police academy a couple of years ago. She moved up to Ashland a few weeks back." Finn hesitated and stared at me. "She took Donovan Caine's position in the police department."

My hands tightened around the padded arms of my salon chair. A man's face flashed before my eyes. Black hair, hazel eyes, bronze skin, and a lean, hard body that had felt marvelous pressed against my own. Detective Donovan Caine. One of the few honest cops in Ashland who actually tried to fight crime, rather than taking a bribe to look the other way. Caine had also been my sometimes lover, until he'd left town a few weeks ago.

Detective Donovan Caine had been upstanding to a fault, with a strict code of justice and morals that never, ever bent. He'd had a hard enough time dealing with the fact that I used to be an assassin—and that I'd killed his former partner, Cliff Ingles, for raping a thirteen-year-old girl. But when I'd gone after coal mine owner Tobias Dawson for threatening an old friend of Fletcher's, Donovan hadn't handled it well at all. He'd known I'd planned to assassinate Dawson, and he'd done nothing to stop me.

After I killed Dawson, well, Donovan's morals, his ideals, started eating away at him. He'd come down to the Pork Pit one night and said he couldn't be the man he wanted to be and be with me at the same time. Donovan Caine had broken off our complicated affair and left town to get away from me and the attraction between us—and the fact that he still wanted to fuck me despite a) his precious morals and, b) all the bad things I'd done.

I'd been willing to share my life, my heart, with Donovan, and he'd walked out on me. On the possibility of *us*.

Maybe it was a good thing he'd left town. Otherwise, I might have been tempted to do something stupid. Like try to seduce him into giving us just one more chance. And be pissed off all over again when he said no.

"Gin?" Finn asked. "Are you still with us?"

I shook my head to banish my troubled, unwanted thoughts. "Yeah, I'm still here. So my mysterious sister took Donovan's place in the department. What else do you know about her?"

Finn shrugged. "Not much. I've only been digging for an hour. But Bria's got a reputation for being a real hard-ass. Cleaning up corruption, sticking up for the little people, that sort of thing."

So Bria was a crusader, just like Donovan Caine had been. Just what I needed. Another honest cop complicating my life. Especially when I was still trying to figure out why Mab Monroe had murdered my mother and older sister all those years ago—and how I could kill the Fire elemental now without getting dead myself.

"And, of course, we know that Bria is drop-dead gorgeous," Finn said in a dreamy tone. "That picture of her that Dad somehow got his hands on does not do the woman justice."

Finn was referring to a photograph Fletcher Lane had left for me. It had been in a thick folder, along with all the other information about my mother's and older sister's murder at the hands of Mab Monroe. Autopsy photos, police reports, newspaper clippings. Jo-Jo had given me the file after the old man's death. Bria's picture—which made me realize she was still alive—had been the only nice thing in the gruesome folder.

I rolled my eyes. "Do me a favor, Finn. Don't look like that when you talk about my sister."

"Like what?"

"Like you're thinking about her naked and in your bed."

Finn grinned. "Would I do something like that?"

"Absolutely."

"Mmm-hmm." On my left, Sophia grunted her agreement. That was about as expressive as she ever got. Unlike most folks, the Goth dwarf preferred to communicate in short, monosyllabic bursts.

Finn put his hand over his heart. "Oh, Gin, you wound me with your jaded cynicism."

"Yeah, yeah," I said. "My words are like knives. Just let me decide what I want to do about Bria before you start hitting on her, okay?"

Finn gave a reluctant nod of his head. "All right. But figure it out soon. You know I have a thing for hot blondes."

I snorted. "You have a thing for anyone with breasts."

We might have kept squabbling, but Jo-Jo cleared her throat. I turned my head to look at the dwarf.

"So what are you going to do about your sister?" the older dwarf asked in a soft voice. "Are you going to tell her who you really are? What you've been doing all these years? What your plans are?"

"You mean am I going to tell Bria that I'm her long-lost, big sister, Genevieve Snow? That I was a renowned assassin known as the Spider? Or that Mab Monroe killed our mother and sister and that I've sworn to take my revenge on the Fire elemental?" I shook my head. "Call me crazy, but I think that might be a bit much to process all at once."

Just the thought of telling Bria who I really was made my stomach tighten and the spider rune scars on my palms itch and burn. Even though I didn't often feel it, I knew what the emotion was. Dread.

"I don't know. Bria's your sister, after all. That counts for a lot," Jo-Jo murmured.

The dwarf stared at me, but her eyes had taken on a milky white, faraway look that told me that she wasn't really seeing me but peering into the future. In addition to using their magic to heal people, most Air elementals had a bit of precognition as well. Folks like Jo-Jo could sense, listen to, and interpret the emotions, feelings, and actions that permeated the air and wind. Just like I could hear the emotions, feelings, and actions that had sunk into any stone that I was near—brick buildings, granite furnishings, even the gravel underfoot. My Stone magic whispered of things that had occurred in the past. In Jo-Jo's case, her Air elemental magic often gave her flashes of what might happen in the future. At least enough of them to make me listen to her.

I rubbed my head. "I don't know what to do about Bria right now. I just don't know."

Jo-Jo reached over and squeezed my hand. "Whatever you decide, we'll support you—and welcome Bria with open arms if that's what you want."

Sophia nodded. "Welcome her," the Goth dwarf rasped in her low, broken voice.

"Oh, yeah," Finn grinned. "In fact, I volunteer to be the very first one to welcome Bria to Ashland."

I raised an eyebrow. "With what? Your suave good looks? Or perhaps you were going to whip out that smooth charm you claim to possess, along with your dick?"

Finn's grin widened. "Whatever works, Gin," he drawled. "Whatever works."

4

"I can't believe you dragged me down here tonight," I muttered. "We have things to do, remember? Long-lost sisters to investigate, Mab Monroe assassination plans to make, her pesky minions to dispatch. Or have you forgotten about all that?"

Finn pulled his bright green gaze away from a busty blond hooker long enough to glance at me. "Did you say something, Gin?"

I rolled my eyes. "Nothing important, apparently."

"Good." Finn's gaze zoomed back over to the hooker, who was gyrating along with several other women on the edge of the dance floor.

I sighed. Two days had passed since I'd been attacked at the community college by Elliot Slater and his giants. Finn had come by the Pork Pit earlier today and announced that he was treating me to a night out. I'd hoped for a nice quiet dinner somewhere, maybe that new Mexican place that served the spicy-hot fajitas over on St. Charles Avenue.

Instead, he'd taken me to Northern Aggression.

Located in Northtown, the rich, highfalutin part of the city, Northern Aggression was Ashland's most renowned nightclub. Not because it was the epitome of class and sophistication, but because you could get anything you desired here—blood, drugs, sex, smokes, alcohol. The club offered all that and more—for the right price. Not surprising, given the fact the club was managed by Roslyn Phillips, a vampire hooker who'd spent years turning tricks on the rough Southtown streets before she'd put enough cash together to open up her own gin joint.

Just before midnight, yuppies packed the place. Men in suits, women in as little as was legal. Everybody with a drink or ciggie in one hand and someone's ass in the other. All of the yuppies were being egged on by the nightclub's staff of scantily clad, impossibly buff men and women. Most of the staff members were vampires, and all of them were hookers. They were easy to identify since each one wore a necklace with a rune hanging off the end—a heart with an arrow through it. The symbol for Northern Aggression.

The hookers roamed through the club, offering guests trays of free champagne and chocolate-covered strawberries and hinting at the other delights that could be found on the premises. Especially in the private rooms upstairs that were rented out by the half hour—or less.

Of course, some folks weren't too particular about their privacy. Couples of two and three and sometimes four or more huddled close together in the club's booths.

Kissing, caressing, licking, moaning. Several of the tables twitched and shook, not from the raucous music but from the people fucking on the floor underneath.

Finn and I sat in a booth a few feet away from the dance floor, where folks bumped and ground their way through a rocking song by The Killers. Despite my ambivalence toward Northern Aggression and the heavy, sweaty smell of sex that permeated the air, even I had to admit the nightclub had an unabashed, decadent style to it. Crushed red velvet drapes covered the walls, and the floor was a soft, springy bamboo that cushioned your feet as you walked across it.

But to me, the most impressive thing was the bar that ran down one wall—an elaborate sheet made entirely of elemental Ice. Intricate runes had been carved into the surface of the bar, mostly suns and stars—symbolizing life and joy. Both of which could be found in abundance here tonight if you had enough cash or plastic to pay to play.

Behind the counter, a man mixed drinks. His eyes glowed blue-white in the semidarkness. The Ice elemental responsible for tending bar and making sure his cold creation stayed in one piece until the end of the evening. Besides the giant bouncers, he was the only staff member who wasn't wearing the heart-and-arrow rune necklace. The Ice elemental couldn't take time away from mixing drinks to fuck someone behind the bar. There'd be a riot if the booze didn't keep coming.

"Tell me again why we're here?" I asked.

Finn's eyes never left the blond hooker. "To have a good time, of course. Because you got the shit beat out of you, and you deserve a night out on the town."

Under the table, I kicked his shin. "And why don't I believe you?"

"Because you're cynical that way."

I kicked him again, harder this time.

"All right, all right," Finn said, leaning down to rub his leg. "If you must know, I was planning on talking to Xavier about something."

I raised an eyebrow. "And you dragged me along because . . ."

A shadow passed over Finn's face, and his green eyes darkened. "You'll see."

He didn't volunteer any more information, and for once I wasn't in the mood to be curious and pry. I took a sip of my gin and grimaced. For some reason, the cold liquor tasted bitter tonight. Or maybe that was because I was still brooding about Bria.

Finn had kept his promise to dig into my long-lost sister. Yesterday he'd given me a fat folder of information on Bria and told me that another was on its way as soon as he heard from the rest of his contacts in Savannah. But I hadn't opened the folder yet. It had remained closed and untouched on the coffee table in Fletcher Lane's den.

For once, I wasn't sure that I wanted to learn someone else's deepest, darkest secrets by scanning a piece of paper. Part of me—a big part of me—preferred to think of Bria the way that I'd always remembered her. As my sweet little sister. The innocent girl I'd played hide-and-seek with and made countless mugs of hot chocolate for. I didn't know that I wanted to read about everything Bria had been through, growing up as an orphan. My childhood had been traumatic enough living on the Ashland streets. I hoped Bria hadn't suffered as much as I had over the years. Either way, I wasn't sure I wanted to find out. Because the answers could be . . . ugly.

The truth was that I didn't know how I felt about my long-lost baby sister being in Ashland, much less the fact that she was a cop. A good one, at that. Somebody who actually tried to help people, who wanted to make a difference in a city as dirty and corrupt as Ashland—while I'd spent my entire adult life killing people for money. The idea that we shared the same DNA boggled the mind. Guess there was something to that nurture stuff after all.

I threw back the rest of my bitter gin. The alcohol slid down my throat and started its slow, pleasant burn in my stomach, but it didn't improve my mood.

"Find Xavier and let's get on with this," I told Finn.

His turn to raise an eyebrow. "Cranky much?"

I smiled. "You're going to see how cranky I am when I start ordering the most expensive champagne on the menu and guzzling it down like water. After I charge it to your tab, of course."

Finn held up his hands. "Fine, fine. Xavier was supposed to swing by our booth, but I'll go see if I can find him."

Finn got to his feet, straightened his tie, smoothed down his walnut-colored hair, and stepped into the swirling crowd. He strutted toward the Ice bar, probably to ask the bartender about Xavier. His path took him close to the edge of the dance floor. The blond hooker he'd been eyeing blew Finn a kiss. He grinned and veered in her direction. Less than three minutes later, the two of them were ensconced at the bar, drinking martinis and making goo-goo eyes at each other.

I drummed my fingers on the tabletop. A pretty face and tight body could distract Finnegan Lane from his own funeral. I should have just told him I was leaving. I reached for my cell phone to text him that news flash, when a shadow fell over me.

"Why, Gin, what a lovely surprise," a male voice murmured.

I looked up to find Owen Grayson standing in front of my booth. Like Finn, Grayson wore a rich suit, black in his case, with a charcoal gray shirt underneath. The fabric accentuated his compact, sturdy figure, which always reminded me of a dwarf's stocky physique. But at six foot one, Grayson was far too tall to be a dwarf.

His glossy, blue-black hair gleamed under the club's muted lights. So did his eyes, which were a light violet. A white, thin scar slashed down his chin. The faint mark would have ruined the look of another man's face, but it added a hard, sexy, dangerous edge to Grayson's features, giving him a roguish, rakish air. So did the crooked tilt of his nose. Or maybe that was just because I liked the rest of the package so much. Owen Grayson knew how to wear a suit very well, and I couldn't help but speculate what lay beneath his designer duds. Somehow, I knew it would be as appealing as the rest of him.

Still, despite the slick, expensive threads, Grayson looked like the kind of guy who'd taken more than one punch in his time. A real fighter through and through. The strong, self-assured way he carried himself only made him more impressive to me. I'd always admired confidence—

especially when the person actually had something to be confident about. Since Owen Grayson was one of the richest businessmen in Ashland, he had millions of reasons to smile.

I'd met Grayson a couple of weeks ago, back in November. His younger sister, Eva, had been eating at the Pork Pit when Jake McAllister had tried to rob the restaurant. Grayson thought he owed me something since I'd saved Eva from getting dead.

"Hello, Owen," I replied. "What brings you here tonight?"

He shrugged, his broad shoulders straining against the fabric of his suit. "Eva wanted to come dancing."

My eyes flicked over to the dance floor. Sure enough, I spotted Eva Grayson grooving in between a guy and another girl. Eva had the same coloring that Owen did, which made her look like a real-life version of Snow White. Add her rocking figure on top of that, and Eva attracted plenty of attention. She whirled away from one guy to turn and smile at another waiting at the edge of the dance floor. Eva crooked her finger, and the young man eagerly stepped into the fray surrounding her.

I looked back at Owen. "And you came along to babysit her?"

"I like to watch out for her," he rumbled in a low voice. "Besides, she said I needed a night out of the house. Evidently, running my various business interests and adding to her trust fund isn't exciting enough for her tastes."

I smiled. Like most college-age girls, Eva enjoyed flirting with the opposite sex. Dancing the night away at Northern Aggression would be right up her alley—

even if big brother Owen would be watching her every move.

"Care if I join you?" Owen asked.

I shrugged. "Suit yourself."

Grayson unbuttoned his jacket and settled on the opposite side of the booth so he was sitting across from me. He signaled one of the waiters and ordered an expensive scotch. I requested another gin on the rocks, with a twist of lime this time. Maybe that would cut the bitter taste in my mouth.

Our drinks came back, and I took a healthy pull off mine. Nope, still bitter. I sighed and rubbed my index finger down the side of the glass, leaving a trail in the condensation that had already formed there.

"Something the matter?" Grayson asked, taking a sip of his scotch.

I shrugged again. "Just not in the mood to party tonight, I suppose."

Owen stared at me with his violet eyes. "Perhaps you and I could go somewhere else. Make our own party."

"Let me guess where that party would end . . . your bedroom?"

Grayson smiled. "Actually, I was thinking the nearest hotel myself. Why drive that far?"

"Back to wanting to sleep with me again?"

Grayson's smile widened. "I figured it couldn't hurt to give it a shot."

I snorted. For some strange reason, Owen Grayson had taken a shine to me. Sure, I'd saved his sister from getting fried extra crispy by a Fire elemental. Sure, I was an attractive woman. But I just couldn't understand why the businessman was so interested. More than half the women here tonight were hotter, skinnier, younger, and had bigger breasts than I did. Any one of them would have been thrilled to be Grayson's entertainment for the evening. Hell, just for an hour.

More importantly, I wasn't quite sure whether his dogged interest was genuine. Trust didn't come easily to me, which is why I suspected Owen Grayson had some ulterior motive for wanting to get up close and personal with my nether regions besides the obvious one of simply getting his jolly on.

But mostly, I wasn't sure how I felt about him. With his black hair and violet eyes, Grayson was definitely attractive, in a rough, sexy way. But that sort of thing had never much mattered to me. Over the years, I'd had my share of ill-fated flings with the boys at the community college where I took so many classes. Even a grad student and a professor or two. I could do Owen Grayson tonight and forget about him tomorrow as easily as I could wash blood out of my hair. Actually, the blood would be more of a challenge.

No, the problem wasn't Grayson and his murky motives, whatever they might be. It was the small fact that he wasn't Donovan Caine. Despite my best intentions, I'd fallen for the detective, felt something for him. A warm softness in my chest that went beyond mere lust. And when Donovan had left town, when he told me that he was leaving because of *me*, well, it hadn't exactly done wonders for my ego. Or made me eager to start up something new with someone else.

Even assassins needed time to lick their wounds.

But Owen Grayson stared at me very much the way I had looked at Donovan Caine. With pure, focused interest—and the determination to get what he wanted. Me. Despite my doubts about him, it was . . . nice to be looked at that way. Instead of with the cold suspicion that the detective had almost always shown me.

Owen reached over and slipped his hand in mine. His palm was pleasantly cool against my skin, and I felt a little surge of magic brush against the spider rune scar embedded in my palm. Grayson's eyes brightened, as though someone had struck a match in his violet gaze. In addition to being a successful businessman, Owen Grayson also had an elemental talent for metal. To be considered a true elemental, you had to be gifted in one of the four major areas—Air, Fire, Ice, or Stone. But lots of folks were magically skilled in offshoots of the four elements, like electricity or water. In Owen's case, his talent for metal, a branch of Stone magic, let him sense all kinds of metal and ore, control them, and even forge them into whatever he wanted.

"The silverstone's still in there," I said in a wry tone. "If that's what you were looking for."

Owen shook his head. "I'll admit I'm curious as to exactly how you could get so much of the metal melted into your skin like that—especially shaped like a spider rune. And why you carry so many silverstone knives on you all the time. Curiosity is a trait of mine, I'm afraid. But I was much more interested in just holding your hand."

"What are you? Twelve?"

Grayson flashed me another smile. "Sometimes the most sensual pleasures are the simplest ones."

I looked at him a moment. Then I threw back my head and laughed. "Wow. That was lame. Do you try that line out on all the ladies? Or just me?"

Instead of being insulted, Grayson's smile deepened, and his violet eyes glowed with warmth. "Just you, Gin. You're the only one who's ever called me on it."

Owen made me laugh, I'd give him that. So I sat there and let him hold my hand instead of telling him to get lost.

Grayson's thumb traced over the circle embedded in my palm, the center of the spider rune that marked my skin. A little tingle of interest sparked to life in the pit of my stomach. A small sizzle of awareness, of potential, of possibilities. I regarded Owen a little more closely, letting my eyes drift over his powerful shoulders, thick arms, solid chest. The warm tingle spread out, rippled through my stomach, and drifted even lower. Hmm. Maybe I should take Owen Grayson up on his offer of sex. Maybe that would help me purge these lingering feelings I had for Donovan Caine and get the detective out of my system once and for all.

"I've asked you before, and I'll ask you again," Grayson said. "Go out with me, Gin. Dinner, dancing, a movie. Whatever you want. On me. All I ask is the pleasure of your company."

I took another sip of my bitter drink. "And what if I'm not good company?"

He shrugged. "Then we'll chalk it up to a failed experiment. What do you say?"

I opened my mouth to say . . . something, I wasn't quite sure what, when a woman stopped in front of our booth.

"Owen! What a pleasure to see you here tonight," the woman said.

I recognized her. Roslyn Phillips. The vampire madam and owner of Northern Aggression. Roslyn was a gorgeous woman from head to toe. Full, perky breasts, tight thighs, curved hips, and an ass that looked like it had been sculpted by Michelangelo. With a figure like that, it was no wonder Roslyn used sex to power up, along with blood.

Some vamps were like that, especially the ones who worked in the Ashland flesh trade. All vamps needed blood, of course, drinking it down the way humans might swallow a daily dose of vitamins. But many vamps also got a similar high off sex—or feeding off the emotions of others. Those who charged for their sexual services experienced the buzz *and* got paid for their time and expertise. Win-win for them. Which is why a large majority of the hookers in Ashland were vampires. Well, that and the fact they lived so long. Hooking was a skill that would always be in demand, despite the changing times. Always good to have a plan B to fall back on, in case of recession or lousy stock investments.

Roslyn Phillips was dressed for a night at the club, and the vamp's silver miniskirt and matching suit jacket showed off all her glorious assets to their ultimate perfection. Now I didn't look too shabby tonight in my own form-fitting black pants, blue silk shirt, and designer boots. But next to Roslyn's knockout beauty, I might as well have been a piece of poor white trash wearing a holey potato sack. And the vamp's face was just as attractive as the rest of her. Eyes and skin the color of dark, melted toffee. Cropped, feathered black hair that just brushed the edge of her jaw. A small, pointed nose. Blindingly white teeth capped off by two perfectly pointed fangs.

Owen got to his feet and kissed the vamp on her cheek. "Roslyn. Good to see you too. Let me introduce you to my companion. Roslyn, this is—"

"Gin," the vamp said in a neutral tone.

Owen frowned. "The two of you know each other?"

I smiled. "Oh, Roslyn and I are old friends. Aren't we, Roslyn?"

"Of course," she murmured. "Of course."

Owen sat back down next to me, but Roslyn stood where she was. She regarded me with her toffee eyes. After a moment, she sank her teeth into her lower lip. Thinking about something.

Roslyn Phillips and I didn't have the best relationship in the world. Once upon a time, I'd killed Roslyn's abusive brother-in-law to stop him from beating the vamp's sister and young niece. I'd done the job on the down low, but Roslyn had still figured out it was me. She'd whispered about my particular brand of services to one of her girls. That information had reached the wrong ears, which had eventually resulted in Fletcher Lane being murdered inside the Pork Pit. At the old man's funeral, I'd told Roslyn point-blank that she owed me big-time for her loose lips, that anything I wanted or needed, she was going to give to me—or she was going to get dead.

Roslyn had taken our heart-to-heart seriously. When I'd come calling a few weeks ago, she'd given me everything I'd needed to masquerade as one of her hookers and sneak into Mab Monroe's exclusive party so I could get close to Tobias Dawson—and she'd held up when Elliot Slater and his men had come to question her after the fact. I figured we were pretty much square now, but I wasn't about to tell Roslyn that. Especially when she was staring at me like she was considering something important.

"Is there something I can do for you, Roslyn?" I asked.

Roslyn chewed her lip for a few more seconds. Then she nodded. "Yeah, actually there is—"

"I thought I told you to wait in the back for me, baby," a low voice cut through the crowd.

Roslyn's eyes widened, and she froze. Pure, undiluted fear filled her toffee eyes. The emotion rolled off her the way magic might an elemental. I could feel the cold chill of it just like I could the one emanating from the Ice bar several feet away.

I looked past Roslyn to the man speaking. Seven-foot frame. Pale, albino features. Light hazel eyes. And fists the size of hams. Elliot Slater regarded the lovely vampire with a cold expression that indicated that she'd done something very, very wrong.

Fuck. What was the giant doing here? I palmed one of my silverstone knives under the table. Beside me, Owen Grayson frowned, but he didn't move or say anything. Smart man. If he even hinted to Slater that I had a weapon, Owen would find himself drinking through a straw for the rest of his life—at the very least. Despite the hot tingle of attraction that still sizzled in my stomach.

Roslyn plastered a fake, strained smile on her face and turned to face the giant. I scooted a little closer to the edge of the booth, just in case I needed to get up and stab Slater in a hurry.

"Hello, Elliot." Roslyn's voice was as silky as ever, but an undercurrent of fear and stress colored her tone.

Before I knew what was happening, Elliot Slater reached forward, grabbed Roslyn by her neck, and yanked her up against his body. "I told you to wait in the back for me, baby. Not be strolling around out here for every dick to get a good look at you. You're mine now. Or have you forgotten that?"

His? Roslyn was his? What the hell was going on here?

Roslyn tried to smile, but it didn't come off very well. "Now, Elliot, we've talked about this. You know I have to come out into the club at night and mingle with people. It's expected of me."

The giant shook her the way a terrier might snap a rat's neck. "And I've told you that nobody sees that hot ass of yours but me. Understand, baby?"

By this point, other people had noticed the confrontation, including Finn. He'd pushed away from the bar and the blond hooker and was headed in Roslyn's direction. What did he think he was going to do? Other than get beaten to a bloody pulp by Elliot Slater?

Somebody else was also interested in the situation. Xavier, part-time cop and the nightclub's main bouncer, pushed through the crowd. The giant stepped up to Slater.

"Let her go," Xavier's voice boomed out through the club. The giant's hands clenched into fists, ready to lay a hurt on the other man. "You're not welcome here anymore."

A hush fell over the crowd. The dancers stopped dancing, the smokers stopped smoking, the drinkers stopped drinking. Even the people getting busy under the tables paused in their passionate embraces. Everyone focused on the scene before them, and everyone backed away from the two men. Nobody wanted to get in the middle of a dispute between two giants.

Elliot Slater regarded Xavier with the same cool expression he had Roslyn a moment ago. Then he used his incredible speed to sucker punch the other giant. Xavier didn't see it coming, and Slater's fist hit him square in the throat with enough force to kill a cow. Xavier crumbled to the floor, gasping for air. A couple of the club's other bouncers stepped forward to come to their boss's defense. Slater snapped his fingers, and two giants shouldered through the crowd so that they stood behind him, guarding his back. They were the same goons who'd held my arms while Elliot Slater had beaten me two nights ago.

Xavier wheezed on the bamboo floor, and Elliot had Roslyn's neck pulled so far back he could snap it with a thought. I looked at Finn. He grabbed a beer bottle off the closest table and nodded at me. I nodded back. Underneath the table, Owen Grayson's hand settled on my leg. I glanced at him. The businessman had his hand wrapped around his glass of scotch, ready to use it as a weapon. Grayson winked at me. Whatever Finn and I were going to do, he was up for it. I had to admit the wink was kind of sexy. It made me like him a little more.

Elliot turned his attention back to Roslyn. "Now, baby, we're going to go in the back and talk about you disobeying me yet again."

Elliot leaned down and planted a gentle kiss on Roslyn's trembling lips, as though she was the love of his life. As though she was actually *precious* to him—and he wasn't an inch away from ending her existence.

I tensed, getting ready to strike while he was distracted.

But before I could move, I heard the distinct *click* of the hammer being thumbed back on a gun in the hushed silence. Well, that certainly made things much more interesting.

Slater heard it too. He broke off the kiss and turned, moving his body enough that I was able to see past him and get a look at the person pointing a gun at his head—Bria.

❋ 5 ❋

Elliot Slater didn't seem particularly concerned that Bria had a gun leveled at his head. No real reason to be. Giants had thick skulls. Only way to do much damage was to put something through their eyes and up into their brain. Most people just couldn't shoot that well under pressure.

As for her part, Bria didn't seem particularly concerned that Slater was looking at her like he was going to rip her head off her body, scoop out her spine, and eat it for dinner. Instead, she regarded him with a cold gaze, her eyes like sapphire chips of ice in her lovely face.

"I think the lady wants you to leave her alone," Bria said in a hard voice. "So why don't you do that? Right *now*."

Elliot released his hold on Roslyn, who stumbled away. Owen slid out of the booth and caught the vampire before she hit the floor.

"Do you know who I am?" Slater rumbled. "Who I work for?"

Bria smiled, and her eyes iced over even more. "Elliot Slater. Head of security for Mab Monroe. And, given what I've seen here tonight, a prime-A bastard who enjoys intimidating women."

The giant's hazel eyes narrowed with malice. Shocked murmurs rippled through the crowd. No one could believe what they were seeing—someone standing up to Slater and his goons.

"In case you don't know who I am, let me share." Bria reached into the pocket of her black leather jacket and came up with a gold badge. She held it up so the crowd could get a look at the shiny metal. "I'm a detective with the Ashland Police Department."

Despite the situation, I couldn't help the spurt of warm pride that filled me. Not because I had any great love of the police, but because of Bria. My little sister was actually standing up to Elliot Slater, actually trying to help Roslyn, who was so obviously in trouble. It might have been stupid, taking on someone as powerful and well connected as Slater, but I didn't see any fear in Bria's face—just cold, hard determination. She wasn't a pushover any more than I was, which made me like her all the more. Maybe we had more in common than I'd thought. Maybe a lot more.

"Aren't you off duty tonight, detective?" Slater asked.

"I was enjoying the music and a mojito—until you started making trouble," she snapped. "But cops like me never really go off duty. So unless you leave the premises immediately, Mr. Slater, I'm going to arrest you for assault, among other things."

Slater crossed his arms over his chest, considering the

situation. I gathered my legs under me, ready to leap up and strike. If Slater made a move toward Bria, he was dead. I'd climb on his back, reach around, and slit his throat if he so much as touched her. The giant wasn't going to hurt my sister like he had me at the community college. I'd deal with the consequences—and Mab Monroe—later.

I glanced at Finn. He still held the beer bottle down by his side. He'd slipped through the crowd so that he was behind the two giants Slater had brought along for backup. Finn and I had tag-teamed more than a few people in our time. He'd deal with the underlings and keep them busy, while I went after Slater.

Elliot stared at Bria a few more seconds, then uncrossed his arms. "Fine. I'll leave. Wouldn't want you to have to work any overtime tonight, detective." The giant turned toward Roslyn, who huddled on the floor next to Owen Grayson. Slater put two fingers to his lips and blew a kiss to the vampire. "Later, baby."

People scurried to get out of Slater's way as he strolled across the dance floor. His two goons gave Bria the hard stare a moment longer, before they followed their boss out into the night.

Bria kept her gun level with the giants' broad backs until the three men exited the club. Then she lowered and holstered her weapon. Bria let out a breath and tucked her blond hair back behind one ear. Her fingers twitched with the motion. Natural to feel a little shaky after threatening to kill one of the most dangerous men in Ashland.

But Bria put her game face back on and went over to check on Roslyn. My sister knelt down beside the vampire and murmured to her. Roslyn shook her head and hugged her arms to her chest. Once again, that spark of warm pride filled me at Bria's caring actions. She really was good, strong, determined. Reminded me of me. Well, except for the good part.

Since I didn't want to get in the middle of the two of them, I drained the rest of my gin, dumped the ice in a cocktail napkin, and went over to Xavier. The giant slumped against the side of a booth, just trying to breathe. His black eyes looked dull and defeated underneath the club's soft lights. A sneer twisted Xavier's lips, as though he was disgusted at himself for not being able to get rid of Slater all by his lonesome.

"Here," I said, holding out the ice-filled napkin. "Put this against your throat. It'll help with the swelling."

The giant still couldn't talk, but he nodded his head and took the napkin. Finn worked his way through the chattering crowd and hunkered down beside us.

"Is he going to be okay?" Finn asked in a soft voice.

"He's still breathing, isn't he?" I snapped.

Normally, I wouldn't have been so harsh with Finn. But now I knew exactly why he'd dragged me to Northern Aggression tonight and what that little problem was that Finn had promised to help Xavier with—Elliot Slater's creepy fixation on Roslyn Phillips. Finn had brought me here so I'd see it firsthand, so I'd see exactly how terrified Roslyn was of Slater. Finn had set me up. Brought me here to have my heartstrings plucked.

And it had worked.

I stared at Finn, the knowledge blazing in my eyes. He dropped his gaze from mine. Guilty as charged.

"Is there anything I can do for him?" Finn asked in a low tone.

"Go get that tub of Jo-Jo's healing ointment you keep stashed in your car. Xavier needs it more than you do tonight."

Finn nodded, got to his feet, and left. I turned back to the giant, who was staring at Roslyn. Concern filled his dark gaze, along with other soft, warm emotions. The poor guy could barely squeeze in enough air through his bruised throat to keep going, and his only thought was the vampire. If he could have, I imagined Xavier would have crawled over to her and cradled her in his massive arms. Xavier's being in love with Roslyn was going to make all this that much more difficult.

"Xavier."

The giant's head swiveled back around to me.

"I want you and Roslyn to come down to the Pork Pit tomorrow for lunch so we can talk about some things," I said. "Understand?"

Xavier slowly nodded. Surprise flickered in his black gaze, along with another emotion that made my stomach twist. Hope.

"Let's make it a late lunch, say around two o'clock."

The giant nodded again.

"Good," I said. "See you then."

It wasn't long before the music cranked back up, and everyone returned to their previous occupations. Smoking, drinking, dancing, fucking. As though the events of a few minutes ago had never happened. Some folks in Ashland had real short attention spans.

Finn came back in with the ointment, which I slathered on Xavier's throat. In addition to healing with their hands, Air elementals like Jo-Jo Deveraux could also infuse their oxygen-rich magic into certain products to give them an extra kick, like antibiotic ointment. Xavier sat still while the shiny grease worked its magic. Less than a minute later, the ugly, purple, fist-shaped bruise on his throat faded, the swelling went down, and his breathing eased into a wheeze-free pattern of inhalation and exhalation.

As soon as he could, Xavier got up and went over to Roslyn, who was still talking to Bria. Or rather still not answering Bria. The vampire had pulled herself up into a booth, where she sat staring off into space. Bria perched beside her, speaking in low tones. Probably talking to Roslyn about Elliot Slater and trying to get the vamp to press charges against the giant. But Roslyn wasn't answering.

Frustrated by the vamp's lack of response, Bria got to her feet and paced back and forth in front of the booth for the better part of a minute before sitting back down next to the vamp and trying again. Her mojito and night of clubbing were long forgotten. My sister seemed to take her job as a member of the po-po seriously. As proud of her as that made me, I also knew it was something that could be problematic for me later on—for any number of reasons.

Since Roslyn was otherwise occupied, Owen Grayson drifted in my direction. By this point, I'd moved over to the Ice bar and ordered another gin. One that tasted even more bitter than my first two. But it didn't much matter, since Finn had gone out to get his car and take me home. I'd seen what he'd wanted me to see. No more reason to stick around the club tonight. Besides, I'd never been one to stay and gawk at the messy aftermath and cleanup. My former profession as an assassin had precluded that sort of thing anyway.

Grayson took the stool next to me and ordered another scotch. His violet eyes cut to his sister Eva, who was once again grooving with the rest of the folks on the dance floor. After he'd made sure she was okay, Owen turned his gaze to me.

"You know, Gin," he said. "You never did answer my question."

Owen Grayson was persistent, if nothing else. I thought of the way he'd been ready to back me up against Elliot Slater—and how he'd caught Roslyn after the giant had shoved her away.

"All right," I said. "I'll have dinner with you, Owen."

A smile stretched across his face, softening the hard cut of his features. "Excellent. One night this week?"

I shrugged. "Sure. I'll call you."

"Try not to sound too enthusiastic," he replied in a dry tone. "Or I won't be able to contain myself. My ego might get inflated or something."

I grinned at his sardonic humor. My eyes drifted over his broad shoulders and strong body again. I remembered the way Owen had held my hand—and the surprising warmth it had stirred in me. I finished the rest of my gin and got to my feet.

Then I leaned over and put my mouth close to Owen's ear. "Actually, I prefer to save my enthusiasm for more worthwhile pursuits—like those in bed."

"Can I get that in writing?" he murmured.

Owen turned his head so that his lips were an inch away from mine. I stared into his violet eyes, and his scent washed over me—a rich, earthy aroma that made me think of metal. I leaned forward and brushed my lips over his. It was a light, brief contact, and nothing like the frenzied, tongue-driving kisses I'd shared with Donovan Caine. Still, more sparks sizzled to life in the pit of my stomach at the feel of Owen's mouth on mine, at the warmth of his body mingling with my own. Mmm. Maybe having dinner with Owen would be more fun than I'd imagined. Maybe so would a lot of other things.

I pulled back. Desire brightened Owen's eyes so that they almost glowed, but I found myself looking for other emotions in his gaze. For the guilt and grief and tinge of fear that had always swirled in Donovan Caine's eyes whenever he looked at me. But I didn't find them. Only desire and determination.

"If that's a taste of what's to come, I can hardly wait for dinner," Owen murmured.

"Try not to sound too enthusiastic," I quipped. "Or I won't be able to contain myself."

He grinned. "Can I get that in writing too?"

I laughed. Owen joined in with his own throaty chuckle. Feeling strangely lighter than I had in a long time, I winked at him and strolled away.

*   *   *

Thirty minutes later, Finn drove up a long, snaking drive-way that wound up one of the many steep ridges of the Appalachian Mountains that cut through Ashland like rows of sharks' teeth. We hadn't spoken since we'd left Northern Aggression. Finn realized I was royally pissed at him for snookering me into going to the club in the first place. He had the good sense not to try to weasel his way out of it. Tonight, at least.

The driveway opened up into a small clearing on top of the ridge, and Finn stopped his Aston Martin in the gravel outside Fletcher Lane's house.

In addition to leaving me the Pork Pit and a fat chunk of change in his last will and testament, the old man had also bequeathed me his house, a three-story, clapboard structure that had been built before the Civil War. Over the years, the home's various owners had added on to the original structure in a variety of styles. In addition to its white boards, the house was a mishmash of gray stone, brown brick, and red clay. A tin roof covered the entire structure, along with black shutters and blue eaves. The whole thing resembled a ragged doll's house that had been constructed with leftover pieces. But it was home to me. Always had been, always would be.

Finn sighed in the darkness. "Gin, I—"

"We'll talk about it tomorrow," I said, turning to look at him. "When Xavier and Roslyn come to the restaurant for lunch."

Finn blinked. "They're coming to the Pork Pit?"

"At two. Be there."

He hesitated, then nodded. "Thank you, Gin."

"Don't thank me yet. I haven't done anything."

"But you will," Finn replied. "And that's all that matters."

He reached over and squeezed my hand. Despite the fact I was still angry at him, after a moment I squeezed back. Like it or not, Finn was like a brother to me—and in the end, that was all that really mattered.

☼ 6 ☼

Finn promised to be at the Pork Pit tomorrow when Roslyn and Xavier showed up; then he drove back to his apartment in the city. But instead of immediately heading toward the house, I stood in the driveway, listening to the gravel underneath my feet to see if I'd had any unexpected visitors today. I might not be the assassin the Spider anymore, but there were still plenty of people who'd like to get their hands on me, including Jonah McAllister.

But there were no sounds in the small, loose stones that shouldn't be there. No shrieks of danger, no notes of worry, no trills of anxiety. Just the gentle creak of the trees, the light tread of squirrels, chipmunks, and rabbits, the whistle of the wind around the ridge. Soft, soothing murmurs. But the comforting whispers still didn't stop me from checking the black granite that framed and composed the front door to see if anyone might be lurking inside Fletcher Lane's house.

I spread my fingers over the cool stone that made up the main entrance. The granite's hum was low and muted, just like always. No one had been near the sprawling house all day. Good. Even if someone had come up to the house, she would have had a hell of a time getting in through the front door, thanks to its sturdy dead bolts and solid construction. As added protection, thin veins of silverstone ran through the black granite door, and silverstone bars covered all the windows. Silverstone could absorb any kind of elemental magic—Air, Fire, Ice, or Stone—as well as power by folks gifted in other elemental areas, like metal, water, electricity, or even acid. Someone with enough magic could eventually overcome the silverstone and granite door and force her way inside the house, but she'd lose a lot of juice doing it. Which would make her that much easier to dispatch with one of my knives.

I unlocked the front door and stepped inside. Since so many additions had been tacked on to the house over the years, the interior layout was a bit of a labyrinth. Square rooms, oval ones, even an area shaped like a pentagon, all connected by twisting hallways that curved around, doubled back on each other, and often led to the other side of the house entirely. Another advantage, as far as I was concerned. Even if someone could break through the granite around the front door, she'd have a hard time finding me before I slipped out through one of the many secret passages—or came around behind her. All the elemental magic in Ashland wouldn't save you from a silverstone knife in the back. Win-win for me, either way.

I tossed my keys into a bowl by the front door, toed

off the stylish, designer Bella Bulluci boots that Finn insisted I just had to have for my birthday, and headed for the kitchen in the back of the house. After I poured myself another glass of gin, I padded into the downstairs den and plopped down on the sofa. As always, my gaze drifted up the mantel, where a series of rune drawings stood. Four drawings total, three that I'd done for one of my many community college classes and another, more recent one.

The first three runes were the symbols of my dead family. A snowflake, my mother, Eira's, rune, representing icy calm. A curling ivy vine, which had belonged to my older sister, Annabella, symbolizing elegance. And a delicate primrose that had been Bria's rune—the symbol for beauty.

The fourth rune was a bit different in that it was shaped like a pig holding a platter of food—my own rendering of the colorful neon sign that topped the entrance to the Pork Pit. It wasn't exactly a rune, not like the other three, but I'd sketched it in honor of Fletcher Lane. In my mind, Fletcher and the Pork Pit were one and the same, and both were symbols of home, comfort, safety.

My eyes skipped over the runes, then settled on the primrose. Bria's symbol. When we were kids, our mother had given each of us a rune to match our personalities and had them made into small silverstone medallions for us to wear. I couldn't quite believe that Bria still had her necklace—and that she was wearing it all these years later. I did the math in my head. Bria had been eight years old the night our mother and older sister had died, so she'd be twenty-five now. At thirty, I was five years older.

I sighed, took a sip of gin, and grimaced. Still bitter.

I put the glass aside and leaned forward, staring at a manila folder lying on top of the scarred coffee table, along with a single picture. The photo was of Bria, of course. Blond hair, blue eyes, hard mouth. She looked the same in the color picture as she had in the flesh two nights ago and earlier this evening at Northern Aggression.

Finn had written a single word on the folder's tab— *Bria*. The folder contained all the information he'd been able to dig up on my sister so far. Her work history, financial records, habits, hobbies, vices. Finn had already read through the information, but for some reason, I just couldn't look at it.

I wanted—I didn't know what the hell I wanted. Maybe the chance to get to know Bria as a real, live person, instead of flipping through the neatly ordered pages of her life the way I would when I was scouting out a potential target, trying to figure out how to get close enough to kill him. Maybe even for Bria to tell me all her secrets herself, the way that a true sister might.

I didn't consider myself a sentimental person. Watching my family get fried to a crisp as a kid and then being forced to fend for myself on the mean streets of Ashland was more than enough to shock the sentiment right out of me forever. But ever since I'd found out that Bria was alive, ever since I'd seen that picture of her that Fletcher had left for me, I'd been daydreaming about what she would be like. About what it would be like when we saw each other again.

I'd even fantasized about Bria immediately recognizing me, smiling, and running over to give me a big hug—while some sort of uplifting music swelled in the background. Instead, my baby sister had seen me at my worst—playing the part of the victim. I wasn't sure which one was the greater evil—my twisted fantasy or the harsh, bloody reality.

My fingers traced over Bria's name, and I hooked a fingernail underneath the tab, ready to flip it open and see what secrets my baby sister had been keeping. But I just couldn't bring myself to do it. Not tonight. Maybe it was sentimental of me, but I wanted to put off more of the harsh realities the folder was sure to contain—at least for tonight.

So I left the folder where it was, swallowed the rest of my bitter gin, and headed upstairs to bed.

The fist came out of nowhere. One minute I was running through the smoky interior of our house trying to get away from the men who were chasing me. The next I was con-fronted with a giant's fist, larger than my head. It filled my vision for half a second before slamming into the side of my face. Pain exploded in my body, and the force of the blow threw me ten feet through the air. I landed hard on a patch of sooty, smoldering carpet.

I groaned, rolled over, opened my eyes—and found myself staring at a charred, blackened husk of a body. My mother, Eira. Even through the crispy, ruined skin and flaky ash, I could see the white gleam of her teeth, her mouth open in one last scream. The only other thing the Fire elemental's magic hadn't melted was my mother's silverstone snowflake rune, the one she always wore around her neck. The symbol for icy calm. The rune gleamed like a silver diamond against my mother's burned skin. Tears filled my eyes at the horrific sight. I turned away and tried not to vomit.

An hour ago, I'd woken up to find giants breaking into our home. And they hadn't been alone. A Fire elemental was with them—a woman. Her laughter rang through the house like a dark dirge, along with the hot, pricking feel of her magic. The Fire elemental and her men had stormed into our house and left a path of death and destruction in their wake. My mother had gone down to try to stop the Fire elemental. So had my older sister, Annabella.

Through the smoke and haze, I'd seen my mother duel the elemental, using her Ice magic to try to overpower the other's Fire. But the other elemental had been stronger, and my mother had vanished in a ball of Fire. Furious, Annabella had thrown me off and rushed to our mother's defense. Annabella had died a few seconds later in another explosive ball of flames—her white nightgown lit up like a macabre candle. The Fire elemental had laughed all the while.

I'd run.

Away from the elemental, away from the fire, away from the nightmarish, burned figures that had been my mother and older sister. I'd raced down the hall, snatched Bria out of bed, and pulled her through the house as fast as I could. We had to get away. We had to get out of the house. I'd shoved Bria onto a stone terrace that overlooked the gardens, hoping to get out that way. But there were more men waiting outside the house. They'd seen me and given chase. So I'd hidden Bria in one of our favorite spots and run back into the house, leading them away from her.

But one of them had been lying in wait for me inside—the giant who'd just punched me. I tried to get to my feet, to run *away again, but someone grabbed my long, tangled, brown hair and pulled me upright. It was hard to see through the smoke that blackened the room, but I saw the giant draw back his fist to hit me again. Maybe it was the smoke, but he seemed to be a pale, ghostly figure, like some sort of horrid ash golem come to life.*

Even as I whimpered and waited for the blow, I found comfort in one thing. Bria was safe, hidden in the spot where I'd left her. The Fire elemental's men would never find her, and she'd be safe from the flames spreading through the house. That was all that mattered—

I must have blacked out, because the next thing I knew, I was sitting upright. I jerked, but heavy ropes held me down. My hands felt like they were lashed together too, with something cold and metal stuck in between them. I concentrated on the shape and realized it was my spider rune. Someone had taken the silverstone medallion off my necklace and stuck it between my hands. But why?

I tried to open my eyes to see what had happened to me, to try to figure out where I was and how I could get away, how I could get back to Bria. But something scratched against my eyelids and weighted them down. Cloth, maybe. Was I blindfolded?

"There's no use in struggling," a female voice said in my ear. "I've made sure those ropes are quite secure."

The low, sibilant voice reminded me of a copperhead's rasp. A fingernail slid down my cheek, leaving a ribbon of fire in its wake. I yelped and jerked my head back from the burning sensation. The Fire elemental had me. I could tell it was her by the way her hot magic lashed and pricked against my skin, even if I couldn't see her.

"What do you want?" I whispered. "Why are you doing this?"

She laughed. A low, mocking sound that told me exactly how helpless I was. "Because I can. Because your bitch of a mother took far too many things from me over the years. Because the very existence of your happy little family sickens me. Because it needed to be done before the Snow sisters became any kind of threat to me. But mainly, because I wanted to."

How could anyone want to hurt us? Why? What had we ever done to her? Sour bile filled my throat. Somehow I choked it down. Throwing up would only make her angrier.

"Now, dear, sweet Genevieve," the Fire elemental purred. "I need you to do something for me."

"Wh—what?" I stammered.

"Tell me where your sister Bria is."

So the Fire elemental and her men hadn't found my baby sister yet. She wouldn't be asking about Bria otherwise, and I wouldn't still be alive. Relief filled my body, along with a small bit of determination. A cold little knot deep in my stomach. I wasn't going to tell the elemental where Bria was, I vowed. No matter what she did to me. I wasn't going to kill my sister. Not now, not ever.

The elemental dug her cruel fingers into my hair and yanked my head back. "Tell me now!"

Just the touch of her hand against my head made it feel like she was scalping me with a red-hot knife. Tears of pain filled my eyes and soaked the blindfold, but that small knot of determination tightened inside me.

"No," I whispered. "I'll never tell you."

Silence.

After a few seconds, the Fire elemental let go of my hair.

Footsteps sounded, and I had the sense she was circling me the way a vulture would fly around a carcass. The footsteps stopped. I turned my head this way and that, trying to figure out where she was and what she would do next. No use.

"Fine," she murmured. "We'll do it the hard way. It's always more fun. In case you haven't realized, I took the liberty of removing that quaint little rune you wear around your neck. I had one of my men duct-tape it inside your hands. You're going to tell me where your sister Bria is, or I'm going to use my magic to heat the rune. I trust you know what burning flesh smells like by now. Imagine that being your own. The stench, the excruciating pain, the knowledge that your own skin is melting away into nothing. Tell me, is your sister worth all that?"

I thought of Bria. Sweet little Bria with her chubby fingers and big blues eyes and shy smile. She was worth it. Worth all that pain and more.

"Go—go to hell, bitch," I said in the strongest voice I could muster. "I'm not telling you anything."

"So brave, so young, so very stupid. Have it your way then," the Fire elemental said.

For a few seconds, nothing happened. Then I felt a hot, pricking sensation gather between my palms. The silverstone spider rune grew warm between my hands, and I started sweating, more out of fear than the heat. She was really going to do it. Really going to torture me. Really going to heat the rune until it burned my palms. I wondered if it would actually catch fire, and if I'd be engulfed in flames along with it.

For a moment, I wavered, ready to tell her where I'd hidden Bria. Then I thought of my mother and Annabella, of their burned, smoking bodies lying on the floor. No, I vowed.

I wouldn't do that to Bria. I wouldn't give her to the Fire elemental.

The rune continued to heat up. I felt blisters form on my palms. I tried to move, tried to slip the metal out from between my hands, but they were taped together too tightly. All I could do was sit there and endure it. The blisters popped and turned into a burning sensation. I gritted my teeth, even as more tears streamed out of my eyes, and sweat dripped off my fingers. The burning intensified. What came after burning? Scorching? Scalding? Searing? The acrid smell of my own melting flesh filled my nose, along with sour sweat and fear.

The Fire elemental's low chuckles washed over me. She was enjoying this, enjoying my suffering, this hot, searing, excruciating pain that felt like it would never, ever end.

Finally, I couldn't stand it any longer. I screamed. And again. And again. And again—

I woke up, my mouth open in a silent scream. My eyes flicked around the dark room, and it took me a moment to come back to myself. To remember that I was safe in Fletcher Lane's house. That it was just a dream, just a memory, and nothing more. Nothing that could physically hurt me now. I drew in a ragged breath and flopped back against my damp pillow.

I'd been having these sorts of dreams ever since Fletcher's murder a couple of months ago. The old man had been tortured to death by an Air elemental who'd hired me to do a job, then decided to double-cross and murder me so the hit couldn't be traced back to her. I'd killed the Air elemental, of course, but it hadn't brought Fletcher back to me—or stopped the dreams. If anything, it was like the old man's death had opened a floodgate to my past, and the images kept spilling out no matter how much I wanted them to sink back into the darkness.

Only they weren't really dreams so much as memories of my past. Of that fateful night when my mother and older sister had been murdered—by Mab Monroe. Of when the Fire elemental had tortured me to get me to give up Bria's hiding place.

I opened my hands and stared at my palms. A bit of moonlight slipped in through the bedroom window and highlighted the silverstone scars on my hands. A small circle surrounded by eight thin lines. A spider rune. The symbol for patience. I'd born the marks for seventeen years now, but tonight, it felt like they'd just been made yesterday. Everything had felt fresh and raw and sore since Bria's reappearance in my life.

I thought of that folder of information Finn had compiled on my sister. Of what secrets it might hold. I wondered what Bria remembered of the night our mother and older sister had died. If she knew Mab Monroe was the one who was responsible for it all. Why Bria had come back to Ashland. Why now, after all these long years?

But instead of getting out of bed, going downstairs, turning on a light, and looking at the file like I should have, I pulled the sheet up to my chin, as though the soft, warm flannel could protect me from, well, everything. All the horrible things that had happened, and all the ones that were yet to be.

Tomorrow, I thought. I would look at the information tomorrow.

Tonight, I only wanted to sleep—and forget.

7

At exactly two o'clock the next afternoon, Xavier pulled open the front door of the Pork Pit, making the bell chime. Punctual. I liked that in a man.

The giant held the door out wide so Roslyn Phillips could maneuver around him and step inside. The vampire madam and nightclub owner was dressed down today in a pair of black wool pants and a thick, ivory turtleneck sweater. A black and ivory checked coat covered her slim shoulders, and silver glasses perched on the end of her nose. Roslyn was still a striking woman, even without the party clothes and heavy makeup she wore when working the floor at Northern Aggression.

Catalina Vasquez, one of my best waitresses, heard the bell chime too. Her head snapped up from the chemistry textbook she'd been reading. Like me, Catalina was a student at Ashland Community College who worked part-time at the Pork Pit to make ends meet. With her long black hair, hazel eyes, and full-bodied figure, Catalina was quite popular with my male customers—especially Finnegan Lane, who always stopped to admire her assets whenever he came by the restaurant.

Catalina grabbed a couple of menus off a holder on the back wall and hurried behind the long counter that ran down one side of the barbecue restaurant. She reached the end, where I perched on my usual stool behind the old-fashioned cash register. I put down the copy of *The Adventures of Huckleberry Finn* that I'd been reading and signaled Catalina to stop.

"The lunch crowd has died down," I said. "Why don't you go on break now? I know you've got some errands to do. Take a couple hours if you want. I'll handle them. I was thinking about closing down until four anyway."

Catalina flashed me a wide, grateful smile. "Thanks, Gin. You're the best."

"Hmph."

A grunt sounded from the middle of the counter, where Sophia Deveraux stood slicing a thick wedge of Jarlsberg cheese, one of the key ingredients in the Pork Pit's most excellent grilled cheese sandwich. The dwarf was dressed in her usual black jeans and boots. Her T-shirt was also black today with a large silver heart on the front that was broken in two and dripping crimson blood. A thick silver choker ringed Sophia's throat, and several matching rings flashed on her fingers.

Catalina Vasquez bit her lip and looked over her shoulder at the Goth dwarf. Catalina had only been working at the restaurant a few weeks, and she was still getting used to Sophia—and interpreting what the dwarf's grunts really meant. Of course, I knew that Sophia was mocking Catalina's assertion that I was the best boss ever, but I wasn't about to share that knowledge. I had a hard enough time keeping waitresses, given the dwarf's dour persona. I wasn't about to let a responsible, punctual, hard-working jewel like Catalina slip through my fingers because of Sophia Deveraux and her monosyllabic method of communication.

"Sophia agrees," I said. "You should definitely go on your break now."

"Um, okay. If you're sure."

Catalina handed the menus over to me, grabbed her black wool pea coat off the stand in the corner, and headed out the front door. I waited until she was gone before I stepped over to Xavier and Roslyn.

"This way, please." I led them to a booth in the very back of the restaurant, out of sight of the glass storefront windows.

Finnegan Lane was already seated there against the back wall, wearing another one of his ubiquitous suits. Black, with a faint gray pinstripe today. A cooling cup of chicory coffee perched on the table in front of Finn, along with the remains of his lunch—a half-pound cheeseburger with all the fixings, steak-cut fries, and a triple chocolate milkshake that would go straight to anyone else's ass but his. I always envied Finn his ability to eat whatever he wanted and never gain a pound.

Roslyn slid into the opposite side of the booth across from Finn. Xavier sat next to her. I gave both of them menus and went to check on my only other customers—a couple of construction workers grabbing a late lunch before heading back out into the December cold. The two men were ready to pay up and leave. Once I got their change, I went back over to the others. Behind the counter, Sophia kept slicing cheese, her knife *thwack-thwack-thwack*ing against the countertop.

"So what'll it be?" I asked, pulling a pad and pen out of the back pocket of my blue jeans.

"I'm not hungry," Roslyn murmured, tapping her French manicured nails on top of the laminated menu.

"Me either," Xavier rumbled.

"I don't care whether you're hungry or not," I snapped. "You're in my gin joint now, and you're damn well going to eat something. So tell me what you want, or you'll find yourself at my mercy."

I might be a stone-cold killer, but no one could ever accuse me of lacking in the hostess department. Still, I gave them the hard stare to show them I was serious. Xavier ordered two barbecue pork sandwiches, coleslaw, baked beans, and a blackberry lemonade. Roslyn requested an ice water with lemon, a grilled cheese sandwich, and a fruit tray.

I cocked my hip to one side and looked at her. "Sweetheart, does this look like the kind of place that serves fruit trays?"

Roslyn's dark eyes flicked over the barbecue restaurant. I didn't have to look behind me to know exactly what she was seeing. Clean, but well-worn blue and pink vinyl booths. Matching faded pig tracks on the floor that led to the men's and women's bathrooms, respectively. A long counter lined with stools where people could watch their food being prepared on the opposite side. A framed, blood-covered copy of *Where the Red Fern Grows* on the wall next to the cash register, along with an old faded picture of two young men holding fishing rods. Cumin, red pepper, and other spices from the afternoon's cooking flavored the air, along with a healthy dose of pure, heart-stopping grease.

The vampire's wide mouth quirked. "No, I suppose not."

"The only fruit I have in here is in the cherry pie. You can have some of that. With vanilla bean ice cream. Be back in a minute."

I scribbled down their orders, tore off the paper, and took it over to Sophia Deveraux. The Goth dwarf had moved on from slicing cheese. Now she cut through a pile of tomatoes with a long, curved, serrated knife, making precise, neat little rounds for the rest of the day's sandwiches.

"Another order," I told her. "I'm going to flip the sign over to *Closed* for the next hour or so and lock the front door. And I'll be sending Finn and Xavier your way in a few minutes. Keep them busy in the back while I talk to Roslyn."

"Hmph." Sophia gave me her usual noncommittal grunt.

This morning, I'd told Sophia that Roslyn and Xavier were coming by to talk about a problem they were having—a problem I was thinking about helping them with in my own special way. The Goth dwarf's black eyes had actually sparkled a little bit at the thought of disposing of another body for me. Jo-Jo might take care of healing me, but Sophia was the cleanup crew. No matter how bloody a scene was, no matter how much tissue, brain matter, and other nasty bits were lying around, the dwarf could make the area look pristine. No blood, no hairs, no fibers, no DNA or fingerprints of any kind were ever left behind.

I'd often wondered if Sophia had the same sort of Air elemental magic that Jo-Jo had. Air magic was great for sandblasting things—like getting blood off a wall. But I'd never seen or felt Sophia do any magic. I didn't even know what the dwarf did with all the bodies I'd sent her way over the years. Didn't know where she took them or what she did with the remains. I didn't even know why Sophia enjoyed getting rid of the bodies in the first place. I had a feeling it had something to do with her ruined voice, which rasped worse than a chain smoker with a collapsed lung.

I'd never come right out and asked the dwarf. Fletcher Lane had instilled a healthy dose of curiosity in me, but I valued Sophia's and Jo-Jo's services and friendship too much to pry. At least for now.

Sophia put her tomatoes aside and started working on the order. I fixed Roslyn's water and Xavier's lemonade and took the drinks back over to the booth.

". . . and then I said, 'Of course I didn't sleep with your wife. She was too busy screwing your business partner to even notice me.' " Finn let out a laugh at his lame joke.

Xavier stared at him with a blank expression. Roslyn ran a fingernail back and forth across the tabletop.

I plunked the drinks down on the table. "Food's coming up in a minute."

By the time I locked the front door and walked back over to the counter, Sophia had dished up Xavier's coleslaw and baked beans, and Roslyn's cherry pie with ice cream. I fixed the vamp's grilled cheese, while the dwarf worked on the two pork sandwiches. A few minutes later, I carried the plates of food to the table and set them down. Then I slid in on Finn's side of the booth.

"Nothing for me?" Finn asked.

"You've had your lunch already. Don't be greedy."

Finn stuck out his lip and pouted. I rolled my eyes. Roslyn and Xavier dug into their food.

The four of us didn't speak while they ate. Xavier hesitated, but after the first few bites, his claim of not being hungry vanished—along with all the food on his plate. Roslyn merely nibbled at her grilled cheese and only ate a few bites of her pie. A shame, really. Golden crust, warm filling, a perfect blend of sweet and sour. I'd made the cherry dessert fresh this morning. Cooking was one of my great loves and skills in life, along with being rather handy with my knives.

I waited until they'd both pushed their plates away before I got down to business. "Finn, Xavier, why don't you boys go help Sophia? I think there were some boxes in the back she needed help unloading."

Xavier frowned, and his dark eyes flicked to Sophia. The dwarf had gone back to slicing tomatoes, and the muscles in her arms bulged with her swift, precise movements.

"You're kidding right?" the giant rumbled. "Sophia's a dwarf, the strongest one I've ever seen. She could probably bench-press me if she wanted to."

"Go help her, Xavier. Now."

Finn opened his mouth to argue, but I cut him off. "You too, Finn."

The two men grumbled, but they got to their feet and shuffled over to Sophia, who led them through the swinging doors and into the back of the restaurant. The dwarf would keep them occupied while I talked to Roslyn. Once I'd settled myself in the booth again, I stared at the vampire.

"Now that the boys are gone, you want to tell me what that little scene at Northern Aggression was about last night? And why Elliot Slater thinks that the two of you have some kind of relationship?"

Roslyn tapped her fingers on the tabletop. After a few seconds, her hand stilled. She drew in a breath and raised her dark eyes to mine. "Because the bastard's stalking me."

* ❁ * **8** * ❁ *

"Stalking you?" I asked.

The news wasn't unexpected, given the creepy display of affection I'd seen last night, but I was mildly surprised that she came right out and said it. Roslyn Phillips wasn't my biggest fan, especially since I'd threatened to kill her if she ever talked about me being an assassin to anyone ever again. The vampire must be more upset or desperate than I'd thought to spill her problems to me with so little provocation. I hadn't even given her the hard stare yet.

Roslyn bit her lip and nodded. "Stalking, domination, possession, call it whatever you like. The bastard's obsessed with me."

"When did this happen?"

"It started a couple of weeks ago," the vampire said. "When Elliot Slater came to question me about Mab Monroe's party and how someone was able to get their hands on one of the invitations for my girls—and her heart-and-arrow rune necklace. After that, well, I guess you could say he took a liking to me."

The beginnings of a migraine stirred behind my eyes. Elliot Slater had come to question Roslyn because she'd helped me get into Mab's party so I could go after Tobias Dawson. Slater had seen, gotten close to, and become obsessed with the vampire because of me. All of which meant that Roslyn's suffering was my fault. All my fault. The vamp had kept up her end of our deal—given me the help I'd needed and kept quiet about it after the fact— and now she was being stalked as a result.

I'd done a lot of bad things in my time. Killed a lot of people, had a lot of blood on my hands. But Roslyn suffering like this because of me—it made me sick to my stomach. Physically ill. Because she didn't deserve it. Even when she'd blabbed about Fletcher Lane to the wrong person, Roslyn had only been trying to help someone else. This time, she'd listened to me about keeping quiet, and look what it had gotten her. My stomach twisted a little more at the thought. I didn't often feel this particular emotion, but I knew what it was. Guilt.

"At first, I thought it was just a passing thing, you know?" Roslyn said in a low tone. "Slater's not the first guy who's wanted to fuck me. I've had my share of wacko stalkers over the years. I always make it crystal clear that I don't hook anymore. That all I'm interested in doing is running my club. Then I steer them to one of my girls. Usually that's the end of it. If someone persists or really starts bothering me, Xavier encourages him to reconsider the matter."

"But not Elliot Slater." A statement, rather than a question.

"No," she whispered. "Not Slater. After he questioned me about Mab's party, he started coming to the nightclub. He'd get one of the booths on the main floor, order some drinks, and just watch me. All night long. He tried to get me to sit with him a couple of times. Dance with him too. I always politely refused. I sent other girls over to him to try to distract him, but Slater just passed them off to his giant friends. He never so much as looked at them."

"So when did he go from watching you to something else?"

Roslyn dropped her eyes and stared at the tabletop again. "One night about a week ago. I sent Xavier home early and stayed late to go over some of the books. I thought nobody else was in the club but me. I was wrong. Slater came into my office. He said he was tired of waiting for me to realize what a good thing we could have together." The vamp's voice was hard, brittle, remote, as if she was talking about something that had happened to someone else. "I tried to get him to leave. Tried to leave myself, tried to fight him off. Nothing worked."

Although I didn't want to cause the vampire any more pain, there was a question I had to ask. Something I needed to know. "Did he rape you?" I made my voice as soft and gentle as I could.

Roslyn raised her toffee gaze to mine. Her eyes were dull and empty, even though a grim smile tightened her beautiful face. "Not exactly. Slater grabbed me and made me sit on his lap. He was so fucking strong. I couldn't move, I couldn't break free, I couldn't do *anything*. I screamed, over and over again, but I could tell that . . .

excited him, so I made myself stop. I thought he was going to rape me then, but Slater just sat there, watching me. Waiting for me to realize there was nothing I could do to stop him. And when that happened, when he had me where he wanted me, the bastard made me kiss him—over and over again. And the whole time, he told me how beautiful I was. How fucking *special.* He rubbed my back for a while, and then, he stroked my hair. It was almost like . . . I was some sort of doll he was playing with. Some real-life Barbie he could do anything he wanted to. Slater had this look in his eye—this sick, satisfied look. It was the scariest damn thing I've ever seen."

There was no sorrow in her voice, no pity, no feeling sorry for herself. Just a cold recitation of the facts. A calm retelling of the way she'd been forced to submit to Slater. The way he'd overpowered, controlled, and humiliated her. The way he'd made her feel so helpless. Maybe there hadn't been any body parts involved, but Slater had subjected Roslyn to his own twisted form of rape.

Two tears rolled down Roslyn's lovely face. She used a crumpled, discarded napkin to wipe them away, then took off her silver glasses and started cleaning them. The only thing that gave her away were the slight tremors that shook her hands as she worked.

The cold, sharp knife of guilt in my stomach twisted in a little deeper at all the things Roslyn had endured because of me. All the horrors that I hadn't even known about until right now. All the pain that I'd accidentally inflicted on her without even knowing it.

But as much as I might want to, I couldn't change the past—only the future. So I leaned back in the booth.

Waiting. Just waiting for Roslyn to pull herself together enough to tell me the rest of it. I'd been the assassin the Spider for years. I was very good at being patient.

After about two minutes, Roslyn put her glasses back on and set the crumpled napkin to one side of the table.

"Since then, Slater's been at the club every night," Roslyn said. "Now he gets a private room. As soon as he comes in, I go and meet him. He usually stays about two hours. I don't leave until he does, and no one interrupts us. No one."

"What does he make you do?" I asked.

"Everything, nothing. Slater makes me sit on his lap and fix him drinks while he tells me about his day. About working for Mab Monroe. Then he asks me about the club. It's like we're playing fucking house or something. Hi, honey, how was your day? But he always has his hands on me, touching me, stroking my hair, kissing me. Every night, he kisses me a little harder, touches me a little longer. It's only a matter of time before—"

Roslyn bit off her words, but I knew what she'd been about to say. That it was only a matter of time before Elliot Slater raped her. It was clear that was what the sick bastard was building up to. I was willing to bet it was a game he'd played before with other women. Stalking them, dominating them, and finally raping them. Like a cat playing pat paw with a mouse until the poor creature was broken, bloody, and dead.

Except in this case, Roslyn Phillips was the mouse. How Roslyn had endured Slater's twisted attentions this long, though . . . that was something else. The inner strength that took . . . it was something I couldn't even begin to imagine. Something I didn't know if I would have been able to do, if our situations had been reversed.

"What about Xavier?" I asked. "The man's paid to protect you and the club. Why hasn't he gone after Slater himself?"

"Because I asked him not to. I told him that I had a special arrangement with Slater. That the giant was paying me good money for my time and to leave it alone."

I stared at the vamp. "Why would you do that? Xavier's a bouncer *and* a cop *and* a giant. He can take care of himself—and you too."

"Because Elliot told me that he'd kill Xavier if he tried to interfere. If he ever interrupted one of our *dates*." She let out a disgusted snort. "That's what he calls them. Dates. And I—I just couldn't bear it if Elliot ever hurt Xavier. I can bear anything else he does to me, except for that."

Pain darkened Roslyn's eyes, but there was also another soft emotion shimmering in her tight gaze and face.

"You're in love with him," I murmured. "With Xavier."

That same grim smile curved her lips again. "Come on, Gin. Everyone knows it's not love when you're a former hooker," she said, trying to make light of her feelings.

"When did it happen?"

Roslyn shrugged. "I don't even know. Xavier's worked for me for almost five years now. Maybe it was this thing with Slater, maybe it was something else. But one day, I looked up and it was just there. I just cared about him more than I have anyone in a long time. And now I can't do anything about it."

"You know he loves you too, right?" I asked.

Roslyn nodded. "I do."

I thought about what the vamp had said. "So if you told Xavier that you had an arrangement with Slater, why did he tell the giant to leave last night?"

Roslyn sighed. "At first, Xavier was too hurt to question my arrangement with Elliot, which was exactly the way I wanted it. Xavier thought I was just seeing the giant because I wanted to. But two nights ago, Elliot told me I didn't show enough . . . *enthusiasm* when he was kissing me. So he hit me, backhanded me with that diamond pinkie ring he wears. Xavier saw the cuts and bruises before I could get myself cleaned up and healed."

"And he realized that you were with Slater against your will."

Roslyn nodded. Weariness made her features sag. "And so here we are."

"Here we are," I murmured.

Silence.

I stared at Roslyn, who kept her gaze on the tabletop. The vamp had spilled her guts to me, held nothing back, but there was still one more thing I wanted to know.

"That first time when Elliot Slater came to question you about the party invitation, why didn't you tell him that it was me?" I asked. "Why didn't you give me up? Why did you really keep quiet?"

Roslyn lifted her eyes up to stare at me. "I didn't tell Elliot it was you because I made a promise to you, Gin. I opened my mouth about what you do once before, and Fletcher Lane died as a result of it. Finn told me how Alexis James tortured Fletcher before he died. Finn was sick over it. So were you. I know that's why you threatened me the way you did at Fletcher's funeral. He was a good man, and once I'd realized what I'd done, how I'd helped cause his death, I was sick over it too."

"Still," I persisted, not quite ready to let the matter lie. "If you'd told Slater, they would have come after me. They might have even gotten to me before I figured out what was going on. Then at least our arrangement would have been at an end."

Roslyn shrugged. "Finn and I have had some nice times together, and I know how important you are to him. How much like a sister you are to him. Call me sentimental, but I didn't want to hurt Finn again."

Finn and Roslyn were what I referred to as good-time buddies. They often got together for a little evening delight when they were between relationships—or when their current paramour was off doing something else. But more than that, Finn and Roslyn had a real friendship besides the sex. They genuinely cared about each other, much to my amazement.

"So I've answered your questions." Roslyn hesitated. "I know—I know I don't have the right to ask it, not after what happened to Fletcher. But I don't have anyone else to turn to, Gin. I thought maybe if I just put up with Slater for a little while, that he'd get bored with me and move on. But he hasn't. And he won't. Not until he kills me."

Tears gathered in Roslyn's eyes again, but she blinked them back. "I don't care so much about myself and what Slater will do to me. But I'm worried about Catherine and Lisa, what will happen to them if I'm not around to protect them. Lisa looks a lot like me, and Slater, he . . . he might . . ."

Roslyn's voice faded away as she thought about what the giant might do to her younger sister, Lisa, and Lisa's daughter, Catherine. The vamp clasped her hands together, trying to contain her emotions, trying to stop the tremors that shook her body and present her usual calm facade.

I didn't ask Roslyn if she'd gone to the cops about what Elliot Slater was doing to her. She knew as well as I did that the large majority of the Ashland po-po could be bought for a song. Since Slater worked for Mab Monroe, his pockets were a lot deeper than Roslyn's to start with. Not to mention the fact that the giant could just use the Fire elemental's influence and connections to get everyone to look the other way. Unless someone decided to stand up to him. Unless someone decided to stop him.

Unless I stopped him.

This was it. The moment of truth. Up until now, all my talk about getting even with Mab Monroe for murdering my family had been just that—talk. I hadn't taken any concrete action against the Fire elemental. Hell, I still didn't even really know *why* Mab had murdered my mother and older sister in the first place—other than the fact that she enjoyed that sort of thing.

But if I went after Elliot Slater, if I killed the giant for what he was doing to Roslyn, there would be no going back. Offing Slater would be the same as declaring war on Mab and her organization. And then it would be me against the most powerful woman in Ashland. There was only one way that was going to end—with one of us dead. Mab Monroe was rumored to have more magic, more raw Fire power, than any elemental born in the last five hundred years. So I wasn't too optimistic about living through any confrontation with her.

But really, there was only one thing I could do now. Sometimes I wondered if it had all been set the night Mab had murdered my family. If I was like one of the heroes in mythology books I constantly read. Like Oedipus, destined and inevitably drawing closer to doing the thing I was trying so very hard to avoid in the first place.

"The first thing you need to do is send your sister and niece out of town," I said to Roslyn. "Treat them to a trip to Myrtle Beach or something. Make them pack enough clothes and cash for at least two weeks. And tell them to keep quiet about where they're going."

Roslyn stared at me. For the first time, an emotion crept back into her dull gaze. Hope. The one damn thing that made sticking my knives out for others worthwhile. She slowly nodded.

"And you need to pack your bags and go with them."

Instead of nodding her agreement once more, Roslyn shook her head. "No."

I looked at her. "No?"

"No," she said, bitterness coloring her tone. "I know how these things work, Gin. Slater's men know what he's been doing to me. If I leave town, and he's suddenly murdered, how's it going to look? The police will come knocking on my door first thing, if Mab Monroe doesn't beat them to me. No, I have to stay here in Ashland. I have to keep playing along with him."

Roslyn was right, of course. That was exactly what would happen, but I was more concerned about getting her away from Slater right now. Yet I could tell by the hard slant of her mouth and the determination flaring in her eyes that Roslyn wasn't going to leave town.

"You sure you want to do that?" I asked in a soft voice, giving her one more chance to back out. "Are you sure you can handle that?"

Roslyn shuddered, but she nodded her head again. "I can do it. I can . . . stand it a few more days. Besides, I want to be here. I *need* to be here."

In other words, the vamp wanted to be around when I killed the giant so she could make sure he was good and dead. That he would never hurt her again. Couldn't blame her for that.

"All right," I said. "You can stay. But you're going to have to do exactly what I say when I say it. Xavier too. No matter how strange or hard it seems. With no questions and no hesitation. Can you do that? And get him to do the same?"

"I can do it." Her voice was a little stronger now.

"Good," I replied. "We'll start working on it today. Stick to your normal routine, but keep your cell phone with you at all times. You might not see much of Finn and me, but we'll be watching you and Slater."

Roslyn bit her lip. Suddenly, the vamp lurched over the table and grabbed my hand. Her fingers felt like ice against my own. "Thank you, Gin," she whispered. "Thank you."

I squeezed her cold fingers, then drew my hand away. "Don't thank me. I haven't killed the bastard yet."

Once Roslyn and I squared away the details, I went to the back of the restaurant and told Xavier and Finn that they could return to the storefront. The two were more than happy to stop working for Sophia. The Goth dwarf had the pair rearranging bottles of mayonnaise and defrosting the blood stains out of the freezers.

I told Finn and Xavier what Roslyn and I had agreed to. To my surprise, the giant leaned down and enveloped me in a gentle hug.

"Thank you, Gin," Xavier rumbled in my ear.

All these *thank-yous* and sentiment were making me uncomfortable. You'd think I'd just promised to lasso the moon or something the way Roslyn and Xavier were carrying on. Instead of just dragging out the deadly skill set I'd perfected over the years.

I stared at Finn, who grinned and shrugged. So I patted what I could reach of Xavier's back, and the giant pulled away. We said our good-byes, I unlocked the front door, and Roslyn and Xavier left the restaurant.

I watched them walk down the street, and Finn moved to stand beside me.

"What are you thinking about?" he asked.

"Nothing much," I replied. "I'm just wondering how exactly I went from being the Spider to the Robin fucking Hood of the greater Ashland area. Three months ago, I was killing people for money. Lots of money. *Buckets* of it. Now, tell me a good sob story instead and I'll take care of all your problems for free. Instead of stealing from the rich, I'm stabbing them to death for the poor."

"Well, we are going to have to work on the pro bono part," Finn admitted. "But there's nothing wrong with helping people. Dad used to do it from time to time."

I looked at Finn, with his walnut hair, ruddy skin, and

green eyes that always reminded me so much of Fletcher. "Maybe, but the old man's little hobby was something neither one of you ever shared with me."

Finn shrugged. "Dad never told me much about it, either."

"Probably because he knew you wouldn't approve of the free part."

Finn grimaced and clutched his chest. "Please, Gin. You know how the word *free* pains me."

There was a reason Finnegan Lane was one of the best investment bankers in Ashland—he loved money. The feel of it, the smell, manipulating it, watching it grow, and, of course, all the pretty things he could buy with it.

"But as much as it hurts me to say it, I hardly think we can charge Roslyn for this job," Finn said.

"You mean since I'm the one who brought Elliot Slater down on her to start with? That Roslyn's situation is all my fault? That her pain and everything—*everything*—she's had to endure is all my fault?"

Finn grimaced again. "I didn't say that, Gin."

"No, but we both know it's true. So let's get to work."

Finn squeezed my shoulder and moved off to get a refill of his chicory coffee. I stood in front of one of the storefront windows. Roslyn and Xavier had long since disappeared, but I peered through the glass and brooded about my latest assignment.

Fucking pro bono work. Going to get me killed one day.

Maybe even today.

"Are you sure he's in there?" I asked.

Finn grinned. "Baby, would I lie?"

I stared at him.

"Okay, frequently," he admitted. "But you can trust me on this. Elliot Slater's in that restaurant, along with Jonah McAllister and Mab Monroe. According to my sources, they're having their weekly powwow. Talking business, counting their money, discussing the latest body count."

"The usual, then," I murmured.

I stared through the window of Finn's silver Aston Martin. It was just after eleven, and we sat parked across and down the street from Underwood's, Ashland's most exclusive and expensive restaurant. Underwood's was the kind of place where a glass of tap water cost ten bucks. More, if you wanted ice. The restaurant was located in one of the city's older brick buildings, a classy, three-story affair in the financial district. Much of the stone had been stripped from the top floor and replaced with floor-to-ceiling windows that gave the restaurant's patrons an impressive view of the Aneirin River that curved through this part of downtown. A crimson awning bearing the eatery's name stretched out into the street, and valets hurried forward to open the doors on the steady stream of limos that pulled up to the curb.

Finn reached over and tapped the manila folder on my lap. "According to my info, the Three Musketeers should be ordering dessert about now. Tiramisu for Mab Monroe, pear cheesecake for Jonah McAllister, and a whole chocolate fudge pie for Elliot Slater."

I opened the folder and flipped through the sheets of paper. As soon as Roslyn and Xavier had left the Pork Pit, Finn and I had gone to work. I'd left the restaurant in Sophia Deveraux's capable hands for the rest of the afternoon, while Finn had fired up his laptop, reached out to his many sources, and started compiling all the information he could on Elliot Slater and the best and quickest way I could kill him.

Just like Fletcher Lane would have done, if the old man had still been alive. Finn even used the same type of plain-Jane folders that Fletcher had. Made me all nostalgic.

Nothing obvious had jumped out of the file, so we'd decided to tail the giant to see if we could spot any potential weaknesses. A bar he liked to frequent, a bookie he did business with, a mistress tucked away somewhere. It was one thing to just walk up to Slater and stab him to death. I could do that easily enough. It would be quite another to make his death look like a random bit of violence on the mean streets of Ashland and not have it traced back to me or Roslyn Phillips.

After Finn had worked his computer magic, we'd swung by Fletcher's house to pick up some supplies for the evening. More silverstone knives for me, an extra laptop battery for Finn, and ski masks and dark, anonymous clothes for both of us. Normally I didn't care if my targets saw my face before they died. It wasn't like they were going to blab about my real identity where they were going. But I wasn't taking any chances with Elliot Slater. Especially since he already knew me as Gin Blanco. It would be just my bad luck to get interrupted before he died and then have him point the finger back at me before he took his last, blood-soaked breath.

I closed the file, placed it on the floor, and leaned my head back against the seat.

"Speaking of files," Finn said. "Did you ever look at that info on Bria that I compiled for you?"

"No."

Finn stared at me with his bright green eyes. "Why not? I thought you'd be eager to see what your long-lost baby sister has been up to the past seventeen years."

I sighed. "Part of me is. But part of me wonders if I should even bother."

"Why?"

"Because Bria's a cop, Finn," I replied. "A real straight arrow, just like Donovan Caine was. I don't think she'd be too thrilled to learn that her big sister has killed more people than the common cold."

Finn looked at me for a moment. "Once again, you underestimate yourself. If Bria can't understand why you've done the things you've done, then she doesn't deserve to know you. Just like Donovan Caine didn't deserve you."

I tried to smile, but I don't think it came off very well. "Sweet of you to say, but we both know that's not true, don't we? I can't blame Donovan for leaving, not really. It's one thing for a guy to want to sleep with me. But hanging around long-term with a former assassin? That's not the kind of thing that makes a man rest easier at night, especially when he's in bed next to me and I've got a knife tucked under my pillow and another one on top of the nightstand."

Finn opened his mouth, probably to argue with me some more, but a movement across the street caught my eye. One of the valets hurried to open the door, and Mab Monroe strolled out into the dark night. The Fire elemental wore a stylish black trench coat, and her coppery hair glistened like wet blood against the dark fabric. Jonah McAllister exited next, followed by Elliot Slater. Both men wore suits, somber ties, and wingtips. I could see the gleam of their shoes even across the street.

Elliot Slater jerked his thumb at the two valets on duty. The kids paled, then hurried around the corner to retrieve someone's car. Slater rejoined Mab and Jonah McAllister, and the Three Musketeers, as Finn had dubbed them, stood on the sidewalk talking. Finn rolled down his window to see if we could hear any of their conversation.

". . . don't care about the consequences. Just get it done," Mab snapped to the other two.

"Perhaps you're being a bit hasty . . ." McAllister began in a fainter voice. He turned around to watch Mab pace back and forth on the sidewalk, and the rest of his words were lost to me.

Mab whirled around on her heel and glared at the silver-haired attorney. "I'm never hasty, Jonah. Elliot and his men need to take care of it. Tonight. Am I understood?"

McAllister nodded his head. So did Slater.

A limo pulled to a stop at the curb in front of them. Mab said something else to her two flunkies, but the rumble of the engine drowned out her voice. The Fire elemental slid into the back of the limo, and a moment later it sped away into the night. One of the valets brought another car around, a late-model Mercedes. Jonah McAllister slipped into the driver's seat, whipped a U-turn, and raced away in the opposite direction.

That left just Elliot Slater standing on the sidewalk. The giant pulled a slim cigar case out of his jacket pocket and lit up a Cuban with the help of a heavy silver lighter. Slater leaned against the brick of the restaurant and puffed away. The giant enjoyed two more cigars in rapid succession, but he made no move to leave.

"What is he waiting for?" I murmured. "Christmas?"

"I don't know," Finn replied.

We sat there and watched Slater smoke. About five minutes later, a black Hummer stopped in front of the restaurant. Slater crushed out his cigar and climbed into the back of the vehicle. Finn and I slid lower in our seats as the Hummer roared down the street past us.

Finn let the driver get a block away before sitting up and cranking the Aston's engine. He turned to me and grinned. "Care to follow the white rabbit down his hole?"

"Sure," I replied. "Let's see what kind of late-night errand the giant is doing for Mab Monroe—and how we can fuck it up."

*   *   *

Finn hung back at a discreet distance, and we followed the Hummer through the downtown district. The vehicle took one of the on ramps to the interstate, so Finn was able to blend in with the rest of the evening's traffic.

"Looks like they're headed for Northtown," Finn murmured.

Ashland might sprawl over the mountainous region where Tennessee, Virginia, and North Carolina met, but the city was really divided into two sections—Northtown and Southtown. The Pork Pit and Ashland Community College lay close to Southtown, which was home to the disenfranchised, down-on-their-luck, and dregs of society. Junkies, vampire hookers, and homeless bums wandered the Southtown streets, along with menial, blue collar workers barely eking out a living.

Northtown was a different story with its cutesy subdivisions, cookie-cutter homes, and sprawling estates. That was the part of the city that the white-collar yuppies and moneyed, social, and magical elite called home. But that didn't make that part of Ashland any less dangerous. I'd rather face down a dozen junkies than have to put up with a self-important yuppie snob who thought he was better than me just because he had little logos on his polo shirts and chinos.

"It's not terribly surprising that Slater's headed to Northtown," I told Finn. "Northtown folks are the only ones rich and dumb enough to make trouble for Mab Monroe."

"Yeah, Mab just ignores Southtown trash like us." Finn snorted.

I smiled. "Going to be the death of her. One day real soon."

Finn stared at me out of the corner of his eye. After a moment, he shook his head and returned my sly smile.

The Hummer carrying Slater and his cohorts got off the interstate. Finn slowed down and followed the black vehicle. The Hummer rumbled past a couple of cobblestone shopping malls filled with pretentious bookstores, overpriced coffee bars, and designer clothing shops. There was just enough late-night traffic to keep us from being spotted. Not that I really cared if Slater realized we were following him. If the giant stopped and confronted us, well, I'd solve Roslyn Phillips's problem on the pavement, witnesses be damned.

But the giant was far too busy plotting his foul deed for the evening to notice us tailing him, because the Hummer never slowed down or did any sort of evasive maneuvers. After about twenty minutes of driving, the massive vehicle turned into a subdivision. A spotlight on the brick entrance highlighted the name—Paradise Park. Finn waited until the Hummer had made the turn into the subdivision before killing the lights on his Aston Martin and following.

I peered at the houses we passed. Mostly two-story affairs with wide porches. Roomy enough for a family, but not enormous. Swing sets, plastic castles, and other toys littered most of the sloping lawns.

"Not as nice as I'd expect for someone causing trouble for Mab Monroe," I said. "These are middle-class homes, not McMansions."

Finn shrugged. "Doesn't matter either way, does it? We're here to watch Slater, not Mab's target."

I returned his shrug. "Not really."

A block ahead, the Hummer's taillights flared red in the darkness. The vehicle made a final turn, coasted halfway down the street, then stopped. I peered out my window. Unlike the other jam-packed avenues in the subdivision, this one only featured two houses sitting on opposite sides of the corner. The Hummer sat several hundred yards away from each one. What was going on? Did Elliot Slater need his exercise or something? Was the giant going for a jog out in the suburbs?

"I wonder why they're stopping here," Finn murmured, voicing my silent question.

"No idea. Let's find out."

I picked up a pair of night-vision goggles from the dashboard and peered through them. The Hummer doors opened, and Slater slipped out, along with four other giants. Elliot Slater ran his hands down his suit jacket, smoothing out the wrinkles. Then he jerked his head at his men. But instead of walking back down the street in our direction, Elliot Slater and his men tromped through the grass to the right of the Hummer. I scanned over and spotted a modest house hidden behind a thin row of freshly planted trees. It looked like it had just been built, given the amount of loose dirt, cement blocks, and two-by-fours that still ringed the structure. The house was the only one on its block, and more than a half mile from the next-closest building.

"Looks like they're slipping up on a house on the next street, Jasper Way, according to the sign at the end of the corner. Going in the back instead of the front," I said.

"Jasper Way?" Finn asked. "What's the name of this subdivision again?"

"Paradise Park," I replied. "Why? Does one of your many conquests live around here?"

"Probably, but the name sounds familiar for some other reason." Finn frowned and tapped his fingers on his thigh, trying to remember something important.

I peered through the goggles again. A light burned in one of the downstairs windows of the home, but the curtains were drawn, so I couldn't see inside. A gleam of white caught my eye, and I looked to the right.

"The name on the mailbox says Coolidge." I frowned. The name tickled my memory for some reason.

"Coolidge?" Finn asked.

"Yeah, Coolidge." I snapped my fingers. "I remember now. After Elliot Slater finished beating me that night at the community college, I heard Mab talking about someone named Coolidge. About how Mab wanted him taken care of—the sooner the better. Must be why Slater and his men are paying him a late-night visit. I wonder what the poor guy did to piss off Mab."

Finn sighed and closed his eyes for a second. "Not him, her," he replied. "Coolidge is a her, Gin."

"How do you know that?"

Finn stared at me, his green eyes flashing like emeralds in the semidarkness. "Because it's in that file of information I gave you."

A hard knot formed in my stomach. "Which file?"

"The one on Bria," Finn replied. "Bria Coolidge. That's the name she's using now."

Oh, *fuck*.

❄ 10 ❄

I dropped the night-vision goggles, grabbed my ski mask from the dashboard, and yanked the black fabric down over my head, hiding my pale face and brown hair from sight.

"Gin—"

Finn said something, probably telling me to wait for him or slow down, but I couldn't make out what it was. I was already out of the car and sprinting toward the house.

Elliot Slater and his giants had a good head start on me— almost a quarter of a mile. I saw the five of them slip through the trees that circled the back side of the house. Another few seconds and they'd be at the back door and surging inside. An icy fist squeezed my heart and lungs, making it hard to breathe. I'd just found my sister again, and now Slater and his men were here to kill her. Why else would they be sneaking around Bria's house this close to midnight?

Run, run, run, run . . . The thought drummed through my head as my boots slapped against the pavement. I chugged past the parked Hummer, leaped over the concrete curb, and ran through the frost-covered grass. The tiny blades crackled like glass under my smashing feet. If Slater and his giants bothered to stop and listen, they'd hear me coming for sure. But I didn't care. All that mattered was getting to Bria before she got dead.

I broke through the line of spindly pecan trees, and Bria's house rose up in front of me, two stories of charming gray brick. I blocked out the blood roaring through my ears and reached out with my Stone magic. But the house was freshly constructed, and the stones were too new to tell me anything about Bria—or what might be happening inside.

I was a hundred feet away from the back door when lights flashed and a series of *pop-pop-pop*s sounded. The distinctive sights and sounds of someone firing a handgun. A window shattered, and a series of loud curses spilled out into the night air. Bria was putting up more of a fight than the giants had expected.

A few seconds later, an intense, bluish white glow filled the downstairs windows and burst through the open back door. Even though I was outside, I could still feel the cold caress of Ice magic surging through the house. A sensation so like my own Stone and Ice power that it made me want to weep. Not surprising, even if it was something that I hadn't thought about in years. Because Bria was an Ice elemental, of course. Just like our mother, Eira, and older sister, Annabella, had been. I was the only one who'd inherited our father, Tristan's, Stone magic as well.

I just hoped Bria had enough juice to hold off Elliot Slater and his men until I could even the odds.

The Ice magic flowed around me a second longer before snuffing out like a candle. Either Bria didn't have much power or something had broken her concentration—like a fist to her face or a bullet to her gut.

The brass hinges of the back door barely clung to the stone frame. One of the giants must have just shouldered his way through it, rather than bother with the pretense of knocking. Although my heart screamed at me to keep running, to get to Bria as quickly as possible, I slowed my steps and paused just outside the door. Me barging into whatever fight was going on inside wouldn't help Bria. That's not how I'd operated as the assassin the Spider, and I wasn't going to do it now. Besides, there was always the off chance that Bria could mistake me for one of the giants and turn on me. Being killed by one's own sister would be a shitty way to die.

So I stood there and listened. Another series of *pop-pop-pop*s sounded, followed by three more shots. Two people exchanging gunfire.

"Fuck!" A sharp, masculine cry. One of the giants had been hit.

Then silence.

I crept a few feet inside the door, taking care to be exceptionally quiet. The back door opened up into a kitchen, and the white tile floor and countertops gleamed like they were made of ivory. The fight had started in here, judging from the black splashes of blood on the floor. Sharp, melting pieces of elemental Ice also littered the tile underfoot like a wet carpet.

But what was most surprising was the refrigerator. The top door had been blown off, and a rune shimmered with a bluish white light inside the frosty depths of the freezer. The symbol zigzagged up and down like the teeth of a saw. That's what it was called—the saw. Symbolizing pure, biting force. In addition to using runes to identify themselves, elementals could also imbue runes with magic. In other words, make the symbols come to life and perform some specific function.

The saw was a defensive rune that could be used by any elemental and was especially popular as a sort of magic trip wire and bomb rolled into one. Since Bria was an Ice elemental, she'd drawn the saw symbol in her freezer, using the rune and appliance to contain her frosty magic. When the giants had broken into her house tonight, she'd most likely sent a burst of her Ice power into the freezer, triggering the explosive saw rune inside. And then—*boom*! The freezer door had blown open, spraying the giants with sharp, jagged icicles. Hence the blood on the floor.

I recognized the trick. I'd done it myself with stone a time or two. Baby sister had booby-trapped her own freezer. Despite the situation, I found myself grinning underneath my ski mask. *Nice.*

I saw all this in the three seconds it took me to creep to the opposite side of the kitchen. I crouched down and peered around the doorjamb. A long hallway stretched out before opening up into the front of the house. Rooms branched off either side of the hallway, which was now littered with debris. A couple of porcelain vases had been shattered, chairs overturned, a table splintered, a mirror knocked off the wall and broken. More blood glistened on the wooden floor, and a couple of bullets had punched into and blackened the walls. I started forward—

"Give it up, Coolidge!" Elliot Slater's voice rumbled through the house like thunder. "We've got you surrounded, and it's only a matter of time before you run out of ammo. We'll kill you quick, I promise."

"Fuck you, Slater," Bria snarled.

Not the most original of retorts, but it was hard to be witty under pressure. Still, I frowned. Despite her bravado, Bria's voice had sounded high and thin, like she was in pain or injured. But she was still breathing. As long as she kept doing that, Jo-Jo Deveraux could fix the rest of the damage. From the sound of things, Elliot and his men had Bria trapped somewhere in the front of the house. Which meant they wouldn't be expecting a sneak attack from the rear. Excellent.

I tiptoed down the hallway, a silverstone knife in each hand. Although I still wanted to charge forward, I moved slowly, calmly, carefully. Just because I thought Slater and his men were at the end of the hall didn't mean that he hadn't left someone behind to guard their rear. Slater had worked for Mab Monroe for a long time. He wasn't dumb by any stretch of the imagination. So I checked every room that branched off the hallway, looking for trouble.

Two doors up from the kitchen, I found some. A giant slouched over a sink in a small bathroom. Judging from the long, needlelike bits of elemental Ice sticking out of his face, it looked like he'd been the one who'd taken the brunt of the blast from the booby-trapped freezer. The giant held a white towel up over his eye socket. At least, the towel had been white at one point. Blood had turned the cotton fabric a dull crimson. The giant had also been shot a couple times in the chest, and a tight cluster of wounds just above his heart oozed blood. Baby sister was a good shot. She just hadn't had time to finish him off before the other giants had rushed her.

Good thing her big sis Gin was here to take care of that.

I drew in a breath, then burst into the bathroom. My sudden appearance startled the giant so much that he dropped his towel, giving me a good look at the icicle that had skewered his right eye like a toothpick through an olive. The wounded giant opened his mouth to yell for his friends just as my silverstone knife slammed into his throat. The scream turned into a coughing, choking wheeze. My other knife ripped into the giant's stomach. His warm blood splashed all over my ski mask and dark clothes.

But the giant wasn't down for the count just yet. The bastard lashed out at me, flailing wildly with his fists. One clipped my shoulder. The other hit my left kidney. Even weakened, the solid blows still hurt. Being an elemental, I could have reached for my Stone magic and used it to harden my skin into an impenetrable shell. Almost nothing could hurt me when I did that. But I didn't know if Elliot Slater or one of his other men had any elemental power, and I didn't want to tip them off to my presence just yet. Besides, I reserved my magic for the main event. This barely qualified as the warm-up bout.

So I just stood there, slashing the giant with my knives.

By the time I'd made my third pass with the silverstone weapons, the giant's pink guts could be seen through the ripped fabric of his shirt. Not to mention the fact that his throat was open almost to his spine. He quit fighting, and his one good eye glazed over. I lowered his heavy body to the floor and tiptoed back to the door.

"What was that?" one of the giants muttered.

"I don't know—" Another man started to respond when another series of *pop-pop-pop*s shattered the quiet.

Someone else returned fire, and I used the noise and distraction to slip out of the bathroom and forward to the end of the hallway. It opened up into a large, square living room that looked like a tornado had ripped through the area. Broken lamps, overturned furniture, shattered knickknacks, cardboard packing boxes that had been split open from things falling on top of them.

To my surprise, a giant lay dead just inside the doorway. He slumped against the wall, staring up at the ceiling. I spotted a couple of bullet wounds clustered in the middle of his chest, but that wasn't what had killed him—it was the Ice. The giant's face looked blue and brittle, an inch of white frost had gathered in his hair, and his eyes resembled frozen marbles. Large icicles hung off his nose and chin, and his mouth was open in a silent scream.

The human body is mostly water. Flash-freeze that water using elemental Ice magic, and, well, you've got yourself a human Popsicle. Not a pretty way to die, but an effective method of dealing with an enemy who's bigger and stronger than you. That bluish white flash I'd seen before must have been Bria laying her Ice whammy on the giant. The temperature was also at least ten degrees colder in here than in the rest of the house, due to Bria using her Ice power. My breath frosted in the air.

But the Iced giant was the only person I saw. A short wall ran out into the middle of the room, hiding the other half from sight. *Pop-pop-pop.* Bria and the giants were still exchanging gunfire, and the stench of cordite hung in the air, along with my frosty breath. I crept over to the wall and peered around it. Elliot Slater and his two remaining goons crouched behind an overturned couch about fifteen feet in front of me. Only one of the giants had a gun. Slater and the other man just huddled there, waiting for an opening.

I looked past the couch. Through a tangle of upended tables and chairs, I spotted an oversize stone fireplace. Bria had taken refuge inside the hollow space. I could just see her toes peeking out from behind the stone. She was trapped. Slater had been right. It was only a matter of time before she ran out of ammo. Then the three giants could just charge her and rip her apart with their bare hands. From the smile on Elliot Slater's face and the way he kept flexing his hands, he seemed to be looking forward to that prospect.

A hard smile curved my own lips. Just like I was looking forward to gutting the giant. For Roslyn Phillips, and now for Bria too.

The shooting stopped, and I heard a hollow *click*. Bria let out a soft curse. She was out of bullets, which meant it was time for me to make my move. A knife in either hand, I stepped around the short wall and let out a low whistle. The giant closest to me turned at the sound, and I threw one of my knives at him. The weapon sank into his left shoulder socket. He growled in pain, and the gun he'd been holding slipped out of his numb fingers. Slater and the other man whirled around in surprise.

"Who the fuck are you?" Slater snapped, his eyes flicking over my blood-spattered clothes and ski mask.

I grinned and grabbed another knife from the small of my back. "Your worst nightmare."

His hazel eyes narrowed. "We'll see about that, bitch."

Slater started toward me, but the giant I'd winged had other ideas. He pulled my silverstone knife out of his shoulder and stepped in front of his boss. Slater stopped and pointed over his shoulder at the fireplace where Bria was still hiding.

"Get the cop!" Slater roared at the third man. "Get Coolidge before she gets away! Now!"

The other giant nodded and turned toward the fireplace. I threw one of my knives at him. The weapon sank into the giant's back, and he grunted. From the way he moved, I knew I hadn't done any major damage, but maybe it would slow him down enough for me to take care of Elliot Slater and the other man coming toward me.

The giant I'd winged crossed over to me in three steps and slashed at me with my own knife. I ducked the wide blow. Even as I lunged down, I slashed his femoral artery on his right leg. Black, arterial blood sprayed in my face, but I ignored the warm, stinging sensation and grabbed a fourth knife out of one of my boots. As I came up, I used that weapon to open up the artery on his left leg. The giant howled again and staggered back. I slammed my boot into one of his knees. The change of tactics surprised him, and he stumbled away and flipped over the lopsided couch. He wasn't dead yet, but he'd bleed out quick, especially if he kept thrashing around.

Meanwhile, Bria had crept out of the fireplace. She grabbed one of the long, metal pokers and held it out in front of her like a sword. I could see blood on her face and clothes, but I couldn't tell how badly she was injured. The giant I'd thrown my weapon at reached around, pulled the knife out of his own back, and advanced on her. I scurried to one side to go help Bria, when a flash of movement caught my eye. I instinctively threw myself to the left. Elliot Slater's ham-size fist whistled past my cheek, and I turned to face the quick giant.

Slater regarded me with his cold hazel eyes. "You know you're going to die for interfering with me."

"Really? Tell that to your two buddies that I've killed—so far," I mocked.

Slater regarded me another moment, then snapped his hand up. I'd been expecting the punch and jerked back, but he still managed a glancing blow to my stomach that forced some of the air from my lungs. It was bad enough that Slater had a giant's inherent strength and toughness. Why did he have to be so fucking quick too? That just wasn't fair. Slater came at me again, and I was too busy dodging his blows to lament the fact that he was so much faster than me.

Another flash of motion caught my eye. On the other side of the room, the front door swung open, and a figure dressed in dark clothes stepped inside. The figure paused a moment, taking in me fighting with Elliot Slater and Bria swinging her fireplace poker at the other giant.

"Hey, buddy," the figure called out. "You want some help with her?"

The giant turned, and Finn shot him in the face four times. Fletcher Lane might not have trained his son to be an assassin like me, but the old man had taught Finn everything he knew about weapons—including how to shoot a gun. Hell, Finn was a better shot than I was. Which is why Finn's first bullet went through the giant's right eye and up into his skull. The giant's head snapped back, and he was already on his way to dead when Finn's next three bullets shattered his face. Bria flinched as the giant's blood, bone, and brain tissue splattered on her face and body. But she didn't scream. For some reason, that made me even prouder of her than the freezer trick.

And then there was one—Elliot Slater.

The giant looked over his shoulder at his dead minions and Finn, who was rapidly advancing on us. I wouldn't have thought him capable of it, but Slater actually did the smart thing.

He ran.

I surged forward, wanting to kill him right here, right now, and take care of Roslyn Phillips's problem. But once again, Elliot Slater was quicker than I was. The giant slammed his fist into my stomach again and shoved me out of the way. Then, he dove headfirst through the nearest window and out into the dark night.

❋ 11 ❋

I just lay where I'd fallen, sprawled halfway over a table. Gun at the ready, Finn rushed over to the window and looked outside.

"Slater?" I croaked, still trying to suck down as much oxygen as I could. The giant had connected with his last blow, and it felt like he'd broken a couple of my ribs—again.

Finn drew back and shook his head. "Gone already. He moves fast for a giant."

I nodded. I'd gone fist-to-fist with him, so Slater's speedy getaway didn't surprise me. Even if it was damn inconvenient. But the giant was just going to have to get dead another night. Right now, I had Bria to think of—and the bodies and blood that littered her house like old newspapers.

"So now what?" Finn asked.

"Time to call in the cleanup crew," I said. "Get both of them over here right now."

Although his black ski mask obscured his features, Finn still managed to raise his eyebrows at me. "Both of them? Not just our dark and twisty friend?"

I nodded. "Both of them."

"You're the boss." Finn pulled his cell phone out of the pocket of his black khakis, moved to the other side of the living room, and started dialing Sophia Deveraux.

I drew in a breath and turned to face Bria. My baby sister stood in front of the fireplace, the long metal poker clenched in her hands and propped on her shoulder like it was a baseball bat she was eager to swing at my head. Bria must have been getting ready for bed when Slater and his men had burst through the back door. She wore a pair of faded, flannel, baby blue pajama pants with a matching shirt. Her feet were bare, although her toes were painted a dark magenta. Jo-Jo Deveraux would have approved of the color.

Despite the late hour, Bria still wore her primrose rune on a chain around her neck. I wondered if she ever took off the necklace. I was guessing no. The silverstone medallion caught the light and flashed at me like a traffic signal. Warning of danger, in more ways than one.

My eyes flicked over her body, looking for injuries. A couple of rough scrapes marred Bria's beautiful features, probably from where she'd thrown herself into the fireplace. More cuts and bruises dotted her arms and hands, and the sleeves of her shirt had been ripped and shredded in places. Purple circles of exhaustion ringed her blue eyes, and blood had matted in the ends of her shaggy, layered, blond hair. But what concerned me most was the ever-increasing circle of blood on the right side of her body, parallel with her belly button. She'd been shot, judging from the bullet hole that blackened the fabric of her shirt.

Anyone else probably would have been whimpering on the floor by now, but Bria stood there, as though the gut wound was of no more consequence to her than what she'd eaten for dinner. Whatever else she might be, whatever secrets she had, I knew one thing—my sister was one tough cookie. Just like me.

Bria stared back at me. Wariness shimmered in her blue gaze. "Who the hell are you? What are you doing here?" she demanded, tightening her grip on the fireplace poker.

The motion made three rings glint on her left index finger—thin bands stacked on top of each other. Silverstone, from the way they caught the light.

"Saving your ass." I moved around the couch so that I stood directly in front of her. "Why? What does it look like we're doing?"

Her bruised features tightened. "I didn't need your help."

I stared down at the giant in front of the couch, the one whose femoral arteries I'd severed with my silverstone knives. He'd clamped his hands over his legs to try and stem the blood flow, but it hadn't worked. The giant's dead, glassy eyes fixed on the ceiling fan.

"Really?" I asked. "And here I thought you were trapped in a fireplace with three very large, very strong giants just waiting for you to run out of bullets so they could come over and beat you to death. Or am I misinterpreting the situation?"

Bria's mouth twisted. Whether it was from pain or annoyance, I wasn't quite sure.

"Tell me," I asked, bending down to examine the giant. "What exactly did you do to piss off Mab Monroe enough for her to send Elliot Slater and his goons out here to kill you? Now, Mab isn't lacking for flunkies, but she sent her numero uno after you tonight."

"That's between me and Mab," Bria said in a frosty voice. "I don't see how it's any of your business."

I was mildly surprised that Bria didn't deny the fact that she'd done something to upset Mab. "In case you couldn't tell from the bodies, I've decided to make it my business. So you might as well tell me."

Bria's eyes narrowed. "I'm not telling you a damn thing. If I were you, I'd think about leaving—right now. I'm a homicide detective, and I've already called for backup. A couple of units should be here any minute."

I finished my examination of the dead giant, got to my feet, and turned to face my sister once more.

"You didn't have time to call for help, detective," I replied. "Because you went for your gun instead of reaching for the phone. Nothing wrong with it. I prefer to take care of my own problems too."

"How the hell do you know that?"

I shrugged. "Because if you'd used it to call for help, it would be lying somewhere in this mess."

Bria's gaze flicked to the left. A cordless phone sat in a charger on a table that had somehow escaped the battle.

"Not that calling 911 would have done you any good," I continued. "Slater probably put the word out for the po-po not to respond to any distress calls in the area tonight."

"Elliot Slater doesn't run the police department," she snapped.

I snorted. "No, Mab Monroe does. But since Slater is her number-one enforcer, he can call in any favors he needs any time he needs them. I don't know how long you've been in Ashland, but you need to realize right now that the cops are useless. Your boys in blue don't care about you. They would have been perfectly content to come out here tomorrow, photograph your corpse, and eat some doughnuts while they were at it."

Bria's mouth tightened, but she didn't say anything. Looked like she had already figured out exactly how things worked in Ashland. Good. The knowledge, distasteful though it might be, might help keep Bria alive until I figured out exactly why Mab wanted her dead—and what I could do to keep it from happening. I might not know my sister, might not have any inkling as to the kind of woman she was now, but I'd be damned if Mab Monroe was going to murder another member of my family.

"But my associate and I are here now, and we've decided to take an interest in your situation," I said. "Now, why don't you sit down and let me take a look at that gunshot wound before you pass out from the blood loss?"

Bria stared at me. Emotions flashed like icy fire in her blue eyes. Suspicion, mistrust, wariness. No fear, though. Despite everything that had happened tonight, she wasn't screaming at the top of her lungs, or worse, bawling her eyes out. Her calm demeanor, even when injured, made me admire her a little more. I didn't know why I felt so proud of my sister every time I saw her, every time I realized just how tough she was. It wasn't like I'd done anything to make Bria the strong, independent woman she was today. But the feeling was there, just like my love for her was—two things I knew that I'd never be able to quash no matter what had happened between us in the violent, murky past or here in the troubled present.

But blood had soaked the bottom half of Bria's shirt by now, which meant I didn't have time to screw around and keep talking until she decided to trust me. Not that she ever would.

"Look," I said in a soft voice. "I have zero love for Elliot Slater and his men, which is why I came to your rescue here tonight. I just want to help you. That's it. Nothing more, nothing less. So let me, okay? Nothing else bad will happen to you tonight, I promise."

Finn finished his call to Sophia Deveraux and moved to stand beside me. "You should listen to her, detective. She doesn't offer her assistance lightly or often. And her promises? Better than money in the bank."

I looked at him. "Better than money? That's high praise coming from you, since there's nothing you love more than C-notes."

Finn just grinned at me.

Bria snorted at our banter. "Maybe I'm old-fashioned, but I have a hard time trusting two people who broke into my house, killed a couple of giants, and are now chatting to me like we're out having cake and coffee—while wearing ski masks."

I shrugged. "You do what you want, but how much

longer do you think you can stand there? You can either trust us not to kill you, or you can bleed out in a few minutes. If I were you, I think I'd pick option A. But that's just me."

"Oh, I'd definitely go with option A too," Finn chimed in. "Because it would be a crying shame to let that sweet body of yours get all cold and stiff, detective." Finn smiled at her, his white teeth flashing through the slit in his ski mask.

I rolled my eyes. Here my sister was, bloody, battered, and brandishing a weapon, and Finn was using the lull in the action to hit on her. Sometimes I thought Finnegan Lane had a death wish, thinking with his dick as much as he did.

Bria glowered at Finn, but she took the fireplace poker off her shoulder and lowered it to the floor, using it as a sort of crutch. By this point, she was having a hard time just keeping herself upright. Her body swayed from side to side, and tremors shook her arms and legs.

"Fine," Bria muttered. "But keep your hands where I can see them."

She lowered herself down so that she was sitting on the bottom shelf of the fireplace. I jerked my head at Finn, and the two of us moved over to the front door.

"Keep an eye out for our dwarven friends," I murmured. "And go around back and see if Slater's Hummer is still parked on the street behind us. I'm willing to bet that he's gone, at least for tonight, but I want to be sure."

Finn nodded and walked out the front of the house, closing the door behind him.

"Charming associate you have there," Bria sniped.

"Does he always storm into people's homes and shoot men in the face?"

"Not always," I replied. "Sometimes he just talks them to death."

Bria's mouth twisted again, but this time, the corner of her lips lifted up into a faint smile. Perhaps my sharp wit wasn't completely lost on her.

"Now, let's take a look at that hole in the side of you," I said.

I moved over to the fireplace and got down on my knees in front of Bria. Apprehension flared in her face again, and she still had a firm grip on the fireplace poker. But I kept my movements slow and nonthreatening, and she let me lift up the corner of her ruined shirt. A small, neat hole marred Bria's pale flesh just above her hip bone. Blood leaked out of the wound with every breath she took, but it wasn't gushing as badly as I'd feared. She'd be all right until Jo-Jo Deveraux could come and heal her.

"It's a through-and-through," Bria muttered. "Bullet's probably buried in my fireplace somewhere."

I knew it was. I could hear the stones' muttering about the violence that had taken place in here tonight. I nodded and looked around the ruined living room. A pale blue afghan covered with white snowflakes lay among the mess on the floor. Using one of my knives, I cut off a swath of the fabric. It would have been easier to go into the bathroom and find a towel, but I didn't want to leave Bria alone so she could do something stupid—like call the cops for real. Bria tensed at the sight of me ripping into the afghan, so I tucked the bloody knife into my boot before I approached her again.

"Here," I said, showing her the fabric. "Let's put this against your wound until my friends get here."

"More friends? Are they as charming as the other fellow?"

I shrugged. "Depends on your definition of *charming*. But one of them is a healer."

"Convenient," Bria muttered.

I smiled. "Very."

Bria leaned back against the outer wall of the fireplace and lifted up her shirt. I carefully placed the fabric against the gunshot wound, then wrapped it around her waist so it would plug the exit hole too. I pulled the fabric as tight as it would go, making Bria grunt with pain, then tied the whole thing together with a neat bow. Bria rested her head against the stone. Her breath came in short pants, and sweat glistened on her neck and forehead.

"Sorry," I said. "But it had to be done."

She nodded. "I've . . . had worse."

She sat there a few seconds, eyes closed, resting, getting her strength back. Once her breathing eased into a more normal pattern, Bria opened her eyes and stared at me again. "Who *are* you? Why did you come in here after Elliot Slater and his men?"

Ah, the moment of truth. I sat down on the floor in front of her and crossed my legs, considering my options. I could lie, of course. Make up some fairy tale about being a good Samaritan who just happened to hear the noise, put on a ski mask, grabbed several knives, and jumped into the fray against five giants and a pissed-off Ice elemental. Not that Bria would believe me. Hell, I'd probably start laughing halfway through a story like that. Finn would certainly get a chuckle out of it. Since I couldn't think of a somewhat convincing lie, I decided to go with the truth.

"I have a certain interest in Slater," I replied. "I've been following him all night."

"And what would that interest be?" she asked.

"I'm going to kill him."

Silence.

I sat there and waited for the angry condemnation to fill Bria's blue eyes. For my baby sister to look at me the disappointed, reproachful way that Detective Donovan Caine always had—like I was a dog who'd betrayed its master.

Instead, Bria tilted her head to one side and regarded me with a thoughtful expression. "You're an assassin, aren't you?"

Not a huge leap of logic to make, considering what she'd seen me do tonight. I shrugged. No reason to lie now. "I used to be. I retired a while back."

"So why go after Slater now?"

I shrugged again. "An old friend called in a favor, and I owe her big-time. Besides, my retirement's been rather boring for the most part. I like to keep my hand in things, and my blades sharp. So I help the little people, as it were, every once in a while."

Bria snorted. "What are you then? Some sort of guardian angel?"

"The angel of death, maybe," I replied. "People who have guardian angels generally don't need my services."

She smiled at my grim humor. We sat there staring at each other. Five seconds ticked by. Then, ten. Twenty. Thirty. Forty-five . . .

"Why don't you take off that ski mask?" Bria asked.

I raised my eyebrows. "And let you get a good look at my face? I think not, detective."

She smiled again. "Can't blame me for trying."

"Of course not," I replied. "So is this the part where you tell me what a bad, bad girl I've been, murdering people for something as common as money? Vow to bring me to justice no matter what and do the whole honorable cop shtick?"

Bria shrugged and winced at the pain the motion brought along with it. "Why would I do that? If it wasn't for you, I'd be dead right now. Beaten to death by Slater and his men. Believe me, I'm grateful for the intervention, even if it is by a self-proclaimed angel of death."

Well, that certainly wasn't the answer I'd been expecting. Donovan Caine would have already been planning which cell to stick me in down at the police station. Seemed my sister's morals were a little bendier than the detective's. But what surprised me more than her attitude was the emotion her words stirred in me—hope. Hope that maybe one day I could tell Bria who I really was and what I'd had to do to stay alive over the years—and that she would accept me despite all the bad things I'd done. And what I was prepared to do now to keep her, Finn, and the Deveraux sisters safe from Mab Monroe, Elliot Slater, and anyone else stupid enough to threaten them.

Fucking hope. Next thing you'd know, I'd be getting soft and sentimental and teary-eyed over puppies and kittens and rainbows.

"So you're okay with your savior being a bona fide assassin?" I asked.

Bria shrugged and winced again. "You saved me for whatever reason. I'm not prepared to think too much about it tonight. I know there are worse things, worse people in the world. I'll stop them first. Then, when that's done, maybe I'll get around to you—"

That was all Bria got out before the blood loss caught up to her, and she toppled over in a dead faint.

✻ 12 ✻

"Knock, knock," Finn called out as he opened the front door to Bria's house. "Honey, I'm home—" He stopped at the sight of me kneeling over Bria's inert body. "What happened to her?"

"She passed out from the pain and blood loss," I said.

"Good thing," Finn replied. "Seeing as how we have company."

He stepped to one side, and Sophia and Jo-Jo Deveraux entered the living room. The two dwarven sisters stood in the doorway and surveyed the destruction and dead bodies in front of them. Sophia wore a pair of thick, black coveralls and heavy boots, while Jo-Jo was clad in a pink robe that looked fuzzier and softer than a baby's blanket. The older dwarf had stuck her feet into a matching pair of house shoes. She wasn't wearing socks, though, despite the chill of the December night.

Jo-Jo let out a low whistle. "Finn told Sophia that

you'd made a mess, but I didn't think it would be quite this bad, Gin."

"You know me. I never do anything halfway," I quipped. "Now, come over here and see to Bria before she gets any worse."

Sophia pulled a pair of black rubber gloves out of one of the pockets on her coveralls and snapped them on with obvious relish. The Goth dwarf didn't smile, not really, but there was definitely a sparkle in her black eyes and a lightness to her steps. She was eager, happy even, to get to her disposal work. At least I'd made someone's night. Sophia dragged the bodies of the three dead giants over to the front door and flipped the couch back into its normal upright position. Then the Goth dwarf picked up Bria and put her on the sofa.

Jo-Jo found a chair that hadn't been splintered and carried it over so she could sit down and examine my blood-covered sister. Finn grabbed a tall lamp out of a corner and plugged it in so Jo-Jo could have enough light to see exactly what she was doing while she healed Bria. I moved around the living room, righting overturned furniture, picking up broken pieces of glass, stuffing the other splintered, bloody debris into some trash bags that I'd found under the kitchen sink.

Sophia bent down, put one of the dead giants over her shoulder in a fireman's carry, and got to her feet. The giant weighed several hundred pounds, but Sophia could have been carrying around a stuffed bunny rabbit for all the effort she seemed to be exerting.

Still, I thought I'd be polite and see what I could do to aid the Goth dwarf. "Do you need any help with them?

Carrying them outside? Or doing whatever you're going to do to them?"

Sophia gave me a flat look with her black eyes. "Nuh-uh." The dwarf's grunt for *no*.

With the giant still slung over her shoulder, Sophia opened the front door and stepped out into the dark night. Despite my curiosity about what the Goth dwarf did with the many bodies she disposed of, I didn't follow her outside. Even though I knew that Jo-Jo Deveraux was the best Air elemental healer in Ashland, I didn't want to leave Bria's side. Not until the bullet holes in her had been sealed shut, and she was sleeping peacefully.

"Nasty bit of business this is," Jo-Jo murmured. "Bullet nicked one of her kidneys, among other things."

The middle-aged dwarf had already unwrapped the crude afghan bandage I'd wound around Bria's midsection. Blood stained most of the fabric a dark crimson. Jo-Jo reached for her Air elemental magic, and her eyes began to glow a milky white in her face. The dwarf held her palm over Bria's midsection.

Air elementals could tap into all the natural gases in the air, including oxygen. That's how they healed people—by forcing and circulating oxygen in, around, and through wounds, using all those helpful little air molecules to sew ripped, torn, and ruined flesh back together again.

Jo-Jo reached for her Air magic again, and her palm began to glow the same milky white color as her eyes. The dwarf's power always felt like hot tingles washing over me, like part of me had fallen asleep and was just waking up. Tonight was no exception. I gritted my teeth at the odd sensation.

Jo-Jo's magic didn't cause me actual physical pain, not like being in the presence of Mab Monroe's Fire power did. But it still made me uncomfortable. Air and Stone were opposing elements, just like Fire and Ice. Jo-Jo's Air magic just felt strange to me, just like my Stone and Ice power would to her. The magical, elemental equivalent of nails on a chalkboard all the way around, as it were.

Jo-Jo's magic also made the silverstone spider rune scars on my palms itch and burn. Silverstone was a very special metal, capable of absorbing all kinds of elemental magic. In a way, silverstone was hollow, empty, and hungering for enough magic to fill it up. Lots of elementals had charms or medallions made out of the metal, in which they stored bits and pieces of their power. Sort of like magical batteries. My mother had used her snowflake rune that way. I eyed the primrose medallion that rested in the hollow of Bria's throat. I wondered if she had learned how to do that trick too, along with booby-trapping her freezer.

The primrose wasn't the only silverstone Bria wore. I picked up her hand and looked at the three rings on her left index finger. They were nothing fancy, just three thin bands stacked on top of each other, although there seemed to be patterns in the metal. I squinted at the bands and realized that they had tiny runes carved into them. Small snowflakes ringed one of the bands, while ivy vines curled through another. The final ring, the top one on Bria's finger, was stamped in the middle with a single spider rune—my rune.

My heart twisted. Baby sister wore a ring, a symbol, for each of us. My mother, Eira's, snowflake. Our older sister, Annabella's, ivy vine. And my spider rune. Somehow I knew she wore them all the time, just like she did her own primrose medallion. She still remembered us, still remembered me, all these years after that horrible night. She remembered what I wished I could forget. I let out a tired breath and gently put Bria's hand down by her side.

Jo-Jo passed her hand over Bria's midsection several times before releasing her grip on her magic. The milky white glow on her palm faded, and the dwarf's eyes returned to their normal translucent color.

"There," she said. "Good as new."

I peered over the dwarf's shoulder. Sure enough, the nasty hole in Bria's side had vanished, replaced by smooth, pink skin. Jo-Jo had also taken the time to get rid of the scrapes and bruises that had dotted my baby sister's arms, hands, and face.

"Thanks, Jo-Jo," I said. "I'm sure Bria would tell you that too, if she were awake."

"No problem, darling." Jo-Jo reached over and tucked a lock of Bria's blond hair behind her ear. "After all, she's family now."

For some reason, the dwarf's soft words made me shiver.

By the time Sophia dragged the remaining bodies outside and the rest of us straightened up as much of the bloody mess as we could, it was well after midnight. I hauled another garbage bag outside and dumped it in the plastic pickup container. My eyes scanned the darkness, but I didn't see anyone or anything moving in the black night. Bria's house was more than a half mile from the others at the end of the street. At this late hour, everyone else in the immediate vicinity had long ago retired to their bedrooms. Only a few security lights mounted over garages and outbuildings broke through the night. Low, thick clouds obscured the moon and stars, and a metallic scent filled the air that told me snow was on the way.

But a couple inches of the white stuff wouldn't be nearly enough to cover up the bloody bit of violence I'd done in Bria's house tonight—and what I was planning to do to Elliot Slater as soon as I got the chance. I was going to make sure the giant got dead before he had the opportunity to hurt Bria or Roslyn Phillips again. And there were plenty of other people in Ashland who wouldn't mind living in a world without Slater in it. All this pro bono work I was dabbling in really was turning into public service. The mayor so needed to give me a medal.

As I peered into the night, the front door opened and Jo-Jo Deveraux stepped outside. The dwarf settled herself on the steps that led up to the porch, draping her fuzzy pink housecoat over her knees. I stood at the base of the steps and leaned against the handrail.

"You did a good thing tonight, Gin," Jo-Jo said. "Saving your sister like that."

I shrugged. "It wasn't so much a good thing as it was sheer luck. I had no idea Slater was coming here to kill her. If Finn and I hadn't been following him . . ." My voice trailed off.

I didn't want to think about how close I'd come to losing Bria again tonight. That I'd almost missed my chance to get to know her again before I'd even been ready to take it in the first place, to risk telling her who and what I really was. My sister might be a stranger to me now, but I couldn't let go of the memory of the sweet little girl she'd once been—a girl that I would have done anything to protect. Back then and especially now.

Besides, Fletcher Lane had left me a photo of her for a reason. The old man had wanted me to find Bria, to get to know her again. Even if I hadn't wanted to do those things on my own, I would have gone through with them just to honor Fletcher's wishes. He'd done so much for me over the years. I was going to do everything I could for him now—even if he was cold, dead, and buried.

I shook my head and chased away my melancholy thoughts. Fletcher Lane was gone. Mooning about his murder once more wasn't going to bring him back. Right now, I needed to focus on the problem in front of me— Elliot Slater and his amazing quickness. So I told Jo-Jo how fast the giant was and asked if perhaps Slater was using some sort of elemental magic that I couldn't sense to help his fists connect with my ribs. The dwarf frowned for a few seconds, thinking.

"It's possible," Jo-Jo said. "But to do what you're describing, Slater would have to be doing one of two things. One, he'd have to be an Air elemental and using his magic to affect the gases in the air. Air has weight, you know, even though we don't usually realize that it does. Slater could be using his power to move the air, the molecules, out of his way so he has less resistance to go through when he swings his fists. Simple physics, really."

"And two?" I asked.

"He'd have to be an Ice elemental and using his power to momentarily freeze his opponents. Using just enough magic to give himself that second's advantage, that seeming bit of speed," Jo-Jo said. "But I don't think he's an elemental."

"Why not?"

Jo-Jo shrugged. "Because those are both very, very subtle skills that would take years to master. Elliot Slater doesn't strike me as having that much patience. Besides, given your high sensitivity to elemental magic, Gin, you'd still be able to feel him using his power, even if there was only a teaspoon of it in his whole body. More than likely, Slater's quickness is just a genetic quirk that he's honed over the years. There are very few people who can use elemental magic without others sensing it."

For a moment, a distant light flashed in the dwarf's pale eyes, as though she was thinking about something that had happened a long time ago. Maybe it was the droop of her shoulders or the way Jo-Jo fingered her string of pearls, but something about the dwarf's last words bothered me—and her too.

"Do you know anybody who can completely hide their elemental magic from others, even while they're embracing or using it?" I asked in a soft voice.

Jo-Jo's eyes cleared, and she gave me a small, sad smile. "Just one person. Although, I think you could do it too, Gin, if you really needed to."

I blinked. "Me?"

Jo-Jo nodded. "You."

The dwarf looked at me, a knowing light in her eyes, and I shifted on my feet. Jo-Jo Deveraux claimed that I was one of the strongest elementals she'd ever met, a notion that always made me uncomfortable. My mother had been an extremely strong Ice elemental, and yet all her magic hadn't saved her from a horrible, fiery death at the hands of Mab Monroe. My sister Annabella's magic hadn't done her any good against Mab either. And Bria would have been dead, beaten to death by Elliot Slater, if Finn and I hadn't intervened tonight.

So while Jo-Jo might claim that I was strong enough that my Stone and Ice magic would never fail me, I didn't really believe the dwarf. Which is why I carried so many silverstone knives. Sure, blades might break, but they always left some sort of jagged edge behind that I could shove and twist into someone's flesh.

Once you were out of magic, you were done for. Especially if the person you were fighting still had some juice left. Hence the fact that so many elementals died in duels. Elementals fought by flinging raw magic at each other—Air, Fire, Ice, and Stone—until somebody ran out of power, strength, will. When that happened, the other elemental's magic washed over the loser. Lose an elemental duel, and you were going to get suffocated, burned, frozen, or perhaps even entombed in your own skin.

Either way, you got dead. Just like my mother and older sister had, thanks to Mab Monroe and her Fire power.

"Come on," I said, pushing away my troubling thoughts. "It's getting cold out here. Let's go back inside."

Jo-Jo got to her feet, and I opened the door for her. We stepped into the living room, and I stopped short. A few minutes ago, large, sticky patches of blood had covered the hardwood floor like a new coat of varnish. But now the golden wood looked pristine. Sophia Deveraux was down on her hands and knees, gloves off, scrubbing at one last spot. But instead of using a rag or brush, the Goth dwarf slowly moved her bare finger back and forth over the bloodstain, staring at the spot as though she could burn it away with her mind or some hidden magic deep inside her.

And that's exactly what she was doing.

Sophia made one pass with her finger, and the blood under her hand dried. On the second pass, the stain looked brittle, as though it had been on the floor for years instead of just an hour. Sophia kept casting her finger back and forth over the stain with slow, precise movements. While I watched, the bloodstain underneath her hand turned a rusty brick color, then a pale pink. A minute later, the wood gleamed with its original golden hue as though the blood had never even been there at all.

I'd been right when I'd thought that the Goth dwarf had the same kind of Air elemental magic that her older sister Jo-Jo did. But instead of healing, instead of mending all those tiny molecules back together, Sophia used her power to tear them apart, to break them down and then slowly sandblast them away into nothingness. I imagined she could do the same to just about anything that crossed her path—blood, bones, bodies.

But the most amazing thing was that I didn't feel her using the slightest bit of elemental magic.

Sophia's black eyes didn't spark and flash with power the way that so many elementals' eyes did. The tip of her finger didn't glow. Her skin didn't become pale, chalky, or sweaty. Hell, she didn't look like she was exerting any effort at all. Sophia's Air elemental power was completely self-contained—and completely undetectable.

Sophia sat back on her heels and nodded, pleased by another job well done.

I looked at Sophia, then at Jo-Jo. "Just one person, huh?"

Jo-Jo's lips turned up in that sad smile again. "Just one. A skill she learned out of necessity rather than by choice."

I thought about asking Jo-Jo what she meant by that cryptic remark, but she went over to Sophia and patted her sister on the shoulder. Sophia glanced up, smiled, and squeezed her big sister's hand. Some emotion passed between them that I couldn't quite identify. Pride perhaps, tinged with sorrow. Whatever it was, I wasn't going to interrupt it tonight.

The sisters always came when I needed them. That's all that mattered, and that's all I needed to know. They'd tell me the rest in time. When they were ready. Besides, I wasn't exactly the most forthcoming person, especially when it came to my emotions.

I glanced to my right. Finn paced back and forth in front of the fireplace, his cell phone stuck to his ear. Bria rested on the couch, sleeping off the effects of being healed by Jo-Jo. My sister looked like an angel relaxing there on the sofa—despite the clumps of blood that had matted in her shaggy hair.

"I see. I owe you one. Thanks. Bye." Finn snapped his phone shut and turned toward me. "Good news. One of my sources says that Elliot Slater's gone home to lick his wounds for the rest of the night."

"Wounds? The bastard didn't have any wounds, as far as I could tell," I muttered and rubbed my side. After she'd finished with Bria, Jo-Jo had used her Air magic to restore my ribs to their previously unbroken state.

Finn jerked his head at Bria. "Seems your sister winged him in the shoulder with her gun. Either way, he's not coming back here tonight, according to my source."

I raised an eyebrow. "And which source would this be?"

Finn grinned. "This would be Leslie, the lovely young lady who happens to be the daughter of one of the maids who works at Slater's mansion. Evidently, Slater came home a while ago, went straight to his bedroom, and rang for an Air elemental healer to come force the bullet out of his shoulder."

"Is this Leslie reliable?" I asked.

Finn's grin widened. "In all sorts of ways."

I rolled my eyes. I didn't want to hear about more of Finn's sexual conquests. Not tonight. So I focused on more important matters. "So Slater's tucked himself in bed for the rest of the evening. Good. Did Leslie or any of your other sources say anything about why Mab sent the giant out here to kill Bria?"

Finn's smile slid off his face. "No, but they didn't have to. I already know."

"How—" I started.

Finn crooked his finger at me. "Follow me. There's something you need to see, Gin."

Curious, I followed Finn down the hallway. Jo-Jo and Sophia stayed in the living room to keep an eye on Bria. Finn walked back to the kitchen, then climbed a set of stairs to the second floor of the house. More cardboard boxes lined the hallways up here, stacked so high that they formed another set of walls in some places. Looked like Bria had only gotten the downstairs part of her things unpacked.

"While you were busy cleaning up, I took the liberty of exploring the rest of the house," Finn said.

"You mean you rifled through Bria's stuff to satisfy your own rampant curiosity," I corrected.

Finn looked over his shoulder at me, his green eyes as bright as Christmas lights in his ruddy face. "You're just jealous you didn't get around to it first."

I shook my head. "Not really."

"Anyway, your sister has some interesting quirks," Finn replied.

I still couldn't even bring myself to read the file of information that Finn had compiled on Bria. I certainly didn't want to paw through her personal, private things like the cheapest kind of thief, especially when she was downstairs, unconscious on her own sofa, recovering from a gunshot wound.

Finnegan Lane had no such qualms. He loved finding out information about other people, ferreting out all their secret hobbies, habits, and vices—and using them to his own advantage if the situation called for it. To him, it was a grand game, one in which he always came out the winner. Groundhogs couldn't dig as well as Finn could.

So I knew there was nothing I could do but sigh and go along with him. "What kind of quirks?"

He stopped in front of a box with open flaps, reached inside, and pulled out a frilly white negligee. "For starters, she likes girly underwear. Lace, ribbons, soft, feminine colors. The whole shebang. Expensive brands too." Finn rubbed the silk between his fingers. "Makes me look forward to the future."

"For what? When you try to seduce her?" I pulled the negligee out of his hand and put it back in the appropriate box.

"Of course," he replied in a smug tone. "And it won't be a matter of merely *trying*. No one can resist the charms of Finnegan Lane for long."

Finn definitely wasn't lacking in the self-confidence department. But as annoying as he was, he was also pretty good at figuring out what made people tick. Just like his father, Fletcher, had been.

"What else?" I asked.

Finn reached into another box and pulled out a small, round sphere. "For whatever reason, she collects snow globes. I've found three boxes of them so far."

My breath caught in my throat, and I took the globe from his outstretched hand. A charming winter scene lay underneath the smooth, domed glass—a couple of tiny brown horses pulling two laughing young girls in a silver sleigh. Evergreen trees lined the back of the snowy sphere, surrounding a miniature house. But another image flashed in my mind—more globes just like this one, their glass shining like stars underneath a fading sunset.

"My mother used to collect snow globes too." I shook the glass and watched the fake flakes of snow drift down and settle on top of the horses and two girls. "She had dozens of them all lined up on top of the fireplace mantel. Bria and I used to go down and shake them, trying to have the snow flying in all of them before the first one settled back down. A silly game we played. I'd almost forgotten about it."

My voice dropped to a whisper, and my fingers tightened around the globe, threatening to punch through the thick glass.

"Are you okay, Gin?" Finn asked.

I shook my head, loosened my grip, and passed the globe back to him. "Why wouldn't I be?"

He just looked at me. I dropped my sad, gray gaze from his searching green one and gestured at the boxes.

"And what does all that tell you about her?"

A thoughtful light flared in Finn's eyes. "That Bria Coolidge's icy shell is merely a mask to hide the soft, warm, sentimental woman that she really is deep down." He paused. "Kind of like you. Black and crunchy on the outside, marshmallow-soft on the inside."

I gave him a hard stare. "I am not a fucking *marshmallow.* And I am especially not sentimental."

"Of course not. That's why you just hacked and slashed your way through several giants to save a long-lost sister you haven't seen since you were thirteen." Amusement colored his placating tone.

My eyes narrowed to slits, but Finn just grinned at me. My angry face had long ago lost its effect on him. Finn knew that I'd rather hurt myself before I did him.

"But come here, I've saved the best for last," he said, gesturing for me to follow him once more. "What's most interesting about Bria is this."

Finn opened a door at the end of the hallway, and we stepped into Bria's home office. Wooden desk, computer, stapler, sticky pads, lots of books and papers stacked everywhere. I didn't see anything out of the ordinary—until Finn snapped on the light. And there it was, pushed against the back wall.

An eight-by-ten picture of one of the spider rune scars on my palms.

The photo was stuck in the middle of the biggest dry-erase board I'd ever seen. And it wasn't alone. There were more pictures, ones that I recognized from the file of information that Fletcher Lane had left me—autopsy photos of my mother and my older sister. The burned husks of their bodies. Mounted right next to the photo of my scar.

My stomach clenched, and that icy fist started squeezing my heart again.

"What the hell is this?" I whispered.

Still shocked, I moved closer to the dry-erase board. In addition to the photos, notes had been scribbled all over the surface in a variety of colors. *Murdered, burned, bodies reduced to ash* in red. *Physical evidence* in black. *Possible suspects* in navy blue. *Motive?* in a bright green.

"What the hell is this?" I repeated.

My eyes went up and down and all around the dry-erase board. Everywhere I looked there was another piece of information about the night my family had been killed, about the night that Mab Monroe had burned our house to the ground.

"I believe some folks call it a murder board. It's a visual representation of all the evidence found in relation to a crime. Some cops use them to help connect the dots or keep track of leads." Finn leaned against the doorjamb.

"From the looks of it, I'd say Bria is investigating the murder of your family. Just like you started to, after Dad left you that file."

"All right. I can understand her doing that, wanting to know the truth, who was behind the murders and why. But where did she get all this information?" I asked. "Especially that photo of the spider rune scar on my palm?"

I peered at the photo, wondering how I'd been so sloppy as to let someone take a picture of my hands. Oh, every once in a while, someone eating at the Pork Pit caught a glimpse of my scarred palms. But I was always able to pass the marks off as burns I'd gotten working in the restaurant. It wasn't like I ever stopped, held them up for everyone to see, and posed for pictures—

And then I remembered. Fletcher Lane had bought a digital camera a few months before he died. He'd brought it to the Pork Pit one day to show it off to me. A fancy newfangled device, he'd called it in his gruff voice. The old man had started taking my photo, and I'd finally put my hand out in mock surrender to get him to stop. He'd snapped a final picture and smiled before putting the camera away.

"Fletcher," I murmured. "He's the one who took the photo."

I told Finn about the camera incident and how I hadn't thought anything of it at the time.

Finn's green eyes drifted over the murder board. "That's not all Dad did, is it? He sent Bria the same folder of information that he left you, Gin. He sent her the exact same file about Mab Monroe murdering your mother and older sister."

"With a twist. Fletcher sent Bria a photo of my scar instead of the lovely headshot of her that he provided for me. Very thoughtful of him not to send her a glossy of my face." I shook my head. "I can understand Fletcher leaving me the information. I've made my peace with that. But why would he send it to Bria too? What did he hope to accomplish?"

"I don't know," Finn murmured. "Maybe he wanted to see how she'd react to the knowledge that you were still alive. Maybe he wanted to bring Bria to Ashland on her own terms."

I dropped my eyes from the board. "Doesn't much matter now, does it? Fletcher's gone, Bria's in town, and Mab wants her dead. Whatever the old man started with Bria, she's come to Ashland to finish it. If Mab doesn't get to her first."

"Speaking of finishing things, there's one more thing you should see," Finn said.

He moved to the right side of the board, put his hand on the top edge, and slowly turned it over. The board was constructed in such a way that it could be flipped over without moving the entire structure around. The back of the board was filled with just as many photos and scribblings as the front side. Only there was one distinct difference.

The back of the board dealt entirely with Mab Monroe and her organization. It was organized like a classic Mob pyramid. Mab's picture sat alone on top of the board. Underneath her photo were shots of Elliot Slater and Jonah McAllister. Below them were even more pictures of the various goons that made up Mab's organization. Bria had written notes beside each photo, with words like *Indicted, Arrested,* or *Dead.* There were more *Dead* notations than anything else. Not surprising, given Mab's dislike for failure.

"I think we know why Mab sent Slater to kill your sister," Finn said. "One of the reasons anyway. Looks like Bria's set her sights on the Fire elemental."

"Why?" I asked. "Because she wants to clean up Ashland? Or because she knows Mab murdered our mother and sister?"

Finn shrugged. "Does it really matter at this point?"

I rubbed the spider rune scar on first one palm, then the other one. Damn things were itching and burning again the way they always did when I thought about things that upset me, like my murdered family and crusading sister. "No, it doesn't matter why Bria's here or what she knows. All that matters now is keeping her safe—and away from Mab Monroe and her minions."

Finn snorted. "Are you kidding? Based on all this, I'd say that Bria's eager to get down and dirty with Mab. Maybe even more so than you are, Gin. Remember that scene in Northern Aggression last night? Bria looked like she'd be happy to put some bullets in Elliot Slater's head."

I stepped forward and turned the board back over to its original position. "Well, then, I guess I'm just going to have to get to Mab before Bria goes and does something stupid—like get herself killed."

Finn sighed. "I was afraid you were going to say that."

I gave him a hard smile. "Come on, Finn. We both know going after Mab will be fun."

"Oh, sure," Finn replied in a dry tone. "It'll be a barrel of laughs, right up until she kills us."

Finn wasn't entirely joking. He knew as well as I did that going after Mab would be tricky at best and most likely lethal. Even Fletcher Lane had never dared to take on the Fire elemental. For years the old man had compiled information on Mab, looking for any weaknesses, any sliver of opportunity he could take advantage of to kill her. But Mab always had too many people, too many guards around her. Even if I'd been able to get her alone, she could always kill me herself with her elemental power. Mab's own strength was the real reason she'd survived all these years.

Still, I couldn't help but stare at the photos on the board—the ones that showed the blackened husks that had been my mother and older sister before Mab had used her elemental Fire magic to burn them to ashes. And somehow, I knew that I was going to try to do the impossible—no matter what.

"Not if I kill her first," I murmured. "Not if I kill the bitch first."

Finn and I went back downstairs. Jo-Jo and Sophia had finished the last of the cleanup and stood by the front door ready to go. Bria was still asleep on the sofa. Once again, I was struck by how angelic she looked lying there, how calm and peaceful. You'd never guess that she spent her free time digging up dirt on the most dangerous woman in town.

"How long will she be out of it?" I asked Jo-Jo.

The dwarf stared at my sister. "That shot to the kidney

took a lot out of her, but she should wake up within the hour. Two, at most."

I eyed a clock on the wall. Just after two in the morning. Finn said Elliot Slater was busy getting patched up himself, which meant the giant wouldn't be back for Bria. Not tonight, anyway.

"All right, we need to be gone before she wakes up," I said. "So grab whatever supplies you brought in and leave. Finn, you help them, please. I'll be out in a minute."

Finn opened the front door, and Jo-Jo and Sophia gathered up their gear and went outside. Finn followed and shut the door behind the three of them.

I moved over to the sofa and stared down at Bria. Sleep eased out the sharp planes of her face, and a dewy pink color freshened up her cheeks, thanks to Jo-Jo's healing elemental Air magic. At this moment, Bria didn't look anything like the icy professional I'd seen that night at the community college or the calm cop holding a gun on Elliot Slater at Northern Aggression. She seemed younger, softer, like this. More like a grown-up version of the sweet little girl that I'd once known.

And she was going to stay this way, I vowed. I was going to lullaby Elliot Slater very, very soon. Once the giant was removed, I'd go after Mab Monroe. The time for keeping to the shadows like a tiny spider had passed. It was time to show Mab and her minions that I had some bite—and that they were next on my fucking to-do list.

I looked at Bria a moment longer, then turned away.

"Sweet dreams, baby sister," I murmured before walking out the front door.

* 13 *

The next day it was business as usual at the Pork Pit. Crowds of customers. Harried waitresses. The hiss, spit, and sizzle of the grill. The spicy smells of baked beans and barbecue sauce flavoring the air. Sophia Deveraux cooking up a storm.

And me plotting someone's demise.

"I just don't see how you're going to do it," Finn said, wiping a bit of barbecue sauce off his mouth. "Elliot Slater's sure to be on his guard now. Not only against you, but Bria too. You could try to snipe him from a distance, but as big and strong and tough as he is, you'd probably have to put several bullets or arrows in him in just the right places. Which you probably wouldn't have time to do before he started ducking for cover."

I nodded my head, agreeing with him. I'd killed people with rifles and crossbows before, but I preferred using my silverstone knives. It was just easier to make sure someone got good and dead that way.

"As for something more personal, which we both know you prefer anyway, he'll be looking suspiciously at any woman who's trying to get close to him in a dark alley, in a dark room, in a dark car. Anywhere dark, basically," Finn continued. "Which is where you do your best work, Gin."

It was after three the next afternoon. The lunch crowd had already come and gone, and it wasn't quite time for the dinner rush yet. Which is why Finnegan Lane sat on a stool beside the cash register shooting the breeze with me. In between scarfing down two hot dogs loaded with spicy chili, onions, shredded Cheddar cheese, and sweet honey mustard, along with baked beans and a big slice of my still-warm chocolate-chip pound cake.

I looked up from my copy of *The Adventures of Huckleberry Finn* and stared at my partner in crime. "Don't worry. You'll find an opening for me. You're my handler now. It's what you do, remember?"

"I *am* the best," Finn said in a not-so-modest voice. He chewed another bite of his hot dog. "But even I can't make you invisible, Gin. And that's what it's going to take to get close to Elliot Slater right now."

"I'm good at being invisible, remember?"

"True," Finn agreed. "But people tend to notice pesky little things like screams and bloodstains. Especially when there's a body to go along with them."

I rolled my eyes and went back to my book. Finn had come over for an early dinner and to help me brainstorm how I could get close enough to Elliot Slater to bury my silverstone knives in his broad back. So far, all Finn had done was eat my food and muse about how difficult it was going to be making sure the giant got dead before he killed Roslyn Phillips—or Bria. Finn's defeatist attitude wasn't helping, and since I hadn't come up with any bright ideas of my own, I'd turned to Huck in hopes that something would spring to mind while I was reading about someone else's adventures. But nothing had so far—

The front door opened, causing the bell to chime. I looked up from my book, ready to greet my potential customer. To my surprise, Roslyn Phillips stepped inside the restaurant. Today the vamp wore a short, plum-colored coat over a pair of winter white pants, which looked both elegant and sexy on her at the same time. A silverstone pin gleamed on the lapel of Roslyn's jacket—a heart with an arrow through it. The symbol for her nightclub, Northern Aggression. Like most magic types, Roslyn wore her rune with pride.

The vamp paused in the doorway a moment, her toffee eyes sweeping over the interior. Roslyn had come during the postlunch lull, so the waitresses that had been working were in the alley behind the restaurant taking a long smoke break and eating their own dinner. Several customers still sat at the tables and booths against the windows, finishing up their meals, lost in their own bubbles of conversation. When she realized no one was within earshot of Finn and me, she nodded, yanked the door shut behind her, and stomped over in our direction. The vampire's high heels clattered against the floor like falling silverware.

Roslyn slammed her small handbag down on the counter next to Finn, startling him and making him jiggle the spoonful of baked beans he'd been ready to shove into his mouth. The beans slipped off his spoon and splattered on his gray suit jacket, along with a healthy amount of barbecue sauce. Finn cursed and reached for a white paper napkin.

But Roslyn didn't care about Finn's fashion emergency. The vamp only had eyes for me—eyes that flashed with hot anger.

"What the fuck did you do to Elliot Slater last night?" she snarled.

"Lovely to see you again too, Roslyn." I marked my place in my book with a wayward credit card receipt and set it aside. "Care to take a seat?"

Roslyn plopped down on the stool next to Finn's, her back as tall and straight as the arrow in her rune pin. The vamp's hot gaze never left my face.

"I ask again," she snapped in a low voice only the three of us could hear. "What did you do to Elliot Slater last night?"

I shrugged. "Nothing much. Killed a couple of his men. I was going to do him too, but the bastard ducked out a window and ran away before I could get down to business with him."

My confession didn't appease Roslyn. If anything, it made her angrier. I could tell by the way the vamp bared her pearl-white fangs at me. Finn gave Roslyn a sidelong glance and kept trying to rub the barbecue sauce out of his suit, more concerned about the stain setting in his jacket than the danger presented by the pissed-off vampire. He was rather impractical that way.

"I take it there's a problem with Slater?" I asked in a quiet tone. "Beyond what you told me yesterday?"

Roslyn stared at me. I met her gaze with a calm one of my own. If anyone else had busted into my gin joint and bitched about the way I handled my bloody, dangerous business, I would have set her straight, perhaps with the point of my knife. But Roslyn was the victim in all this, had suffered so much because of me, I was going to be as gentle with her as I could. Even if gentle was something I didn't really know how to do—or that I hadn't been myself in a long, long time.

After a few seconds, the vamp made a visible effort to get herself under control. Finn gave his stained jacket up as a lost cause. He sighed and tossed his crumpled napkin in the middle of his plate. Dinnertime was officially over.

"Would you care for something to eat or drink?" I asked, trying to be the responsible hostess once more.

"No," Roslyn muttered.

I ignored her curt answer and moved over to a glass cake stand resting on the counter against the back wall. I cut Roslyn a piece of the chocolate-chip pound cake and put the dessert in front of her, along with a tall glass of milk and a fork. Since no one liked warm milk, I wrapped my hand around the glass and reached for my Ice magic. A silver light glowed on my palm, centered on the spider rune scar embedded in my flesh. Ice crystals immediately formed on the surface of the mug, and a moment later, it was as cold and frosty as if I'd just taken it out of the freezer. Steam curled up from the lip of the glass.

Not so long ago, doing something as simple as cooling a drink had been about the extent of my Ice magic.

Now it wasn't any harder than breathing. Jo-Jo Deveraux claimed that the silverstone metal melted into my palms had inhibited my Ice magic, since Ice elementals tended to release their power through their hands to make cubes, daggers, and other shapes—or just to blast someone with their cold magic.

But I'd finally overcome the blockage during a desperate moment when I was facing off with another elemental, when my life had been on the line. Now, doing things with my Ice power was far easier than it had been before. I was getting stronger in it too. Jo-Jo claimed that my Ice magic would continue to grow until it was just as powerful as my Stone power, making me the rarest of elementals—someone who was equally strong in two elements.

I wasn't exactly comfortable with that idea for a variety of reasons. Mainly because I'd seen my mother, Eira's, Ice magic let her down when she'd gone up against Mab Monroe. I wasn't so sure I wanted to tempt fate by relying on my own Ice magic when Mab and I had our inevitable confrontation. Because it would be damned ironic if Mab killed me the exact same way she had my mother and older sister. Irony. Always out to get you.

Roslyn eyed me some more, and I realized that I'd never done any kind of magic in front of the vamp before. That she hadn't even known I was an elemental until now. The other customers were all still too busy with their food to notice my small magical display.

I wasn't worried about Roslyn telling anyone, though. She'd agreed to keep quiet after what had happened to Fletcher Lane, and she'd held up once already under Elliot Slater's questioning. Her word was good.

Roslyn opened her mouth to turn down the food I'd just shoved her way, but I cut her off.

"You're welcome," I said. "Now, you want to tell me what's going on? And why you decided to storm in here like Sherman marching through Atlanta? I know you've been around a while, but the Civil War ended a long time ago."

Roslyn sighed, and some of the angry fight sagged out of her slim shoulders. "Elliot called me last night, around three in the morning, demanding to know where I was, what I was doing, and if there was anyone with me."

I frowned. "Why would he want to know all that?"

Finn snorted. "You mean besides the fact that the bastard's obsessed with her? That he wants to know and control her every movement?"

I ignored Finn's snide comment. "What did Slater want?"

Roslyn fiddled with the fork I'd set down in front of her. "He said he had some trouble with someone last night. That someone had come after him, and he was worried that they'd come after me in order to get to him." Her mouth twisted. "Because everyone knew how much he *cares* about me. How fucking *precious* I am to him."

The vamp's hand tightened around the fork, and her eyes darkened like she was wishing she could shove the silverware into Elliot Slater's jugular. I admired her spirit, if not her practicality. Roslyn would have been much better off using a butter knife, if death by silverware was going to be her modus operandi.

I filled Roslyn in on what had really happened last night. How Finn and I had been following Elliot Slater when we'd seen him get the order from Mab, get his goons together, and go after Bria.

Roslyn frowned. "Why do you care if Elliot kills some new cop in town? Why interfere?"

I wasn't about to confess my familial connection to Bria to the vamp, so I gave her a flip answer. "I thought I could take him out right then and there and let the cop take credit for things. It worked once before, you know."

Roslyn grimaced. She knew what I was referring to— the night a couple of months ago when I'd killed Alexis James in the Ashland Rock Quarry. Roslyn had been there as one of Alexis's hostages, along with Finn. Roslyn was the one who'd backed up Donovan Caine's claim that he'd killed the Air elemental, instead of me.

I thought about what Roslyn had said. So Elliot Slater thought I'd been there to off him last night, not to save Bria from getting dead. Not surprising. Like Mab Monroe, Slater didn't strike me as someone who thought about other people—except what he wanted to take from them. Still, Finn had been right. Slater would be on his guard now, which would make him that much tougher to kill.

"Anyway, whatever you did, Slater was worried about me. It was all I could do to convince him not to come over to the club and check on me right then." Roslyn shuddered. "Xavier was at the club with me. If Slater had come over, the mood he was in, he would have killed Xavier just for being there."

Finn and I nodded. We both knew that I'd pissed off Slater by killing his men last night, and he would have taken his anger out on Xavier—maybe even Roslyn too. Hell, the giant could do that at any time. Beat the vampire to death with his fists the way he'd almost done to me at the community college. That's the kind of sick bastard he was. And why he needed to get dead as soon as possible.

"So how did you keep Slater from coming over?" Finn asked.

Roslyn grimaced again. "I told him that I'd go out with him tonight. Some charity gambling tournament on the *Delta Queen.*" She closed her eyes. "He said he wants to take me back to his place afterward. So we can finally . . . be together the way we should."

A shiver of fear rippled through the vamp's body, and her hands trembled against the countertop. Roslyn didn't have to tell me that the thought of seeing Elliot Slater, much less playing the part of his doting girlfriend, was enough to turn her stomach. Just the idea of the giant putting his hands on her or anyone else made me want to vomit. Not to mention what would happen when Slater got Roslyn back to his house—alone. The vicious ways he would brutalize her all night long.

It wasn't going to happen, I vowed. Elliot Slater wasn't going to hurt Roslyn ever again. No matter what I had to do or who saw me do it.

"Don't worry," I said. "You're not going to have to go back to Slater's place tonight."

Roslyn's eyes snapped open.

I looked at Finn. "We needed an opening."

He frowned. "You can't be serious, Gin. You can't kill Elliot Slater on the *Delta Queen* in front of who knows how many witnesses. It's a fucking *riverboat,* or have you forgotten?"

"I haven't forgotten, but it's a place like any other," I replied. "Don't make it a challenge. You know how much I like those."

Finn rubbed his chest like he had a sudden case of heartburn. I didn't think it was caused by the onions and grease he'd just eaten. The *Delta Queen* was something of an Ashland institution—a riverboat casino that slowly trolled up and down the muddy waters of the Aneirin River. A big, white behemoth straight out of, well, the Mark Twain novel I was reading.

"Come on, Gin, think about it. Elliot's sure to have some of his men with him," Finn said. "And this tournament? It's a big deal. Or at least the party of the month. All my clients at the bank are going, and all the other Ashland bigwigs are sure to be in attendance."

I sighed. "Look, I know it's going to be tricky. I'm not denying that. But doing Slater on the riverboat does have some advantages."

"Name one," Finn dared.

"One, it's a public place, which will be easier to get into than his heavily fortified mansion. Two, it will be crowded. Three, there will be alcohol on the premises, which means lots of people will be getting their load on. Drunks tend to be lousy witnesses. Four, and perhaps most important, I can dump Slater's body over the side when I'm finished with him instead of trying to stuff him in a closet somewhere." I ticked the points off on my fingers. "Shall I go on?"

Finn rubbed his chest again. "Everything you say is true, but it's still dangerous, Gin. Slater could scream or get away from you before you finish him off. And if he does, if his men or the casino guards hear him, you're the one who won't get off the boat alive."

"I know all that. But those are the same risks I would have with any job."

"So why are you so eager to take those chances?" he asked. "Why now that you've retired?"

"Because I don't want Roslyn to have to go home with that bastard," I said in a quiet voice. "Understand?"

I didn't mention that it was because the whole situation was my fault to begin with. That Roslyn had suffered so much already because of me and that I wasn't going to let her be hurt anymore.

Finn could easily see the guilt in my eyes.

Then his green gaze cut to Roslyn and the obvious strain in her eyes and face and clenched fists. Right now, the vamp resembled a life-size porcelain doll—one that would shatter if you so much as breathed on her. Finn realized what I had—that the vamp was on the edge. That she couldn't take another night of being Elliot Slater's plaything. Not again. Not without cracking and screaming and fighting back with everything she had—and then getting dead because of her defiance.

"All right," Finn said in a low voice. "All right. We'll do it. But how are you going to get close to him? Like I said before, Slater's sure to be on the lookout for any strange woman approaching him after what happened at Bria's house last night. More important, the giant already knows you, Gin. Slater knows who you are, what you look like, and that you have a grudge against him. You won't be able to sweet-talk him and get him alone like you did Tobias Dawson."

"I didn't sweet-talk Dawson. I got knocked out and woke up in a coal mine. What part of that says *sweet-talk* to you?"

Finn gave me a tiny grin, trying to lighten the mood. "Some guys are into that sort of thing."

I rolled my eyes. Finn was so much more disturbed than I was. All I did was kill people with my silverstone knives. Clean, simple, straightforward, to the point. Finn was the one who liked to dabble in the kinky stuff—with any woman who would have him.

The front door of the restaurant opened. The bell chimed, interrupting my unwanted musings on Finn's proclivities. I looked toward the door, grateful for the interruption, until I saw exactly who was standing in the Pork Pit—Detective Bria Coolidge.

My baby sister was here in my gin joint, in my place of business. Bria stood in the doorway, surveying the restaurant much the same way Roslyn had done just minutes before. Blond hair, blue eyes, rosy skin. She looked no worse for wear, despite the fact that she'd been shot and almost killed last night. She sported a long, navy coat over a pair of dark jeans, a black turtleneck sweater, and stylish black boots. Her primrose rune gleamed a bright silver against the inky fabric of her sweater. Bria's eyes flicked over the interior of the Pork Pit before settling on Finn, Roslyn, and me clustered together at the counter. She headed toward us.

Finn shot me a troubled glance. I knew exactly what he was thinking, because it was the same thought spinning through my mind. What was Bria doing here? Had she somehow realized that we were the masked duo who'd saved her from Elliot Slater and his giants last night? Had she somehow, some way, tracked us back to the Pork Pit? Was she here to arrest us for killing the giants?

Bria stepped up to the counter next to Roslyn. She looked at the vamp a moment, clearly surprised to see her here. Her cool gaze frosted over even more at the sight of Finn, who grinned at her. Finally, Bria turned her attention to me. "I'm looking for Gin Blanco."

"That would be me," I replied. "Is there something I can help you with?"

Bria reached into her coat and drew out a gold badge. She flashed it at me, then stuffed it back into her pocket. "I'm Detective Bria Coolidge with the Ashland Police Department. I'm here to ask you a few questions about the beating you took the other night. We met there, if you remember."

Some of the tension eased out of my body. So that's why she was here. Following up about me getting almost beaten to death at the hands of Elliot Slater. Not because of what happened last night. Not because I was the mysterious, masked woman who'd saved her from being murdered in her own home. Not because she'd recognized me. Not because she'd realized that I was really her long-lost big sister, Genevieve Snow.

"Ms. Phillips, why don't you take your cake over to one of the booths so I can speak to the detective?" I asked in my most polite voice. "I'll have the rest of your order ready in a jiffy."

Roslyn stared at me, then Bria. Curiosity filled the vamp's face. She realized Bria was the cop I'd saved from

Slater last night, but Roslyn knew better than to ask questions or make a scene.

"Of course. Take your time," the vampire said, going along with me. She picked up the glass of milk and cake and walked over to a booth in the back of the restaurant.

With Roslyn out of the way, Finn was free to turn around on his stool and give Bria the slow head-to-toe appraisal he reserved for women he was thinking about seducing. Finn smiled his approval. He liked what he saw.

"What are you looking at?" Bria snapped.

"Just you, detective." Finn's grin widened. "Just you."

Her eyes narrowed, but not before I saw a small spark of something flash in the blue depths—attraction. However unwanted it might be, Bria found Finn smug, but appealing. Couldn't blame her for that. Especially since I'd slept with him myself back during my foolish teenage years. With his green eyes, solid figure, and devilish smile, Finn had seduced far more frosty and intimidating women than Detective Bria Coolidge.

But Finn and Bria? That was another complication I didn't need right now.

"There's not much to tell, detective," I said, interrupting their heated staring contest. "Like I told you before, I fell down."

Bria looked at me. Her mouth flattened into a hard line. "You fell down? Original."

I gave her a bland smile. Now was not the time to be a smart-ass. Smart-asses were memorable for any number of reasons, and right now, I needed her to forget all about me. At least until after I'd killed Elliot Slater.

Bria kept staring at me, her gaze sweeping over my features and down what she could see of my body—mainly, my grease-stained blue apron and long-sleeved black T-shirt. "Well, you seem to have healed nicely. Looks like your brother here did in fact get you to that Air elemental healer and the best medical treatment in Ashland."

"I always keep my promises," Finn replied in a mild tone.

Bria raised an eyebrow but didn't rise to his baiting. "Your foster brother seems to care quite a bit about you, Ms. Blanco."

"Foster brother?" I asked, already knowing the answer to my question.

"He is your foster brother, isn't he?" Bria asked. "The son of Fletcher Lane, the man who adopted you as a child? The man who left you his barbecue restaurant to run?"

"You've been checking up on me, detective."

Bria stared at me. "Just doing my job, Ms. Blanco. Just doing my job. Which is why I want to ask you some questions about your attack at the community college the other night."

I gritted my teeth, my admiration for Bria's tenacity warring with my own frustration. Now was not the time for her to be darkening my doorstep asking questions that I wasn't going to answer—ever.

"There's nothing to report. I fell down. End of story. Can I offer you a piece of cake before you go, detective?"

Since I wasn't giving up any information, Bria decided to switch tactics.

"Are you afraid of someone?" she asked in a softer tone. "Would it help if we spoke privately, Ms. Blanco?"

I looked at her. "The only person I'm afraid of is my

cook, Detective Coolidge. And that's only because she puts too much salt in her macaroni salad. I told you before, and I'm telling you again. I fell down that night at the community college—repeatedly. Now, why don't you go out there on the mean streets of Ashland and help someone who really needs it? Because I'm doing just fine."

My tone was harsher than I would have liked it to be for my first real face-to-face meeting with the sister I hadn't seen in seventeen years. But she wasn't going to take no for an answer, any more than I would have in her situation. This was the way it had to be right now. I hated to be rude to my own sister, but I had things I needed to do if I had any chance of taking care of Elliot Slater tonight. The sooner I killed the giant, the sooner I could move on to other things—like figuring out how Bria fit into my life and if I could ever really be a part of hers.

"Is it your foster brother?" Bria asked, turning her cold gaze to Finn. "Is he the one who beat you? The one you're afraid of?"

I laughed. "Finn? Beat me? Hardly. He'd stab himself in the eye before he ever laid a hand on me."

Finn gave Bria another charming smile. "I'm thoughtful that way, detective."

She stared at him another moment. Her eyes flicked to me, then to Roslyn Phillips. The vamp huddled in a booth in the back of the restaurant, pretending to be interested in her cake. Roslyn was a better actress than I'd thought. I might have believed my chocolate-chip pound cake was the best she'd ever had, if I hadn't known she was merely picking at it while listening to our every word.

"You know, a lot of people in Ashland don't seem to remember things that happened to them," Bria said. "Beatings, assaults, intimidations."

"Must be something in the water," I said in a dry tone. "Some chemical that promotes memory loss."

Bria looked at me, and I gave her a level gaze. She returned the stare. Blue eyes on gray. Both as cold and unyielding as they could be.

"Fine. If that's the way you want to play it, I'll take your kind suggestion and go help someone who might actually appreciate it." Bria reached into her jacket and drew out a small business card. "But if you *fall down* again and jog your memory about what really happened that night, give me a call. Day or night. I'll take care of everything. I promise. No one will know you talked to me."

Maybe it was the sincerity in her voice. Or the fact that she seemed so serious about helping people and making a difference. But instead of another dry remark, I merely nodded and took the card from her, trying to end our meeting at least on a neutral note, trying to salvage something good from this.

Our fingers brushed. For a second, the cold caress of Bria's Ice magic touched my skin. Baby sister's magic radiated off her body the same way that Mab Monroe's Fire power did, although the sensation was much weaker. Bria's power felt soothing to me, like a cool washcloth on a feverish forehead. It was nothing like the hot, pricking sensation of Mab's magic.

Bria frowned at the contact, as though it bothered her in some way, but she didn't say anything. I wondered if she'd felt my own Ice magic or even my Stone power. Some elementals literally leaked magic, which meant that other elementals like me could sense their power even when they weren't embracing or using it. Some magic escaped in drips and drabs, while others like Mab Monroe's was a slow, constant burn. My elemental magic was self-contained, unless I did something with it, used it in some way. Still, I wondered if Bria had felt something, sensed something about my magic that was so similar to her own power. After all, we'd both gotten our Ice magic from the same source—our mother.

Bria nodded to me and Finn. She stared at Roslyn a moment, then turned on her boot heel and headed for the front door. The bell chimed once more, signaling her exit.

"That went rather well, don't you think?" Finn asked after the door had closed behind her.

"What part? You hitting on her? Or me telling her to stay out of my business?"

Finn considered my question. "Well, the two of you didn't come to actual blows. And nobody got arrested. That's always a bonus."

"Yeah," I replied, watching Bria stick her hands in her jacket pockets and walk down the street. "But she knows we're hiding something, and I don't think she'll let it go until she finds out exactly what it is."

Once it was apparent that Bria wasn't coming back, Roslyn Phillips took her previous seat at the counter next to Finn.

"What was that all about?" the vamp asked.

I snorted. "Please. Like you didn't hear every word. I know you have enhanced hearing, Roslyn. Most vamps do."

She shrugged. "One of the benefits of drinking blood. Makes some of your senses really come alive."

Vampires were just like elementals in that some were stronger than others, and the blood they drank often had different effects on them, depending on their own power level and whose vein they were chugging from in the first place. A regular pint of O-positive from a normal human would give any vamp a little buzz, enough to sharpen their hearing and improve their eyesight. Give a strong vamp access to a Fire elemental's blood, and, well, that's when you got vampires who were as tough as giants and dwarves—with flames dripping from their fangs to boot. And of course, vampires could be elementals themselves, if they had the inherent magic flowing through their veins, instead of siphoning the ability out of whomever's blood they were drinking.

There weren't many things that turned my stomach, but the thought of sucking down someone else's blood— hot and fresh from his neck or cold and frosty in a glass— was more than enough to do it. Despite whatever extra juice it might give me. But I had other things to think about. Like the fact it was closing in on four o'clock, and I had a giant to stalk and kill this evening.

"Back to our previous conversation," I said. "Roslyn, I want you to do exactly what Elliot Slater wants you to to-night. Go out with him to the event on the *Delta Queen*. I know it's going to be hard, but do you think you can do that?"

Another shudder rippled through the vamp's body, and she didn't say anything.

"I know I'm asking a lot, after everything you've been

through. If you can't, I understand," I said in a soft voice. "There's still time for you to leave town. We can find another way—"

"No," Roslyn said in a grim voice so low I had to strain to hear her. "This is how it has to be. I want him dead. Tonight. I can . . . do it. I can . . . handle it one more night, one more time."

She bit her lip and nodded her head, as if trying to convince herself that she really could calmly go out with the man who'd been stalking her and using her as his own little toy. But Roslyn knew that playing her part was the only way this was going to work—no matter how distasteful it was going to be.

"And what will you be doing, Gin?" Roslyn asked.

I stared at her, my gray eyes as cold as ice. "Hopefully, stabbing the bastard to death before you down your first glass of bubbly."

* 14 *

Just after eight that night, I opened the door, climbed out of the Aston Martin, and smoothed down my dress. I walked around the front of the silver sports car and waited for Finn to lock his precious baby up tight.

Then, when Finn joined me, I put my hand on my hip and struck a pose. "How do I look?"

Finn gave me the once-over. "Nice. Not at all like you plan to commit murder before the night is through."

Since I was going to spend the evening hobnobbing with Ashland's wealthiest citizens, I'd decided to dress up for the occasion. I'd traded in my usual jeans and T-shirt for a simple cocktail dress with a loose, flowing skirt. The garment was made of a heavy, shiny satin that was such a deep blue that it looked black. All the better to hide bloodstains.

Even more important, the dress also featured long sleeves to hide the two silverstone knives I'd tucked up them, and the poofy skirt fell to my knees, hiding the other two knives that I'd strapped to my thighs. Still two more knives rested in the sides of my stiletto boots, and I had another one tucked into my purse. Seven knives was probably overkill, but I wanted to be prepared when I went after Elliot Slater. It just wouldn't do to have the giant in my sights and be unable to finish him off for a lack of adequate weaponry. I might officially be retired from being the assassin the Spider, but that didn't mean I still wasn't a pro.

In an effort to blend in with all the pretty young things and trophy wives sure to be in attendance, I'd gone heavy on the makeup—smoky eyes, deep plum lips, lots of mascara. I'd even freed my shoulder-length hair from its typical ponytail for the evening's festivities. Jo-Jo Deveraux had been all too happy to curl my dark chocolate locks into wavy ringlets. The dwarf always liked it when I played dress-up.

Jo-Jo had also been kind enough to slip me some tubs of her magic-infused healing ointment, just in case Elliot Slater got a couple of licks in before his swan song tonight.

"And me?" Finn asked. "How do I look?"

Finn wore what he always wore to a society function— a classic tuxedo, small diamond cufflinks, and polished wingtips that had a higher luster than some of the jewels the debutantes would be wearing tonight. The black fabric accentuated the bright green of his eyes, while his walnut-colored locks curled around his collar in an artful arrangement that looked both deliberate and effortless. Finn had spent more time on his hair than Jo-Jo had on mine.

"Ever the gentleman," I replied. "Not at all like you plan to assist me in committing said murder tonight."

Finn grinned and held his arm out to me. "Ready for an evening of murder and mayhem?"

I grinned back. "Always."

Arm in arm, Finn and I left the parking lot and strolled toward the *Delta Queen*.

The riverboat was docked in the middle of the downtown district, where the Aneirin River curled like a ribbon past the city's skyscrapers and cultural buildings like the Ashland Opera House. Several years ago when the riverboat casino had first come to town, the city planners had constructed a wooden boardwalk lit with old-fashioned iron street lamps. Despite its proximity to the mean streets of Southtown, the gentrification had stuck, mainly because the casino had its own ever-vigilant security staff who kept an eye out for the riffraff who might mug their customers before they could get on board and blow their money in high style.

No gang runes or graffiti could be seen on the boardwalk itself, and several artsy shops and restaurants had sprung up opposite the river on the far side of the weathered wooden planks—overpriced antiques stores and cafés determined to suck as much money as they could out of passersby before they boarded the casino and lost that week's paycheck. Ah, progress.

The *Delta Queen* featured six decks, each one more lavish and opulent than the last. Even from this distance, I could see the gleam of polished wood, heavy brass, and delicate crystal through the wide windows that lined the upper levels. Tasteful bits of red and blue trim glistened in various spots on the riverboat's white exterior finish, marking it as an all-American place to lose your life savings. Globe-shaped lights wrapped around the mahogany and brass railings and dipped from one deck to the next like the strings of an electrified cobweb. The third story formed an open U shape that jutted out past the other decks and formed the bow of the boat. Meanwhile, a giant paddlewheel that rose all the way up to the sixth deck anchored the back of the vessel.

I stared at the paddlewheel. Hmm. That had possibilities. Like me shoving Elliot Slater through it. But the riverboat wasn't scheduled to leave the dock tonight. Even if a cruise had been planned, the boards were too wide to do the necessary amount of damage to the giant, and I doubted the fall alone would kill him. He'd probably scream a lot on the way down, though.

Too bad. I'd never killed anyone with a paddlewheel before. I might not officially be the Spider anymore, but I was always on the lookout for new experiences—and new skills to add to my deadly repertoire. Elliot Slater was going to die tonight, but that didn't mean I couldn't have a bit of fun helping him quit breathing.

Thanks to his position at his bank and the fact that so many of his wealthy clients would be in attendance tonight, Finn had been invited to the party. I was tagging along as his plus-one. Finn handed his engraved invitation to the man checking names on the shoreline, who ushered us on board with little fanfare.

"Hmph," Finn sniffed, sounding exactly like Sophia Deveraux. "He didn't even tell me to enjoy myself this evening."

I patted Finn's arm. "That's because you're not one of the important people who are coming tonight. He's saying his fawning for them."

Finn sniffed his displeasure again.

As the two of us walked up the gangplank to the riverboat itself, I glanced over the railing. Below, the murky waters of the Aneirin River washed by, heading toward the far-away Mississippi River and ultimately the Gulf of Mexico. Oil slicks shimmered royal blue, purple, and green on the water's surface, and all the soft, artful lights on the riverboat couldn't hide the odd bits of wood, soggy fast-food wrappers, and other flotsam that clogged the shoreline. Or the stench.

I wrinkled my nose. The air reeked of rotten catfish. Ugh. The scent reminded me of the last time I'd been this close to the river—when I'd taken a nosedive off the top of the Ashland Opera House to escape the cops after a botched hit. It had taken me several hot showers to get the stench of rotting fish out of my hair.

Finn and I reached the top of the gangplank and found ourselves on the third, open deck, the epicenter of the event. The deck itself was larger than two ballrooms put together. Blackjack, baccarat, poker, and other gaming tables had been set up out in the open. The *slap-slap-slap* of cards being shuffled could be heard, along with the *clink-clink* of chips hitting each other on the felt tables and the whirring *clack-clack-clack* of the slot machines. Heaters tucked against the railing and under some of the tables kept the December chill at bay, helped immensely by the inflated egos of those already on board.

People dressed in tuxedoes, gowns, and flashing jewels

were already waiting their turn to lose their money—all of which was supposedly going to charity tonight. I rather doubted that, since Phillip Kincaid was one of the riverboat casino's primary owners.

Kincaid was another of Ashland's underworld sharks, just like Mab Monroe was, with his own network of enforcers and heavy hitters. He was already on deck, a six-foot-tall man with a chest that looked as dense as concrete beneath his white tuxedo. His sandy blond hair was slicked back into a low ponytail, all the better to show off his chiseled cheekbones and striking blue eyes. I'd never had any dealings with Kincaid, but rumor had it that his father had been a dwarf, his mother a giant. Hence his solid physique. I didn't know where he'd gotten the pretty face from, though. Didn't much matter. I put Kincaid out of my mind, since he wasn't my target tonight.

According to Finn's sources, a formal sit-down dinner would be held later in the evening. Through the open doors that led inside the riverboat, I spotted waiters hurrying to and fro with glasses, silverware, floral centerpieces, and more in the dining room. The inside of the ship was hollow and ringed with balconies, so the folks on the fourth, fifth, and sixth decks could look all the way down to the third floor, where a stage had been erected for dinner shows. The lower two decks were enclosed. That's where the kitchen was housed, along with the money cages. I knew because Finn and I had spent the past few hours going over the riverboat's schematics, among other things.

Finn grabbed two champagne flutes from a passing waiter and handed one to me. "How do you want to play this?"

I took a sip of champagne. "Let's split up. I want to take a stroll around the deck, see what the security is like in person, and find a cozy spot where Elliot Slater and I can chat privately later on tonight. You keep an eye out for Roslyn and the giant. Call me when you spot them."

"Okay," Finn said. "I'll be around if you need me."

We broke apart. I sipped champagne and meandered through the gaming tables and small cliques of self-important people clustered together on the deck. The trophy wives, debutantes, and rich divorcees stood tall and resplendent in their jewel-colored designer dresses, peacocks preening for the penguin-suited men in attendance. And practically everyone—male and female—wore some small bauble that weighed in at several carats, whether it was a diamond choker or a ruby cufflink slyly winking from the end of a tuxedo sleeve. My Stone magic let me hear the gemstones' proud whispers of their beauty, elegance, and fire, as vain and boastful as the people wearing them.

I shut the sound of the gemstones out of my mind and focused on the security detail for the evening. Several giants wearing dark suits roamed through the crowd, as was to be expected at one of these things. Several more stood with their arms crossed over their chests, keeping an eye on the players at the higher-end gaming tables. I counted five on this deck alone, and I knew that at least a few more would be patrolling the other levels and the interior of the riverboat, watching out for drunks and other potential problems. Each of the giants wore a large pin in the middle of his long tie that marked him as part of the security staff. The gold pins were shaped like the casino's rune—a dollar sign superimposed over an outline of the riverboat. Classy.

The amount of security was troublesome but not surprising. The *Delta Queen* was a casino, after all, and there were lots of whales here tonight with cash to lose.

Including Owen Grayson.

The businessman sat at a table at the very tip of the boat playing poker with a couple of other high rollers. Instead of the plastic red, white, and blue chips some of the other gamblers were using, stacks of solid gold chips sat in front of each player, marking their value as hundred thousand dollar tokens. Given the stakes they were playing for, a crowd had formed around the table. I edged my way close enough to get a good view of the action.

Like every man in attendance, Owen Grayson had dressed up for the evening in a tuxedo, but his choice of navy fabric made his eyes seem more blue than violet. Even though he was sitting down, I was once again struck by how compact, sturdy, and strong Owen's frame was. His violet eyes glittered in his face, even as his blue-black hair disappeared into the shadows cast by the lights wrapped around the railing behind him. The scar under Owen's lips was a thin white line, but it wasn't unappealing. If anything, it added more character to his features. Hard and tough and sexy, that's how he looked to me.

I wasn't the only woman studying him. Several regarded Owen with open, predatory interest, mentally weighing his figure and pocketbook against the other gentlemen to determine who was most worthy of their attention this evening. But evidently the others found him as appealing as I did, because none of them made a move to leave or go trolling past the other tables for more potential victims.

The dealer shuffled a fresh hand, and Owen used the lull in the action to scan the crowd around him. He stopped when he spotted me. Owen's violet eyes trailed down my body, one slow inch at a time. Breasts, stomach, thighs, legs. He took it all in. A smile spread across his face, softening his hard features. I gave him a cool nod, acknowledging his approval of my dress. Owen's smile widened, and he tipped his head in return.

"Sir?" the dealer asked Owen.

Owen looked at his cards and raised whatever bet had been given before. The man sitting to his left hemmed and hawed a minute before folding, and the others placed their bets. Owen's violet gaze stayed on me a moment longer before focusing on his cards again. I moved on.

I walked through the hollow interior of the riverboat, where the staff was still busy setting all the tables for the evening's dinner. The enclosed portion of the upper decks wrapped around a square, open area that featured a large, parquet stage fronted by black velvet curtains. The riverboat's dinner shows were almost as popular as the gaming tables.

Once I'd acquainted myself with all the entrances, exits, and possible cubbyholes where I might quietly kill Elliot Slater, I did another swift circuit of the open deck. But the giant and Roslyn Phillips weren't in attendance yet, so I went in search of Finn to see if he'd heard anything from Roslyn this evening.

As always, he was easy to find. Finnegan Lane had planted himself at the end of the bar that had been set up on one side of the deck. Bars were one of Finn's favorite places, rife with booze, gossip, the occasional salty snack, and pretty, inebriated women open to the raw suggestion in his hungry smile. I found him chatting up a sweet young thing who barely looked old enough to drink, much less afford the emerald drops dangling from her ears or the C-cups spilling out of the top of her dress. Somebody had a generous sugar daddy.

I tapped the girl on the shoulder and gave her a hard smile. "Sorry, sugar, but you need to move along now. My dear *husband*'s already taken for the evening."

Finn huffed his disapproval. The girl's brown eyes darted between the two of us. Evidently, she didn't like the trouble she saw brewing in my cold face because she grabbed her strawberry daiquiri and scooted down to the other end of the bar in search of an easier prospect.

Finn sighed. "Did you really have to do that?"

"No." I smiled. "But it sure was fun."

"C'mon, Gin. You could have at least scared her off some other way. You know how I feel about the word *husband*." Finn gave a delicate shudder. Any romantic commitment longer than a couple of hours was enough to make him jumpy.

I rolled my eyes. "We're here to do a job, in case you've forgotten. You can hit on the young stuff once everything's been taken care of for the night. *Capisce?*"

"Capisco," he muttered.

I leaned against the bar and surveyed the sparkling, laughing, chattering crowd before me. I recognized a lot of the faces, mostly through my time as the Spider. Sisters, mothers, brothers, husbands, stockholders. I'd helped a lot of people on this boat get rid of their familial and business problems over the years in Ashland and beyond.

"Any sign of our friends yet?" I asked.

"No, but they should be here soon. Roslyn texted me a few minutes ago and said that Elliot Slater had just pulled into her driveway—" Finn jerked his head. "Hey, there they are."

I looked to the left just in time to see Elliot Slater crest the top of the gangplank. The giant had one arm curled possessively around Roslyn Phillips's hourglass waist. For her part, the vamp hung limp at his side like she was seasick and five seconds away from throwing up whatever she'd eaten today. Couldn't blame Roslyn for that, after all she'd been through. I didn't know that I would have made it this far in her shoes.

Two giants also dressed in tuxes followed Slater on board, moved ahead of him a few feet, and stopped, scanning the glittering crowd before them. Must be Slater's de facto bodyguards for the evening.

Elliot Slater stepped to one side and turned, speaking to someone behind him. A moment later, two more figures stepped up and onto the riverboat—Jonah McAllister and Mab Monroe.

✸ 15 ✸

Finn saw my face tighten and my eyes darken with anger. "Something wrong?" he asked in a mild tone, even though he already knew the answer.

"I didn't think Mab would be here tonight, since this is Phillip Kincaid's casino," I muttered. "The two of them hate each other. I thought Slater would be here alone, since gambling is one of his pastimes, according to your file on him."

"Kincaid had to invite her, just like he had to invite Elliot Slater. Leave Mab Monroe and her flunkies off your guest list? That's unthinkable in this town, even if Kincaid would be happy to dance on all their graves and take over Mab's operations." Finn nodded his head in that direction. "And in addition to Jonah McAllister, looks like Mab brought two more bodyguards along with her."

Sure enough, two giants stepped onto the riverboat behind Mab and Jonah. The rear guard, as it were.

"No wonder poor Roslyn looks faint," Finn murmured. "Besides Slater, who knows how long she's had to listen to Jonah McAllister this evening? His arrogance would be enough to drive anyone mad. And Mab isn't exactly a shrinking violet herself."

We sat at the bar and watched the four of them. Elliot Slater led Roslyn Phillips out onto the deck, stopping every few feet to shake hands with someone he knew. The giant wore a black tuxedo that made his seven-foot physique seem even larger and more intimidating than usual. Tree trunks would look small in comparison to him.

So far, Roslyn seemed to be playing the role of the devoted date this evening. The first part of which was to look smashing. The vampire had donned a floor-length scarlet evening gown dotted here and there with matching sequins. Somehow, the slinky, tight-fitting gown managed to be tasteful and still show off Roslyn's perfect figure.

More than a few eyes turned in the vampire's direction, but a quick glower from Slater was enough to end the appreciative gazes. The giant's hazel eyes also followed the interlopers, as though he was committing their names and faces to memory so he could beat the stuffing out of them later. He crooked a finger at one of the two giants hovering near him and whispered something in the other man's ear. The giant nodded and moved off into the crowd. A few seconds later, one of the men who'd been staring at Roslyn was discreetly escorted off the riverboat. If I had to guess, I'd say he was going to get the same kind of treatment that I'd received the other night on the community college quad.

Elliot Slater stayed close to Roslyn the entire time, only letting her out of arm's reach long enough to grab them both a glass of champagne. Once he was done holding court, Elliot pulled Roslyn over to one of the blackjack tables, where they both sat down. The giant picked up Roslyn's hand and cooed sweet nothings into her ear whenever he wasn't busy betting or looking at his cards.

Despite her makeup, the vamp's face looked pale and sweaty underneath the strings of lights. I had the sense Roslyn was very close to bolting. And though I couldn't blame her for it if she did, it would only make things worse in the end.

Jonah McAllister and Mab Monroe also worked the crowd. Or rather, they stood in the middle of the deck and let their admiring sycophants come by one by one and suck up.

Jonah also wore a tux, his silver hair a bright, gleaming contrast against the black fabric. Mab wore a black cocktail dress not too dissimilar from my own. The dark color made her hair look like burnished copper against her creamy shoulders. As usual, she sported her gold sunburst necklace. The ruby that made up the center of the ornate design gleamed like fresh blood against her skin. Even across the open deck, my Stone magic let me hear the gemstone's harsh, powerful murmur—one of fire, death, destruction. The awful sound made me grind my teeth together. The primal, elemental part of me wanted to smash that damn ruby and destroy its proud, horrid murmurs almost as much as I wanted to kill Mab.

"Now that you've had time to scope out the place, how do you want to do this?" Finn asked in a low voice. "Want me to cull Slater from the herd? Spill a drink on him so he has to take a convenient trip to the men's room?"

"No," I replied. "We both need to leave with plausible deniability. You spilling a drink on Elliot Slater, and then him disappearing adds up to the right conclusion real quick. Throw me into the mix, and they'll even think they have the right motive. Just keep an eye on them, especially Roslyn. She looks like she's about ten seconds away from screaming and trying to claw out Slater's eyes."

"Wouldn't you be?" Finn asked in a quiet voice. "Xavier told me about Roslyn's so-called meetings with the giant. All the ways that he's been terrorizing her. About how he's been making her play house with him, as though they're a real couple. It's one of the sickest things I've ever heard."

I thought about how calm Roslyn Phillips had been when she'd told me what Slater had been doing to her. How the bastard was controlling and scaring and hurting and abusing her. How he was playing with her before he finally raped her.

"I would have cut his heart out of his chest with one of my knives—or at least tried to," I replied.

"So why hasn't Roslyn done that?"

"Because Roslyn isn't a former assassin like me. She didn't have the benefit of Fletcher's training. But more importantly, she has her sister and niece to think about. Xavier too. Her dying doesn't help them one bit."

Finn looked at me with his bright green eyes. "And you don't have people who love you too?"

I shrugged. "It's not the same. You, Jo-Jo, and Sophia know what I am, what I can do. And you've seen what other people have done to me."

"You were a mess after Alexis James and Tobias Dawson got done with you," he agreed.

I continued on like he hadn't spoken. "The three of you know the risks by now. That one night, I might not come home. The three of you have each other to lean on. Roslyn's the rock in her family. Her sister and her niece depend on her. She was trying to protect them."

Finn kept staring at me. "And you're our rock, Gin. You should think about that too."

I didn't respond. Because the funny thing was, Finn, Jo-Jo, and Sophia were my rocks—and I'd kill anyone who even thought about hurting them. Even if it meant my own death.

It was a price I'd be happy to pay.

Finn strolled off into the crowd, planting himself at a slot machine just in front of Slater's blackjack table. Roslyn gave him a wan smile, but some of the tension eased out of her slim shoulders. At least the vamp knew we were here and ready to play. Her toffee eyes skimmed over the crowd, looking for me, but she couldn't see me from where she was sitting. I made sure of it. I stayed at the bar, drinking a gin, watching the flow of traffic around the blackjack table, and thinking about everything I'd read about Elliot Slater in the past few days.

Finn had compiled quite a file on the giant, looking for any way to get to him, any weakness, vice, or hobby that he might have. We'd even dug into the folder of info that Fletcher Lane had compiled on Mab Monroe. The old man had included Slater in the mix with his boss, for obvious reasons. All the information had been interesting but not very helpful. Slater hadn't become Mab Monroe's top enforcer by accident. He was a crafty, cold-blooded bastard who liked using his fists to hurt people—a fact I'd felt for myself twice now.

Sadly, Roslyn Phillips wasn't the first woman Elliot Slater had terrorized. Finn had dug up a dozen investigations involving missing women in Ashland just in the last two years alone. Slater's name had been connected to all the cases, with him almost always listed as being the victim's *boyfriend*.

Tall, short, curvy, or not. Giant, dwarf, vampire, human, elemental. Black, white, Hispanic, Asian. None of those things mattered to Slater. The only thing he seemed to care about was beauty. That was the one thing all his victims had in common—they were all exceptionally beautiful women, just like Roslyn was. Eye-catching and striking with the kind of perfect features you just couldn't look away from.

The pattern was the same every single time. Slater would see a beautiful woman, become obsessed with her, and start stalking her. Showering her with his own twisted brand of attention and inventing the same sort of sick relationship with her that he had with Roslyn. In every single case, the woman turned up dead—raped and beaten to death a few weeks after she started *dating* Elliot Slater.

Finn had gotten his hands on some of the crime scene photos. They weren't pretty. They made what the giant had done to me that night at the community college seem like a gentle massage. Slater seemed to enjoy destroying the women's beauty just as much as he did admiring it to start with.

Some of the women had tried to fight back, of course. They'd gone to the police and tried to get a restraining order against Slater. But nothing ever came of their cries for help. In those cases, the women ended up dead within days instead of weeks. Slater didn't like being disobeyed.

The simple fact was that Elliot Slater was a serial killer who enjoyed stalking, terrorizing, and controlling women before he finally raped and ultimately murdered them. He liked their fear, liked the feeling of power it gave him. It was probably the only thing that could get a sick bastard like him off.

Of course, nothing ever came of any investigation into Slater, thanks to the giant's working for Mab Monroe. Hell, she probably gave him carte blanche to go out and find himself a certain kind of *distraction* every once in a while. A reward for all the bloody jobs he did on the Fire elemental's behalf.

But I had seen a sliver of opportunity in the file, one possible window to get the giant alone tonight—Elliot Slater liked to smoke cigars. A fact I'd witnessed the other night outside of Underwood's restaurant. Not an unusual habit among the moneyed, muckety-muck types in Ashland.

But in a crowd like this, lighting up a Cuban would be frowned upon. Trophy wives didn't like their designer dresses to reek of tobacco. And they'd create enough fuss to make even someone like Slater realize it was better to smoke away from all the silks and satins, if only to keep from listening to their bitching. So if the giant wanted his nicotine fix tonight, Slater would have to seek out a less crowded location to puff away to his heart's content. And when he did, I'd make my move—

"Is this seat taken?" a voice rumbled to my right.

I turned my head and found myself staring into Owen Grayson's violet eyes. "It is now."

Owen tipped his head, settled himself next to me, and ordered a tonic water.

"No scotch tonight?" I asked.

The bartender slid his drink over, and Owen rattled the ice cubes in the glass before he took a sip. "I don't drink when I'm gambling."

"Didn't look like much of a gamble," I replied. "Since you were up several hundred thousand dollars last time I saw you, and the other players desperately looked like they wanted you to move to another table."

Owen grinned. "I should probably mention that I'm excellent at bluffing."

"I just bet you are."

We sat there in companionable silence for a few moments. Owen leaned back, his gaze slowly tracking up and down my body. Admiring the view. I had to admit the unabashed attention pleased me. Especially when there were so many more attractive women on board. Even assassins had egos.

"You know," Owen said in a casual tone. "We're going to have to stop meeting like this."

"Like what?"

He gestured. "At a bar."

This time, I leaned back against said bar and cocked an eyebrow. "You didn't seem too upset last time we were at a bar together. The other night at Northern Aggression."

"That's because you promised to call me," Owen replied. "Which you haven't done yet."

I shrugged. "I've been busy."

"With what?"

Across the deck, Elliot Slater raked in a pile of gold chips.

"This and that."

Owen drained the rest of his tonic. "You know, I'm not used to waiting for a woman to call."

"Well, then this new experience will be good for your ego," I replied. "Keep it from getting too inflated. I think we also discussed that last time we met."

Owen chuckled, then scooted forward and put his hand on top of mine. It was a light touch, as gentle as a breeze. But to me, the feel of his warm skin on mine whispered of possibilities—and the pleasure that could be found in more full-body contact.

"What do you say we get out of here, Gin? Go have that dinner you promised me?"

"Dinner?" I replied.

"Dinner," he said, his eyes darkening to a rich, plum color. "And maybe some dessert too. If you'd like."

I knew exactly what he meant by *dessert*. My eyes drifted over Owen's face, down his chest, and over his strong, capable-looking hands. Once again, a hot tingle of desire sizzled to life in the pit of my stomach.

Donovan Caine wasn't coming back. The detective had made it perfectly clear that I wasn't what he wanted. That he valued his precious morals more than what he could have with me. And Owen Grayson was here, ready, willing, and able—and his violet eyes free of the guilt that had always darkened Donovan's golden ones.

Owen's thumb stroked over the back of my hand, another light, delicious touch that made me want to say yes to him, just to see what would happen between us—

Out of the corner of my eye, I saw Elliot Slater get to his feet. He murmured something in Roslyn's ear, then snapped his fingers. The two giants that had been hovering around the blackjack table moved closer to Roslyn, ordered to watch her instead of Slater. The giant traced a finger down the side of Roslyn's cheek. The vamp attempted to smile through the touch, but it came off as more of a grimace. Slater didn't seem to notice, though. He pulled a heavy silver case out from inside his jacket, opened it, and plucked out a long, fat cigar.

My window of opportunity had just opened. I wouldn't get a better chance than this all evening. I might not get another chance all evening.

Owen's thumb kept up its long, sure strokes, a promise of what could come later with other, more interesting parts of his anatomy. My pleasure or Roslyn's pain. No choice, really.

I smiled at Owen, pulled my hand away from his, and got to my feet. "Hold that thought. I see someone I just have to speak to. Please excuse me for a few minutes."

Surprise flashed in his eyes, and Owen opened his mouth, probably to ask what I thought I was doing turning down his open invitation yet again. I wasn't sure I knew myself.

I might even have been sorry if I hadn't already turned and walked away.

✲ 16 ✲

I kept to the perimeter of the deck, drawing as little attention to myself as possible as I headed after Elliot Slater. By this point, the benefit was in full swing, with at least three hundred people milling about in the open air, playing poker, pulling the slot machines, and drinking themselves into a fevered tizzy. More than enough traffic and noise to conceal my movements to all but the most devoted observer.

The key to making it look like you're not following someone is to pretend like he doesn't even exist. That the two of you are just out for a stroll, coincidentally in the same direction with the same destination in mind. So I walked along at a sedate pace, smiling at the men and women who wandered past me. I even paused a few seconds and pretended to be interested in the outcome of a baccarat game.

Finn had seen Slater get up, and he spotted me moving

through the crowd after the giant. Finn nodded at me, encouraging me to keep going. I nodded back. I had no intention of stopping until the giant was dead and feeding the catfish in the Aneirin River.

Thirty feet ahead of me, Elliot Slater rounded the corner of the deck and disappeared from view. I watched the end of another baccarat game, waited a few more seconds, then followed him.

Around the corner, the wide deck narrowed to a long walkway that ran the length of the entire riverboat. This side of the boat faced into the Aneirin River, and a few couples had slipped away from the rest of the maddening crowd to take in the view and murmur hot suggestions into each other's ears. I ignored them, my eyes fixed on my prey.

Ahead of me, Slater continued to walk at a casual pace that suggested he was out for a smoke and a stroll and nothing else. He broke free of the last remaining couple and stepped through an open door. It was quieter here, and I took care to put my heels down as softly as I could on the wooden deck. I eased up to the door and peered inside.

This part of the walkway had been enclosed in glass, probably so folks could still see the river and stay dry during a rainstorm. The walkway fronted a small, recessed salon complete with tables, chairs, and a bar inside the riverboat itself where passengers could relax and watch the landscape go by during cruises. The glassed-in section ran for about thirty feet before opening back up into the night air.

Slater had walked through the entire room and now

stood beyond the other open door. The giant shook a lighter in his hand, as though it was low on fluid and he was trying to coax one more burst of flame out of it. There was no one here but the two of us this far back on the riverboat. Perfect.

I walked forward. I made it through the glassed-in salon and stepped back out into the night air. Ahead of me, Slater still fussed with his lighter. I put my arm down, ready to palm one of my silverstone knives.

Just then, a restroom door opened to my left, and a man stepped out onto the deck ahead of me—putting him between me and Elliot Slater. The man turned in my direction, as though to walk back down to the open deck. Silver hair, hard hazel eyes, wrinkle-free face. He spotted me immediately, and his eyes widened for a second before narrowing.

Jonah McAllister looked just as pissed to see me as I was to see him.

"What the hell are you doing here?" he barked.

I wasn't particularly surprised that Jonah McAllister was here. After all, I'd seen him board the riverboat earlier this evening. And if there was one thing I'd learned during my years as the Spider, it was that the universe always conspired to fuck up the best-laid plans of mice, men, and most especially, assassins. Like the slick lawyer choosing this exact moment to step in between me and my target. I could practically hear the cosmic chuckles ringing my ears. Ha, ha, fucking ha.

For a moment, I debated palming my knife, lunging forward, and stabbing Jonah McAllister where he stood.

Just for interrupting me. I could do the lawyer, step over his body, and then take care of Elliot Slater. Two-for-one special. But I knew I wouldn't be able to get away clean after the fact. McAllister could scream, Slater could hear the struggle and charge at me, or even worse, run to get his boss, Mab Monroe. The Fire elemental would have no qualms about frying me right there with her magic. Not when what I had done would be so obvious.

No, Jonah McAllister was going to have to live to see another day. And now, so would Elliot Slater. Which meant Roslyn Phillips's suffering wasn't over yet, if it could ever truly be over, given what the giant had done to her.

Fuck.

I crossed my arms over my chest and gave the lawyer a cold look. "What does it look like I'm doing? I'm taking a stroll around the riverboat. Is that a problem?"

Elliot Slater's head snapped around at the sound of my voice. The giant frowned, put his cigar and lighter away, and headed in our direction. Fantastic.

Jonah McAllister's hazel eyes narrowed even more at my snide tone. "I specifically meant how did someone like you get on board? The *Delta Queen* is very exclusive, and loath as I am to admit it, Phillip Kincaid's parties even more so. Helps keep the white trash out."

"White trash? Do you really think that's an insult?"

"Not to someone like you," he sniffed. "Which is what makes you trash."

"At least I look my age," I snapped, referring to his wrinkle-free face. "Tell me, exactly how much a week do you blow on Air elemental facials? A thousand bucks?

Two? I'm guessing more. After all, you're a man of advancing years now."

I knew I should have kept my mouth shut, that it would have made things easier if I'd let McAllister take his shots at me and had just slinked off into the darkness as if I was utterly demoralized and defeated. But I was getting real tired of the lawyer needling me at every single turn just because it amused him. And for keeping me from killing Elliot Slater tonight and at least helping Roslyn Phillips in that small way.

An angry red flush spread up Jonah McAllister's neck at my words, something even the best Air elemental facial couldn't disguise. The silver-haired lawyer opened his mouth to lambaste me some more, when Slater stepped up behind him.

The giant stared at McAllister a moment before his hazel gaze cut to me. His eyes narrowed as well in recognition. Slater might be obsessed with Roslyn, but I noted the giant wasn't above checking out my breasts and legs, even though they were nowhere near as spectacular as the vampire's.

"Gin Blanco," Slater rumbled. "You clean up nice."

The back-assed compliment made the gin that I'd just drunk roil in my stomach.

"Elliot," Jonah said. "I'd like you to escort Ms. Blanco off the boat please. It seems she just hasn't learned her lesson about insulting us—or being where she doesn't belong. I think she needs you to remind her exactly what her place is."

Elliot grinned. "Shall I toss her over the side? Right here?"

"Don't be thuggish," Jonah replied. "We have an image to maintain. Ms. Blanco deserves the walk of shame past all of tonight's guests. And then you can deal with her any way you like on shore. Seems that beating you gave her just didn't take. Perhaps you'd like another chance to get it right."

The giant's grin widened.

So Jonah McAllister wanted Elliot Slater to hustle me off the riverboat, take me to a dark alley somewhere, and beat me—again. Not my original plan for the evening, but sometimes, you had to roll with the punches.

Before I could move or react, the giant used his speed to surge forward and clamp his hand around my upper arm. His long, hard fingers bit into my flesh like steel bolts, but I gritted my teeth against the pain. I wasn't going to give him the satisfaction of screaming and begging for mercy. Not again.

Let Slater drag me off the boat and into one of the alleys that surrounded the riverfront. He'd be in for a nasty surprise. So would McAllister, if the lawyer decided to tag along and watch the show. Because I was tired of tiptoeing around them. Mab Monroe too. I wanted to kill the Three Musketeers and proceed with things— namely getting Roslyn Phillips some help for the brutal trauma she'd been through and figuring out a way to tell Bria who and what I really was.

Killing McAllister and Slater tonight would at least solve a few of my problems. More than that, though, it would just be *fun*. Unlike other assassins that I'd run into over the years, I didn't kill people because it brought me any great pleasure. I did it because it was a job that I happened to excel at. But even the most consummate professional could be excused an indulgence or two, and I was thinking about making McAllister and Slater mine.

"Come on," Slater said. "Let's go."

Jonah McAllister stepped aside, and Elliot Slater pushed me down the walkway toward the front of the riverboat. I didn't make a sound. Didn't scream, protest, or try to jerk my upper arm out of the giant's grip. Mainly because I didn't want Slater to move his hand any lower and find the silverstone knife nestled against my forearm. Besides, screaming would be useless. No one would come to my aid. Everyone knew Elliot Slater worked for Mab Monroe. And with the Fire elemental in attendance here tonight, no one would dare question why the giant was strong-arming me—or what he might do to me once he got me off the boat.

"It's a shame you're just not willing to learn, Ms. Blanco," Jonah McAllister said in a conversational tone. The lawyer walked behind me. "That you just can't accept the way things work in Ashland."

"Learn? Accept?" I looked over my shoulder and glared at him. "What you really mean is you don't understand why I'm not cowed by you and yours, why I don't just roll over and let you do whatever you want to me."

McAllister shrugged. "Call it what you like. But every time you forget, you're going to get another reminder, like the one at the community college. Until you either remember to pay us the respect we're due, or until you're dead. Either option is perfectly acceptable to me."

We rounded the corner and stepped back out onto the main deck. Elliot Slater was a hard man to miss, and more than a few people looked in our direction. But once they realized the giant had his hand clamped on my arm like a vise, folks quickly went back to their drinking and gambling.

Everyone except Roslyn Phillips. Even though she was fifty feet away from me, I could see the vampire's face tighten. Roslyn thought I'd been caught trying to assassinate Slater. She didn't realize that I'd just had the bad luck to run into Jonah McAllister, who still suspected I had something to do with his son, Jake's, death.

Luck. Capricious bitch. She'd gotten me into trouble more times than I cared to think about.

Finn also spotted Slater holding on to me. Our eyes met for a second before I cast my gaze down and shook my head a tiny bit. *No,* I was telling him. Don't interfere. Not yet. Finn's hand tightened around the handle of the slot machine he'd been pulling down, but he didn't move. I knew he'd be there when I needed him, though.

Slater bent down to murmur in my ear. "Do yourself a favor and don't make a scene, Blanco. Or I'll hit you even harder when we get off the boat. Just because." His breath reeked of onions, which made his threat that much fouler, so to speak.

Oh, yeah. I was going to enjoy stabbing the giant to death. Just because.

But I played the part of the cowed victim and let the giant push me toward the gangplank on the opposite side of the deck. Slater crooked his finger, and his two giant minions left Roslyn's side to come over and flank me. Of course. Slater would need someone to hold me up while he beat me again. Because doing it himself would be such a *bother*.

Jonah McAllister nodded his head in satisfaction, then strolled to the center of the deck, where Mab Monroe was still holding court. Elliot Slater strong-arming me toward the exit had also caught the Fire elemental's interest, and her black eyes tracked me across the deck. McAllister reached her side and whispered something in Mab's ear. After a moment, the Fire elemental nodded her approval, rubber-stamping my impending beating and possible death. Good to know where I stood, at least.

But Mab wasn't the only one watching us. Phillip Kincaid was interested in the drama as well. The casino owner leaned against one of the blackjack tables, staring at me with obvious curiosity, trying to figure out who I was and why Elliot Slater was dragging me off the riverboat. He looked across the deck at Mab, who gave him a flat stare, a clear warning not to interfere with the giant. After a moment, Kincaid shrugged and turned back to the table. He didn't know me so he didn't care what Mab's men did to me. This might be Kincaid's casino, but even here, he knew he was no match for the Fire elemental.

But there was one more person on the deck who wasn't busy pretending I was invisible—Owen Grayson. He must have seen Elliot Slater out of the corner of his eye, because he glanced at the giant. Then his head snapped back again when he realized that the giant had a death grip on me. Owen's violet eyes stayed on me as he watched Slater walk me past the gaming tables and slot machines. I didn't look in Owen's direction or try to signal him in any way. This was my problem, my mess, my punishment for antagonizing Jonah McAllister instead of keeping my mouth shut.

But to my surprise, instead of going back to his tonic water, Owen Grayson got to his feet, threw a couple of chips on the bar to cover his tab, and headed toward us.

Well, this was going to be interesting.

Owen met us in the middle of the deck in an open space behind one of the blackjack tables. Since Owen stood in the center of the aisle, Elliot Slater had to stop or run over the businessman. Slater decided to stop. The other man was important and rich enough for that small courtesy.

"Is there a problem?" Owen asked. His voice was low and deep, with a dangerous, aggressive edge, and his eyes flashed like dark amethysts in his face.

Elliot tightened his grip on my arm, his fingers digging into my flesh in a clear warning for me to keep my mouth shut. "No problem, Mr. Grayson. Just taking out a bit of trash that got onto the riverboat by mistake."

Trash wasn't the worst thing I'd ever been called. Hardly enough to make me roll my eyes. But the word made Owen's gaze simmer with violet fire. For a moment, I felt a blast of cold emanate from his body. A manifestation of his elemental talent for metal—and his anger. Owen's face remained smooth, except for the scar under his chin. It whitened under the strain of his clenched jaw.

"Ms. Blanco is my date for the evening," Owen replied in a mild tone. "She's hardly trash. I suggest you let go of her arm. Most ladies don't like to be manhandled."

"Only in bed," I quipped. "And even then, I still like to be on top."

His mouth quirked at my flip remark, and our eyes met and held. Gray on violet. Desire simmered in Owen's eyes underneath his anger, and I knew he could see the emotion reflected in my gaze. But there was something else, another emotion in his cold face that surprised me—concern. For me.

My chest tightened, and I couldn't breathe. It had been so long since someone besides Finn, Fletcher, or the Deveraux sisters had cared about what happened to me that it took my breath away for a moment. Even if Owen Grayson was probably just playing the part of the gentleman in order to get laid tonight. Right now, it was working for him.

Owen turned his attention to Slater and smiled at the giant, letting a bit of ugly violence show through his hot gaze. The giant frowned. It was one thing to take me onshore for another beat-down when it seemed like I was here by myself or had somehow snuck in. It was quite another to accost the proclaimed date of one of Ashland's wealthiest businessmen. Enough even to make Elliot Slater think twice.

Footsteps smacked, fabric swished on the deck behind us, and I felt another blast of elemental magic—Fire magic. Dozens of tiny, hot, invisible needles pricked my skin, and my jaw locked even tighter as I struggled to keep my face impassive. To show no sign that I felt anything out of the ordinary. Especially not Mab Monroe's elemental Fire magic dripping off her body like hot candle wax. Slater stepped back, dragging me with him, to make room for his boss, Mab Monroe. Evidently the giant was making too much of a scene, and the Fire elemental had decided to get involved and see exactly what was going on.

"Is there a problem here?" Mab asked, repeating Owen's words. The Fire elemental's low, breathy voice always reminded me of delicately rasping silk. But there was also power in her tone, raw force that couldn't be denied, a clear presence that said *fuck with me and you're dead*.

For a moment, the Fire elemental regarded me with her black gaze. Unlike most elementals, whose eyes glowed brighter when they reached for their magic, Mab Monroe's darkened. The blackest ink would have seemed pale in comparison to her ebony orbs. A flicker of recognition sparked in Mab's gaze. She realized who I was and seemed just as surprised to see me here as Jonah McAllister had. Hardly shocking. After all, I was just a lowly restaurant owner. It wasn't like I moved in her rich, highfalutin circles. At least, not as Gin Blanco anyway. As the Spider, I'd had my share of dealings with a good portion of those in attendance tonight.

I met the Fire elemental's gaze with a steady one of my own. I wasn't going to pretend to be cowed by her. Not by the bitch who'd so viciously murdered my mother and older sister, who'd taken such glee in torturing me all those years ago, who'd ordered the murder of my sister Bria just yesterday. No, I wasn't going to pretend that Mab Monroe scared me anymore. Not now, not ever.

"No problem at all," Owen replied in a smooth voice. "Seems your giant mistook my date for someone else."

He reached over and tapped on Slater's hand with his index finger. The giant looked at Mab. The Fire elemental stared at Owen, who looked right back at her. Owen's gaze never wavered. Neither did Mab's. All around us, conversation had stopped. Even the slot machines were quiet as folks stopped feeding coins into them to watch this much more interesting gamble by Owen Grayson.

After a moment, Mab jerked her head. The motion made her coppery hair spill over her shoulders like a bloody fan unfurling. Elliot Slater huffed his disappointment at his boss's obvious order, but the giant released his grip on me. Owen held out his hand, which I stepped forward and took, slipping my palm into his.

Slater stared at me, but I didn't rub my upper arm where the giant had held me. I wasn't going to give him the satisfaction of realizing that he'd bruised me to the bone with his hard, unrelenting grip.

"If there's nothing else, we'll go back to the bar," Owen told Mab. "Before we try our luck at the gaming tables again. Seems I'm on a roll tonight."

A spark of anger flared in Mab's eyes. Owen was poking at the sleeping bear with a sharp stick, and she was seconds away from ripping off his head. I tensed, ready to palm one of my silverstone knives. I didn't know what agenda Owen had, why he'd decided to save me from Elliot Slater. I supposed the most logical assumption would be that he simply liked me. But things were rarely what they seemed in my line of work, and I'd learned long ago to look out for hidden motives. Even if it did make me slightly paranoid. Better that than dead.

Still, I felt somewhat protective of the sexy businessman. Even though it had been a stupid thing to do, Owen had stepped forward and stood up for me. If Mab made a move toward him, I'd bury my knife in her heart and worry about the consequences later. Or at least try to kill the bitch before she toasted me with her Fire power.

But the Fire elemental smothered her anger and made her face as remote and impassive as before. "Of course," she murmured. "But the next time you decide to gamble, Mr. Grayson, perhaps you should think about exactly what you're risking. A man like you has a lot to lose. Money, status, family."

By *family*, Mab meant Owen's younger sister Eva—who was the most important person in the world to him. Another cold blast of elemental magic exploded off Owen's body, momentarily driving away the feel of Mab's Fire power pricking my skin. Mab felt the surge of magic and smiled. She knew that she'd gotten to Owen with her casual threat.

I curled my fingers even tighter around his hand, lightly digging my nails into his skin. Warning him.

Owen squeezed my hand back. He didn't relax, but he did manage a curt nod to Mab. He wasn't going to push the issue any more tonight. Couldn't blame him for that. A guy could only play the part of the white knight for so long before he was overwhelmed by enemy forces. Too bad Owen didn't realize that I didn't really need rescuing. That I would have been happy to cut into Mab right here, right now if I thought I could get away with it. Still, the display of chivalry pleased me in an odd way. Donovan Caine had certainly never done anything like it for me.

Mab stepped back, and Owen turned and led me over to the bar. As we walked, we passed Finn, who was still sitting at his slot machine. He studied Owen, a thoughtful, assessing look in his green eyes. Finn's gaze flicked to me. I shrugged my shoulders. It was too late to do anything about the situation now. All I could do was go along with things and pretend to be the businessman's date for the evening.

People parted to let us walk by, and we reached the bar without incident. The folks sitting on either side both scooted farther away, as though they were afraid of catching something from us. Owen ordered another round of drinks. Tonic water for him, gin for me. We didn't speak until after the bartender had filled our order.

"So," Owen murmured. "You want to tell me why you followed Elliot Slater to the other side of the boat in the first place? Or perhaps you'd like to start with why he looked like he was going to rip your arm off and beat you with it?"

So the businessman had realized I'd been after Slater. Nothing was going as planned this evening. Nothing at all.

I looked at Owen. Curiosity simmered in his violet gaze along with something else—respect. For what? Me? Why? I hadn't done a fucking worthwhile thing. Hadn't killed Elliot Slater, hadn't killed Jonah McAllister. Hell, I hadn't done anything noteworthy the entire night.

Still, Owen had stuck his neck out for me, risked Mab Monroe's wrath because of me. I owed him some sort of explanation, even if it was going to be complete fiction. I opened my mouth to start spinning a story—

And that's when my cell phone rang.

* 17 *

For a moment, Owen and I just looked at each other. My phone rang again, and his eyes narrowed. I knew who it was, of course, and that he wouldn't have interrupted me unless it was important.

I held my finger up, telling Owen that I'd be with him in a minute, then pulled my phone out of my purse and flipped it open. "What?"

"We've got a problem, Gin," Finn's voice sounded in my ear. "Look who just stepped on board."

I turned my head to the right. Detective Bria Coolidge stood at the top of the gangplank. Bria wore a long, strapless, flowing gown made out of an ice blue silk. The color brought out her eyes and the rosy flush in her pale cheeks, and a matching wrap covered her bare arms. Bria's blond hair had been swept up into a complicated bun. Her only adornments were her primrose rune necklace and the three rune-stamped rings on her left index finger. The silverstone medallion glinted as Bria turned her neck from side to side, scanning the crowd before her. She looked stunning, cold, regal, and beautiful all at once.

And she wasn't alone.

Xavier was right by her side, dressed in a white tuxedo jacket. The giant's bald head gleamed like polished ebony underneath the soft lights.

Bad to worse. That was definitely the theme of the evening.

"What are they doing here?" I muttered.

Beside me, Owen leaned forward so he could get a look at whom I was talking about. I didn't bother to block his view. He was too smart for that. He studied Bria and Xavier a moment, then turned his attention back to me.

"Beats me," Finn replied. "Maybe they're just crashing the party."

"You remember what the old man said about coincidences?"

Finn sighed. "That there are none."

"Exactly," I replied. "Those two are here for a reason. Keep an eye on them. I'll be with you in a minute."

I hung up and turned back to Owen. "I'm sorry. I have to go."

"Then I'm going too," he said.

"This doesn't involve you, Owen. Things have just taken a turn for the worse, and they're probably going to get even uglier before the night is through. You should walk away while you still can."

A crooked smile stretched across his chiseled face. "And let you get away without telling me what the fuck is going on? I don't think so, Gin. You owe me that, at least."

His violet eyes glittered with a hard, determined light, and I realized that I'd peaked the businessman's curiosity even more with my mysterious words and furtive actions. Curiosity. Another double-edged sword that had cut me more than once in my life. Even now, the blade whistled toward my head. I just wondered which way it would slice tonight.

Still, Owen was right. He'd stood up to Mab Monroe for me in front of all the city's movers and shakers. I did owe him something. What that was, I wasn't sure. But if Owen wanted to come along for the bumpy ride tonight, that was his business. I had no doubt that he'd want to get off afterward. Donovan Caine certainly had.

"Fine," I said. "But follow my lead, and do what I tell you to when I tell you to do it. Understand?"

His smile deepened. "Yes, ma'am."

Owen and I left the bar. Finn spotted us moving through the crowd and discreetly waved us over. He'd moved from his perch at the slot machine to a shadowy spot where he could put his back against one of the walls that formed the interior dining room. I looked out over the crowd, but I didn't see Bria or Xavier anywhere.

"Where'd they go, Finn?"

Instead of answering me, Finn raised his eyebrows in Owen's direction.

"He's with us for the remainder of the evening," I replied. "Just talk, Finn. We can sort out everything else later."

By *everything*, he knew that I meant Owen Grayson and whether we could afford to let the businessman keep breathing if things went bad. Something I was going to have to decide before the night was through. Because while Owen might want to sleep with me, he didn't know what he was getting into tonight. And I didn't know if he could keep his mouth shut about it. But it was a chance I had to take right now.

Finn nodded. "Bria's over by the railing, sipping champagne and looking absolutely stunning."

Sure enough, my sister was doing exactly what Finn said she was. Since Bria seemed to be okay for the moment, I moved on to the other players in the game.

"Where's Xavier?"

"Xavier said something to Bria a minute ago and left her standing there alone," Finn answered. "The giant walked into the dining room."

I frowned. "Why would he go in there? Dinner isn't until later. All the action is still out here right now."

Finn cleared his throat. "I wondered that too—until I noticed that Roslyn's conveniently disappeared as well. She's gone, Gin."

My head snapped around to the blackjack table where the vampire had been. I'd been so busy with Mab Monroe and then Owen Grayson that I hadn't kept track of Roslyn. Her chair was empty. Xavier's sudden appearance started to make a little more sense to me.

"Roslyn," I muttered. "She must have told Xavier that she was coming here tonight with Elliot Slater."

"And Xavier couldn't stand that and came to rescue her," Finn finished. "With or without her knowledge?"

"Doesn't matter," I muttered. "Because if Slater sees them together, they're both as good as dead."

Owen stood still and silent by my side, listening to everything Finn and I said. The businessman didn't say anything, didn't interrupt and ask what the hell was going on, or who we were talking about. He just listened and watched the crowd around us. Most people didn't know enough to keep quiet. My respect for Owen ratcheted up a few more notches.

"What do you want to do, Gin?" Finn asked in a soft voice.

I stood there thinking, my eyes scanning over the crowd again, this time looking for three very specific people. I spotted them almost instantly.

Mab Monroe, Elliot Slater, and Jonah McAllister had moved to the right side of the riverboat and were deep in discussion about something. Slater's giant guards stood close to them, focused on their boss, ready to jump when he gave the order. My gaze cut back to Roslyn's empty chair at the blackjack table. It would only be a matter of time before Slater realized that she was missing and started looking for her. Only one thing to do.

I blew out a breath. "Finn, you stay out here and keep an eye on Bria. Call me if it looks like she's going to get herself into trouble. Owen and I will find Roslyn and Xavier and get them off this boat."

Finn stayed where he was against the wall. I jerked my head at Owen.

"Come on," I said. "They've got to be inside somewhere."

He nodded and followed me through the open doors into the dining room. I stalked past the rows of tables.

A few people had drifted inside to sit down, but none of them were Roslyn or Xavier, so I walked on. Owen moved quickly and quietly behind me. He didn't ask questions or offer any input. He just followed me.

I thought about my earlier tour of the riverboat this evening. Where would I go if I wanted to have a quiet meeting away from the crowd? Only one spot I'd seen this evening had been conducive to lovers.

"Come on," I said. "I know where they are."

Owen nodded, and we walked on. I went through another door, stepping out into the walkway that lined the back side of the riverboat. My stiletto heels slammed against the wood. The time for being quiet was over. Because if I didn't reach Roslyn and Xavier before Elliot Slater did, they wouldn't be getting off this boat alive.

Up ahead, I noticed the door to the glassed-in section of the boat was closed. Some of the blinds had also been drawn, providing a bit of privacy for whoever might be inside the salon. I didn't bother knocking, instead twisting the knob and throwing the door to one side. Inside, Roslyn sat in a chair, shoulders shaking, tears trickling down her tight face. Xavier perched on his knees before her, holding her hands, as though he'd been pleading with her.

"What do you two think you're doing?" I snapped.

"Gin—" Xavier started.

"Do you know what you've done? How much danger you've put yourself and Roslyn in by coming here tonight?"

The giant bit his lip. "I couldn't help myself, Gin. Knowing that Roslyn was here with that *bastard*—"

"I know, Xavier. I know. But I need you to be quiet right now and listen to me. Okay?"

The giant pressed his lips together, but he slowly nodded.

I turned my gaze to Roslyn. "I told you to keep Xavier out of it, that I'd take care of Slater. You said you could handle it."

"I'm sorry," she whispered. "But I—I just couldn't lie to Xavier about where I was going tonight. And what might happen if you failed. If I . . . if I had to go home with Slater."

I tapped my toe on the wooden floor. A migraine throbbed in my head in time to the sharp, staccato motion. Because I had failed Roslyn. I'd had my chance at Elliot Slater, and I'd let Jonah McAllister get in my way. I should have just killed them and dumped their bodies over the railing, despite the consequences. That way, at least Roslyn and Xavier would have been free of this mess.

Owen Grayson stood in the doorway behind me, still looking and listening. I had no idea what the businessman was thinking at this point, and I had no idea what I was going to do about him after the fact. Right now, though, I had to focus on Roslyn and Xavier. Like it or not, I was responsible for them, and neither one of them was going to get dead tonight if I could help it.

I stabbed my finger at Xavier. "You. You get out of here right now. Go back to your partner, Detective Bria Coolidge, who I assume you dragged to this thing for cover, and tell her that there's some emergency you have to take care of. Then you get off this boat and go straight to this house." I rattled off Jo-Jo Deveraux's address to the giant. "You stay there, and you wait for me to show up. No matter how long it takes. Understand?"

The giant closed his eyes and slowly nodded.

"Good. Get going. Now."

Xavier looked at Roslyn another moment before getting to his feet. Owen stepped to one side so the giant could leave the salon. I waited until the echo of Xavier's footsteps had faded away before I turned to Roslyn.

"What about me?" she asked, tears still streaming down her face. "Do you want me to go back out there? Back out to—Slater?" Roslyn's voice broke on the last word.

Instead of answering her, I pulled my cell phone out of my purse and dialed Finn.

"Yes?" his voice sounded in my ear.

"I found them. Xavier's coming your way. Make sure he talks to Bria, then gets off the boat. Go get your car without drawing too much attention to yourself. Roslyn will meet you in the parking lot. Take her to Jo-Jo's. Owen, what's your address?"

The businessman told me the information, which I passed on to Finn.

"Once you get Roslyn settled at Jo-Jo's, come over to Owen's house and pick me up," I told him.

"Got it," Finn said and hung up.

I stuck my phone back in my purse and pulled out some tissues. I drew in a breath and turned to Roslyn, reminding myself to be gentle with the vampire. Yes, she'd put herself and Xavier in danger by telling the giant she was coming here tonight, by not trusting me to do what I'd promised. But I couldn't fault her for it. Not after everything that she'd already been through.

"No, you're not going back to Slater," I said in a quiet voice, handing her the tissues. "We're getting you out of here and away from the giant for good. Now, let's get you cleaned up before we go."

Once Roslyn wiped away her tears and runny mascara, the three of us left the salon. I curled my arm through Owen's, and we strolled back toward the hustle and bustle of the main deck. Owen still hadn't said anything, and I was grateful for his silence. Roslyn walked behind us, moving at a slow, steady pace just the way I'd told her to.

I glanced over my shoulder at the vampire. "Five more minutes, and you'll be safe in Finn's car. Five more minutes. Just remember that, Roslyn."

The vamp nodded, but her toffee eyes were dull and flat in her face. Exhaustion and fear tightened her features.

Owen and I rounded the corner and stepped onto the main deck once more. Roslyn joined us. Owen and I moved toward the gangplank, drawing as little attention to ourselves as possible. We walked several feet away from the wall, creating a sort of human screen for Roslyn, trying to shield her enough so no one would realize that she was leaving.

At this point, we were five hundred feet away from the gangplank. Four hundred. Three.

We walked on, Roslyn picking up speed with every single step. She pulled ahead of us, moving out into the open for everyone to see, but there was nothing I could do to call her back without drawing even more attention to the vamp.

Two hundred feet. One hundred—

"Roslyn!" Elliot Slater's voice boomed through the crowd.

She hadn't been quick enough. Roslyn froze at the sound of the giant's voice, fifty feet away from the edge of the gangplank that led down into the dark night and to her freedom.

The giant used his speed to maneuver through the crowd. Five seconds later, he reached Roslyn's side. I pulled Owen back against the wall that fronted the dining hall. We stood ten feet away from the other couple.

"Where are you going, baby?" Slater asked. "I told you to wait for me at the blackjack table."

Somehow, Roslyn managed a trembling smile. "I got cold. I was just going down to get my coat out of the limo. I'll be back in a minute."

She started to walk past the giant, but he put his hand on her arm, stopping her. Roslyn flinched at the touch. The giant's hazel eyes narrowed. He wasn't buying her excuse.

"I'll have one of my men get it," Slater said. "Until then, you can stay right here next to me where it's warm."

Roslyn stared past Slater at me. Emotions whirled in her dark eyes. Panic. Fear. Hate. Disgust. Rage. So much rage. The vampire dropped her gaze from mine and shuddered out a breath. For a moment, I thought she might give in, might go with Slater and erode a little more of her soul in the process.

Roslyn huffed out another breath. Her whole body stilled, as though she'd been frozen alive by an Ice elemental. Another breath, this one so shallow that her shoulders barely lifted. Then, her spine slowly straightened, and her whole body lifted up, as though she was gathering her strength for what was to come. Roslyn raised her head last. For a moment, she swayed side to side, like a delicate flower tracking the movement of the sun. Then her eyes snapped open. Hate made Roslyn's dark gaze burn as bright as any Fire elemental's.

"Don't put your hands on me."

Slater frowned. "What did you say, baby?"

"I said don't put your fucking hands on me!" Roslyn screamed.

She shoved the giant as hard as she could. Like all vampires, Roslyn had above-average strength. But Slater was a giant, and a big one at that. He took only two steps back. But Roslyn didn't care. Everything that she'd been suppressing these past few days—all the anger and rage and fear and helplessness—all of it just erupted. Spewed out of her like foul venom from a copperhead's pointed fangs. And Roslyn finally let out the heavy, terrible secret she'd been carrying.

"You're never touching me again!" the vampire screamed. "Never! Do you hear me, you sick bastard? You're never putting your filthy hands on me again! I'd rather die first!"

All conversation on the deck stopped. All the drinking, all the gambling, everything. Everyone in attendance focused on Roslyn Phillips. With her clenched fists, trembling body, and hard mouth, the vampire resembled some beautiful Valkyrie or goddess, angered beyond the point of all reason.

Roslyn realized that everyone was watching her. But instead of being cowed into silence by the attention, the hate in her eyes blazed even brighter, a bonfire burning out of control.

"Do your rich friends know what a bastard you are?" Roslyn screamed. "How you've been stalking me? How you've been coming to my club every single night and making me fix your stupid drinks and kiss you like a lover? Does your boss know what kind of sick fuck you are? How you made me come here tonight and pretend to be your fucking girlfriend even though I hate you, even though I *loathe* you?"

A lot of bad things happened in Ashland on a daily basis. Robberies, beatings, murders. Still, shocked gasps rippled through the crowd at the vampire's words. Every eye landed on Elliot Slater. The giant turned his head this way and that, feeling the heavy judgment of all in attendance, before his gaze snapped back to Roslyn.

"Calm down, baby."

Slater's voice was soft, but his eyes were cold, flat, hard. His right hand clenched and unclenched into a massive fist, and his knuckles cracked with the movement. The pale, chalky skin of his cheeks turned a mottled red with rage, and his thin mop of blond hair bristled with anger. Roslyn had just called Slater on his predilections in the most public and humiliating of ways. The bastard was seconds away from hitting her—or worse, snapping the vamp's neck outright.

I palmed one of my silverstone knives and got ready to move. He wasn't going to touch her. Not as long as I still had a breath left in my body.

The giant stretched out a hand to do something to Roslyn. Hit her, draw her closer. But Roslyn didn't give him a chance. Even as he reached for her, the vampire picked up her long skirt, turned, and ran away as fast as she could. Her heels clattered against the deck and then the gangplank, the echo growing fainter with every step.

Slater stood on the deck, momentarily stunned. Then, he shook his head and started after the vamp. I shifted my weight forward, ready to follow him—

"Elliot."

That single, breathy word was enough to stop Slater and make him jerk back like a dog on a leash. The crowd parted, and Mab Monroe stepped forward. The *swish-swish* of her black silk dress sounded as loud as a vacuum cleaner in the absolute silence. The Fire elemental stopped at the giant's shoulder and patted his arm. Mab's black eyes seemed to suck in all the available light as she studied her number-one enforcer.

"Let her go, Elliot," Mab said in a voice loud enough for everyone to hear. "You know how troubled poor Roslyn is. All those pills she's on for her mood swings and depression. I'm sure she'll come to her senses. When she does, she'll be quite embarrassed about those horrible things she just said. I'm sure she'll offer you a very sincere, very *public* apology."

At this point, Mab was speaking to the crowd as a whole, rather than to the giant. The Fire elemental was letting everyone know that Roslyn Phillips was persona non grata, as Finn would say. As for all the talk about Roslyn being troubled, I imagined Mab would trot out those same tired lines when the vampire's body was pulled out of whatever dark hole Slater was planning to plant her in.

Because that's what the giant had in mind. Whatever twisted obsession or feeling he'd had for Roslyn was gone, burned away by her bitter truths. Now, only hate filled Slater's face. Pure, simple, murderous hate.

Mab looked at Phillip Kincaid first, since the riverboat was his gin joint, giving him the courtesy of at least pretending to defer to him on his home turf. After a moment, the handsome casino owner nodded at her, accepting her statement, even though he knew it was all so much bullshit, just like everyone else did. But there was nothing he or anyone else could do about it.

The Fire elemental stared at one person after another, daring anyone to challenge her phony words. After a few seconds, all but the bravest souls dropped their eyes from Mab's and went back to whatever they'd been doing before. Talking, drinking, gambling. Slowly, the noise level returned to normal. Mab pulled Slater toward the back of the deck, where Jonah McAllister stood. The three of them put their heads together and started talking to each other once more.

I waited, but Slater made no move toward the gangplank, and he didn't summon over any of his men to go chasing after Roslyn. Well, that was something at least.

I tucked my silverstone knife back up my sleeve and turned to Owen Grayson. The businessman's eyes were dark and hooded, and I didn't feel like reading the emotions swimming in the depths of his gaze. Time enough for that later. Right now, there was only one thing to do.

"C'mon. Let's get out of here," I whispered to Owen.

He stared at me a moment before replying with a single word. "Gladly."

⁂ 18 ⁂

Owen and I walked down the gangplank. After the heated crush of people on board the riverboat, the night air felt cold and empty. Or perhaps that was just my heart after seeing Roslyn Phillips's raw, naked pain. Only one thing was for sure—Elliot Slater was going to die. The giant would never put his hands on Roslyn—or anyone else—ever again. I'd make certain of that.

I might have moonlighted as an assassin for years, but despite popular misconceptions, I'd never taken any great pleasure in killing people. To me, it had been a job, just like any other. Something I'd been good at, no matter how twisted and wrong and evil it might have been. But this time, this time, I was going to enjoy gutting Elliot Slater. Going to enjoy ripping into him, carving his heart out of his chest, and making him watch while I squished the black, bloody organ between my fingers. Maybe I'd even take a few pictures for Roslyn. The vamp could use them on her Christmas cards this year. Happy holidays.

Owen and I stepped off the gangplank and onto the riverside boardwalk.

"My car's this way," Owen said, heading toward the parking lot where Finn had left his Aston Martin.

I walked by his side, scanning the shadows. The iron street lamps did little to drive back the darkness, and the parking lots stretched out before us like the thick gray slabs you might find on top of graveyard tombs. A few other couples had decided to leave the riverboat soiree early as well, and they waited in small clusters for the tuxedo-clad valets to retrieve their vehicles or for their limos to pull up near the gangplank entrance.

I looked for Xavier, but I didn't see him lurking around anywhere. The giant should have been long gone if he'd followed my instructions. I did, however, spot Roslyn. The vampire had stopped running and stood about a hundred feet ahead of us on the boardwalk. Beyond her, in the parking lot, I saw the headlights flicker on Finn's Aston Martin, signaling her. Roslyn hugged her arms to her chest and walked toward the silver sports car, weaving her way around the other vehicles in the lot.

A scuffle sounded, and loud footsteps clacked on the boardwalk behind us in a rapid rush. Someone was running toward us. I looked over my shoulder to see who it was. Her ice-blue dress whipped around her legs, and the silverstone primrose rune bounced up and down against her throat with every stride she took. My sister just didn't know when to leave well enough alone.

Owen heard the footsteps too. He turned, saw Bria

running toward us, and pulled me to one side, out of her way. Bria sprinted past us. Up ahead, Roslyn reached Finn's car, opened the door, and got inside. A moment later, Finn steered the vehicle out the far side of the lot, away from the pursuing Bria.

Baby sister realized that the vampire had gotten away from her. She slowed to a stop and smacked her hand against the closest street lamp. "Fuck!"

She turned around and saw Owen and me standing on the boardwalk staring at her. Bria reversed direction and hurried our way, her heels spiking into the wood one step at a time. Bria reached into the small purse whose strap she'd looped over her shoulder and pulled out her badge. The gold gleamed like an old coin in the lamplight.

"Detective Bria Coolidge," she announced. "Did the woman in the red dress speak to you? Did she say where she was going?"

I tightened my hand on Owen's arm in a warning. He looked at me and nodded. He was going to go along with whatever I said. Smart man. He might just live through the evening.

I looked at Bria. "She didn't say anything to us. I have no idea where she went."

Bria must have recognized my voice because she frowned and peered closer at me. She studied my face for several seconds, before her gaze flicked down my dress, then slid over to Owen Grayson. I could almost see the wheels spinning in her mind as she tried to figure out what I'd been doing on board the riverboat.

"Ms. Blanco," Bria said. "This is the second time we've run into each other today."

"Detective Coolidge," I replied. "You look lovely. That color really brings out your baby blues."

Bria's mouth tightened, as she tried to decide whether or not I was being sincere. "Who's your friend?" she asked.

Owen stepped forward and extended his hand. "Owen Grayson. Gin's date for the evening. It's a pleasure, detective."

If Owen wanted to keep up the charade of pretending to be my date, fine with me. It gave me a plausible reason to be here in the mix tonight.

Bria shook his hand, then turned her attention back to me. "You don't know where Roslyn Phillips went? I find that hard to believe, Ms. Blanco. Especially since she was at your restaurant earlier today. The two of you seemed quite cozy then."

I shrugged. "Lots of people eat at my restaurant, detective. The food happens to be excellent. You should come try it for yourself sometime. I'll fix you a barbecue sandwich so good, it will make you slap your mama."

I said the words without thinking, in the joking sort of way I had to so many other people over the years whenever I was boasting about the Pork Pit. But I knew I'd made a mistake the second they were out, because Bria's face went cold and blank. Of course it would. Mine would have too.

"My mother's dead."

Those three simple words each felt like a silverstone knife ripping into my heart. My eyes dropped to the delicate primrose rune around Bria's neck, then the rings on her finger, and my stomach tightened. Damn. Sometimes I really could be a cold-hearted, insensitive bitch.

Bria shook her head, as if chasing away a bad memory. I knew the feeling.

"You have no idea where Ms. Phillips went?" she repeated her earlier question.

"None," I replied. "If it makes you feel better, detective, I was just as shocked as you were to hear what she said about Elliot Slater."

"As was I," Owen cut in. "As was I."

I looked at Owen, but his face was just as closed off as Bria's was.

Bria stared at me again, and I returned her gaze with a cool one of my own. She must have realized she wasn't getting anything out of me tonight, because she gave me a curt nod.

"Fine," she said. "I'll track Ms. Phillips down myself. You have my card, Ms. Blanco. If you see Ms. Phillips, please tell her that I'd like to speak to her regarding what she said about Elliot Slater. That I'd like to help her press charges against the bastard, and that I'll protect her no matter what."

Bria's eyes burned with cold, blue fire. The cop in her meant every word she'd just said. She'd protect Roslyn from Slater, even if it resulted in her own ostracization from the police department—or even her death. Finn had been right when he'd pegged my sister as a crusader. I admired the fact that she wanted to help Roslyn, even if I knew nothing would ever come of any charges filed against Slater. Besides, the giant wasn't going to live long enough for all that. Not if I had my way about things.

Bria gave me another hard stare. "If Roslyn Phillips

is your friend, if you care about her at all, you'll tell her what I said."

"Sure," I replied. "If I see her."

Bria's lips flattened into a thin smile. "Sure. If you see her."

"Now, if you'll please excuse us, detective, Owen and I were just leaving."

Bria stared at me a moment longer, then stepped to one side. "Enjoy the rest of your evening, Ms. Blanco."

"You too, detective," I murmured. "You too."

Thirty minutes later, Owen Grayson pulled his navy blue Mercedes Benz to a stop in the driveway that ringed his mansion. I stared out the window at the building before me. Like most wealthy Ashland businessmen, Owen lived on a sprawling estate, although he was out more in the suburbs than truly being entrenched in the glorified confines of Northtown.

Owen's place also wasn't quite as pretentious as I'd thought it would be. The mansion boasted a simple, sturdy facade of only four stories instead of the usual eight or so the rest of the city's power players preferred. I opened my door, got out of the car, and stood in the driveway a moment, listening to the whispers of the gray cobblestones under my feet and the larger rocks of the mansion above my head. The soft murmurs spoke of pride and power, tempered with wary caution. The sound fit with what I knew of Owen Grayson. Wealthy, strong, cautious. I rather liked it.

Owen walked past me toward the front door. I followed him. He dug his keys out of his pants pocket, and

I eyed the knocker mounted on the front door—a large hammer done in hard, black iron, just like the enormous gate that ringed the house and grounds.

Most magic users in Ashland used some sort of rune to identify themselves, their family, their power, or even their business. Jo-Jo Deveraux, for example, used a puffy cloud to identify herself as an Air elemental. From previous encounters, I knew that the hammer was Owen Grayson's personal and business rune. The symbol for strength, power, and hard work. A curious choice for a rune. Most people of Owen's wealth and stature would have gone with something flashier, like Mab Monroe with her ruby and gold sunburst necklace.

Owen opened the door and stepped to one side. "Welcome to my parlor."

"Said the spider to the fly," I finished the old saying.

For a moment, I wondered how Owen would react if he knew that I was the Spider and that he was the poor fly caught in my sticky web. I pushed the thought away and headed inside.

Owen led me through the interior of his mansion. He didn't speak as we walked, and I used the silence to examine my surroundings. One, for practical reasons. I still hadn't decided what to do about Owen and everything that he'd seen and heard tonight. So I made note of the passageways and potential exits, just in case I had to kill him and leave in a hurry. But I also studied the interior to learn what I could about the mysterious businessman.

Fletcher Lane had instilled a healthy dose of curiosity in me, and Owen Grayson's behavior over the past few weeks had only deepened my desire to know even more about him—and if he might be suitable enough to help me start forgetting about Donovan Caine. I liked recreational sex as much as the next gal, but it always helped if my bed partner was someone I wanted to stick around after the fireworks ended.

Just like the exterior of the house, the furnishings were much simpler than I'd expected. Dark, heavy, sturdy woods, thick rugs in cool blues and greens, lots of interesting iron sculptures. I got the sense everything was picked more out of love for the object itself, rather than an inflated desire to be sophisticated and stylish.

Owen led me to a downstairs living room, dominated by an enormous flat-screen television on one wall. Eva Grayson and Violet Fox sat in the middle of an oversize sectional sofa in front of the television, watching *The Princess Bride* and eating a large tub of popcorn. The smell of butter and salt drifted up to me.

The two college girls were best friends—and about as different as different could be. With her black hair, blue eyes, porcelain skin, and tall, lithe figure, Eva always reminded me of a real-life version of Snow White. Violet, on the other hand, was short and curvy, with a mop of frizzy blond hair, black glasses, and bronze skin that hinted at her Cherokee heritage. Both girls sported soft, fuzzy pajamas, apparently in for the evening.

Owen leaned over the back of the sofa and ruffled Eva's hair.

"Are you watching that again?" he said, his voice light and teasing. "If I'd known you were going to make Violet watch it every time you girls had a movie night, I would have bought you something else."

"It's not my fault you have no taste in movies," Eva teased back.

I stood off to one side and watched them. Their good-natured squabbling reminded me of my own relationship with Finn. And the sort of easy camaraderie that I longed to have with Bria someday.

But then Eva spotted me lurking in the shadows. "Gin? Is that you?"

I stepped forward. "In the flesh."

"Gin, it's so good to see you!" Eva got up on her knees, leaned over the back of the sofa, and hugged me.

"It really is," Violet echoed.

Violet put down the popcorn and also got up on her knees and hugged me. I accepted the girls' greetings. Eva had considered me a friend ever since I'd saved her from being fricasseed by Jake McAllister when the Fire elemental had tried to rob the Pork Pit a few weeks ago.

Violet also considered me a friend but for another reason—I'd killed Tobias Dawson, the dwarf who'd sent his brother to rape and murder her when her grandfather, Warren, wouldn't sell his land to Dawson. Doing pro bono work had some perks. Saving Eva and Violet from getting dead had been two of them.

Once we got the hugs out of the way, the two girls sat back down on the sofa.

Eva gave me a critical once-over. "You look smoking hot tonight, Gin. I didn't know you were Owen's date for that boring riverboat thing."

I looked at Owen. "Oh, it was sort of a last-minute arrangement."

His lips twitched. "Very last minute."

"Well, it's about time you went out with my big brother," Eva said. "Even if he wouldn't know a good movie from a hole in his head."

I laughed. "I'm glad you approve, Eva. How come you're not out on the town this evening?"

Violet answered me. "Finals are over, and we decided to veg out."

"Totally," Eva agreed.

I nodded at the screen. "With *The Princess Bride,* I see. A classic. I approve."

I chatted with Violet and Eva a few minutes, asking them about their classes and finals, before Owen finally cleared his throat.

"Sorry, girls, but Gin and I need to talk." He mussed Eva's hair again. "Don't stay up too late."

Eva rolled her eyes at her brother's instructions. Violet just snickered.

Owen and I left the living room, and he led me to the back of the house. A heavy wooden door sat closed at the end of a hallway. It bore the same simple hammer rune as the front door. Once again, Owen opened the door and stepped to one side. I entered the room, my gaze sweeping over everything. Big desk, leather chairs and couches, books, maps, crystal lamps, a stone fireplace. Your typical office.

Except for the weapons.

They adorned one entire wall of the room, mounted there in a simple display. Swords, axes, hammers, the occasional mace, and knives. Lots of knives. Some of which could have been carbon copies of my own silverstone instruments. As a former assassin, I always admired well-crafted weapons. Even across the room, I could tell that these were all finely made. Hmm. So Owen hadn't been lying when he'd once told me about his interest in crafting weapons. The businessman became more interesting by the minute.

I walked over to the wall and gestured at a long sword, one of a matching set. "May I?"

"Of course."

I took the weapon from its perch and examined it. Light, lethal, strong, perfectly balanced. Besides size, the only real difference between the sword and one of my own knives was the small rune stamped onto the hilt— Owen Grayson's hammer. No doubt every silverstone weapon on the wall bore the same rune, the mark of its maker. Evidently Owen was quite the craftsman. He'd probably made the iron sculptures I'd seen throughout the house as well.

Owen had much more than a modest elemental talent for metal, if these weapons were any indication of his skill. I knew I could take any weapon off the wall and use it with the utmost confidence that it wouldn't bend, break, or shatter the first time I shoved it into someone's chest. To me, that was the real sign of a master craftsman. I'd always been practical that way.

"Do you like it?" Owen asked, moving to stand beside me. "You should. It's just a bigger version of the two knives you have hidden up your sleeves, the other two you have strapped to your thighs, the two more hidden in your boots, and the one in your purse."

Owen's violet eyes glowed with a faint light, and I felt the faintest bit of magic trickling off him. A cool caress, not unlike my Stone magic. Not surprising, since metal was an offshoot of Stone. He was using his elemental talent for metal to scope out how many silverstone weapons I currently carried on my person. Couldn't blame him for that. Not after everything that had happened this evening.

Owen leaned against the wall and crossed his arms over his chest. He regarded me with a cool gaze. "So," he said. "You finally want to tell me what you were doing on that riverboat tonight? With all those knives on you? Because I'm guessing you didn't go just to play poker."

I put the long sword back into its slot on the wall, then turned to face him.

"No," I replied. "I wasn't there to play poker. I was there to kill Elliot Slater."

❋ 19 ❋

Owen Grayson stared at me. He tensed at my blunt words, and emotions flashed in his amethyst eyes. Wariness. Curiosity. Caution. But surprisingly, no fear. And no condemnation.

Seconds ticked by as he looked at me. Ten, twenty, thirty, forty-five . . .

"I could use a drink," he finally said. "How about you?"

I nodded. "Sure."

Owen walked across the room and opened a tall wooden cabinet, revealing a variety of expensive, colorful liquor bottles tucked away inside. "What do you want?"

"Gin. On the rocks. With a twist of lime too, if you've got it."

Owen fixed my drink and poured himself a healthy amount of scotch. I watched him while he worked, but his hands didn't tremble or shake the way most folks' would have when they realized they were alone with someone who'd just announced her murderous intentions. But Owen Grayson seemed as calm as ever.

I could have lied, of course. Could have told him some fairy tale about carrying the knives for protection or other such nonsense. But Owen had heard what I'd said to Finn, Roslyn, and Xavier, and he'd seen the vamp's confrontation with Elliot Slater. Owen hadn't become one of the richest businessmen in Ashland by being stupid.

If I hadn't told him, he would have put two and two together and come up with five on his own. At least this way, I could judge his reaction to my dark intentions—and decide what I was going to do with him. Because fuck potential or not, if I thought Owen Grayson was any kind of threat to me, Finn, or the Deveraux sisters, I'd pluck one of his own weapons off the wall and gut him with it.

Owen handed me the drink and held out his own glass. "To new friendships," he murmured.

An odd thing to say, given my revelation, but I clinked my glass against his and took a sip of the gin. It went down cold, then spread a sweet heat through my stomach. It still tasted bitter, though. Or perhaps that was just because of my own sour mood—and the fact that I was about to drive away another man by confessing my deepest, darkest secret to him. Might as well get on with it.

I threw back the rest of my gin, set the empty glass on the desk, and walked around to the other side. The bitter taste filled my mouth and spread down my throat. "I've got a long night ahead of me, dealing with Roslyn, Xavier, and everything else. So go ahead and ask me whatever you want to ask me."

"Fair enough." Owen drained the rest of his scotch and put down his own glass.

We stood there, staring at each other across the desk, him behind it, me in front of it. The steady *tick-tick-tick* of an elaborate iron clock on the wall filled the silence.

"So you were there to kill Elliot Slater," Owen finally said. "I suppose I don't have to ask why, given Roslyn Phillips's reaction to him."

I shrugged. "That's one of the reasons. But don't think I'm doing it purely out of the goodness of my heart. I've had some problems with the giant myself. Figured I'd do myself and Roslyn a favor at the same time."

Owen's lips flattened into a thin smile. "So you're a practical sort then."

"Always." I drew in a breath. "Assassins have to be."

Silence.

To his credit, Owen didn't flinch or grimace or even look away. He just kept staring at me, his violet eyes sharp and shrewd in his cold face.

"Assassin, eh? I thought as much, given the knives," he said. "That much silverstone is hard to come by, especially when it's that well crafted."

"You're only as good as your tools."

He nodded. "Of course."

More silence.

"So do you have a name, Gin?" Owen asked, crossing his arms over his chest. "What do people call you?"

"Ah, you want to know if you've heard of me."

Assassins went by code names, for a variety of reasons. The good ones, anyway. You weren't much of an assassin if you let yourself get caught after the fact. Something that would happen sooner, rather than later, unless you adopted some sort of anonymous moniker. A code name made things so much easier. Booking jobs, getting paid, keeping the po-po in the dark, living long enough to spend the money afterward.

Fletcher Lane's code name had been the Tin Man, because he never let his heart or emotions get in the way of a job. The old man had dubbed me the Spider because of the scars I bore on my palms and because I'd reminded him of a spider hiding in the corner when he'd first taken me in off the streets—all long, thin, gangly arms and legs. Over the years, Fletcher had taught me how to be the embodiment of the spider rune that marked me—how to be patience itself. To wait and watch and make my own plans, spin my own webs, instead of reacting to others' schemes.

Owen shrugged. "What can I say? I'm curious."

"Curious? Most men would be running for the door at this point," I replied. "Blubbering and screaming all the while."

He grinned. "I'm not most men."

No, he wasn't, a fact that intrigued me more and more, as did the complete lack of judgment in his violet gaze. I could have told Owen that I was a librarian and gotten the same reaction—or lack thereof. Not surprising. He'd seen me after I'd used my Stone magic to collapse Tobias Dawson's coal mine on top of the dwarf. Owen knew that I'd somehow survived and dug my way out of the rubble. Maybe he hadn't realized that I was an assassin at that point, but he'd known that I was a survivor. Not much difference, really.

"Besides," Owen continued. "If you're as good as you say you are, I wouldn't make it to the door anyway."

"No, you wouldn't," I replied in a quiet voice.

His grin widened. "You know you're not helping my ego, Gin."

"Oh," I said in a lighter tone. "I think you've got plenty of confidence to spare, Owen."

He kept grinning at me, the expression softening his rough features into something more pleasant—and enticing. I looked at his solid frame, his broad shoulders, the apparent strength in his arms. Too bad Finn was on his way over to pick me up. Otherwise, I might have stepped forward and explored this attraction that sparked between Owen and me. Provided, of course, that Owen wasn't really quaking with terror on the inside over my gruesome revelations. Somehow, though, I didn't think his calm facade was an act.

"But to answer your question, yes, I do have a name." I drew in another breath. "One that you've probably heard of."

The grin dropped from his face, and he was serious and somber once more. "And what would that be?"

Instead of answering him, I slowly uncurled my hands and held them out face up, so that he could clearly see the spider rune that marked each one of my palms. A small circle, surrounded by eight thin rays. The symbol for patience. Owen knew what the rune was as well as I did.

"The Spider," he said in a quiet voice. "You're the Spider."

"I was." A grim smile curved my lips. "I actually retired from the business a couple of months ago. But it doesn't seem to have sunk in yet."

Owen's eyes narrowed, and he regarded me with another shrewd, knowing look. "Tobias Dawson. You killed him too. That's why you were at Mab Monroe's party and asked me to introduce you to him. So you could get him alone and kill him."

I nodded. "That didn't quite work out the way that I'd planned, but since I'm still breathing and he's not, I can't complain too much."

Owen crossed his arms over his chest and tilted his head to one side, as if trying to get a better look at me. As if trying to see past the cold mask of my face and into the blackness that coated my soul. "And did you kill Jake McAllister that night as well? Are you the one who stuffed him into one of Mab's bathtubs?"

So he'd heard about Jake's body being found at Mab's party. Seemed like the Fire elemental hadn't squashed that pesky rumor nearly as well as she would have liked to. Or maybe she was just putting it out there herself to see who would be stupid enough to take credit for Jake's death so she could pay him a personal visit. Either way, there was no point in denying anything now.

"Seemed like a good idea at the time," I said.

I didn't tell Owen that Jake McAllister had threatened to rape and murder me. I wasn't going to make excuses for myself. I'd made that mistake with Donovan Caine. Tried to make the detective see that while I might be something of a monster, there were worse ones out there than me. That occasionally, I took out the big bads to make things better for folks. That Ashland needed someone like me. Someone who could work outside the corrupt legal system. Someone who couldn't be bought or bribed or intimidated into backing down. Donovan hadn't been able to understand, much less accept that simple fact. It went against everything the detective had believed in—about the system and himself.

I wasn't going to make the same mistake with Owen Grayson. Whatever this thing was between us, he was going to know exactly what kind of person I was, what kind of cold, calculated violence I was capable of and had executed so many times throughout the years. I wasn't going to sugarcoat anything for him or try to explain away all the bodies that I'd left in my wake.

Owen could draw his own fucking conclusions and act accordingly. And when he told me to get the hell out of his office and never come back, I'd go quietly and without anger or malice. Because before he'd left town, before he'd left me, Detective Donovan Caine had taught me an important, if painful lesson—that anyone who couldn't accept me for who and what I was wasn't worth wasting my time on.

So I stood there, and I waited for Owen to tell me to leave.

"I suppose I should thank you for killing Jake McAllister," he said. "After I found out that he'd threatened Eva that night at your restaurant, I wanted to snap the little bastard's neck myself. I might have too, if not for Jonah McAllister and his connection to Mab Monroe."

Owen uncrossed his arms and flexed the fingers on one hand, then the other, as if he'd still like to get his hands on Jake McAllister, even though the Fire elemental was currently rotting in his grave.

"Don't thank me," I said. "I didn't do it for you."

"No," he replied. "You did it for yourself. Because Jake McAllister was going to keep on making problems for you. Just like Tobias Dawson was making problems for Violet Fox and her grandfather, because Warren Fox wouldn't sell his land and store to Dawson."

Surprised, I frowned. "You knew about the Foxes' troubles with Dawson?"

Owen nodded. "Eva told me about it. I offered to intercede on Warren's behalf, but he wouldn't hear of it. Grumpy old bastard."

"Warren T. Fox is definitely all that."

We shared a smile, and for the first time, a bit of hope flickered in my chest. Because instead of the cold disgust I'd expected to see, warm respect filled Owen's violet eyes. He kept studying me, that strange, thoughtful expression on his face once more.

"You don't remember me, do you, Gin?" Owen asked.

I raised my eyebrows at the sudden change in conversation. "Should I?"

He shrugged. "Maybe I'm a sentimental fool, but when a girl saves your life, you hope she remembers you after the fact."

I'd saved Owen Grayson's life? When had that happened? And why had I done it in the first place? I wasn't in the habit of saving anyone but myself. My eyes narrowed. "Sorry. Not ringing any bells."

The corner of his lips lifted into a half smile. "I thought not. Given all the other . . . excitement you've confessed to just tonight, I suppose I shouldn't be disappointed."

I just stared at him, searching my memory for anything that would tell me what he was talking about, but I came up blank. As far as I could remember, the first time I'd ever set eyes on Owen Grayson was the night he'd come to the Pork Pit to pick up Eva after Jake McAllister had tried to rob the restaurant. Oh sure, I'd seen his picture in the newspaper and his face on the evening news, since he was one of the movers and shakers in Ashland. But that night in the restaurant was the first time I'd ever been up close and personal with him.

Owen sighed, walked around the desk, and sat down on the far edge. He gestured for me to do the same, so I perched on the opposite corner.

"I don't know how much you know about me, Gin, but my parents died in a fire when I was a teenager. There wasn't any money or insurance or other relatives we could stay with, so Eva and I were out on the streets. She was little more than a baby then."

I knew what it was like to live on the mean streets of Ashland. Cold, hard, depressing, constantly cowering in dark corners so the bigger and stronger wouldn't decide to take an interest in you. It had been hard enough by myself at thirteen. I couldn't imagine being responsible for someone else as well back then.

"Anyway," Owen said. "We didn't have any money for food, so I begged mostly or stole what I could. One night, I found myself in the alley behind this barbecue restaurant near Southtown. It was winter and cold, and Eva and I hadn't eaten in days."

A tiny flicker of memory sparked to life in the back of my mind. A fuzzy image that I'd all but forgotten. I remembered that snowy winter—and the scrawny teenager

I'd seen behind the Pork Pit one night, digging through the cold trash for something to eat.

"The back door of the restaurant opened, and this girl stepped out, carrying a black trash bag. She was a few years younger than me," Owen said in a low voice. "She saw me digging through the trash and stopped. Then she spotted Eva huddled across the alley in this little crack in the wall that I'd set her down in. The girl stared at Eva, then at me for the longest time."

The image sharpened in my mind. A boy wearing tattered clothes, his hands raw, red, and chapped from the cold. And a little girl, bundled up tight in layers of rags, staring at me with her big, blue eyes that reminded me so much of Bria's curious gaze. The surprise of seeing her in my old hiding spot, in the little crack between buildings where I'd slept so many nights in the frosty air.

My stomach twisted now, here in Owen's office, just as it had done that night.

"The girl went back inside. I thought she was going to get the owner of the restaurant. That he'd tell us to move on—or worse call the cops and report us. Instead, she came back with this cardboard box. The top of it had been cut off, and the girl had stuffed the whole thing with food. More food than I'd seen in weeks." Owen's eyes never left mine as he spoke. "More food than Eva and I had eaten in weeks."

I remembered the warmth of the Pork Pit that night. How I'd grabbed the box from one of the rooms in the back and raced into the storefront, packing up all the sandwiches and beans and fries and cookies that hadn't been eaten that day. How I'd been filled with some terrible emotion I couldn't explain, that the only thing I could do to get rid of it was to try and help that little lost girl in the alley. Fletcher Lane had been sitting behind the cash register, reading one of his many books. He'd watched me box up the food in silence, his bright green eyes filled with thoughts I couldn't begin to comprehend.

"And how did you come to the conclusion that it was me? That I was the one who gave you some food that night? That was years ago." My low tone didn't completely disguise the emotion that thickened my voice.

"Because after I took the box from the girl, she handed me a jacket," Owen continued. "A black leather jacket nicer than anything I'd ever owned, even when my parents had been alive."

Finn's jacket. I'd grabbed it from the coat rack on my way back out to the alley. He'd just bought the coat a few days ago, and he'd been pissed when he'd realized that I'd given it away. To the point where he'd started around the counter after me. One of the many times Fletcher had to separate us, in the beginning.

"After she gave me the jacket, the girl turned to go back inside, but I reached out and grabbed her hand," Owen said, his own voice raspy now. "She let me hold her hand maybe three seconds before she jerked away from me and went back inside. But that was long enough for me to feel the metal in her hand—the silverstone embedded in her flesh."

I remembered that cold, faint, desperate touch. It had burned me in a way nothing else ever had, not even when Mab Monroe had melted the spider rune into my palms in the first place. I'd gone back inside the restaurant, not quite crying. Fletcher hadn't said a word. The old man had just sat there reading his book, waiting for me to compose myself once more. After I'd told him what I'd done, Fletcher had just nodded his head and gone back to his book. We never spoke of it again.

Owen reached over, picked up my cold hand, and turned it over, so my palm was face up, the spider rune scar visible for all to see.

"Just like the silverstone you have in your palms, Gin," he said. "I've known it was you from the moment I shook your hand that first night at the Pork Pit. And I've been watching you and trying to think of some way to repay you ever since."

"Why?" I asked. "So I felt sorry for you one night and gave you some food. So what?"

Owen shook his head. "It wasn't just that. I came back the next day, hoping to thank you. But instead of you, an older guy was there, drinking coffee and waiting in the alley. He said he knew about my situation and that he also knew someone who needed a good, strong apprentice. A dwarven blacksmith who lived up in the mountains. He drove Eva and me up there that day. The dwarf took a liking to me, and I worked hard for him. And now, well, we have all this." Owen gestured at the office with its fine furnishings.

Fletcher. He was talking about Fletcher Lane. The old man had helped Owen just the way he'd aided me so long ago. I wondered why. It was one thing to take a single stray in off the street after she'd saved your life, like I'd once done for Fletcher. But helping others? Every time I thought I had a handle on who and what Fletcher Lane had been, I found out something else unexpected or met someone like Owen who told me another story of the old man's kindness.

"Well, you're right," I said. "That was me. I gave you the food. But you don't owe me anything for it. Hell, I didn't even do it for you. I did it for me. Because I'd once been in that alley digging for garbage to eat."

Owen nodded. "I thought it might be something like that."

His thumb stroked soft and slow over the scar on my palm. A pleasant warmth spread through my stomach, then moved lower, as I thought about other places where Owen could touch me. But I didn't want him like this. Didn't want him to feel that he needed to pay me back—for anything. I wanted him to want me, Gin Blanco, as I was now. Cold heart, bloody hands, iron will. Not because of some soft sentiment he felt for a girl who didn't even exist anymore.

"So that's what this is all about?" I asked. "You asking me out, you wanting to get to know me better. You actually think you owe me something for some random act of kindness years ago?"

"I owe you everything, Gin."

I shook my head. "No, you don't. Sure, I gave you the food and the jacket. But the job with the blacksmith? That was all the old man. Fletcher Lane. He owned the Pork Pit before me."

Owen frowned. "Lane? As in Finnegan Lane?"

I nodded. "Finn's father. He was the one who got you that job, Owen. Not me. I didn't have anything to do with it. Fletcher never said a word to me about it."

"I see."

"So you don't owe me anything. Not one damn thing," I said, letting him off the hook and ignoring the bitterness that filled my mouth—and heart. "Because I would have done the same thing for anyone who'd been in that alley looking the way you and Eva did that night. So whatever debt you think you've accrued with me over the years, cancel it. I certainly have. Just keep your mouth shut about Elliot Slater and what I told you tonight, and we'll be more than square."

I started to pull my hand out of his, but Owen tightened his grip, the strength of his fingers pressing against mine. His eyes burned with violet fire.

"You think that I just want you now because of something that happened back then? That I'm coming on to you to pimp myself out to pay off some debt?"

I raised an eyebrow. "Not a big leap to make, given our conversation tonight."

Owen shook his head. "You're wrong, Gin. Dead wrong."

"Really? Would you still be holding my hand if I were old, toothless, and had a face like a piece of leather?"

He had the good grace to wince.

"That's what I thought," I said. "Besides, I've been down this road before. In case you haven't been listening, let me recap. I'm an assassin, Owen. A very, very good one. I've spent my entire adult life killing people for money, a lot of money, and after I leave here tonight, I'm going to go plot how I can slit Elliot Slater's throat and get away with it. Do you really want to be with a woman who sleeps with a silverstone knife under her pillow? And would use it on you at any time if she thought you were a threat to her? Because that's me, in a nutshell."

Instead of answering my question, Owen regarded me with another thoughtful stare. "Donovan Caine really did a number on your self-confidence, didn't he?"

He had, but I'd be damned if I was going to let Owen know how badly the detective had wounded me when he'd left. So I shrugged.

"The detective and I came from two different worlds. The twain met, and one of them decided that he couldn't handle it. I don't want to waste my time going over the same old ground with someone new. Assassins aren't known for their exceptionally long life spans. Even retired ones like me."

Owen stared at me another moment, then pointed toward the wall of weapons. "Do you see that axe to the left?"

"Yes," I replied, not sure where he was going with the sudden change in conversation.

"I chopped off a man's fingers with that," Owen said in a calm voice. "Because he was Eva's first-grade teacher, and he touched her the wrong way. And then, when he was screaming at me to stop, I took his head off with it. I used that mace over there to smash a guy's kneecaps to splinters because he wanted me to pay him protection money when I started my own blacksmith shop. I have other stories I could tell you. The point is that I haven't gotten to where I am today by being kind and gentle. I did what I had to in order to survive and protect my sister. I imagine you've done the same."

I didn't say anything.

"I don't judge you for what you've done, Gin. Why are you judging me for another man's mistakes? Because Donovan Caine did make a mistake," Owen said in a soft voice. "Letting someone like you go."

"Someone like me?"

Owen got to his feet and moved until he was standing in front of me. "Someone strong and tough and smart and sassy and sexy as hell. That's why I'm interested, Gin. Because you're all of those things and more. Not because of a small kindness that you showed to me in the part of my past I'd like to forget."

Owen's words made my heart ache. Because these— *these* were the words that I'd longed to hear from Donovan Caine. I'd wanted the detective to understand me, to accept my actions and be able to look past them toward the future we could have together.

But Donovan was gone, and he wasn't ever coming back. Instead, Owen Grayson stood before me, a silent but clear offer burning in his violet eyes. Once more, my gaze drifted over his broad shoulders, his solid frame, his strong, capable hands. And I made up my mind. I'd take what I could have tonight and damn the consequences and feelings I might wake up with tomorrow.

I scooted off the desk and stood so that I was directly in front of Owen. We stared at each other, gray eyes on violet ones. The seconds ticked by. Ten, twenty, thirty, forty-five . . . Owen opened his mouth to say something. What, I didn't know, and I didn't care.

Instead of listening to him, I grabbed his jacket, pulled him to me, and crushed my mouth to his.

* 20 *

Owen seemed startled by my sudden movement, but I flicked my tongue against his lips, and he got with the program. There was no hesitation with Owen, the way there had been with Donovan Caine. Owen kissed me just as hard and long and deep as I did him, until we were both panting for breath and aching for more—much more.

Owen was gentle and fierce at the same time. His hand gliding through my hair, softly massaging the back of my neck, even as his hot tongue wrestled with and thrashed against mine. His fingertips skimming down my throat and chest before boldly cupping my breast through the satiny fabric of my cocktail dress. At his light but aggressive touch, those little twitches and tingles of desire I'd felt with Owen before flared higher than ever, coalescing into a tight ball of fiery want and aching need that settled between my thighs. His smell filled my nose—that rich earthy scent that made me think of cold metal. I breathed in and felt my own Stone magic quicken in response to the elemental scent of him. Mmm.

But I just didn't sit back on the desk and let Owen have his way with me. I was too busy with my own explorations for that. I ran my fingers through his ebony hair, enjoying the coarse, bristlelike feel of it under my fingertips, before sliding my hands lower. His shoulders and biceps were wider and stronger than I'd realized and coiled tight with pent-up tension, as though he were holding back. As though he were afraid of hurting me or scaring me off. I didn't want him to hold back, so I upped the game, sliding one hand down to cup and rub his bulging erection.

Owen hissed with pleasure

"Do you like that?" I murmured.

He hissed again, then pulled back and smiled at me. His eyes sparked with violet fire and mischief. "Probably just as much as you like this."

Owen's hand slid down my leg and up under my short dress. He ignored the silverstone knives strapped to my legs and went straight to the sweet spot, drawing his finger up and down the junction of my thighs. I moaned in response, wanting him to rip away my silken panties so he could really touch me.

But instead, Owen drew his finger away and smoothed my skirt back down.

"But we'll get to that in a little while," he said. "I haven't finished my work up top yet."

"You're such a tease," I muttered.

His grin widened, and he leaned forward to kiss me again. I wrapped my arms around his neck and drew him closer, tighter, so our bodies were flush against each other, his erection pressing between my thighs. I rocked my hips forward, grinding against him, letting him know exactly what was waiting for him, if only he'd get on with things. Owen's shoulders bunched and tightened that much more under my fingers—along with other parts of him.

"Now who's teasing?" he rasped.

I laughed.

Owen started kissing my neck, nibbling at it the dainty way a rabbit might work on a carrot. One hand held me close to his chest, while the other one started its exploration of one of my breasts, then the other.

Somewhere between that first kiss and Owen's hand sliding up my leg, a funny thing had happened—I realized that I wanted him. Not just for a round of hot sex, though that was in the immediate offing. Somehow over the last few weeks, Owen Grayson had worn me down with his open, unabashed interest, playful banter, and calculated determination. I wanted to see what could happen between us—starting tonight.

As Owen worked his magic on my neck and breasts, I opened my eyes and weighed the options. The desk I was sitting on was wide enough, but the leather couch to the side would be much more comfortable—

The doorbell rang. A low, sonorous chime that echoed through the mansion. A moment later, the bell sounded again, and then again, as though someone was jabbing it repeatedly.

I sighed. "That's probably Finn."

Owen pulled back. "And he can't wait, can he?"

I sighed again. "No. More like Roslyn can't wait."

I didn't often feel guilt, but a sort of shame filled me. Roslyn Phillips had been stalked and worse, and instead of figuring out how I could kill the bastard who'd tortured her, here I was getting busy with a man I knew almost nothing about. Fuck. I was getting soft in my pseudoretirement.

I scooted off the desk and got to my feet. Owen stepped back and watched me finger-comb my hair and put my dress back into its proper position.

"Duty calls," he murmured. "Even for an assassin."

I gave him a tight smile. "Sadly, yes."

Owen Grayson escorted me to the front door and opened it. Sure enough, Finn stood outside leaning against the doorjamb, his Aston Martin parked in the driveway behind Owen's Mercedes.

Finn's green eyes took in my flushed faced and red lips. A sly smile filled his face. "I do hate to interrupt," he said. "But we have work to do, Gin."

"I know."

I turned to Owen. "Sorry to cut the evening short. Rain check?"

His violet eyes glittered with a hot promise. "Definitely."

Owen grabbed my hand, his thumb tracing over the spider rune scar on my palm. I enjoyed the sensation for a moment, before squeezing his hand and slipping mine free.

I didn't look back as I slid into Finn's car, but I could feel Owen's eyes on me as I got inside and buckled up. Finn hopped into the driver's seat, cranked the engine, and roared down the driveway away from the gray stone house.

"Well, I see someone ended the evening on a high

note," Finn said as he drove through the iron gate that ringed Owen's property.

"Not really. You rang the bell before I could get mine done," I sniped.

"Sarcasm does not become you, Gin," he replied. "So I take it Owen took the news well? What exactly did you tell him?"

"Just about everything."

Finn looked at me out of the corner of his eye. "Why would you go and do something like that?"

I shrugged. "Seemed like the thing to do. He knew I was involved with Tobias Dawson's death, and he had his suspicions about me killing Jake McAllister at Mab Monroe's party. He would have put it all together anyway when Slater's body turns up cold and rotting somewhere in the next few days."

"Do you think he'll talk?" Finn asked in a low voice.

I thought about Owen's confession that he'd wanted to kill Jake McAllister himself. About the other men that he had hurt and killed to protect Eva and himself. About what he thought he owed me for giving him food that night all those years ago. About the hard, passionate way he'd kissed me even after I'd told him exactly who and what I was.

"No," I replied. "Owen has his own reasons for keeping his mouth shut."

I told Finn what Owen had said about living on the streets and how Fletcher Lane had gotten him his first job as a blacksmith.

"Dad helped Owen and Eva?" Finn asked. "I never knew about that."

"Me neither," I muttered. "It would have been nice for Fletcher to mention his altruistic streak before he died."

Memories of Fletcher Lane flooded my mind. The knowing look in the old man's green eyes. The way he so thoughtfully and carefully studied everyone and everything around him. My heart ached, the way it always did when I thought of all the things I wanted to say to him, all the things I wanted to ask him—and would never get to.

Finn and I didn't speak for a few minutes, but I could tell he was still thinking about Owen and the possible risk the businessman represented to us.

"Don't worry about Owen, Finn," I finally said. "Besides our past history, he wants to fuck me now, remember? Spilling news of my secret identity is only going to get him a knife to the chest. He knows that. And I seriously doubt he wants Eva to finish growing up without big brother around to keep her safe and in line."

"And what happens if you're wrong?" Finn asked.

My stomach tightened, and I stared out into the darkness. "Then I'll fuck him once, and when we're done, I'll stab him where he lies."

"That's hard core, Gin," Finn replied. "Very hard core. Kind of kinky too."

A grim smile tightened my lips. "That's me. Gin Blanco. Hard core and kinky to the bitter end."

* 21 *

Finn and I arrived at Jo-Jo's about twenty minutes later.

Jo-Jo Deveraux lived in one of the less pretentious parts
of Northtown, as befitting someone of her Air elemental
power, wealth, and social connections. Finn made the
turn into a subdivision named Tara Heights, then coasted
down Magnolia Lane and pulled into a long, sloping
driveway. Jo-Jo's three-story plantation house perched on
top of a large hill, giving a clear, sweeping view of the
other houses located on the street.

It was after midnight now and normally, at this hour,
only one or two lights would be on inside the dwarf's
house. Jo-Jo might be an Air elemental, but she needed
her beauty sleep just like the rest of us. But not tonight.
The whole first floor of the antebellum structure glowed,
indicating that everyone inside was still wide awake. I
doubted any of us would get much rest tonight.

Finn parked his car in the driveway, and I scanned

the shadows around the house and its long, wraparound porch. Elliot Slater shouldn't have been able to track Roslyn Phillips to Jo-Jo's, but the giant had gotten away from me twice now, and I wanted to be prepared for anything. But nothing moved or stirred in the darkness, not even a lone bullfrog bellowing despite the December cold.

Finn headed for the front door, but I stood where I was and took a moment to listen to the murmurs of the white cobblestones that paved the driveway. Searching for even the slightest hint of trouble, the smallest note of worry or alarm. But the stones only whispered of the wind and frost and cold. Slater and his goons hadn't found Roslyn—yet.

We stepped up onto the porch, and Finn banged the cloud-shaped knocker against the front door. Heavy footsteps sounded, and Sophia Deveraux opened the door. The Goth dwarf wore a pair of black sweatpants, topped with a sweatshirt that had bloody, broken hearts all over it. For once, Sophia wasn't wearing one of her leather collars, and her black hair was mussed, like she'd been asleep at some point during the evening. She carried a long length of metal pipe, perfect for dealing with any unwanted visitors who might darken the doorstep this late at night.

I eyed the sturdy weapon. "Nice to see you too, Sophia."

"Hmph." Her usual noncommittal grunt.

Sophia stepped back, letting Finn and me inside the house. "Kitchen," she rasped and closed and locked the door behind us.

I walked down the hallway in that direction, with Finn

behind me, and Sophia bringing up the rear. I reached the doorway to the long, skinny room and stopped. Roslyn Phillips sat tall and upright on a stool at the rectangular, butcher's block table that took up the middle of the kitchen. Her back couldn't have been any straighter than if she'd had a board attached to it. The vamp still wore her crimson party dress, although the fabric now seemed drab, crumpled, lifeless. Even the sequins that dotted the dress were muted, as though the events of the evening had robbed them of all their sparkle. Roslyn had been crying again since I'd seen her last, her eyes almost as red as her dress, her usually flawless face a mess of smeared makeup and dried tears.

Xavier perched on a stool next to her, not quite touching her, but clearly aching to do so. The giant kept his dark eyes on the vampire, who stared at the tabletop in front of her. Neither one spoke or moved. They looked frozen, like they were figures in a painting that had somehow been propped up among the pastel-colored appliances.

"About time you got here," Jo-Jo Deveraux drawled.

The dwarf stood at the stove on the other side of the table, waiting for a teakettle to whistle its piping note. Old-fashioned sponge rollers ringed Jo-Jo's head like rows of plastic pink soldiers. The dwarf wore one of her flowered pink housecoats, and her usual string of pearls gleamed around her neck, despite the late hour.

"I had things to do," I replied, sitting down on a stool across from Roslyn.

"More like people," Finn said in a low voice.

I shot him a dirty look, but Roslyn and Xavier didn't

seem to notice. The vamp kept staring at the table, and the giant kept looking at her.

"Did they tell you what happened tonight?" I asked Jo-Jo.

The dwarf nodded and opened her mouth to respond. But before she could say anything, the teakettle shrieked that it was ready. Jo-Jo rushed to pick it up to cut off the noise, but the pot chirped out another high-pitched whistle. The harsh, unexpected sound made Roslyn flinch, as though someone had slapped her. Xavier reached over and put his massive hand on top of hers. That made the vamp flinch too. Xavier froze and slowly drew his hand away.

Jo-Jo poured hot water into several cups and added some tea bags. The cups went onto an antique sterling silver serving tray, along with milk, sugar, cream, and a plate of blackberry muffins that I'd baked yesterday at the Pork Pit. When everything was arranged to her satisfaction, Jo-Jo set the tray on the table in front of Roslyn.

"Have some tea, darling," the dwarf said in her light, warm voice. "It will make you feel better."

Roslyn automatically reached for a cup and took a polite sip, going through the motions. But after a moment, the vamp's shoulders eased down, and her face relaxed. Roslyn let out a long breath. My nose twitched. I knew alcohol when I smelled it. I glanced over my shoulder. Sure enough, a half-empty Mason jar of what looked like home-grown moonshine sat on the counter next to the cloud-covered cloth that hid the toaster. I looked at Jo-Jo, who winked, gave me a small smile, and handed me my own cup of tea. I shrugged and took it from her.

Finn skipped the tea and poured himself some chicory coffee from the pot that Jo-Jo always kept on for him. Sophia leaned against the doorway and stared at Roslyn. For once, emotions flashed in the Goth dwarf's dark eyes, but I was too tired to try to figure out what they were.

The six of us sat in silence for several minutes. Jo-Jo kept refilling Roslyn's tea cup, urging the vamp to eat one of the muffins that she'd set out. Finally, Roslyn agreed, breaking the muffin apart with her hands and chewing one small bite at a time. But the spiked tea and the sugary confection revived her a bit. Her cheeks flushed and lost some of their pallor, and her body slowly unwound into a more normal position.

"Feeling better?" Jo-Jo asked in a soft voice.

Roslyn looked up and gave the dwarf a small smile. "A little. Thank you."

Jo-Jo waved her hand. "You're more than welcome, darling."

The vamp gave Jo-Jo another smile and dropped her eyes. Everyone stilled once more, giving Roslyn the time she needed—

The muted chirp of a cell phone broke the silence. I turned my head. The sound came from a bench that hugged the back wall of the kitchen. I spotted a small red purse sitting among several coats that had been thrown over the low wooden bench.

I looked at Jo-Jo, who shook her head.

"That's my phone," Roslyn said, answering my silent question. "Elliot's calling me. He's been calling ever since I left the riverboat."

"Tell me you haven't answered him," I said.

"No," Roslyn whispered. "I haven't answered him."

"Good."

After five rings, the sound stopped—only to start again a few seconds later. Despite the alcohol that she'd drunk, Roslyn's face tightened once more, and tears filled her eyes.

"Why won't he stop?" she asked in a shaky voice. "Why won't he just *stop*?"

I leaned over, grabbed the vamp's cold hand, and squeezed it. "He's going to stop, Roslyn. Elliot Slater is never going to bother you again. I promise."

The vamp stared at me and shook her head. "Even if you kill Slater now, everyone will know it was me. That I had something to do with it. I'm never going to be free of him. Never." Her voice dropped to a whisper.

I looked at her, feeling small and helpless for the first time in many years. Roslyn was right. As soon as Slater's body turned up, Mab Monroe would start asking questions—and Roslyn would be the first person the Fire elemental would interrogate.

Unless I could think of some way to stop it.

Roslyn was done for the night—physically, mentally, emotionally—so Jo-Jo led the vamp upstairs so she could shower, put on some more comfortable clothes, and crash in one of the guest beds. Finn, Sophia, Xavier, and I stayed in the kitchen. I didn't speak until I was sure that Roslyn was out of earshot.

"I'm going to need some help to pull this off," I said in a soft voice. "A place for Roslyn to stay, someone to watch over her while I take care of business. Will you guys help me? Please?"

"Of course, Gin," Finn replied. "Whatever you need, anywhere, anytime. You know that. That's what families do for each other. And we're all family here."

Sophia murmured her agreement as well.

I nodded my head in gratitude, then looked at Sophia first. "Roslyn stays here until I deal with Elliot Slater. You take the night shift guarding her. Jo-Jo can keep an eye on her during the day. Roslyn doesn't go out, she doesn't talk to or see or call anyone. Okay?"

The Goth dwarf nodded. She knew the drill.

"Good. I'm also going to need you to come down to the Pork Pit and work your usual shift tomorrow. I'll be there too."

Xavier frowned. "You're going to have the restaurant open tomorrow? Why? You should be busy plotting how to get to Slater, not serving up barbecue."

I looked at the giant. "Don't worry, I will be. But everyone involved in this thing needs to stick to their normal routines. Go to work, go home, whatever. Be seen by other folks. That way, when Slater's body turns up and Mab Monroe starts asking questions, we all have some plausible deniability. We were far too busy being normal to even think about killing the giant. It might just save our asses."

Xavier shook his head. "That might work for the rest of us, but it won't for Roslyn. Not if she's cooped up here the whole time."

"That's where Finn comes in."

I turned to face Finn, who was pouring himself yet another cup of chicory coffee. The warm caffeine fumes flooded the kitchen, reminding me once again of Fletcher

Lane. The old man had drunk the same coffee that his son did. It might have been nothing more than silly sentiment, but the smell comforted me, even during this long, tense night. Not for the first time, I wished the old man were still alive. Fletcher Lane had been a master tactician. He'd know exactly the best way to handle Elliot Slater—and get away clean afterward. Instead of fumbling around with things like I was doing. Like I'd been doing for days now.

But Fletcher was gone, and I was here. It didn't much matter what happened to me after the fact—only that the others were clear. And if I had to die to make sure they were, well, at least I'd seen Bria again before I kicked off to hell.

I breathed in once more, enjoying the rich aroma a final time, before pushing all thought of Bria and the old man away. "Finn, I need you to get busy constructing an alibi for Roslyn."

"Alibi?" Sophia rasped in her ruined voice.

I nodded. "Alibi. Back when this whole thing started, Roslyn sent her sister and her niece down to Myrtle Beach to get them out of the way. Well, after the scene last night on the riverboat, Roslyn decided to get out of town and join them."

"Impromptu vacation?" Finn asked. "I can do that. Hotel bill, restaurant receipts, shitty souvenirs, sand in a suitcase. Shouldn't take more than a couple of hours to fake it all. I can even rig up some security footage from the hotel that Roslyn's supposedly staying at if you want."

For a moment, I wondered exactly how Finn was going to get his hands on not only sand but tacky beach T-shirts and conch shell necklaces this close to midnight. But if there were any to be had in all of Ashland, Finnegan Lane would find them. Like me, Finn had many skills, most of which weren't exactly legal.

"Do the whole package," I answered. "And make it look good. *Very* good. Enough to stand up to whatever scrutiny Mab Monroe might bring to bear. Or the police."

Finn toasted me with his coffee mug. "Consider it done."

"What about me?" Xavier asked in a low voice.

Xavier had his elbows on the table, and his hands laid out flat in front of him. The giant's arms were so long that he could have leaned forward and grabbed the opposite edge of the counter. The broad, coiled muscles of his back and biceps pressed against his white tuxedo jacket, threatening to split the material at the seams. Shadows darkened his black eyes, and his strong jaw clenched and unclenched. A vein throbbed on the top of Xavier's shaved skull, the blue tint of his blood visible even through his ebony skin.

I knew the signs and could read the rage in Xavier's eyes like a pirate scanning a treasure map. X marked the spot. This was a man who wanted to rip into something, or rather someone—Elliot Slater—and slowly tear the skin from his bones, pound it back on, and start again. Couldn't blame Xavier for that. Not after what the bastard had done to Roslyn. But it was my job to keep him in line, so I could take care of Slater once and for all. And so we could all walk away clean after the fact.

"Your job is going to be the most difficult," I said. "You need to go to Northern Aggression tomorrow and open the nightclub as usual. Work the door, keep an eye on the crowd, everything you usually do."

"Why is that going to be difficult?" Xavier growled.

I stared at him. "Because sooner or later, Slater's going to come by the club looking for Roslyn—and you're going to have to deal with him."

Xavier's hands curled into two massive fists. "I'll deal with the bastard, all right."

"No," I said in a sharp tone. "You will not fucking touch him, unless you want to get dead. Slater's sure to have backup with him. Even if you took him out, one of his buddies would get you in the end."

Xavier's face hardened, and his eyes glinted with rage. At Slater, mostly, but I wasn't in the giant's good graces right now, either.

"Look," I said. "I'm not questioning your skills or your strength or how much you care about Roslyn. We all know that you wish you could kill Slater yourself. And we all know that you can't do that without dying, either there at the scene or later on, when Mab Monroe gets involved. We all want the same thing—Elliot Slater cold and rotting in the ground for what he's done to Roslyn. But more importantly, we want everyone to be able to walk away after the fact. What's it going to be, Xavier? You want to play the hero and die for your woman? Or you want to do things my way and live long enough to go spit on Elliot Slater's grave? Decide. Right now."

Xavier looked to the others for support. First, his eyes cut to Finn, who took another slug of coffee and moved to stand behind me. Xavier turned to Sophia. The dwarf grunted, gave him a flat stare, and also walked over to my side of the table. Finally, the giant stared at me. Rage still glinted in his eyes, but another emotion shimmered in his dark gaze. Resignation. Despite his feelings for Roslyn, Xavier was smart enough to realize that I knew what I was talking about—and that I'd do everything in my power to keep my promise to him and especially to Roslyn.

"Fine," Xavier said in a low voice. "We'll do it your way. But if Elliot Slater's not dead in two days—"

"Then you can go after him and damn the consequences," I said.

Xavier stared at me a moment longer, then nodded. "All right. What do you want me to do?"

"When Slater comes to the club looking for Roslyn, you tell him you don't know where she is and that you don't care anymore. That you hate her, and he's welcome to her."

Xavier flinched at my harsh words, but he nodded. "All right. I can do that."

"You have to do more than just do it," I snapped. "You have to *sell* it. Make Slater think that you're done with Roslyn. For good. I'm not going to lie to you, Xavier. Slater's probably not going to believe you. Things will get ugly. He'll probably get his goons to beat you or do it himself. He could hurt you real bad. Maybe even kill you just for the fun of it."

Xavier stared at me, his black eyes as hard as granite. "I don't care how bad he hurts me as long as Roslyn is safe. That's all that matters to me."

I nodded. "Good. Is there anyone at the club you can trust? Anyone there who will back you up?"

Xavier thought a moment. "Vinnie. The Ice elemental who works the bar. He's a stand-up guy. And he owes me."

"You tell Vinnie to watch the door and to call the cops as soon as Slater shows up. Specifically, your partner, Detective Bria Coolidge."

Finn and Sophia both stared at me, surprised by my order. I didn't want Bria anywhere close to Elliot Slater, but she was the only cop I knew who'd take on the giant and his men. Who would do something besides stand there and let Slater beat Xavier to death. Like it or not, I had to get my sister involved in this. Bria could keep Xavier alive long enough for Jo-Jo Deveraux to get to the giant and heal him. After that, Sophia would be there to watch over everyone.

Xavier nodded. "All right. I'll tell Vinnie. One question, though. What will you be doing during all of this?"

"Following the bastard," I replied in a cold voice. "Tomorrow night, the second he's alone, I go after him with everything I have."

Everyone knew their part in the drama that was about to unfold, and there wasn't anything else to say. So we stayed in the kitchen, drinking tea, sipping coffee, and eating muffins in silence.

A few minutes later, Jo-Jo came down the stairs. The middle-aged dwarf looked at Xavier. "Roslyn's asking for you," she said. "Second door on your left."

The giant nodded, put down his tea cup, and headed up the stairs. Finn wandered in that direction and waited until the heavy tread of Xavier's footsteps stopped and the upstairs door creaked closed before he turned back to me.

"Correct me if I'm wrong, Gin," Finn said. "But you didn't explain exactly *how* we're all going to get free and clear of this after you make a pincushion out of Elliot Slater."

I nodded. "I didn't want to say anything in front of Xavier, but we're going to make Mab Monroe forget all about Roslyn."

"How?" Sophia rasped.

"We're going to give her someone else to worry about."

I told Finn, Sophia, and Jo-Jo exactly what I was planning on doing after I killed Slater. The crazy, dangerous way that I was going to take the heat of Mab's fury off Roslyn and direct it squarely on me. I laid it all out for them. Everything I was going to do—now and when I finally made my move against the Fire elemental.

When I finished, the three of them looked at me. Finn's eyes a bright green. Sophia's face flat and expressionless as usual. Jo-Jo's head cocked to one side, a thoughtful light in her pale gaze.

Finally, Finn let out a low whistle. "You're serious, aren't you?"

I shrugged. "If you can think of a better plan, please, enlighten me."

"Don't get me wrong," Finn said. "I think it's brilliant. Stupid and dangerous and cocky, but brilliant too. Even though it goes against everything that Dad taught us about drawing attention to ourselves, everything that he taught *you*."

I blew out a breath. "I know. Which is why I need to know if you're all on board with me or not. Because it's not just me who's going to be on the line this time. You guys will all be on the hook too. If Mab figures it out before I'm ready to deal with her, she'll come after us—all of us. And she won't stop until we're all dead. If you don't want to be a part of it, I understand. This thing with Mab, it's my fight, my problem, not yours. It always has been."

Finn, Sophia, and Jo-Jo didn't even have to look at each other.

"Nonsense," Jo-Jo said. "We're family, darling. Always will be."

"Family," Sophia repeated.

"Family," Finn echoed.

I stared at them. Handsome Finn, who looked so much like his father that it made my heart twist in my chest. Dark, remote Sophia, who kept all her secret dreams and hurts and fears to herself. Soft, pink Jo-Jo, the smartest and wisest of us all. I'd already lost Fletcher Lane. I didn't want to lose them too. But my confrontation with Mab Monroe was inevitable now. Hell, maybe it had been ever since the night she'd murdered my family. Like Oedipus killing his father, no matter how hard he struggled not to. Nobody did tragedy like the Greeks. Or me.

"I'm glad you're with me on this." My voice shook only a little. "But mostly, I'm glad that you *are* my family."

I turned away from them and took my tea cup over to the sink so they wouldn't see the tears in my eyes. When I turned back to face them, I was cold, calm, and composed once more.

"All right," I said. "Let's get this party started."

❋22❋

We all spent the night at Jo-Jo's house, and the next day, we put our plan into action. That is to say, everyone did what they would normally do in the morning.

Sophia got up early and drove to the Pork Pit to bake the bread for the day's sandwiches. Finn donned one of his many suits and went to work for the money men at his bank. Xavier headed home to rest so he'd be ready to open Northern Aggression later on tonight. Jo-Jo fired up her hair dryers, tanning booths, and curling irons for her salon clients. I planned to go to the Pork Pit and work a full shift as usual.

Before I drove home to shower and change, I looked in on Roslyn Phillips. The vamp sat cross-legged on the bed in one of Jo-Jo's guest bedrooms staring out the window at the skeletal branches of the trees that surrounded the antebellum house. Roslyn wore a pair of Sophia's black sweats, somehow making the fabric seem rich and expensive instead of the sturdy, sensible cotton that it was. She wore no makeup, her beautiful face smooth and dull, like a stone that had been worn down by the steady rush of water over time.

I sat down on the end of the bed. Roslyn didn't turn in my direction, but she knew I was there. If nothing else, she'd felt the mattress dip under my weight.

"Feeling better?" I asked in a soft voice.

She shrugged.

A soft *thump-thump-thump* sound caught my ear. Roslyn's cell phone lay on top of the nightstand next to the bed, moving ever so slightly.

"I got tired of the constant ringing, so I put it on vibrate," she said in a flat voice. "He must have called me a hundred times since last night. And no, I haven't answered it."

"You should turn it off."

She bit her lip. "I can't do that, Gin."

I knew she couldn't. Roslyn realized that Elliot Slater was out there searching for her, using all the resources he had to find her. As long as the phone kept ringing, she could tell herself that he hadn't found her yet. That she was safe for a little while longer. In a twisted way, that phone was Roslyn's lifeline—the only thing keeping her from going completely crazy.

I'd never been good at helping people, comforting them. That was more Jo-Jo's line of work. There was only one thing I could say to comfort Roslyn, only one promise I could make to her that would mean a fucking thing.

"Leave it on then," I said in a quiet tone. "Listen to it. Make sure your battery doesn't die."

After a moment, Roslyn turned to stare at me. "Why?"

I let her see the cold, violent resolve in my gray eyes. "Because when your phone quits ringing, you'll know the bastard's finally dead."

That afternoon, I sat on my stool behind the cash register at the Pork Pit and reviewed all the information that I had on Elliot Slater. Mostly, though, I thought about my previous encounters with the giant, visualizing the way he'd hit me that night at the community college, the way he threw his punches, how he placed his feet, how he distributed his weight. Analyzing his style, his technique, looking for any weakness that I could exploit, looking for any way that I could kill him without letting him put his hands on me first. The giant had beaten me twice now. He wasn't going to do it again.

"Anything?" Sophia rasped.

I closed the folder and shook my head. "It says the same thing that it's always said—that Slater is one tough customer."

"Hmph." Sophia grunted and went back to wiping down the back counter.

It was after six. Darkness had already spread its black blanket over Ashland, and most folks were heading home from work, eager to get in from the cold. It had been slow all day, so I'd sent the waitresses home early with pay. My last customer had left ten minutes ago. Those who passed by the storefront windows invariably had their heads down, chins tucked into the tops of their jackets, with no time or inclination to stop for hot barbecue tonight. Outside, the street lamps had already flickered on, illuminating the gray sidewalks and bits of snow that floated in the frosty air. Time to leave the restaurant and get on with my mission for the evening—killing Elliot Slater.

I turned to Sophia to tell her to close up shop when the front door opened, making the bell chime—and Detective Bria Coolidge stepped into the restaurant.

Bria shut the door behind her and headed in my direction. She looked beautiful as always. Shaggy blond hair, ice blue eyes, cheeks flushed from the cold air. Once again, she wore her long navy coat over jeans, a sweater, and black boots. Her primrose rune flashed like a ball of silver fire in the hollow of her throat. It matched the glint from the rings on her index finger.

"Hello, detective," I said in a calm voice. "Good thing you got here when you did. Sophia and I were just about to close down for the evening."

Bria's gaze flicked to the Goth dwarf, who was still wiping down the long countertop. "Kind of early for that, don't you think?"

I held out my hands and gestured at the empty storefront. "Not tonight. The cold tends to make people want to head home to their loved ones instead of stopping off for something to eat."

"Point taken. But I'm not here for the food."

"More's the pity," I murmured. "The strawberry pie is excellent today."

Bria looked at the glass cake stand where I always put the dessert of the day. But even the lush strawberries glinting from their golden crust weren't enough to make her stray from her appointed mission.

"I want to talk to you about Roslyn Phillips," Bria said.

Not surprising, given the fact that Bria had been chasing after the vamp last night after Roslyn told everyone on the riverboat what Elliot Slater had been doing to her. I'd been half-expecting Bria to come barging into my gin joint all day, demanding to know where the vampire was. And she had finally shown up.

I had no doubt that Bria wanted to help Roslyn. Given what I'd seen so far, she would have done the same for any woman that she thought had been stalked and victimized the way Roslyn had. I admired her for that.

But the cold, cynical part of me wondered how much of Bria's determination to help was personal. Because Bria didn't have any witnesses to the fact that Slater had tried to kill her, and Sophia had made sure that no evidence of any kind had been left behind at the scene. If Bria wanted to lock up Slater—and she surely had to, given the fact that the giant had tried to kill her—then Roslyn was her best shot at making that happen. And somehow, I didn't think she was going to give up on the vamp without a fight.

"What about Roslyn?" I asked.

"Have you seen or talked to her today?" Bria asked.

"No."

An easy lie. And I didn't volunteer any more information or even ask why Bria was so interested in finding Roslyn in the first place. When dealing with the po-po, it was best to follow the example of Sophia Deveraux and speak only in short bursts—if at all.

Bria studied me, her blue eyes cold and icy. "I think you're lying. You and Roslyn looked particularly friendly when she was in here yesterday."

"That was yesterday," I replied. "Roslyn was here for the food. Nothing more, detective."

"That's funny because no one seems to know where Ms. Phillips is," Bria replied. "She's not at home, and no one's seen her at that nightclub she owns, Northern Aggression."

"Perhaps you should ask your partner if he's seen her," I said in a snippy tone. "Since Xavier actually works for Roslyn."

Normally, I wouldn't have sicced Bria on Xavier. But better for her to be at the nightclub questioning him than standing here accusing me. I had work to do tonight. And the sooner I killed Elliot Slater, the sooner Roslyn could sleep easier and return to her regularly scheduled life, instead of being holed up in Jo-Jo Deveraux's house.

"I've already been to the club," Bria replied. "And Xavier claims he hasn't seen her either."

I cocked my head to one side. "You sound like you don't believe him."

Her face hardened. "What I do or don't believe is none of your business. Now, why don't you tell me where you were last night?"

"You think I did something to Roslyn Phillips?" I laughed. "Oh, please."

Bria's eyes iced over, even more. "You know, we could have this conversation down at the police station."

I crossed my arms over my chest. "Really? On what grounds? That I was at the same party as Roslyn last night? That she came into my restaurant and had a meal? I see you've already taken up the bad habits of the rest of the Ashland Police Department, detective."

"And what would those be?"

I stared at her. "Interrogating people for no reason."

Bria had the good grace to flinch at my insult.

As much as I would have loved to continue this verbal smackdown with my long-lost sister, I needed to get on with things. Finn was due to pick me up at seven so we could start tailing Elliot Slater and look for a place to kill the giant. Which meant that I needed to get rid of Bria. So I decided to give her what she wanted—some answers.

"Yes, Roslyn came in here yesterday, but only to get some food. Yes, I saw her last night on the riverboat, including that awful scene with Elliot Slater. No, I haven't seen the vamp since then, and I don't expect to," I said. "Whatever you think you saw here yesterday, Roslyn and I are not best friends, merely casual acquaintances. I go to her club on occasion, she gets barbecue here sometimes. That's the extent of our relationship, detective. As for where I was last night, I went home with Owen Grayson. We had a very *stimulating* evening in his office, if you absolutely have to know."

Bria studied me for several seconds. "You don't like me much, do you, Ms. Blanco?"

It wasn't that. It wasn't that at all. If anything, I was proud of how well Bria seemed to have turned out, despite everything that had happened to her. She just didn't realize that I had to keep her at arm's length. That my jumbled feelings for her were still too fresh and raw for me to do anything but antagonize her. That sarcasm was the gentlest and least deadly of my many defense mechanisms. That I had a cold, hard, bloody job to do tonight, something that she could never know about or be a part of.

I shrugged. "I don't know enough about you to like or dislike you, detective. What I hate is when someone comes into my gin joint and starts threatening me. I don't respond well to threats, from the police or anyone else."

She sighed. "I'm not threatening you. All I'm trying to do is help Ms. Phillips. You heard what she said about Elliot Slater, what she accused him of. I've spent the whole day trying to track her down. Surely you know about Slater's reputation, who he works for. I want to find Ms. Phillips before he does. That's all I want to do."

Bria had that same tired note in her voice that I'd always heard in Donovan Caine's. That same tone that told me how many brick walls and dead ends she'd run up against today—many of them in her own police department. Like she said, she was just trying to do the right thing, just trying to help a woman who so obviously needed it. Bria was trying to do things the legal way. In Ashland, all it would get her was dead. And I just couldn't allow that to happen. Not to my baby sister. Better I deal with Slater than Bria. Better for Roslyn, and better for Bria, whether she knew it or not.

"That's very noble of you," I said in a kinder voice. "It really is. But I can't help you. I don't know where Roslyn is, and I didn't know anything about her problems with Slater until I heard about them last night on the riverboat, like everyone else. Even if I had known before, there's nothing I could do to help her. Not against someone like Slater. You said it yourself. You know who he works for. But I truly am sorry for Roslyn, detective. I truly am. More than you will ever know."

Bria opened her mouth to say something, when a

sharp ring cut her off. But it wasn't the telephone next to the register that had sounded. It was my disposable cell phone. Which could mean only one thing—trouble.

"Excuse me." I dug my cell phone out of my jeans pocket and answered it. "What?"

"Gin?" Jo-Jo's voice flooded the line. "We've got a problem."

The tight, worried note in the dwarf's tone told me exactly what she was going to say.

"Roslyn's gone," Jo-Jo said.

❊23❊

Roslyn Phillips gone? Fuck.

Bria saw my face tighten. Her blue eyes sharpened with interest.

"Gin?" Jo-Jo asked. "Are you still there?"

"I'm sorry to hear that," I said in a calm voice. "Tell me what happened."

"I was busy with clients most of the day. I checked in on her at lunchtime, and Roslyn was fine. Well, as fine as she could be, given the circumstances. Quiet, but fine," Jo-Jo said. "I went upstairs to ask her what she wanted me to make for supper, if she needed some blood, if she wanted to talk about anything, and she was gone. She must have slipped out while I was doing my last perm of the day."

"Do you have any idea why she decided that she didn't like her perm?" I asked.

Jo-Jo knew enough to realize that I didn't want to speak

openly in front of whoever might be standing nearby. "She left her cell phone behind. There was a text message on the screen from Elliot Slater. He said for Roslyn to meet him on the street outside Underwood's restaurant in half an hour or he would start killing the people close to her—starting with Xavier. He also threatened to kill her sister and niece whenever they came back to Ashland."

So the giant had decided to play hardball. And instead of coming to me, instead of trusting me to handle things, Roslyn had gone straight to him. She might even be dead already.

"When did she leave?" I asked. "Right after you gave her the perm?"

"I finished up at six. I heard her moving around upstairs as late as five thirty. She can't have been gone more than thirty minutes, forty tops."

I glanced at the clock on the wall. Creeping up on six fifteen now. Which meant that Roslyn had been gone almost an hour. The restaurant was only about a twenty-minute cab ride from Jo-Jo's house, which meant Roslyn had to have reached Slater by now.

"I'm so sorry, Gin," Jo-Jo said, shame and worry in her voice. "I thought that she'd let you handle things. I had no idea that she'd take off."

I sighed. "It's not your fault that she didn't like her perm. Some people just don't know good work when they see it. We'll talk about it later. I have a customer waiting right now. But keep your door open, okay? I'll probably stop by later."

"Sure," Jo-Jo replied. "I'll have everything ready, including myself. Whatever you need, Gin."

What Jo-Jo really meant was that she'd be on standby, ready to heal Roslyn Phillips when I got the vamp away from Elliot Slater. If I got the vamp away from the giant before he killed her.

"Great. See you then."

I hung up and looked at Bria.

"Something wrong?" Bria asked.

I smiled at her. "Nothing serious. A friend of mine runs a beauty salon. Seems like one of her clients didn't like the curl in her hair today."

Bria didn't look like she believed me for a second, but there wasn't much she could do about it. She'd already called me a liar to my face and threatened to take me to the police station. I hadn't blinked at either one of those threats, and she was smart enough to realize that it would take a lot to rattle me. So she drew a card out from her coat pocket and put it on the counter between us. I didn't pick it up. I didn't want to risk brushing my fingers against hers and feeling her Ice magic again. I didn't need the distraction of that and all the emotions that came with it right now.

"Another one of my cards," Bria said. "Please call me if you hear anything about Ms. Phillips. I'd consider it a personal favor."

"Of course," I lied. "You have a good evening, detective."

"You too, Ms. Blanco."

I thought Bria would turn around and leave, but instead, she just kept staring at me with her cold, icy eyes.

"Is there something else, detective?" I finally asked.

"It's funny," she murmured. "But ever since I came here

a few days ago, I've had the strangest feeling of déjà vu about you. Almost like I . . . know you from somewhere."

Years of training kept any emotion from showing on my face. The first time Bria had come to the Pork Pit, when our fingers had touched and I'd felt her magic, I'd wondered if she'd sensed anything about me. If she'd felt my Ice power that was so similar to hers. Whether she had or not, something about me had tickled her memory.

Bria and I had been exceptionally close when we were kids, but I wasn't particularly worried about her recognizing me as her big sister Genevieve Snow. With my dark, chocolate brown hair and gray eyes, I looked like our father, Tristan. He'd died when Bria was a baby, and she'd never known him. Bria was the one who'd looked the most like our mother, Eira. And I'd changed a lot from when I was thirteen. I'd lost all the baby fat that had softened my features. The planes of my face were much sharper, harder, and more angular than they'd been when I was a kid. Then again, so were Bria's.

But more than that was the fact that Bria had already looked into my background, already dug into my rock-solid cover identity as Gin Blanco. There was just no reason for her to think that I was her long-lost sister Genevieve. Especially since I hadn't acted anything like she probably thought Genevieve would. I hadn't exactly been welcoming toward Bria, even though I longed to just wrap my arms around her and hug her tight, just to make sure she was real. But too many things, too many secrets, lay between us right now for all that.

Bria shrugged. "I suppose it's nothing. Just like the help that you've given me today, Ms. Blanco."

My sister stared at me a second longer, then turned and walked out of the Pork Pit.

The first thing I did was go over to the front door, lock it, and turn the sign over to *Closed*. I stared out the storefront windows, but Bria had already disappeared from sight. Good. I didn't need her hanging around distracting me from what needed to be done. A long, bloody night lay ahead, and I needed to focus, needed to forget about everyone and everything that I cared about, and morph into the Spider once more, so I could get through what lay ahead. So I could get Roslyn Phillips through it—before she got dead.

So I pushed all thought of Bria away and turned to face Sophia. The Goth dwarf stood behind the counter, a dish towel draped over her shoulder, just watching me with her flat, black eyes.

"That was Jo-Jo on the phone," I said.

"Problem?" Sophia rasped.

"Roslyn left the house and went to meet Elliot Slater. He threatened to start killing the people she was close to. Slater has her now, and I have to figure out where he took her—before he kills her." I looked at the Goth dwarf. "I need you to go babysit Xavier for me. If he finds out Roslyn went to Slater, he'll go crazy and start looking for her himself. And I can't have that."

Sophia nodded. She knew that Xavier would only get in my way—and probably get Roslyn killed in the process.

While the dwarf turned off the french fryer and shut everything else down for the night, I called Finn and told him the situation.

"Fuck," he said.

"Fuck, indeed." Then, I asked Finn the most important question—of Roslyn Phillips's life. "Where would Elliot Slater take Roslyn for one last hurrah before he kills her?"

"You don't think she's dead already?" he asked. "He's had her at least an hour by now."

I thought of the hot rage that I'd seen flashing in Slater's hazel eyes last night on the riverboat. Of the embarrassment that Roslyn had caused him with her screamed accusations. Of the way that the giant had started after her, only to be called back by Mab Monroe. Of all the incessant calls that he'd bombarded Roslyn with during the long night.

"No," I replied. "Slater will want to play with her first, punish her for what she did to him. At least for a couple of hours. That's what he did to all those other women in his file. Which means I still have time to get to Roslyn— if I can find her. So where do you think Slater would go? You're the one who compiled that file on him, who dug up all of Fletcher's old information on him. You would know better than me."

Asking for direction, for guidance, for a target to strike out at. It was something that I would have asked of Fletcher Lane, if he'd still been alive. But the old man had taught Finn everything he knew about how to gather information on a member of the opposition, analyze it, and predict how he would react in a certain situation. In some ways, Finn was even better at it than Fletcher had been, because Finn innately understood things like greed and desire and avarice. He saw them every day at the bank where he worked, and again at night, while he hobnobbed with his rich, deadly clients.

Through the cell phone, a slow, slurping sound filled my ear. Finn, drinking yet another cup of coffee and thinking about my question. I could picture him leaning back in his expensive office chair, his green eyes bright with thought, the warm scent of his chicory coffee adding to his caffeine high. I let him think. Roslyn's life depended on his coming up with the right answer. After about a minute, the slurping stopped, and I knew that Finn had come to a conclusion.

"Elliot Slater has a mansion up in the mountains north of the city," Finn said. "He calls it Valhalla, if you can believe that. It's large, remote, secluded. Dad used to speculate that Valhalla was where Slater disposed of certain bodies for Mab Monroe. I bet he's gotten rid of some of his own victims up there as well. The Aneirin River cuts through the area. Lots of gorges, lots of hollows, lots of places to dump a body where it'll never be found. If Slater wanted to spend one more night with Roslyn before he killed her, that's where he'd take her. I'd bet my life on it."

"You're not betting your life," I replied. "Just Roslyn's."

"I know that, Gin." Finn's voice was as dark and somber as mine. "Believe me, I know."

We didn't speak for a moment.

"Everything you need to know about Valhalla is in that file I compiled on Slater. Maps, roads, blueprints of the mansion and outbuildings," Finn said. "Do you have it with you?"

I looked at the papers that I'd spread out on top of the counter. "I'm looking through it right now."

"Where do you want me to meet you? Because I'm coming with you, and that's not up for discussion." There was no hesitation or give in Finn's voice. Just the determination to finish this and save Roslyn. No matter what.

I eyed the clock on the wall. Creeping up on six thirty now. Roslyn had been gone an hour. By the time I got to Valhalla, close to another hour would have passed. If I waited for Finn here at the Pork Pit, it would be closer to ninety minutes. I didn't know how long Slater would keep Roslyn alive, but every minute, every second I waited, was another one that the vamp would be in pure agony—and another one closer to her eventual death.

"All right, but we're running out of time. I'm leaving right now to drive up there." I looked at the maps of the area. "Looks like there's some sort of gas station at the bottom of the mountain where the mansion sits. Grab your gear and meet me there as soon as you can."

"You got it," Finn said and hung up.

I gathered up all the papers on Elliot Slater and his mountain hideaway and stuffed them back into Finn's manila folder. While I'd been talking to Finn, Sophia Deveraux had slipped into the back of the restaurant. The dwarf came out through the swinging doors carrying an anonymous black duffel bag. She handed it to me without a word.

"Thanks, Sophia."

I took the bag from her, listening to the comforting *clink-clink-clink* of weapons rattling around inside. The bag contained just about everything I needed to do a quick, dirty job—silverstone knives, money, dark clothes, fake IDs, credit cards, tins of Jo-Jo's healing salve. There was only one more thing that I needed to stop and get on my way to Elliot Slater's mansion. I unzipped the bag and put the folder of information in on top of my other supplies. Then I hefted the bag over my shoulder and headed for the swinging doors that led to the alley behind the restaurant.

Sophia moved to one side to let me pass. The dwarf reached out and put her pale hand on my arm. For a moment, I thought she meant to stop me from going on what basically amounted to a suicide mission. If anyone could do it, the dwarf could. I wasn't stupid enough to think that I could take Sophia in anything resembling a fair fight. She'd seen all my tricks before, and she was tough as hell. And now I knew that she had Air elemental magic too—powerful magic that she could use to dissolve me into nothingness.

The dwarf stared at me for several seconds. Her eyes were black and flat as usual, but I caught the flash of some emotion swimming in the dark depths. It might have been approval or even pride, but it was gone too quick for me to pin it down.

"Luck," Sophia rasped in her broken voice. She dropped her arm and gestured for me to go on through the swinging doors. The dwarf wasn't going to stop me.

I nodded. "Thanks, Sophia. Tonight, I think I'm really going to need it."

✴24✴

Twenty minutes later, my Mercedes Benz skidded to a halt in front of Owen Grayson's mansion. I climbed out of the car, ran up to the front door, and banged the hammer rune knocker as hard as I could against the thick wood. About thirty seconds passed before I heard the scuffle of footsteps inside. A moment later, Eva Grayson cracked open the door. When she saw that it was me, she swung the door back even more.

"Gin?" Eva asked. "What are you doing here? Do you and Owen have another date or something?"

I didn't answer, instead shouldering my way past her inside the mansion.

"Gin? Gin, what are you doing?" Eva called out behind me.

I ignored her and walked on through the house with all of its comfortable furnishings in their muted colors and the elaborate iron sculptures standing in various nooks and crannies. My boots smacked out a loud pattern, while softer slippers scurried on the wooden floor behind me, as Eva hurried to catch up.

"Gin, what's wrong?" she asked.

I didn't respond. I hurried past the downstairs living room where Eva and Violet had been watching a movie last night. Had it only been last night? Seemed like a lifetime ago.

To my surprise, Violet Fox poked her head out of the living room, clutching a tub of popcorn in her hands. She and Eva must have been having another girls' night in. Violet's dark eyes widened behind her glasses when she saw me, and she started following me down the hallway, just like Eva was.

After about a minute of brisk walking, I came to the door that marked the entrance to Owen Grayson's study. I rattled the knob. Locked. I turned to face Eva.

"Do you have a key for this?" I barked.

Eva started at my harsh tone. "Yeah, somewhere up in my room—"

No time for that. I reached for my Ice magic, and the familiar silver light flashed on the spider rune scar on my palm. Eva let out a small, surprised gasp at my display of elemental power. Violet just stood behind her, watching me.

A few seconds later, I let go of my magic and went to work with the two Ice picks that I'd created. It took me less than a minute to open the office door. I snapped on a light and walked over to the rows of silverstone weapons hanging on the wall. Eva and Violet followed me inside.

"Owen's not here," Eva said in a desperate voice. "I

don't know what you want or what you're doing, Gin, but if you'll just wait for him, he'll be back any minute."

"Sorry," I replied, scanning the weapons for what I needed. "No time to wait."

There. Those would do nicely. I plucked the matching set of long swords that I'd noticed last night from their spots on the wall. I hefted the silverstone swords in my hands, checking their weight and balance. Perfect. Absolutely perfect. Owen Grayson truly was a master craftsman. And I was going to put his weapons to good use tonight.

A black leather scabbard with two slots in it hung next to the swords, and I grabbed it as well. I turned and was headed toward the office door when Eva stepped in front of me.

"Oh no," she said. "Owen's absolutely *insane* about his weapons. He never lets anyone take them out of the office, not even me."

I tried to go around her, but Eva sidestepped in front of me again. She was persistent, if nothing else. Just like her big brother was.

"I don't have time to argue with you, Eva," I snapped. "Get out of my way. Right now."

Her blue eyes narrowed at my sharp tone. "Or what? You'll stab me with one of those swords? I don't think so."

"No," I said. "But I'll shove you out of the way. How about that?"

Eva's face paled at my threat, but she held her ground. Brave, but stupid. Reminded me of Bria. I didn't want to hurt Eva, but I would if it meant I'd get to Roslyn Phillips in time to save the vampire.

Violet Fox stepped up beside her friend and regarded me with her dark eyes.

"You're going after someone," Violet said in a quiet tone.

I let out an angry breath. "Yes."

She nodded. "All right then. That's all I need to know." Violet put her hand on Eva's arm and drew her friend to one side. "Let her go, Eva. Just let her go."

"But Owen—the weapons—" Eva sputtered.

"I don't think he'll mind since Gin's the one taking them. Even if he does, well, I doubt he will for long. Isn't that right, Gin?" Violet gave me a crooked smile.

I found myself smiling back. "That's right, Violet. Thank you."

Eva looked at her best friend, then at me. Violet slowly pulled the other girl to one side. Eva had a decidedly dazed expression on her lovely face, but I knew Violet would fill her in on what she needed to know. I nodded at Violet and walked past them, out of the office, and back down the long hallway. The girls followed me, but neither one said anything, and Eva didn't try to stop me again.

I reached the front door, which was still open. Outside, my car beckoned, a silver beacon telling me to get on with things. But I found myself pausing, turning around, and staring at Eva. "If I don't come back, tell your brother, tell Owen . . ."

I struggled to find the right words. Spouting mushy sentiment on command had never been one of my skills. Besides, I wasn't even sure what I felt for Owen Grayson, other than a prurient desire to feel his naked body pressed against my own.

"Tell him what?" Eva asked.

A grim smile tightened my face. "Tell Owen that he's a hell of a kisser."

With those words, I stepped outside and shut the door behind me.

Thirty minutes later, I turned off my Benz and clicked on a small flashlight that I kept in the glove compartment. Using the information in Finn's file, I'd driven up into the most rugged section of the Appalachian Mountains that cut through Ashland, way up north, well above the genteel confines and estates of Northtown. Technically, I was still in the city, but there were more mountains up here than people.

I'd parked the car to one side of a small gas station that lay at the foot of this particular ridge. My Benz hid between a rusted-out pickup truck that might have had green paint at one time and a white Dodge van propped up on cement blocks, its tires long since rotted away to bare rims. It was only seven thirty, but the station had already closed for the evening, probably due to the cold and hard bits of snow that continued to coast around on the night wind. The old, clapboard station reminded me of Warren T. Fox's store, Country Daze, which wasn't too far from here.

I played my flashlight over the maps that Finn had compiled for me. Finnegan Lane might be a designer-suit-wearing, caffeine-addicted womanizer of the highest degree, but when he dug into someone, he got every single bit of dirt there was on them. Which is why the folder of information on Elliot Slater contained not only glossy magazine spreads of his mountain retreat but more useful topographical maps as well, along with the blueprints to Valhalla itself.

I sat in the car, feeling the cold creep in through the doors and windows, and studied the maps, searching for the best way to slip into the mansion. First, though, I'd have to hike up the mountain. Only one road curved up the rugged hillside, and whatever guards Slater had posted would be able to see the headlights from any car a half mile from the mansion—something I couldn't afford to have happen. Like so many of my other jobs over the years, the element of surprise was the key to my success, more so tonight than ever before, since the giant was holding Roslyn Phillips hostage and was doing or had already done who knew what to her.

Depending on what kind of shape Roslyn was in, I might have to come back and drive the car up to get her, but flashing my headlights wouldn't matter then, since I would have killed everyone in the mansion at that point.

I'd just decided to follow a dry creek bed up to the mansion, when the headlights of another car appeared in front of the gas station. The car slowed, and I spotted Finn behind the wheel of his Aston Martin. I flicked my headlights on and off, so he'd know that I was already here. Finn parked his silver sports car on the other side of the rusted pickup truck. A minute later, he opened the door on the passenger's side of my Benz and slid inside. He too carried a black duffel bag of supplies.

"Your timing is impeccable," I said. "I've only been here a couple minutes."

Finn grinned. "Isn't it always?"

His green eyes flicked to the maps and flashlight in my hands, and the smile dropped from his handsome face. "You found a way in yet?"

"I've found a way up the mountain. We'll worry about getting inside after we reach the mansion."

I showed Finn the creek bed that we'd be hiking up. He took the map from me and studied the terrain. But after a minute, he put the map down and stared up at the mountain before us. His fingers tapped out a staccato pattern on his thigh.

"What are you thinking?" I asked.

Finn sighed, and his hand stilled. "That I hate that it's come to this. That it's all my fault. I didn't expect things to get so complicated. Not with Roslyn or Elliot Slater. If I'd known just how badly the giant was obsessed with her, how messy this whole situation was going to get, I never would have told Xavier that we'd help them. I would never risk you like that, Gin."

"I know," I said in a soft voice.

We didn't speak for a few seconds.

"We don't have to do this," Finn finally said. "*You* don't have to do this. Roslyn left Jo-Jo's of her own free will, even after you told her not to, even after you told her that you'd take care of Slater. The best-case scenario is that Slater has just beaten her. But we both know that Roslyn's probably dead by now, that we could be risking ourselves for absolutely nothing."

Everything that Finn said was true, and he was only voicing the same troubling thoughts that I'd had on the drive up here. But there was one more thing that we both had to think about before we made our decision.

"And what would Fletcher do if he were here?" I asked. "What would the old man say?"

Finn stared up at the mountain a few more seconds, before turning to face me. "He'd say that we made a promise to Roslyn, and that you can never go back on your word." A smile tightened Finn's face. "And he'd grouse that it's about damn time somebody gave Elliot Slater exactly what he deserved."

"Exactly," I replied. "I gave Xavier my word. More importantly, I gave it to Roslyn too. Even if she might not be alive to appreciate it."

"I know." Finn reached over and squeezed my hand. "But I'll be with you, every step of the way. I love you, Gin."

"I love you too." I squeezed back. "Now let's go kill the bastard."

I climbed into the backseat of my Benz, peeled off the clothes that I'd been wearing at the Pork Pit, and pulled a fresh set out of the duffel bag that Sophia Deveraux had handed me. Thick, black cargo pants, a long-sleeved black turtleneck, a tight-fitting black vest with numerous pockets, boots, socks. I gathered my dark brown hair into a ponytail, then pulled a black watchman's cap over my head as low as I could and still have a clear field of vision. In the front seat, Finn donned a similar set of black clothes.

Once I was properly attired for the evening's activities, I took a small tin of black grease out of the bag and smeared it all over my face. Wouldn't do much good to dress in black from head to toe and have my pale face shining like a beacon in the night. When I finished, I passed the tin over to Finn. He wrinkled his nose but dipped his fingers into the grease and darkened his own face.

I got out of the car and shouldered the duffel bag with its remaining contents, including Finn's maps, my flashlight, and Owen Grayson's two long swords. I also slid a pair of night-vision goggles on over my head. A moment later, Finn did the same, bringing his own bag and goggles with him. Our heavy boots crunched on the gravel of the gas station's parking lot. Under my feet, the sharp stones whispered of the roll of tires over them, the *chug-chug-chug*s of the gas pumps, the chime of the bell over the door of the station. Normal sounds. Nothing to be worried about—so far.

Finn and I left the parking lot behind and slipped into the woods on the far side of the station. It didn't take us long to find the dried-up creek bed, and we stepped down into the shallow rut and started working our way up the mountainside. By walking up the creek bed, all we had to worry about stepping on were loose stones, and the lack of trees and branches in our path let the two of us move quickly and quietly at the same time. We didn't speak as we walked, saving our breath for the terrain.

We'd only been hiking about twenty minutes when Finn put his foot down on something that snapped with a loud *crack*. We both froze. The sound reverberated through the immediate area before the wind whipped it down the mountain. Finn and I dropped to the ground, waiting, but no one came to investigate the noise.

When I was sure we hadn't attracted any unwanted attention, I shone my flashlight on the ground underneath Finn's boot. To my surprise, Finn had stepped on what looked like a long, brittle femur bone, snapping it in half. Definitely a human bone, probably belonging to a giant, from the length of it. Looked like Fletcher Lane had been right about the mountain being a dumping ground for the bodies of Elliot Slater and Mab Monroe's enemies.

Finn raised his eyebrows. He knew a bone when he saw it too. I shrugged. Nothing we could do for whomever it had been attached to, so we moved on.

The air grew colder, sharper, the higher we climbed, burning my lungs like liquid fire. I kept my mouth closed and breathed in only through my nose, trying to minimize the sensation. The metallic scent of snow gusted on the night breeze, and heavy clouds clung low to the ground, partially obscuring the moon and stars, before being pushed on by the wind. I wanted all the cover I could get, and for once, luck, that cruel, capricious bitch, seemed to be smiling on me. I knew it wouldn't last.

A few birds rustled in the thick branches of the maple, elm, and pine trees over our heads, but our footsteps and movements were small and quiet enough for them to keep a silent watch on us, instead of fluttering up into the darkness and alerting whoever might be watching. Besides, they were safe and warm for the night and didn't want to give up their roosts if they didn't have to. The birds sensed they weren't our prey for the evening and were content enough in their trees and nests to let Finn and me pass without comment or criticism.

I wasn't sure how long we'd been walking before the creek bed veered west, away from the mansion. I climbed up out of the shallow rut and slithered forward into the black shadow provided by a large walnut tree. Finn followed me.

According to Finn's maps, Valhalla lay due east another mile up the mountain. We were still far enough away that I pulled out my flashlight and shone it over the maps, getting my bearings for the final time. Finn peered over my shoulder, doing the same. He nodded, and I turned off the flashlight and stuffed the maps back into my duffel bag. We climbed on.

I took the lead once more, moving more slowly and cautiously than before. Elliot Slater was secure enough in his mountain retreat not to have any exterior security measures, like lasers or dogs. Sloppy, sloppy, sloppy of him, but I wasn't going to complain, as it made things easier for Finn and me. Besides, I'd never liked killing dogs, even if their owner was a cold-blooded bastard who needed to be put down.

Still, the lack of obvious security didn't mean that Slater hadn't come up with some other clever, deadly way to booby-trap the perimeter. I would have. So I kept an eye out for trip wires, small holes, and flashes of light that would alert me to the fact that we were approaching a trap—or worse, had just set off some sort of defensive, protective rune. I had no desire to take a fireball to the chest because I'd put my feet or hands somewhere they shouldn't be. Finn followed my path exactly to further minimize the risk.

But we didn't stumble across anything, and several minutes later, we crested a ridge that overlooked the mansion.

As its name implied, Valhalla was a massive, six-story structure that took up a good portion of this particular mountain. The building was constructed of thick, heavy wood, inlaid with gray granite and river rock. Several balconies and patios wrapped around the structure, offering sweeping views of the surrounding mountains and hillsides below. It would be a gorgeous spot to take in the blaze of fall color as the leaves changed. But with winter approaching, the leaves had already fallen, revealing the bony, fingerlike fragments of the trees, interspersed with the thick, green boughs of the pines and firs that stood up like rows of jagged, mossy green teeth among the bare maples and poplars.

There was enough light up here for me to pull off the night-vision goggles and look toward the mansion with my own eyes. Beside me, Finn took off his goggles as well. Lights blazed in several windows on the first, second, and third floors, and I spotted a tall shadow moving back and forth in one of the windows. Someone was definitely home tonight.

As if I wouldn't have guessed by the two giants standing vigil outside the main, first-floor entrance. I'd been right when I'd thought that they'd be able to see any car headlights climbing up the mountain. Several hundred feet of road was visible from the giants' line of sight, and the area around them had been cleared of all trees and underbrush. It would take me about fifteen seconds to rush from the edge of the forest and reach the giants by the front door—plenty of time for them to alert whoever else was inside the house. We weren't getting in through the front door, so I turned my attention to the second story.

That story was more or less level with the cleared back-yard of the house. An Olympic-size pool stretched out almost to the woods there, probably heated, since it hadn't been covered up for the season yet. Finn and I crouched behind one of the many pine trees on the hillside overlooking the pool. The tangy scent of sap tickled my nose, but I ignored the sensation, focusing on the scene before me, blocking out everything else but the things I needed to hear and see.

Two giants stood on the stone deck next to the pool, smoking cigarettes and talking softly. They didn't seem to be carrying any obvious weapons, but that didn't mean there weren't a couple of guns on them somewhere. Problematic, but still doable.

Finn tapped my shoulder and pointed at the house itself. I scanned past the two giants and spotted another man sitting in a chair just inside the back door. That giant wet his thumb and flipped another page in whatever book or magazine he was reading.

I frowned. The inside man was worrisome. We could creep forward and drop the first two giants easily enough, but the third man would be sure to spot us—and probably be able to raise the alarm before we could silence him too. I'd much rather backstab Elliot Slater than have the giant lying in wait for me—with Roslyn Phillips already dead.

Finn tapped me on the shoulder again and jerked his thumb backward, telling me to follow him. We slithered back away from the ridge, well out of sight and earshot of the two guards by the pool.

"Why does there always have to be a third man?" I muttered.

"Because Elliot Slater's no fool," Finn replied in a soft voice. "You need a distraction, Gin, something to draw at least one or two of the men away from the patio and maybe make the guard inside come out as well. We don't know how many more giants might be in there, and you need to drop as many as you can out here."

Finn stared at me, his mouth set into a determined line.

"No, Finn," I snapped in a fierce whisper. "Forget about it. I'm not using you as bait so I can kill a couple of Slater's men before I slip inside the house. You know what Slater will do to you."

"And I know what he's doing to Roslyn right now," Finn countered. "Every second we're out here arguing is another second that he could be hurting her. Face it. This is the easiest way you can get inside and see if Roslyn is still alive."

He was right. Damn. I hated it when he was right.

Finn's mouth crooked into a smile. "Besides, you're always saying that I need to have some sense beaten into me. I'm sure that Elliot Slater would be happy to oblige you."

I stared at him. "You don't have to do this, Finn. We can find another way inside."

"I know," he replied. "But how long will that take? Every second counts now. Besides, I got us into this mess. Let me do what I can to end it. You're the better fighter. I'm the better distraction. You know it's true."

I couldn't argue with him. Not when he was right. Not when he was so determined to help me to help Roslyn. So I blew out a breath and nodded my head. "All right. But the second I find Roslyn and get her out of there,

I'm coming after you. And you'd damn well still better be breathing when I get to you. Understand?"

Finn's teeth flashed in the darkness. "I understand. You just can't live without me, Gin. There's no shame in admitting it."

If I hadn't been afraid of drawing unwanted attention from the guards below, I would have punched him for spouting that sentimental shit. I settled for rolling my eyes.

"Whatever," I said. "But if you're so determined to get yourself killed, you might as well get started."

Finn snapped his hand up in a mock salute. "Aye, aye, captain."

We didn't speak after that. I moved back into position on top of the ridge so I could see the two patio guards. Finn disappeared in the shadows to my right. I crouched beside one of the trees and hoped that I was doing the right thing, giving up Finn so I had a chance of saving Roslyn. Because if she was already dead, then this was all for nothing—

The *snap-snap* of a fallen tree branch fifty feet to my right sounded as loud as a gunshot in the quiet of the dark night. I stilled, scarcely daring to breathe, even though I knew it had to be Finn, getting into position to do whatever he was going to do.

Below me on the patio, one of the guards crushed out his cigarette. I would have thought the action normal, if I hadn't seen him light it just a few seconds ago. He'd heard the crack too, but he maintained his position. My eyes narrowed. Why would he just stand there? Why wasn't he tromping up the ridge to investigate?

And then—

Silence.

I huddled closer to the tree that I was hidden behind, sinking even deeper into the shadows, and slowly turned my head to the right, keeping the movement small and steady as I looked for Finn. But Fletcher Lane had also taught his son a thing or two about being invisible, and I didn't spot Finn among the tangled trees.

So I looked and listened and waited, counting the seconds off in my head. Ten, twenty, thirty . . . forty-five . . . sixty . . . I didn't hear anything until the ninety-second mark, when another small rustle drifted to my ears. Dead leaves scraping together in the underbrush. Finn pretending that he was trying to be quiet when he was really hoping to attract attention. But the guards on the patio didn't move, still didn't take the bait that Finn was teasing them with.

So I stayed where I was, quiet and hidden in the shadows. Nobody ever got dead by waiting. That's what Fletcher Lane always said, when he was teaching me how to be patient enough to wait out whatever enemy or danger I was facing. The old man's advice had kept me alive over the years—no reason to doubt it now.

I did, however, palm a pair of my silverstone knives. Always better to be armed while you waited out the enemy.

Another minute passed before I spotted a flash of silver light through the dense trees. Just a little glint, but it was more than enough to give away Finn's position. And now I saw him, a shadowy figure easing from tree to tree, creeping forward. The glint came from the gun in his hand. Finn kept up the charade of moving cautiously, not rushing to put his feet down, even though he was purposefully making even more rustling and cracking noises now.

I glanced back down at the patio. The two giants guards stayed at their posts on the patio, unwilling to investigate or unconcerned about the noise. I frowned. Something about their nonchalant stance bothered me. But since I couldn't put my finger on it or do anything about it, I turned my attention back to Finn, who reached the edge of the tree line. A moment later, he broke free of the clutching branches—

The sharp whine of a bullet caught me by surprise.

And then it was on.

❊ 25 ❊

The bullet slammed into the tree trunk next to Finn's ear. He dived back behind the tree and returned fire, his muzzle flash giving away his exact location. My head snapped down to the patio. The two guards stood in the same spot as before, only this time they clutched guns in their beefy fists. Guns that were pointed up at the tree line. Guns that they were firing at will. And I finally realized what had bothered me about them a few seconds ago—the fact that I couldn't see the third man anywhere.

The guard dropping his cigarette must have been some sort of signal to the man inside, who'd slipped off and sounded the alarm, while the two men on the patio had pulled weapons from some hidden spot on their bodies and started shooting. Who knew how many more men Elliot Slater had inside his mountain mansion? However many were inside, in seconds they'd be crawling up the mountainside, closing in on Finn.

And I couldn't do a damn thing about it.

Click-click-click.

The giants on the patio ran out of bullets. One of the men stopped to reload, while the other charged up the hill, fighting up the steep slope to get to Finn.

"Move, damn it," I whispered through clenched teeth. "Move, Finn."

Finn couldn't have possibly have heard me, so his own sense of self preservation must have kicked in. He reloaded his gun, threw down some cover fire, and scurried into the trees, heading back down the mountain. I knew Finn could run fast. Real fast when he put his mind to it. Like when his pants were down, and he was faced with an angry husband. Maybe he'd be able to slip away without getting captured. Then at least he would be safe when I went inside after Roslyn.

The giant who'd been on the patio surged over the top of the hill and crashed into the trees. I glanced down the slope, but his buddy with the gun wasn't making any move to follow him. Instead, he stood against the patio door, out of sight of Finn's original position, although not mine. Smart, not sending all your men into the woods. Exactly the sort of thing I'd expect from Slater.

I waited a few more seconds, but the guard made no move to struggle up the slope like his predecessor had done. But instead of slipping down the hillside and coming up behind him, I palmed another knife and went after the giant who was chasing Finn. It might have been Finn's plan to lure out the giants so I could kill them up here, but I would have followed him anyway. Because despite what I'd told him before, I wasn't going to leave Finn twisting in the wind by himself. Finnegan Lane wasn't dying out here in the woods, even if he was supposed to be a bloody distraction. Not if I could help it.

The giant made no effort to be quiet or conceal his trail, instead crashing through the leaves with as much force as he could muster. He probably thought the louder he sounded running after Finn, the more intimidated and scared Finn would be. He never considered the possibility that all the noise would make it that much easier for someone else, someone like me, to creep up behind him and stab him in the back. Which was exactly what I was going to do when he stopped long enough to catch his breath. Hopefully, Finn would just keep on running, instead of trying to trick more of the giants into coming into the woods.

Up ahead of me, the giant slowed, as if he'd lost Finn's trail. Wouldn't be hard to do in the darkness. I stopped, slid behind a tree, and watched him. After a few seconds of studying the ground with a small flashlight, the giant pulled a walkie-talkie off a clip on his belt and pressed a red button on the side.

"He's heading in your direction."

"Roger that," came the reply.

So the giant had come after Finn to drive him in the direction that the giant wanted Finn to go—and straight into some kind of trap—

Crack! Crack! Crack!

Up ahead, three shots rang out and echoed around the mountaintop. The giant rushed forward. I slipped about fifteen feet off to the left and followed him parallel through the woods. Thirty seconds later, the giant stepped into a large clearing ringed with rocks.

Crack!

A bullet slammed into the giant's chest, and he staggered back.

Crack! Crack!

Two more wounds blossomed—one in his shoulder, another one in his right knee. Not enough to kill him, but enough to hurt. The giant screamed and went down on his one good knee. I stayed where I was, searching the shadows for Finn. Ten seconds later, Finn stepped out from behind one of the rocks. Gun out, he headed for the giant.

"Where's your boss?" he demanded. "And where's Roslyn Phillips?"

The giant spat at him. Finn coldcocked him with the gun, then slammed his boot into the man's blown-out knee. The giant screamed with pain.

"Where is Elliot Slater?" Finn snarled again.

A grim smile curved my lips. Finnegan Lane was never lacking for style, if nothing else—

"Right here, you son of a bitch."

Click.

Finn knew that sound as well as I did—the hammer being thumbed back on a revolver. He froze and slowly turned around.

Elliot Slater stepped out from the shadows, flanked by two more giants. A large revolver glinted pale silver in Slater's hand. The long barrel was exactly even with the bridge of Finn's nose. Finn had lowered his gun to his side when he'd kicked the injured giant. No way he could raise it up in time to get a shot off before the giant pulled the trigger on his own weapon and killed him. Finn knew it as well as I did.

"Drop it, pal," Slater rumbled. "Or I'll kill you where you stand."

Finn's face tightened with rage, keeping up his act, and he slowly leaned forward and put the gun down on the leaf-strewn ground. Slater jerked his head, and one of the other two men rushed forward to pick it up. The fourth man lay moaning on the ground, clutching his shattered knee.

Slater stepped forward, still keeping his gun up. "Well, well, Finnegan Lane. Didn't expect you to show up here tonight."

Finn shrugged. "I love surprises, don't you?"

Slater eyed him. "I'm not going to ask you what the hell you're doing on my mountain in the middle of the night. Not just yet. We'll save that for when we get back to the mansion. You know, I'd already exhausted my previous entertainment for the evening. But you—you'll do just fine as a replacement."

Replacement? My stomach tightened. Had the giant already killed Roslyn Phillips? Were we already too late? Had Finn put himself in danger for nothing? I didn't know, and I didn't have time to puzzle it out. Because Elliot Slater stepped forward and slammed his fist into Finn's face. My foster brother crumpled to the ground and was still.

Elliot Slater stood over Finn's body a few seconds to make sure that he wasn't faking his unconscious state. When he was satisfied that Finn was out, Slater crooked a finger at one of his giants.

"Bob, you carry that son of a bitch back down to the mansion and chain him up in the main room. Phil, you stay here and help Henry," he said. "Did you guys see anyone with Lane? Any kind of backup?"

"No, sir," the one named Phil replied. "We watched to make sure, but it looks like he's alone."

They hadn't watched quite well enough because they hadn't seen me skulking through the woods. Sloppy, sloppy, sloppy of them. Then again, most folks only looked ahead for danger, not behind them.

The first giant, Bob, moved over to Finn, picked him up by his hair, and slung Finn over his shoulder like he was a wet dish towel. Then Bob set off through the far side of the clearing. Elliot Slater tucked his revolver into the waistband of his pants and followed him. Phil, the second uninjured giant, dropped next to Henry, the man that Finn had shot three times.

Part of me wanted to throw caution to the wind and go charging after Finn. To take Slater down like a wolf would a deer and rescue my foster brother. But the part of me that was the Spider, the cold, hard part that would always be the Spider, knew that was a risky plan at best. Slater and his man would be sure to make some noise, and I didn't know how many more giants were out there waiting for them to return. Besides, Finn had sacrificed himself for me so I could see whether Roslyn was still alive. I wasn't going to ignore his gift.

But that didn't mean I couldn't take care of Phil and Henry, in front of me right now.

Better to pick them off one a time rather than find myself in a situation where I could easily be overrun. As much as it made me want to vomit, I had to leave Finn in Slater's hands for a few minutes.

I scanned the surrounding woods, looking for any sign or sound that indicated that Slater had sent more men into the forest. But I heard nothing but the low groans of Henry, the giant that Finn had shot, as his buddy Phil hoisted him upright and put his arm under the injured man's shoulder, taking the weight off his blown-out knee.

It took Phil a few seconds to turn Henry around and point him back in the direction that the ambush had come from. Which gave me plenty of time to get a better grip on my silverstone knives and slip ahead of them. I waited behind a tree on the far end of the clearing. Once again, I looked and listened, but Slater seemed to be satisfied with his capture of Finn. No more giants came crashing through the underbrush, and all sounds of Slater and Bob, his other man, had vanished, swallowed up by the cold trees. Time for me to get into the game, even if it might already be too late to save Roslyn.

"Come on, buddy," Phil said to the injured man. "It's not so bad. I'll drive you back into the city, and we'll get you fixed up with an Air elemental healer. A couple hours from now, you'll be good as new."

Henry just moaned. No surprise there. A blown-out knee hurt like nothing else, especially when you had to walk on it.

"Come on now," Phil said again. "Keep it down. You know how Mr. Slater hates whiners."

At Phil's urging, Henry made some attempt to tone down his whimpering. Too bad. He should have groaned while he had the chance.

The giants' progress was slow, but soon their heavy footsteps approached my hiding place. My hands tightened around the hilt of my knives, and I prepared myself for what was to come. I pushed away all thoughts of Roslyn and Finn and Elliot Slater. All that mattered was the here and now, and taking care of business.

Phil stepped out of the clearing, dragging his buddy alongside him, and walked past me. I let the giants get a couple feet in front of me before I fell in step behind them. Phil was too busy murmuring encouraging words to Henry to hear the whisper of my footsteps on the forest floor. I closed the gap between us. Phil must have seen me move out of the corner of his eye, because his head started to turn in my direction.

And that's when I struck.

My first knife punched into the giant's back, scraping his thick ribs, before I thrust the blade up and into his heart. Sticky, black blood coated my hand like I'd just squeezed a ketchup bottle with all my might. Phil jerked and arched back at the sudden, wrenching pain, opening his mouth to bellow out his anguish. But before he could do that, I drove my foot into the back of his knee as hard as I could. The giant lost his grip on his buddy, who stumbled forward and slammed headfirst into a tree trunk. The already injured Henry let out another low groan of pain and misery.

But I focused my attention on Phil, who'd done his own header into a pile of leaves. He thrashed around, trying to get to his feet even as his body started to shut down from the massive injury that it had just received. By this point, Phil was screaming, but the leaves under his face muffled the sharp sound. Since I wanted to keep it that way, I straddled the fallen giant and put my knees on his back, pinning him on the cold, mossy ground. I dug one hand into his hair, pulling back his head. Phil gulped in a grateful breath, getting ready to scream again.

Too little, too late.

With my other hand, I sliced my silverstone knife across his exposed throat, slashing open his thick neck. Phil moaned and gurgled. With one hand, he flailed back, trying to dislodge me. His other hand went to his throat, trying to stem the steady pump of blood. I paused a second, listening. But Phil's cries didn't appear to have been loud enough to attract immediate attention.

So I climbed off the dying giant's back and went over to Henry, his fallen comrade, who wasn't in much better shape. The giant writhed back and forth, softly moaning in pain. I kicked him over so that he lay on his back, dropped to one knee, and slit his throat, putting him out of his misery. He didn't even try to fight back.

In less than a minute, it was over. Gin 2, giants 0. Just the way I liked it.

But my job wasn't done yet. While the giants bled out, I slid over into the shadows, watching and waiting. But no footsteps sounded, and I didn't hear anyone rustling through the underbrush. I'd taken care of them quietly enough not to attract attention. Good.

I pulled my knife out of Phil's back and made sure both giants were dead before I slipped off into the woods back the way that I'd come. The looking and listening were over. It was time to get on with things—and take care of Elliot Slater once and for all.

❆26❆

I walked back through the woods to my previous spot and grabbed my duffel bag. I slipped the scabbard that I'd taken from Owen Grayson's house over my shoulders. The black leather straps crisscrossed over my chest, and I slid the two long swords into their anointed slots. Once that was done, I grabbed a few more small supplies and left the bag where it was.

I headed to the left, keeping inside the tree line and circling to the far, opposite side of the patio until I faced the very back of the mansion. Only one giant guard remained outside next to the pool, since the others had been pulled away to take care of Finn. Like it or not, Finn's plan had worked.

Since it looked like the shooting was over, the guard had once again lit up a cigarette. He faced away from me, out toward the woods where Finn had been, and I watched while he tucked his gun into the small of his back. The other man that had been sitting just inside the glass doors was nowhere to be found. He was probably somewhere farther inside the mountain mansion, helping Elliot Slater secure Finn for the torture that lay ahead. I wouldn't get a better chance than this.

So I took it.

I hopscotched my way down the slope, skipping from one tree to another. The landscape hadn't been as well cleared on the back side of the house as it had on the front, which gave me plenty of cover to work with. I moved quicker than I had before, but I took care to make as little noise as possible. I still needed every bit of surprise that I could muster. Because now Finn's life depended on it, along with Roslyn's.

Two minutes later, I'd worked my way to the edge of the stone patio, which was set about four feet off the ground. I eased up, letting my head rise just above the surface of the rim. All around me, the stones whispered of wind and water. They also reverberated faintly with the sharp crack of gunshots that had just been fired. But those notes of alarm had already started to fade away. That bit of violence had been too brief and the majority of it too far away for the action to permanently sink into the patio. As for what I was about to do to the man in front of me, well, that kind of violence would probably linger in the stone for quite some time to come.

The guard stubbed out one cigarette with his foot and reached into his suit jacket for another. I wouldn't get a better opportunity—so I took it.

I pulled myself up, rolled over, and came up into a crouch behind some heavy, wrought-iron patio furniture.

The guard drew a lighter out of his pocket and clicked it a couple of times, trying to get more than mere sparks out of the cheap plastic. I rose to my feet and tiptoed forward, a silverstone knife in either hand.

The lighter flared, illuminating the guard's profile. He turned to face me, one hand pressing down on the lighter tab to keep the flame going.

"Finally," he muttered.

Last word he ever said. The giant never even saw me step out from behind the furniture and creep forward so that I was directly in front of him. He lit his cigarette and lifted his head, smoke streaming from his nostrils like he was a mythical dragon. My first knife ripped into his stomach, spilling his guts all over the stone patio. The second knife slammed into his windpipe, cutting off any sound he might make. The poor guy never knew what hit him. He choked on his own blood, even as his body spasmed from the shock of the two vicious, fatal wounds. He went down on his knees, halfway to dead, but I held him up and cut his throat, just to be sure.

Since I didn't feel like dragging his body off the patio, I tipped the dead giant into the pool. He sank to the bottom, blood still spurting out of his wounds, turning the crystal water the ugly brown color of iodine. Under my boots, the stone of the patio took on a harsher note from the giant's spattered blood. A symphony wouldn't have sounded better to me at the moment.

Gin 3, giants 0.

I waited a few seconds, but no one seemed to have heard me take out my latest victim. When I was sure that the kill had been clean and quiet, I eased over to the glass patio door, turned the knob, and slipped inside.

The inside of the mansion looked just as I'd expected it to—lush, elegant, expensive. Thick carpeting, throw rugs, and just enough natural wood and stone to make you think that you were in some rustic oasis instead of a carefully crafted structure. I could tell Slater had had the structure built especially for him because all the door-ways had at least a twelve-foot clearance and were five feet wide. Giants didn't like to be crowded.

I stood inside the patio door a moment, thinking about the blueprints of the place that Finn had procured for me and getting my bearings. In the woods, Elliot Slater had told his man to chain Finn up in the downstairs living room. I currently stood on the back side of the house, which meant the living room was several hundred feet in front of me. I knew that Slater had at least one more man with him right now—the one who had carried Finn out of the woods—but I didn't know how many other giants might be lurking around. Best to do a perimeter sweep and kill as many of them as I could before taking on the big kahuna himself.

Besides, some small part of me hoped that Roslyn Phillips might still be alive. I owed it to the vampire to get her out of here if she was still breathing. Jo-Jo Deveraux could fix anything short of death, no matter what horrible things Slater might have done to Roslyn. I'd promised the vampire that I was going to protect her from the giant. That he was never going to hurt her again. So far, I hadn't lived up to my word, but if Roslyn was still breathing, then I'd be damned if I was leaving here without her.

A long hallway stretched out north and south before me. I tiptoed up the north side, keeping to the shadows and pausing every few feet to look and listen.

Silence.

I didn't hear any movement. No rustle of clothing, no labored breathing, no scratch of shoes on the rugs or carpet. Just silence.

I kept going, eventually coming to a set of stairs that led up to the third floor. Once again, I visualized the blueprints that had been in Finn's folder. If I remembered correctly, the interior of the mansion was hollow. The downstairs living room on the second floor was the focal point of the structure, with the ceilings of the other floors cut out above it. Balconies on every floor led to other rooms while still overlooking the living room below, which featured floor-to-ceiling windows on one side. Since I wanted to see Elliot Slater's setup before I went after him, I headed up the stairs so I could get a bird's-eye view of things. Besides, the master bedroom was located on the third floor. Which is where Slater had probably taken Roslyn first when he'd brought her here.

Again, I heard no one and saw nothing except furniture—until I reached the door that led to the master bedroom. To my surprise, the door was cracked open, and soft murmurs slid out into the hallway where I stood. I cocked my head to one side. A man's voice doing most of the talking, but not Slater's. The pitch was too high. Didn't much matter. Other than Finn and Roslyn, whoever else was in this house was going to die right along with the giant, no matter what his voice sounded like.

I crept closer to the door, and the murmurs sharpened into real words.

". . . know how beautiful you are? It doesn't have to be like this," the man said.

More silence, as if he was waiting for someone to respond.

"I'm talking to you, bitch. Answer me."

More silence.

Slap-slap-slap.

A series of violent blows rang out, and a low moan sounded. My eyes narrowed, even as my heart lifted. Because the moaner was a woman. And it sure sounded like Roslyn Phillips to me.

I eased closer to the door and put my eye up against the crack. The door was only slightly open, showing me a narrow strip of what lay inside.

A bed dominated the room—the biggest bed that I'd ever seen. The sucker had to be at least twenty-five feet square and was covered with an ivory comforter. Thick wooden posts rose up from the four corners of the bed, and I could see some sort of heavy, hemp rope tied to them. The rope creaked, as though someone was tied down by it. A man also stood before the bed, but it wasn't Elliot Slater. His hair was a bright red, instead of the blond wisps of the other pale, chalky giant.

This giant was also naked, with an ass that was so fat, dimpled, and hairy that I would happily have killed him just for inflicting the sight on me.

"Like I told you, Slater's busy right now. Besides, he

doesn't know a good thing when he has it anyway. Smashing up that pretty face of yours, beating on that soft body of yours, what a fucking waste. If you were mine, I would have found something much better for us to do together. Something we're going to do right now," the man drawled in a soft voice, as though he wasn't casually talking about raping someone.

"He'll . . . kill you . . . for this."

The voice was low and weak and raspy, but I still recognized the person it belonged to—Roslyn Phillips. She was still alive—and she was damn well going to stay that way.

I couldn't see the man's face, but I got the impression that he smiled.

"No, he won't because you're not going to live long enough to tell him about it," he replied.

The man moved forward to the edge of the bed. He held a rag in his hand. The bits of rope I could see jerked and spasmed. Roslyn, trying desperately to get free before the bastard gagged and raped her. A cold, calm, familiar sort of determination filled me, and my hands tightened around my bloody knives.

While the naked giant wrestled with Roslyn, trying to get the gag into her mouth, I opened the door and stepped inside the room. The man was too busy with the vampire to hear my soft footsteps on the carpet. I came at him at an angle, so I could see what kind of shape Roslyn was in.

The sight on the bed sickened me.

I'd been right on one count. Elliot Slater had wanted to hurt Roslyn before he killed her. The vampire lay spread-eagled on the bed, her arms and legs tied to each of the four posts. Blood and cuts and bruises covered her body—every single inch I could see of it.

If I hadn't known it was Roslyn, I wouldn't have recognized her. That's how bad she looked, her features all mushed and mashed together, like she'd been run over by a car. Roslyn's skin looked like it had been rubbed raw with sandpaper. Her beautiful face was a mess of pulpy, purple, swollen flesh, and the vamp's blood had long ago turned the ivory comforter a dark crimson. There was so much blood on her that it took me a second to realize that Roslyn was still wearing clothes underneath all the gore. Her pants and shirt were torn in places, and blue-black bruises peeked out from the rips like dark eyes.

I didn't often feel rage, but cold fire burned in my veins at what had been done to the other woman—and what sort of torture Elliot Slater had in store for Finn if I didn't save him. For a moment, I felt almost crazed with this burning need to kill the giant and everyone else here, everyone who had hurt Roslyn and Finn.

The giant put one hairy knee on Roslyn's stomach. The vampire thrashed weakly against him, but he would have been much too heavy for her to dislodge, even if she'd been free of the ropes and at full strength. I gathered my own will and waited until the giant leaned over Roslyn, trying to force the gag into her bloody mouth before I spoke.

"Having fun yet, you sick bastard?" I growled.

The giant's head whipped around to me. His mouth fell open, and he started to sputter out some excuse about what he was doing. But it was too late for that. Much, much too late.

I threw myself at him. My knives flashed like liquid silver in the light. And someone else's blood besides Roslyn's spattered onto the ivory comforter.

Less than a minute later, the dead giant thumped to the floor. I wiped my bloody knives off on the comforter, then used them to saw through the ropes that bound Roslyn to the bed. The vamp turned her head to look at me. I didn't know if she could see me through her battered, black eyes, so I reached forward and gently squeezed her hand.

"It's Gin," I said in a low voice.

"Gin?" Roslyn whispered through her bloody, swollen lips. "You . . . came . . . for me? After . . . I left . . . Jo-Jo's . . . Why . . . would you . . . do that?"

I stared at the vampire's body, at all the horrible things that had been done to her on the outside, and all the other horrible things that I couldn't see on the inside. All the things that might never, ever heal. All the things that I'd brought down upon her when I'd asked her to help me get into Mab Monroe's party. The guilt from it made me sick, and I knew that it always would. I was Roslyn's now, and I always would be. Whatever she needed, I would freely give to her, anytime, anyplace.

Still, I made my voice as gentle as I could, given the cold rage and sharp guilt still burning and twisting through my veins.

"Because I'm the Spider. Because my retirement's been a fucking bore. Because you asked me to do a job, and I never go back on my word. Because we're friends, in a weird sort of way. But mainly because nobody deserves to be treated like this—except the bastards who live here." I paused to let the cold venom seep back into my tone. "And you can believe that I'm not leaving this place until every single one of them is dead."

27

Roslyn Phillips wasn't in the greatest shape of her life, which is why I unzipped one of the pockets on my vest and drew out a tin of Jo-Jo Deveraux's healing ointment. I made Roslyn lie still on the bed while I slathered the ointment on the worst of her wounds on her chest and arms.

It was one of the hardest things I'd ever had to do.

I knew that Roslyn didn't want me touching her, that she might not want anyone touching her ever again, given how badly she'd been beaten. But it had to be done to save her. Roslyn flinched every time my fingers brushed her body and with every single movement of my bloody hands, but she didn't complain, and she didn't ask me to stop.

I'd never seen anything so brave in my entire miserable life.

Still, I did the best I could to distract Roslyn, keeping up a steady stream of chatter, telling her exactly how the bastard who'd been about to rape her had died and exactly how I was going to do the same thing to Elliot Slater. I don't know if it was my cold, measured words or the healing power of Jo-Jo's magic, but Roslyn stilled after a few minutes, only flinching every other time I touched her.

While Roslyn lay on the bed, letting Jo-Jo's ointment patch up the worst of her wounds, I opened one of the closet doors, looking for something else for her to wear—something that didn't have her own blood all over it. To my surprise, a variety of women's clothing was mixed in among Elliot Slater's oversize suits. I grabbed some pants, a sweater, socks, shoes, and even some clean underwear from the interior and tossed them to Roslyn.

"Take off those bloody rags, and put these on," I said in a gentle voice. "And then we'll get you the hell out of here."

The vamp did as I commanded, even though her movements were still slow and stiff, despite the healing ointment. I helped her as best I could. When she finished, I dug another small tin out of one of my vest pockets and handed it to her.

"Here. Put this one on your face. It's more of Jo-Jo's ointment. It'll hold you together long enough for you to get to the dwarf so she can heal you up properly."

Roslyn's hands shook so badly that I took the tin back from her, dipped my fingers into the ointment, and slathered it on her face.

"Sorry for the rush," I murmured. "But Elliot Slater's got Finn downstairs, and I need to get to him before Slater kills him."

"Finn's . . . down there?" Roslyn rasped, letting me work on her face.

"Yeah," I replied. "Seems he had the same idea about rescuing you that I did. Offered himself up as a distraction so I could slip inside the mansion."

Some of the swelling went down on Roslyn's face, and I saw the gleam of tears in her toffee eyes.

"No matter what happens," she rasped. "Thank you . . . Gin . . . for coming . . . for me."

The vamp fumbled about until she wrapped her bloody hand around mine. I gently squeezed her trembling fingers.

"You're welcome," I said. "Now let's get you out of here."

While I waited for Jo-Jo's healing ointment to put Roslyn's face back in some kind of working order, I questioned the vamp about how many more guards there might be inside the house.

"How many have you killed already?" she asked.

"Four."

She nodded. "There should be two left, besides Slater."

"Where would they be?" I asked, checking my silverstone knives and the two swords still strapped to my back.

"If you say he's got Finn, then the two guards will be downstairs with Slater," she replied. "He always likes to have at least two men with him when he's working on someone. That's where he took me first. When he got tired of hitting me, he brought me up here. One of his men came in and got him before he could—"

Her voice broke on the last few words, and I gave her a minute to compose herself, even though every second I delayed was another second that Finn got the shit beat out of him. I didn't know if I could stand it if my foster brother ended up the same way that I had that night at the community college when Slater had pummeled me. Just looking at Roslyn made me want to rewind time, go back, and kill all the bastards who had hurt her again—slowly. But I couldn't do that. All I could do was go forward and hope that I got to Finn in time.

I opened the bedroom door and peered out into the hallway. Everything was just as hushed as it had been before. I whispered to Roslyn to keep close to me and keep quiet. The vamp nodded.

I eased down the hallway. About thirty feet past the bedroom door, the right wall opened up, revealing the enormous living room a floor below. I got down on my hands and knees, crawled forward, and peered around the corner, through the wide slats of the banister that ringed the outer wall.

A floor below me, Elliot Slater stood in the middle of the living room, unbuttoning the sleeves of his pale blue shirt. A giant stood on either side of him, slightly behind their boss. The two men had their hands clasped in front of them, just like good little soldiers would. Their shirt sleeves were already rolled up, their hands already stained with blood—Finn's blood.

Finnegan Lane was chained up to a stone column that supported the ceiling several stories above his head. Silverstone cuffs glinted around his hands. The cuffs had been tied to a matching chain that hung on a hook above his head, keeping Finn's arms up. An uncomfortable position made worse by the obvious beating he'd already taken. Bruises blossomed like purple and blue irises on Finn's cheeks. The two giants had roughed him up a bit already, no doubt getting him ready for Elliot Slater's personal attention, but Finn didn't seem to be in too bad shape. He was still breathing, which was the most important thing.

Cold rage burned in Finn's eyes as he watched Slater start rolling up his sleeves. Every once in a while, Finn rattled his cuffs, testing them for any hint of weakness. But there was none. Still, his face was guarded and watchful. He hadn't given up hope of escaping, of getting the upper hand, even without my help. Finn would never give up any more than I would. The old man had taught him better than that. Still, Finn's fighting spirit warmed my heart.

Once I'd fixed the position of everyone and everything in the room in my mind, I slithered back down the hallway to where Roslyn slouched against the wall, waiting.

"Slater's down there with two of his men," I whispered. "He's got Finn chained up to a stone column."

Roslyn nodded. "That's where he likes to start with people. He's got another room on this floor for really difficult cases. Most people don't make it up here."

"I want you to get the hell out of here," I whispered. "Slip out the side door where the pool is, go to the garage, get one of Slater's cars, and leave. There's a gas station at the bottom of the hill. My Benz is parked down there. Get in, and use one of the cell phones in the glove box to call the Deveraux sisters. They'll come and help you. Xavier too. In case things don't go well for Finn and me up here. Can you do that for me? Can you make it to the garage?"

Roslyn nodded. "I can make it that far. What are you going to do?"

I palmed my two silverstone knives and held them

up where she could see them. "Finish this—one way or another."

Roslyn disappeared down the hallway, and I eased back to where the balcony was. Slater and his men had their backs to me, and I moved to the other side of the hallway, where it was solid once more. They never even looked up. My eyes went to an iron chandelier that hung down from the ceiling. That would work just fine.

"Finnegan Lane," Elliot Slater rumbled, stepping forward so that he was directly in front of my foster brother. The giant had finished securing one shirt sleeve and had gone to work on the other one. "A strange place to meet."

"So it seems," Finn replied in a chipper voice, despite his bruised features.

"Care to tell me what the fuck you're doing up here on my land?" Slater asked.

"Technically, it's not your land, is it? It belongs to your boss, Mab Monroe. You're just the caretaker of the place, so to speak. Part of the cleanup crew. Just like you've always been."

Finn finished his insult with a toothy grin. Slater's fingers stilled on the fabric of his shirt sleeve, as though he was thinking about lunging forward and punching Finn, but the giant wasn't that easily baited.

"I'll ask you again," Slater said. "What are you doing here?"

"I was looking for a friend of mine," Finn said. "Roslyn Phillips. I think you know her. Care to tell me where she is?"

This time, it was the giant's turn to smile. "Oh, Roslyn's a bit tied up at the moment, just like she's been for the past few hours. Just like she's going to be for some time to come. Until I get tired of the bitch and break her neck with my bare hands."

Finn couldn't help himself—he spat at the giant and his vile words. Slater calmly wiped the spittle off his face, then backhanded Finn. The sound of the giant's palm striking Finn's skin was as loud as a gunshot in the quiet house. Finn grunted with pain, and Slater closed his hand into a fist and punched him. A cut opened up above Finn's left eye, and blood covered that side of his face.

My hands tightened on my knives, but I didn't make a sound. I wanted to give Roslyn as much of a head start as possible, in case Slater and his men killed Finn and me and realized that the vamp was missing. Which meant that Finn was going to have to get slapped around some more. My stomach twisted at the thought, but it was something that we both were just going to have to endure. Wouldn't be the first time.

"You know, I thought I was just going to have some fun tonight with Roslyn," Elliot said. "But imagine my surprise and delight when you show up on my doorstep to add to the festivities."

"I know," Finn replied. "I decided to come to you. Save you some trouble. Since you turned tail and ran the last time we met."

Slater froze for a second. The giant finished rolling up his remaining shirtsleeve before he looked at Finn again. "And when was that?"

Finn stared at the giant. "Why, the night you went to kill Detective Bria Coolidge," he drawled. "That didn't end so well for you, if I remember. How many men did you lose that night? Three? Four? It was hard to keep track with all the blood and bodies everywhere."

This time, Slater's hazel eyes were the ones that narrowed with rage. "That was you?"

Another smile spread across Finn's battered face. "Oh yes. Most fun I've had all week."

Slater studied Finn for several seconds. "You were the one with the gun. The one who shot Jim in the face."

Finn tipped his head in acknowledgment.

"I see."

Slater stepped forward and drove his fist into Finn's stomach. It happened so fast, with such speed, I thought for a moment that I'd imagined it. Until Finn spit up a mouthful of his own blood. Elliot Slater had some of the quickest hands that I'd ever seen.

But Slater didn't stop with one blow. Instead, the giant slammed one fist into Finn's face. I heard the *crack* as his nose broke all the way up here on the balcony. Slater's other fist plowed into Finn's stomach again. Finn moaned, and more blood spewed out of his lips. That cold ball of rage began to burn in the pit of my stomach once more.

"I can keep this up for hours, Lane. *Hours,*" Slater rumbled. "Until you are begging me to stop the pain, to just end you. Now, you're going to tell me exactly why you were at Coolidge's house that night, and why you're so fucking interested in my business."

The giant didn't have to add an *or else* to his threat. He and Finn already knew how to play the game—and they both realized that Elliot Slater currently held all the cards. Except for one. Me. The queen of spades.

Finn's head rolled back and up as he tried not to choke on his own blood. I scooted forward just a bit, so that the edge of my knife caught the light and flashed silver. Finn saw the gleam. His green eyes widened for a second before he shuttered them and slowly lowered his head.

"All right," Finn mumbled. "I'll tell you why I was there. Because I know about Bria Coolidge. Because I know who she really is."

That got Slater's attention. The giant's whole body stilled. He didn't even blink. "And just who is she, Lane?"

Finn looked up at him. "Her real name is Snow. Bria Elizabeth Snow."

Elliot Slater didn't react. Didn't move, didn't flinch. Hell, he didn't even take a breath. Then the giant abruptly turned away from Finn and walked around the stone column, moving out of Finn's line of sight. I drew back into the hallway so that Slater wouldn't see me lurking on the balcony above. The other two giants maintained their positions below me, watching the show with detached interest. They looked like the same two goons who had held me up for Slater that night at the community college. Didn't much matter. They were getting dead regardless.

But what I didn't understand was what Finn thought he was doing telling Elliot Slater that he knew who Bria really was. Did he want the giant to kill him before I could take Slater out? Had the giant's blows scrambled Finn's brains even more than they already were? Because Finn was dangerously close to singing not only his swan song but mine too. To telling Slater everything about us, what we did, and why.

Finn coughed up some more blood and spat it on the

carpet. "Come on, Elliot," he said in a friendly voice. "You're not going to deny it, are you? That's hardly sporting, considering that I'm the one in cuffs and you're not."

The giant finished his circuit around the stone column and stopped in front of Finn once more. "So what if Coolidge's real name is Snow? That doesn't mean anything to me."

"Sure it does," Finn countered. "Because that's why you were there to kill Bria. That's why your boss, Mab Monroe, wants her dead. Because she's Bria Snow, and because Mab murdered her family seventeen years ago."

Silence.

Slater held his position, as still and quiet as the stone column before him. But Finn wasn't finished dropping bombs on the giant—or me.

"You've been working for Mab a long time now, haven't you, Elliot?" Finn murmured. "Twenty-five years by my calculation. You've been her right-hand man from the very beginning. Which means you were there that night. You were there the night that Mab murdered the Snow family."

I flashed back to that night, to my frantic run through my burning house, to the giant's fist slamming into my face. I'd only seen him a second before he'd punched me. Just long enough to notice how pale he was. Almost . . . albino.

Slater didn't say anything, but a muscle twitched in his chalky cheek. All the confirmation that I needed. My breath rushed out of my lungs as I realized what Finn was up to. My foster brother was trying to get some answers for me—answers about what had really happened the night that Mab Monroe had murdered my mother and older sister. And I'd be damned if I had the willpower to stop him right now.

Elliot Slater recovered from his shock, and a cruel smile spread across his face. "You're a smart guy, Lane. Figuring all that out for yourself."

Finn shrugged again. "Not too hard. I've had the file on the Snow family for a while now. Mab's one of the few Fire elementals who had enough magic—then or now—to do what she did that night."

The giant circled around the column once more. This time, Finn's green eyes flicked to the other two men standing in front of him. They stared at him without expression, and Finn turned his attention back to Slater, who stopped in front of him once more. Finn didn't look up at me. He knew that I'd make my move when I was ready.

"What do you want, Lane?" Slater barked out. "What's the fucking point of this? You're dead, and you know it. Why all the questions about something Mab did years ago?"

Finn shrugged. "I'm curious. A trait my father instilled in me. Because it doesn't say in the file exactly why Mab killed the Snow family. What she gained from it. Or why she wants Bria Coolidge dead today."

Slater tilted his head to one side. "You might be smart, Lane, but you really don't have a clue, do you? Not about Mab, not about Coolidge, not about anything."

"Please," Finn said in a wry tone. "Enlighten me."

Elliot Slater leaned forward so that his pale face was level with Finn's bloody one. "Mab killed that family because of Bria Coolidge's magic. Because that bitch's Ice and Stone magic was and still is a threat to her."

Despite my years of training, I couldn't help the small gasp of surprise that escaped from my lips. Mab thought Bria had Ice *and* Stone magic? Why would the Fire elemental think that? I'd been the only one of us to inherit both our mother's Ice magic and our father's Stone power as well—

A horrible, horrible thought filled my mind. So horrible, so ironic, so fucking *wrong* I wanted to scream. To weep and wail and lash out and kill everything and everyone that I could get my hands on. But even as the bitterness filled my mouth at the realization, I knew that it was true—and the real reason why Mab Monroe had killed my family. The awful, horrible reason my mother and older sister were dead.

That night, when the Fire elemental had been torturing me, she'd asked me question after question about Bria, demanding to know where my baby sister was above all else. Because Mab had thought that Bria was me—that Bria was the one with both Ice and Stone magic.

Mab Monroe had really been there to kill me—not Bria.

I wasn't the only one surprised by the revelation. Finn's mouth dropped open at Slater's confession. Finn regarded the giant with thoughtful eyes, and I could practically see the wheels spinning in his head. He realized what the giant's words meant as well as I did.

"Mab Monroe thinks that Bria Coolidge has both Ice *and* Stone magic?" Finn asked. "That's why she wants Bria dead so badly?"

Slater frowned. "Why else would Mab care about the bitch?"

"Surely there's more to it than just that," Finn scoffed. "Mab Monroe is the strongest elemental to be born in five hundred years, if you listen to the rumors. She killed a whole family because one little girl had the power to control two elements? Come on, Elliot. We both know that I'm a dead man. Indulge me. Tell me the rest of the story."

Slater cocked his head to one side, trying to read Finn's expression, trying to figure out what he was up to, why he was so curious about something that had happened so long ago. Hard to get a good read on someone's emotions when blood and bruises covered his face like an extra layer of skin. After a few seconds of study, Slater shrugged.

"Mab wanted to kill the mother, Eira Snow, ever since they were kids. The Monroes were always part of the underworld wheeling and dealing, while the Snows were always real straight arrows. Naturally, the two families got involved in some kind of elemental feud along the way. It stretched back decades from what I understand. Hell, it goes so far back that I don't even think Mab really knows how it started in the first place. But somebody killed someone over something, and it just kept going from there. You know how elementals are. Most of 'em can't get along to save their lives, especially the opposing elementals, like Fire and Ice." Disgust filled Slater's voice. Evidently, he didn't hold his boss in quite as high regard as he led everyone to believe. "Fucking elementals. Always fighting over something."

Finn nodded his head in agreement.

"Mab and Eira Snow grew up together," Slater continued. "Even as kids, they were enemies. Mab made sure of that. And when they got older, well, they both went after the same man—a Stone elemental. Supposedly, Snow actually loved him, but Mab, well, she just wanted his Stone magic, wanted to pass it on to their kids."

The giant stared across the living room, staring back into the distant past. He hooked his thumbs through the belt loops on his pants and rocked back on his heels. Lost in his memories.

"But why?" Finn asked, breaking into Slater's reverie. "Maybe the kids would have gotten daddy's Stone magic. Maybe they wouldn't. There was no guarantee of that."

Slater chuckled. "I tried telling that to Mab myself, but she wouldn't listen to me. Magda's the only one that Mab ever took advice from."

Finn frowned. "Who the hell is Magda?"

The silent same question I was asking myself.

Slater shrugged. "Some crazy old aunt of Mab's who lived up in one of the hollows. Magda was an Air elemental. Seeing into the future was her thing. Writing down prophecies, casting stones, reading tea leaves, looking at moss on trees, drinking chicken's blood. Bitch was into some really crazy shit. She told Mab that Snow would have a kid who would be an even stronger elemental than Mab was. Someone with Ice and Stone magic. Someone who would one day kill Mab."

Kill Mab? Well, the mysterious Magda had gotten one thing right. Because that was certainly my plan now.

"After Snow popped out three brats, Mab decided to make her move," Slater finished.

Finn just stood there, digesting the information. On the balcony above, I did the same, trying to swallow the cold, cold bitterness that coated my mouth and heart.

Slater smiled. "So I got some of my boys together, and we went over to the house late one night. My boys and me took care of the servants, while Mab lit up the mother and one of the brats. It was beautiful."

Finn looked at the giant. "But things got out of hand, didn't they? Otherwise, Bria Coolidge wouldn't be alive today."

"The middle brat managed to hide Coolidge somewhere. So I found the brat and took her to Mab to get some answers. Mab tortured the brat, but she didn't squeak," Slater said. "So we left to look for Coolidge, but the little bitch used her Stone magic to weaken the foundation of her own house. Mab and I barely got out before the whole damn thing came crashing down."

"And you thought Bria buried herself in her own tomb," Finn deduced. "Until she came back to town a few weeks ago and Mab realized that she hadn't died that night all those years ago. I bet Mab fucking *freaked* when her sources in the police department told her about Bria, that the detective was digging up dirt on her family's murder. I bet Mab was absolutely livid when she realized who Bria really was. That's how Mab even knew it was her in the first place, right?"

"More or less." Slater shrugged again. "But it's all just a small setback, one I'm going to rectify after I'm finished having my fun with you—and sweet Roslyn."

Instead of getting angry again, Finn just stared at the giant, his green eyes gleaming with secrets that Slater couldn't even begin to guess. Finn's lips twitched, but not with pain. A small chortle sounded, then another, then another, until he was guffawing with laughter. Tears of hysterical amusement cascaded down his bruised cheeks, mixing with his scarlet blood.

Slater looked at Finn, then at his two flunkies. The other giants shrugged their shoulders. They didn't know why he was laughing either.

"What's so funny?" Slater rumbled, turning back to face Finn. "Most men don't laugh when they're about to die."

My foster brother ignored the giant and kept right on laughing. The loud, merry, confident sound grated on Slater's nerves, because he moved closer, grabbed Finn's chin with his massive hand, and shoved his mouth closed, cutting off his gleeful chuckles. It took some effort, but Finn's chest finally quit shaking with chuckles. Slater stepped back and eyed the other man, still wondering at the cheerful outburst.

"You know what, Elliot?" Finn asked. "You're a pretty smart guy yourself, to help your boss cover up such brutal murders for so long. But in the middle of telling your little bedtime story, you forgot one small thing."

"And what the fuck would that be?" Slater growled.

"You know that night that I stopped you from killing Bria Coolidge?"

The giant nodded.

Finn just smiled. "You forgot that I had a partner then—and still do now."

* 28 *

That was my signal to move. So I pulled myself up onto the banister that overlooked the living room and leaped. I hung in midair for a moment before gravity took over. On my way down, I grabbed the edge of the iron chandelier. My momentum propelled me forward, like I was on a old-fashioned rope swing, and I pumped my legs to get the arc I wanted. Elliot Slater's head snapped up at the noise, but the two giants were too focused on their boss to do the same. Slater shouted a warning. Too fucking late.

I dropped right on top of the two giants. One of them stumbled to the left and slammed into a table. My silverstone knife ripped into the other one's back and sliced all the way down, like I was a sailor and his flesh was some sort of heavy canvas I was cutting into to slow my own fall.

He screamed with pain and bucked like a bronco, but I jumped up, grabbed his hair, and climbed on his back.

The man tried to throw me off, but I had a death grip on his greasy locks. The giant paused a second to scream and gather his strength, and that's when I reached around and slit his throat. His scream turned into a gurgle, and I felt the fight and power drain out of his body, along with his blood. The man pitched forward, and I got off the rodeo ride.

One of my knives was still stuck in the giant's back, and the other had fallen from my grasp when he'd lurched forward. So I grabbed the two knives hidden in my boots and turned to face the other man. He'd picked himself up and was getting back into the thick of the fight. The giant roared with rage, charged, and swung at me. *Sloppy, sloppy, sloppy.* I slithered forward and popped up inside his nonexistent defense. One knife went into his heart. The other severed his jugular. I shoved him away and whirled, ready for Slater's onslaught.

But Elliot Slater stood in front of the column where Finn was chained, just staring at me. His hazel eyes regarded the dead bodies of his men, then flicked up to my face. It took him a second to recognize me through the grease and blood that coated my features like a rubber Halloween mask. But once he did, the giant's eyes narrowed, and a red flush crept up his pale, chalky neck.

"Blanco!" he hissed.

"You were expecting someone else?" I mocked. "And here I thought the idea that all giants were big and dumb was just a vicious stereotype."

My eyes flicked behind him to Finn, who was jumping up and down, trying to slip his handcuff chain off the peg that secured it to the stone column above his head.

"I'm the big dumb bastard who's going to rip you to pieces," Slater snarled, his hands curling into fists.

"Promises, promises," I mocked again.

I needed the giant to focus on me. Not do something smart and use Finn as a human shield.

Elliot Slater charged at me. I waited until the last second, then threw myself to one side and rolled up. I turned and immediately flung one of my silverstone knives at him. The weapon sank into the giant's chest. With a low snarl, he ripped it out and threw it to one side. I grabbed the knife in the small of my back and tossed that one at him too. It also landed in his chest, but I wasn't done yet. Two more knives came out of the pockets on my vest and whistled in Slater's direction as well.

Solid chest hits, all of them. If Slater had been human, he would have been dead by now. But he was a giant and a tough one at that. He merely pulled out the knives and let them drop to the floor at this feet. Once that was done, he smiled and started in my direction.

And that's when I drew the swords.

Elliot Slater had kicked my ass twice now—once at the community college when I'd let him and then again at Bria's house the night that he'd come to kill her. But I'd taken something away from both of those beatings—the fact that I couldn't let the giant put his hands on me. Not if I wanted to win. Not if I wanted to live.

Sure, I could use my elemental Stone magic to harden my skin, to make it tougher than granite. But Slater was arguably the strongest man in Ashland. He could keep punching me until my magic wore down. And when it was gone, when my strength and magic were exhausted and my concentration slipped that one precious second, my skin would revert back to normal. And then the giant could kill me with one well-placed blow. I couldn't let that happen, couldn't let him get close to me. Which is why I'd grabbed the two long swords from Owen Grayson's wall of weapons. I needed a way to cut Elliot Slater down piece by piece and keep out of reach of his long arms at the same time.

Now I was going to see if Owen was as good a craftsman as I thought he was. Going to stake my life on it, as a matter of fact.

Slater pulled up short at the sight of the silverstone swords glinting in my hands. Then a cruel smile spread across his face. "You think those little toothpicks are going to stop me?"

I twirled the swords in my hands. "Come here, you sick bastard, and we'll find out."

And then we danced.

Around and around we circled, our shoes squishing into the puddles of blood already on the carpet. Unlike his men, Slater didn't rush at me, thinking his superior strength and size would be enough to carry him through the fight. Instead, the smart, cagey bastard feinted in and out, testing me, trying to see how good I really was with the swords. He got the message when I sliced his bicep with one weapon and nicked his thigh with the other one.

Slater's hazel eyes narrowed. "There's more to you than meets the eye, Blanco."

I smiled. "Every day's a new surprise."

We kept testing each other. I got a few more wounds in, content to slowly bleed the giant out. Slater realized what my strategy was and decided to up the tempo and use his incredible speed to his advantage. He came at me swinging in a lightning-fast pattern. *Punch-punch-punch.* I dodged the first two, but his last quick blow caught me in the shoulder before I could sidestep away. The hard hit rocked my joint, and my arm and hand went numb from the sudden pressure. Owen's beautiful sword slipped from my fingers and thumped to the carpet. I darted forward and kicked it back and behind me, well out of Elliot Slater's reach. The speedy giant was dangerous enough by himself. If he got his hands on a sword, well, it wouldn't be good for me.

"Seems like you lost your toothpick," he mocked.

"And you've lost more blood," I replied, trying to shake the numbness out of my arm. "I'd say that makes us even."

Slater looked down at his shirt and pants. Blood covered both of them, and the rips that I'd made in the fabric made him look like a castaway whose clothes had been shredded by the elements. The giant smiled.

"Not for long, bitch," he replied. "Not for long—"

And then the worst thing in the world happened— Finn decided to get into the fight.

While I'd been circling around and nicking Slater, Finn had managed to get the chain holding his hands up off the peg above his head. Finn's hands were still bound together by the silverstone cuffs, but he used the heavy chain like it was a piece of garrote wire. He leaped up onto a sofa, threw the chain over Slater's head, and crawled up on the giant's back like a monkey.

I'd give Finn points for style, if not substance, because Slater immediately backpedaled and slammed him into the closest wall. Once, twice, three times in rapid succession. Finn groaned, and the chain slackened around Slater's neck. The giant threw off the metal and Finn, who fell to the floor, completely limp. Slater turned and stomped on Finn's ribs with his massive foot.

"I'll deal with you soon, you cocky bastard," he muttered.

I rushed forward, swinging the long sword above my head, but the giant was quicker than I was. So much fucking quicker. Slater used his massive forearm to block my attack, then punched me in the face. Pain and blood flooded my mouth. I wasn't anticipating the blow and staggered back, momentarily stunned. The giant pressed his advantage, charging at me. I managed to bring the sword up to hold him back, but it was only a temporary maneuver. Slater ripped the weapon out of my hands, tossed it to one side, and kept coming.

Since I was out of weapons, I reached for the only thing that I had left—my magic. My Stone power flooded through my veins, and I pulled the power up through my tissue and bones and muscles and joints, letting it pour over my skin, hardening it. Slater stopped short and eyed the gray, chiseled appearance of my skin.

"Fuck, you're an elemental too. Just full of tricks aren't we—" The giant stopped his muttering and glanced over his shoulder at Finn, then back at me. Knowledge shimmered in his hazel eyes. "Well, well, looks like Mab had the wrong sister all the while, didn't she? Just think how pleased she'll be when I tell her that *you're* the one with the Stone magic. What was the middle brat's name again? Oh, yeah—hello, *Genevieve.*"

Fuck. Of all the things that could have happened, Elliot Slater guessing my real identity had not been at the top of my list. Neither was the way the truth energized him.

Slater let out a loud roar and threw himself at me. This time I couldn't avoid him. The giant slammed me to the carpet and started punching me over and over and over again, just the way that I'd feared he would. He peppered my face and chest with blows, never slowing his cadence or losing his rhythm. *Punch-punch-punch.* Every sharp blow threatened to break through my hardened skin. My head already rang from his previous punches, and it took every thing I had to focus on my Stone power to keep myself from being beaten to death. I had no doubt that the giant could keep his promise to Finn. He could hit me for hours without tiring.

In desperation, I threw my hand to one side and reached for my Ice magic. A jagged knife formed in my palm, and I snapped my hand up, determined to drive the weapon into Slater's eye or neck or whatever the hell I could reach. But the giant saw the motion out of the corner of his eye. Once again, his quickness saved him. He grabbed my hand, stopping the forward motion, and glanced at the crude weapon that I had clenched between my fingers.

"An Ice knife. Cute," he said.

Then the bastard snapped my wrist.

It felt like someone had taken a hammer to my bones. I screamed with pain and fury. My control was slipping, and now it was only a matter of time before the giant killed me. But mainly, I screamed because Finn would die along with me. Because I'd brought my foster brother along for backup, and I'd failed miserably to protect him.

Elliot Slater drew back and smiled down at me. "Time to die, bitch—"

BOOM!

Something slammed into Slater's chest and stomach, rocking him back. Blood sprayed onto my chest and face, and the acrid smell of gunpowder filled the air.

BOOM!

Another sharp retort spat out, knocking Slater back and off me. Cradling my broken wrist, I immediately scooted away from the giant, who pulled himself up onto a silver-colored sofa. My head snapped around, looking for my mysterious benefactor.

Roslyn Phillips stood in the middle of the living room, a large shotgun cradled in her hands. The vamp popped two more red shells into the gun and raised it up. I didn't know where the hell she'd gotten the weapon or why she'd come back here when I'd told her to leave, but I was glad she had. Because the vamp had just saved my life.

Elliot Slater just looked at her in disbelief.

"What the fuck are you doing?" he snarled. "You're supposed to be upstairs, bitch."

"Sorry," Roslyn replied. "Gin was nice enough to arrange a change of scenery for me."

While Slater was distracted, I got to my feet and picked up one of Owen's swords. The pain from my many injuries threatened to overwhelm me, but I ground my teeth together and pushed the hot, searing sensations down into the pit of my stomach. I'd deal with the agony later. Right now, I had Roslyn to think about.

I moved to stand beside the other woman. The vamp gave me a curt nod, but she never took her eyes off Elliot Slater.

The giant's gaze flicked from Roslyn to me. His chest looked like hamburger meat—raw, uneven, bloody. A steady torrent of blood gushed from his wounds, not enough to kill him, but more than enough to weaken him. Roslyn was a better shot than I'd realized. Then again, it was hard to miss with a shotgun. Still, I wasn't going to complain. Because I would have been dead by now if not for the vampire.

Slater knew the score just as well as I did, so he changed tactics. "Come on, baby," Slater crooned to Roslyn. "Why are you doing this? I was just trying to teach you a lesson earlier. You know how much I care about you."

"Yeah," Roslyn spat out. "I know exactly how much you care about me, Elliot. The same way you cared about those other women you told me about tonight—all the other ones that you brought up here and raped and killed when you got tired of them."

Slater's chalky face tightened, and his hazel eyes narrowed with rage. "And you're just another notch on my belt, bitch. You really think you're going to get away with this? Mab Monroe will hunt you down and burn you to a crisp. You'll all die for this. Put down the gun, Roslyn, and I'll spare you. I'll tell Mab that you were just trying to help me. She'll believe me. She trusts me. If you don't, you know what will happen. Mab will come after you, and then after that sweet little niece and sister you love so much. Xavier too. You'll all be dead and burned and gone. Charred to fucking ashes by Mab."

Roslyn just stared at the giant, an unreadable expression on her face. I stood beside her, but I didn't say anything. This was the vamp's fight now. She had to stand up to Elliot Slater now, or what had happened these last few days would haunt her the rest of her life. More so, anyway, than it already would. Roslyn swayed side to side, and the shotgun shook in her trembling hands. For a moment, I thought that she was lost. That Slater had won this final round of cruel torture.

But then, Roslyn's face hardened underneath the blood and bruises, and a cold, terrible light filled her dark eyes. Her back straightened, her fingers tightened on the shotgun, and once again, I saw a glimmer of the hard-assed vampire that I remembered. The one who'd bared her fangs at me when I'd once dared to threaten her niece.

"Maybe I won't get away with it," Roslyn snarled. "But at least I'll have the satisfaction of knowing that you're dead. Go to hell, Elliot."

Roslyn stepped forward and fired the gun.

BOOM! BOOM!

Elliot Slater's head exploded in a mass of blood and brains and bone. The giant twitched once, fell to the floor, and was still.

❊ 29 ❊

Roslyn just stood there, staring down at what had been Elliot Slater's melon-size head. I put my hand on the smoking gun and slowly lowered it.

"It's over, Roslyn," I said in a soft voice. "He's dead now. You killed the bastard. You did it. You took care of him—forever. He's never going to bother you again. *Never.* Do you understand me?"

After a moment, Roslyn pulled her gaze away from the dead giant and looked up at me. Tears filled her eyes, and her hands started shaking once more. I pulled the gun out of her hands, let it fall to the floor, and gingerly, slowly, carefully, put my arms around her, not sure if I should hold her, touch her. Not sure how I could help her through this, but determined to try nonetheless. The vamp sobbed and screamed and pounded her fists against my back. I let her, just let her get it all out. All the pain and fear and misery. All the rage and helplessness and terror. All the relief and horror and sorrow.

I don't know how long we stood there, Roslyn screaming and crying, me just holding her. But eventually, her sobs quieted, and the vamp drew away from me.

"He might be dead, but he's right," she whispered. "I'll never get away with this. Mab Monroe will come after me, after my family, after Xavier."

"You're right," I replied. "You won't get away with it."

Roslyn gave me a look of pure horror.

"But then, you're not going to be the one who's done anything here tonight."

She frowned. "What do you mean?"

"This is what we're going to do," I said.

The torture was over—at least for now. I sat slumped in the chair, only the heavy ropes holding me upright. Sweat and tears dripped from my body like rain, and my hands felt like all the skin had been burned off them. Now I was glad that I was blindfolded so I couldn't see my hands. Couldn't see what a bloody, blistered mess had been made of them.

But the Fire elemental had gone, taking her cruel, pricking magic with her, vanished into some other part of the smoking house, leaving me tied where I was. Still, I knew that it wouldn't be long before she came back and finally killed me—

A scream echoed through the house. Faint and small and weak, but I still recognized the high pitch in her voice, still recognized the person that it belonged to.

"Bria," I whispered through my cracked lips.

Another scream sounded, and my breath caught in my

*throat. I strained my ears as hard as I could, listening, trying
to determine where the sound was coming from. Then the
cold realization hit me. The Fire elemental and her men.
They must have found Bria where I'd hidden her. That
was the only reason I could think of why my sister would be
screaming.*

At that horrible thought, new energy flooded my body.
I struggled against the heavy ropes once more, even though
I knew that it was no use, knew that I couldn't get free of
them. I ignored the searing pain in my hands and brought
my stiff, blistered fingers up to my face, managing to slip the
blindfold off my head. Smoke filled the room I was in like a
dark, somber fog.

A third and final scream erupted from somewhere, before
being abruptly cut off. I listened closely, but no more sounds
came. No more sounds. I knew what that meant. That the
Fire elemental had Bria—that my baby sister was being tortured even now.

At that awful thought, something deep inside me twisted
and snapped, like a taut bowstring finally being loosened.
This cold, great, terrible power filled me. More power, more
magic than I had ever felt before. And then I started to scream.

I screamed for everything that had happened tonight. Everything that I had lost. Everything that had been done to me
and my family. The power poured out of me the way my tears
and sweat had a moment ago.

And it felt good . . . right somehow.

I kept screaming, pushing everything that I had left into
that one echoing sound. All my pain. All my hurt and fear
and rage and desperation and helplessness.

I felt the stones respond to me. Felt my magic rip through

them like lightning, shocking them awake from their long, sonorous slumber, shattering them like they were made of the most fragile crystal. A deep rumble began in the earth below my feet, pushing upward, pushing outward. I couldn't control the power, the raw magic flowing out of me, and I didn't really want to. I just wanted to hurt someone, wanted to lash out at anyone who was left, hurt them like the Fire elemental had me and my family.

One by one, the stones above my head began to crumble and fall. My Stone magic spread outward, until the rest of the house's stones were just as unstable. I felt the stones in the other rooms begin to crack, fall, and slip from the ceilings and walls. Once it started, I couldn't stop it, couldn't stop them. I knew the stones would bring the rest of the smoking house down with them, down on top of the Fire elemental and all her men.

I screamed again, this time in cruel, dark pleasure at the cold, awesome power that I was wielding—

"Are you ready?" Finn asked, cutting into one of my darkest memories.

"Yeah," I replied, staring up at the rune before me on the stone wall. "I'm ready."

An hour later, Detective Bria Coolidge was the first one to arrive on the scene. Her city-issued gray sedan skidded to a stop in front of Elliot Slater's mountain mansion. Bria jumped out of the driver's seat. Xavier got out on the other side. Guns drawn, the two cops rushed to the front door, which I'd conveniently left open in anticipation of their arrival.

Five minutes later, Xavier came outside, cradling Roslyn in his massive arms. The giant had wrapped a blanket over her, and he gently placed her inside the back of the sedan. Xavier started to pull away, but Roslyn grabbed his hand. After a moment, Xavier knelt beside her. He didn't leave her side after that, and I knew that he wouldn't for the rest of the night. Maybe for the rest of their lives.

Bria also came back outside, her cell phone clamped to her ear. I couldn't hear her exact words, but the urgency of her tone drifted up to my hiding spot on top of the ridge overlooking the mansion, just inside the tree line. The same spot that I'd been in when Finn and I had first hiked up the mountain.

And that's when the show really started.

More cars carrying more cops arrived on the scene, swarming over the mansion like ants on a crust of honey-covered bread. Spotlights were erected, along with yards of yellow crime scene tape. It wasn't long before a news van pulled up and parked in the driveway. Then another, then another. I smiled. So far, everything was going according to plan.

Standing in the bloody wreckage of Elliot Slater's living room, I'd told Roslyn everything—about my murdered family, about Bria, but most especially about my plan to take down Mab Monroe—or die trying.

The vamp had studied me for several seconds before shaking her head. "You're one crazy bitch, you know that."

"Yeah, yeah, I'm suicidal," I'd replied. "So are you in or out?"

"In." Roslyn gave me a small smile.

And just like that, we were partners. Hell, maybe even friends too.

As I watched the scene before me, I crunched a couple of aspirin between my teeth and shifted the ice pack that I'd strapped onto my broken wrist before leaving the mansion. I had one more thing to do before I could slip away and go have Jo-Jo Deveraux heal me. Finn was already in the dwarf's capable hands, getting his many injuries taken care of.

Forty-five minutes after Bria and Xavier first arrived, a long, black limo pulled up to the very top of the driveway. Finally she was here. The limo driver got out and rushed to open the back door. A moment later, Mab Monroe stepped into view. The Fire elemental looked like she'd been out on the town. I could see the gleam of sequins on her forest green dress even from this distance. Her red hair looked like dull copper underneath the whirling, red and blue police lights, and her sunburst rune necklace flashed like a ring of golden fire around her neck, surrounding the bloody ruby in the center of the design.

At the sight of Mab, one of the cops, a senior captain whose name escaped me, walked over to her, bent down, and began speaking into the Fire elemental's ear. I made a mental note to tell Finn to get me the guy's name, since he was so obviously in Mab's pocket. He might be worth paying a visit to sometime in the near future.

Mab's face remained as smooth and expressionless as ever, but her eyes blackened, sucking in all the available light, instead of reflecting it back. The Fire elemental was pissed. The captain finished briefing Mab and stepped back, dry-washing his hands in nervousness. But instead of frying him on the spot, Mab looked across the driveway, where Roslyn sat, still wrapped in a blanket in the back of the police car. Then the Fire elemental stared at the cluster of media folks gathered behind the yellow crime scene tape. They were already screaming at the cops to tell them what was going on.

Which meant that it was time for me to make my presence known.

With my good hand, I pulled a small detonator out of my pocket and pressed the blue button on top. A second later, a silvery light flashed, bright enough to fill the whole mountaintop. Everyone screamed and shouted, except for Mab Monroe. She just shielded her eyes against the light and looked for the source of it. After a few seconds, the initial burst of light flared down into a shape burning with silver fire in the stone of Elliot Slater's mansion.

A circle surrounded by eight thin rays. A spider rune. The symbol for patience.

I'd never left my rune, my symbol, at the scene of the crime before. Assassins who did that were stupid and bound to be caught, sooner rather than later. But this was my plan, the crazy one that I'd told Finn, Sophia, and Jo-Jo about. My way to take the heat off Roslyn Phillips for Elliot Slater's messy demise. My way to protect Bria from being killed by one of Mab Monroe's henchmen. My way to get the Fire elemental to focus all her attention on me.

My way to finally declare war on Mab Monroe.

The spider rune continued to burn. I'd poured every last bit of magic that I'd had left into making the rune. Some small explosives from my duffel bag of supplies had helped me put enough juice in it to really make a statement. It looked just as large and ominous as I'd hoped.

My eyes sought out Bria in the crowd. My sister stood a little apart from the other cops, just staring up at the rune on the wall of the house, her mouth open in a combination of surprise and something else that I couldn't quite define or explain. Her eyes dropped to the rune-stamped rings on her finger, and she started twisting one of them around and around. I didn't have to guess which one.

After a few seconds, I pulled my gaze away from Bria. Right now, I needed to make sure that my message had been delivered.

So I reached into my pocket, pulled out my cell phone, and punched in the number that Finn had been gracious enough to provide for me. It rang twice before she picked it up.

"What?" Mab Monroe's silky voice barked in my ear.

"Enjoying the show?" I asked, using a bright, cheery tone to help disguise my voice. "I think it's quite something myself. But then again, I might be a little biased, since I'm the one who orchestrated the whole thing."

"Who the fuck is this? What the hell are you talking about?" Mab snarled.

"I'm talking about that very large rune you're looking at right now. I'm talking about me waltzing into Elliot Slater's little vista up here, putting a shotgun to his head, and pulling the trigger enough times so that his own mother wouldn't recognize the pulpy remains."

As I talked, I watched Mab. The Fire elemental's face didn't change, but her hand tightened around the phone. I hoped she didn't make it spontaneously combust before I was through talking with her. That would rather defeat the point of my little display here tonight.

"Who are you?" Mab asked, her voice dropping to a low, dangerous rasp in my ear. "You might as well tell me now, because I'm going to find you, bitch. And when I do, you're going to pay dearly for this stunt you've pulled."

"We've actually met before," I replied. "I have to say I'm rather crushed that you don't remember me. After all, I did proposition you in your own bathroom."

"Candy, the hooker," Mab said, referring to the trashy name that I'd used that night. "You're that blond hooker from my party. The one who killed Jake McAllister and buried Tobias Dawson in his own coal mine."

"Guilty as charged."

Silence. Below me, Mab paced back and forth in the driveway, thinking hard.

"What do you want?" she finally asked. "What's the point of this—this *display*? Why kill Elliot?"

"Because he was a rapist and a serial killer and deserved to be put down," I replied. "Because he got in my way. Because I was bored. Because I wanted to hurt you. Does it really matter? He's dead. He's not coming back. I made sure of that."

"And the others?" Mab asked. "Jake McAllister, Tobias Dawson. Did they get in your way too?"

"Something like that," I replied. "You can interpret my actions any way you like. I don't fucking care what conclusions you draw."

"Who's paying you to do this?" Mab's voice seethed with rage. "Is it Benson? Weston? Phillip Kincaid?"

I recognized the names that she spat out. More of Ashland's underworld power players, each of whom had his own problems with Mab Monroe. Each of whom would be delighted to see her dead so he could take over her piece of the Ashland pie.

"That's the beauty of this whole thing," I replied. "Most assassins are subcontractors, but me? I'm completely self-employed."

"So you have some grudge against me then, some vendetta, some score you want to settle. How tiresome. Why don't you just show yourself, and we can get on with things? There's no need to involve others in your drama."

I laughed. "Funny. And let your police buddies shoot me down? I don't think so. Now listen up, because I'm only going to say this once. This call is the only warning that you're going to get. You're finished in this town, Mab. You and all your cronies and minions. I'm putting you on notice. I'm going to take down your organization one piece, one player at a time, until you're the only one left. And then I'm coming for you."

Mab laughed. Even up here on the ridge, I could hear the deadly mirth in her voice. "I'm so going to enjoy hunting you down and killing you."

I rolled my eyes. That's what they all said.

"At least do me the courtesy of telling me what I did to you," Mab replied. "Because once I get my hands on you, *Candy*, you're not going to be in any position to speak, much less answer questions."

I smiled into the darkness. "Promises, promises, sugar. As for what you did to me, well, you helped make me what I am. So really, you've got no one but yourself to blame for the cold, cold wrath that I am about to rain down on you and yours."

"I'll find you, and when I do, you're going to die," Mab snarled. "Slowly. Painfully."

"That's another bit of beauty about being self-employed," I replied. "It's only me on my crusade. There's no one else to talk to. No one else to squeal, to bribe, to threaten. And I'm very, very good at being invisible. You won't find me until I want you to. But I did do you the courtesy of leaving my calling card, so to speak."

"That fucking spider rune?" Mab asked. "Why a spider rune? It's so simple, so weak."

I hesitated. Didn't she remember my spider rune medallion? How she'd tortured me with it all those years ago? Didn't she realize that I was Genevieve Snow, back from the dead?

Maybe not, I thought. After all, it had been seventeen years ago, and Mab had killed scores of people in the meantime. Hard to keep track of everyone, especially since I'd just been a weak, helpless kid back then. Besides, Mab had been concerned with Bria and my mother that night—not me. Hell, I probably wasn't the only person the Fire elemental had tortured who'd used a spider rune. It wasn't the most common symbol out there, but it wasn't unheard of either.

Maybe Mab had forgotten me. Maybe she just couldn't be bothered to remember right now, given the ugly surprise of Elliot Slater's death. Maybe she'd put it together later. Maybe she did remember and was just screwing with me. Didn't much matter at the moment. All that did matter was making sure my message was delivered loud and clear.

"Why a spider rune? Because it's the symbol for patience," I replied. "And I can wait however long I have to until I get you. So look at the rune, Mab, memorize it and remember it well. Because you'll be seeing it again real soon, sugar. Including the second before you die."

"You stupid, arrogant bitch—" she started.

I shut my phone. I'd said everything that I needed to. But evidently, Mab didn't like the way the conversation ended. Down in the driveway, the Fire elemental stared at her cell phone, a look of disbelief on her face. A second later, a ball of fire erupted in her hand, toasting the phone and flashing up into the night sky. The cops in front of the mansion immediately turned, hands going to their guns, wondering if this was some new threat. A few of the reporters screamed at the unexpected blast, and everyone took a few steps back.

I counted off the seconds in my head. Ten. Twenty. Thirty. Forty-five . . . The fire snuffed out of Mab's hand, and her fingers curled into a tight fist. After a moment, she took a breath, opened her fist, and clapped a bit of ash off her hands. Then the Fire elemental turned on her heel and got back into her waiting limo. Message received.

A cold smile curved my lips before I turned and slipped off into the dark woods.

And now, promises to keep. Promises to keep.

✷ 30 ✷

"Broken wrist, cracked ribs, and more cuts and bruises than I can count." Jo-Jo ticked off my many injuries one by one.

I shrugged. "It was a slow night."

I lay in one of the cherry red chairs at Jo-Jo Deveraux's beauty salon. After hiking back down the mountain, I'd driven myself over to the dwarf's house so she could heal me up once more. Sophia had already positioned herself above me. The Goth dwarf had her hands clamped on my arms, ready to hold me down so Jo-Jo could pour her healing Air elemental magic into my battered body.

In the next chair over, the already healed Finn murmured a quiet good-bye and snapped his cell phone shut.

"That was Xavier, checking in," he said. "Roslyn's given her statement to the cops. She said exactly what you told her too, Gin. She told the police that Elliot Slater kidnapped her from Northern Aggression and took her up to his mansion because of what she said about him on the riverboat. That he beat her before leaving her tied to the bed. They also found the clothes and mementoes of his other victims in that closet you rifled through, the other women that he raped and murdered."

I nodded. That was the cover story we'd gone with, a way for Roslyn to be the victim that she really was in all this, instead of a twisted scapegoat to cover up Slater's many crimes.

Finn drew in a breath. "Roslyn told them the rest of it too. That she heard lots of noise, lots of screaming, and then several gunshots. That a masked figure, a woman, came into the bedroom where she was at and untied her. That the woman told Roslyn that she was the Spider and to tell everyone in Ashland what she had done to Slater and his men. Then the woman vanished into the night. Roslyn passed out, and the next thing she knew, the cops were everywhere."

Finn stared at me, his eyes bright and green in his ruddy face. "It's already all over the news. They've dubbed you a vigilante, some sort of modern day Robin Hood. Except, of course, you kill people instead of just stealing from them."

I nodded again. That's exactly what I'd wanted to happen. To set myself up as a larger-than-life legend, to distract people from the fact that I was just as human and mortal as the rest of them. People looking for legends tended to ignore the mundane, like someone who owned a barbecue joint and took classes at the local community college.

"I'm proud of you, Gin," Jo-Jo said in a soft voice.

"Proud," Sophia echoed in her raspy voice.

"Why?" I replied. "For setting myself up as a target for Mab Monroe? According to Finn, she's already got her people trying to figure out who I am and what I really want from her. She thinks I'm working for someone who's trying to muscle in on her territory. One of her many enemies."

Jo-Jo shook her head. "No. For saving Roslyn Phillips, for putting the blame on yourself instead of on her."

I shrugged. "It was my fault Elliot Slater fixated on her in the first place. I owe her more than I can ever repay for that alone. Besides, there was just no other way to work it out. Otherwise, Mab would have come after Roslyn, even though she knew that the giant was stalking the vampire."

"Still," Jo-Jo said. "It's something that Fletcher Lane would have done. I'm sure wherever he is, he's looking down and smiling at you, Gin."

I thought of the old man, of the file of information that he'd left me on my murdered family, about the fact that he'd gotten Bria to come back to Ashland to look for me. Jo-Jo was right. I felt like I was following in Fletcher's footsteps in a weird sort of way. The old man had done pro bono jobs for folks. Now I was doing one for the whole city of Ashland.

"You know what?" I replied. "I think you're right."

I dropped my head back down against the headrest. "Now, use your mojo to get me up and around again. I need to go see a man about some swords."

Jo-Jo smiled. "With pleasure, darling. With pleasure."

I knocked on Owen Grayson's front door just as the sun rose over the eastern mountains. I'd just let go of the hammer knocker and stepped back when he threw open the door and stuck his head outside. Owen wore a baby blue shirt that made his eyes seem more blue than violet in the gray dawn. His clothes were rumpled, as if he'd spent the night in them.

Owen's eyes widened at the sight of me, and his violet gaze took in my disheveled appearance, bloody clothes, and the two swords that I held out in front of me. After Jo-Jo healed me, I could have gone home, changed, and showered. Probably should have.

But the blood was part of me, part of who I was and what I did. If things were going to work between Owen and me, he had to realize what being with me really meant—and he had to accept me for who and what I was. Donovan Caine hadn't been able to do that. Now I was going to see if Owen Grayson ever could.

"Hi there," I said in a low voice.

"Hi yourself," Owen replied. He looked at my bloody clothes once more before his eyes lifted to my face. "Long night?"

I shrugged. "You could say that. I wanted to come by and apologize. I think I might have scared Eva a little last night when I came over. But there was an emergency, and I didn't have time to explain things to her. I also brought your swords back."

I held out the weapons to him. They were just as bloody as my clothes. So I stood there, and I waited. Because now it was Owen's turn to make a decision.

He stared at me again, taking in my bloody black clothes before he slowly reached forward and took the swords out of my hand. Owen looked at first one weapon, then the other. Dried blood gleamed like dull red ink on both of the blades, making it ever so obvious what I'd done with them during the long night. That I'd used them to cut and hurt and wound and kill. It was one thing to make weapons. Quite another to see their brutal application in the harsh light of a new day.

For a moment I thought that Owen would turn around, go inside, and shut and lock the door on me. That's what Donovan Caine had done, only he'd been the one to leave instead of me. But to my surprise, Owen nodded his head, then looked up and gave me a small smile.

"Come on," he said in a low voice. "Let's get you cleaned up."

Owen stepped forward, slipped his warm hand into my cold one, and pulled me inside.

He led me back to his study, where he laid the weapons inside the door. Then, his hand still in mine, he walked us down another hallway. He opened a door, and I stepped into what was obviously his bedroom. My stomach tightened with anticipation.

But instead of leading me over to the bed with its black silk sheets, Owen took my hand once more and pulled me into the next room, the master bath. I eyed the gray marble and granite that made up the enormous room. The shower was large enough for four people and even came complete with its own seats, each one surrounded by several jets of water. A place to relax and let the scalding streams pound into your muscles, if you so wished. All around me, the smooth stones whispered of water, heat, relaxation.

Owen Grayson didn't say a word as he reached into the

shower and turned on the water. I started to take off my blood-crusted vest, but he stepped in front of me.

"Let me," he said.

He slowly unzipped the silverstone vest and gently dropped it on the floor. His strong, capable hands pulled my black turtleneck up out of my jeans, and I obediently raised my arms over my head so he could get it off me. My boots and socks were next, followed by my jeans. Owen did all the work, wrestling with the buttons and peeling the stiff, sticky, blood-soaked fabric away from my skin. I stared at him the whole time he stripped me. Owen's violet eyes burned brighter with every piece of clothing he removed. The desire in his gaze matched my own.

Finally, I stood there in my black bra and panties. Owen stared at me for several seconds, then removed those too, his hands gliding down my blood-flecked skin in a way that made me shiver. When I was naked, he took my hand again, guided me over to the steamy shower, and directed me to stand under a stream of water. Pink rivulets ran down my body and swirled away down the drain as the water sluiced the blood from my skin.

Behind me, I heard the wisp of more clothing and the hiss of a zipper. I smiled and reached for a bar of soap in a recess built into a wall. A few seconds later, Owen stepped into the shower behind me.

"Let me," he said again.

I turned, and he stood there naked in front of me, the distinctive foil packet of a condom in his hand. Of course, I took my little white pills so there wouldn't be any unwanted consequences. Still, nothing wrong with extra protection.

My eyes drifted over his tall frame, toned biceps, solid chest with its dark hair that ran all the way down his stomach to his cock. Even without his designer suits, Owen radiated strength and confidence. Mmm.

Owen put the condom in the spot where the soap had been. Then he took the ivory bar from me and lathered it up between his hands. Our eyes locked and held for a moment before he stepped forward and began to wash me. My face, chest, stomach. Owen slowly scrubbed the blood from my skin and hair the way someone might wash dirt off a child. But a fire began building between my thighs at his gentle ministrations. A fire that I knew was finally going to be quenched today.

When Owen finished washing me, I stepped under the hot spray of water, rinsed the soap from my skin, and finger-combed my wet hair. He stood there in the rising steam, just watching me with his violet eyes, the grin on his face telling me how much he liked what he saw. I tugged the bar of soap from his hand and smiled.

"My turn."

I washed him much the same way he'd washed me. Slowly, carefully, gently, showing him the same respect that he'd shown me. The same care and tenderness. When I finished, he stepped in a spray of water, watching the soap bubbles foam up and swirl down the drain.

"Now that we're both clean," I said in a sly tone. "Why don't we do something dirty?"

Another smile tugged at Owen's lips, softening the slashing scar on his chin. "I thought you'd never ask."

We moved toward each other and met in the middle of the shower. I threaded my hands in his slick hair and pulled his mouth down to mine. Our lips met in a kiss that was as gentle as the water cascading over our bodies—and that quickly turned into one of white-hot passion, desire, and need.

Owen growled low in his throat and backed me up against the shower wall. His hands were everywhere. My neck, breasts, stomach, hips, back. Kneading, caressing, teasing. Just like mine were all over him. Neck, chest, stomach, ass. Kneading, caressing, teasing. We couldn't get enough of each other, couldn't explore each other's bodies quickly enough to satisfy this hunger, this need that flared between us.

The slow burn between my thighs turned into a steady, building throb. Our movements became even quicker, more frantic. Our hands and caresses harder, longer, more intense. Owen's tongue drove into my mouth, only to retreat when I was breathless. I happily returned the favor. He buried his head against my shoulder, nibbling at the delicate skin of my throat. I nipped his earlobe with my teeth. Owen's hot lips slid lower, closing over first one nipple, then the other, as he sucked and scraped them with his teasing teeth. I moaned at the hot sensations pumping through my body and hiked my leg up, drawing him closer and settling his cock against me.

I slid my hand down between Owen's legs, stroking the hard length of him, lightly circling my nails over his rigid tip. He rocked his hips against me, ratcheting my desire up that much more.

"There you go again," I rasped. "Being a tease."

Owen laughed. "Why should I stop when teasing you is so much fun?"

One of his hands caressed my breast. The other dipped lower, his wet fingers trailing down my stomach and then into the very center of me, going in and out in a quick, elegant dance.

"Enough teasing," I muttered. "Get over here."

I grabbed the condom out of the wall recess, ripped it open with my teeth, and pushed Owen down onto his back on the shower floor. Once he put the condom where it belonged, I climbed on top of him, ready to get on with things. But Owen pulled me down and rolled me over so that I was on the bottom.

I arched an eyebrow. "I prefer to be on top, remember?"

"Next time," he whispered, parting my thighs and sliding deep into me.

I groaned at the sensation of him filling me. I wrapped my legs around his waist, and Owen started that steady, age-old rhythm.

We bucked and thrashed against each other, each one trying to bring as much pleasure, as much feeling, as possible to the other. Our rhythm built and built until we reached that ultimate peak, our hoarse cries drowned out by the steady hiss of the hot water around us.

⁕ 31 ⁕

After we finished in the shower, we wrapped ourselves in thick, terrycloth robes and headed into the kitchen. I made Owen sit while I cooked us an enormous breakfast. Spicy southwestern omelets, light-as-air blueberry pancakes, thick slabs of Canadian bacon, a sweet, mango-strawberry-kiwi fruit punch. Everything was done to perfection and tasted even better than it looked.

"And you cook too," Owen murmured, staring at the platters on the table. "Is there anything you don't do, Gin?"

"I don't know," I replied in a teasing tone. "Ask me, and we'll see."

His violet eyes darkened with heat.

We sat there in companionable silence for several minutes eating breakfast and enjoying each other's company. After we finished our first round of food, Owen looked at me.

"You want to tell me about it?" he asked in a quiet tone. "I've already seen the version on the early morning news. Quite a display you put on up there on the mountaintop."

"That's me," I said in a wry voice. "A real showwoman."

I told him everything. The problems Roslyn Phillips had been having with Elliot Slater, the giant threatening to kill Roslyn's family unless she came to him, my rush to save her. The only thing I changed was the ending, taking credit for killing Slater instead of laying that at Roslyn's feet. The vamp had been through enough already.

Owen sat there, chewing his pancakes, and listening to my bloody tale. "So is it over then?" he asked. "Are you back to being retired now?"

I looked at Owen, with his rumpled black hair and solid chest peeking out of the gap in his white robe. It would be so easy to lie to him. To say of course it was over now. That I was going to spend the rest of my days slinging barbecue down at the Pork Pit. But my lie wouldn't last long. Owen had his own sources of information, just like Finn did. The next time I took out someone in Mab's organization and left my spider rune calling card, Owen would hear about it sooner or later. But more important than that was the simple fact that I didn't want there to be any lies between us.

"No," I said. "It's not over. It's just getting started. I'm going after Mab. Her whole organization, all her flunkies, all the officials and cops she's got in her pocket. And when I've chipped away enough of her protective shell, then I'm going after her."

Owen stared at me. "And why do you want to do all

that, Gin? Why would you risk yourself like that? What did Mab do to you?"

I drew in a deep breath. "The bitch murdered my family. Among other things."

I didn't say anything else. Didn't give Owen the details of my family's murder or who I really was or the fact that Mab had her sights set on killing Bria for magic that she didn't even have. I just wasn't ready to reveal that much of myself to him. Not now, maybe not ever. If Owen even gave me that kind of chance. If he even gave us that kind of chance.

I drew in another breath and readied myself for the rest of my speech. Because as enjoyable as our time together in the shower had been, great sex wasn't enough for me to put Owen in danger—not the kind of danger that Mab Monroe presented.

"This morning was wonderful," I said. "But given what I did last night, given what I plan to do in the coming weeks, if you don't want things to go any further between us, I'll understand, Owen. Going after Mab and her organization will be dangerous, not only for me but for the people I care about as well. Because if Mab finds out who I am before I want her to, she'll come after everyone I know with everything she's got. I know you have Eva to think about. Believe me, I know how important sisters can be, how important Eva is to you. I'll understand if you don't want to take the risk."

Owen stared at me for several seconds, his eyes dark in his strong face. "I appreciate your concern, but I'm a big boy, Gin. I can take care of myself. Eva too. I've been doing it most of my adult life. Besides," his mouth twisted. "Your family isn't the only one that Mab killed."

A pain I was all too familiar with filled his face. I reached over and put my hand on top of his. "Oh, Owen. I'm so sorry. How did it happen?"

He shrugged. "My father was a gambler. He got in too deep to a bookie who worked for Mab. My father was a big, strong guy. The bookie was scared of him, so he called in Mab for reinforcement. She torched our house with the four of us in it to send a message to the bookie's other customers to pay up—or else. Eva and I got out. Our parents didn't."

Owen lapsed into silence, lost in his fiery memories of the past. We just sat there, my hand on top of Owen's larger one. We didn't say anything for almost a minute.

"So whatever you want to do, however you want to fight Mab Monroe, I'm with you," Owen finally said in a low voice. "Because the bitch killed my parents too. But mainly because I'm falling for you, Gin. I know what you do, what kind of violence you're capable of. But also, I know what kind of woman you are."

His words startled me more than anything had in a long time. "And what kind of woman would that be?"

Owen stared at me. "Someone who's passionate and full of life. Someone who's funny and smart. But mostly, someone who'll do whatever the fuck it takes to protect the people she cares about. That's what I like about you, Gin. That's what I admire about you. That's what draws me to you." His mouth quirked up in a smile. "Well, that and the knives. Did I ever mention that I think weapons are sexy?"

A warm, soft feeling blossomed in my chest, a little

tingle of possibilities, of what could be between Owen and me—something far greater than I'd ever dreamed of.

At his suggestive tone, I arched an eyebrow, got up, and sat down in his lap. "Weapons are sexy, huh?" I whispered, my lips just touching his. "Care to frisk me to see if I'm carrying any right now?"

Owen's eyes glittered with violet desire. "I'd love to."

A minute later, Eva Grayson walked into the kitchen in her flannel pajamas to find Owen and me still kissing—among other more prurient things. She immediately clapped her hand over her eyes and started backing out of the kitchen.

"Oops! Owen, sorry, I didn't realize that you had an overnight guest—" Eva peered through her fingers at me. "Wait a minute. Gin? Is that you?"

I pulled my robe closed. "In the flesh."

Eva's eyes narrowed, and she looked from me to her brother and back again. "A sleepover. Cozy." Her gaze flicked to the food on the table. "I take it you're staying through breakfast then?"

I stared at Owen. "Yeah," I said. "I think I'll be here awhile."

Three days later, just after eleven, I was back at the Pork Pit, sitting behind the cash register reading the morning edition of the *Ashland Trumpet*. The headline across the front page read *Police still searching for vigilante*. The story was yet another follow-up piece about the events that had transpired at Elliot Slater's mountain mansion.

"Well, at least they're not calling you an assassin," Finnegan Lane said, reading the headline upside down.

Finn was taking a break from his banking to have an early lunch at the Pork Pit before the usual noontime crowd hit. Sophia Deveraux had already poured Finn his second cup of chicory coffee and was brewing him another pot to take back to the bank.

I shrugged. "It's only a matter of time before it spins the other way and I'm back to being a cold-blooded killer."

"We'll see," Finn replied. "It might take longer than you think."

"Why do you say that?"

"I've had my ear on the underground buzz," Finn replied, taking a sip of his coffee. "Word is that Mab Monroe is looking high and low for you and that she's got all her boys and girls on red alert. But there are also a lot of other people who are interested in seeing if you can pull it off. If you can actually take down Mab and her organization. Obviously, the other power players in town are extremely interested in the outcome. Phillip Kincaid being the most vocal of those. But there are lots of little folks talking too, moms and pops that have felt Mab's heat over the years. You've got the beginnings of a major fan base out there."

"Great," I replied in a wry tone. "Just what I need. Celebrity."

"It can have its uses," Finn replied.

The bell over the front door chimed, and my first real customer of the day strolled in—Roslyn Phillips. Today the vamp wore an elegant lavender sweater over a pair of slim-fitting, gray wool pants. A bit of matching lipstick brightened her beautiful face, and her silver glasses flashed in the morning sunlight. You'd never know by looking at her that Roslyn had almost been beaten to death. Thanks to Jo-Jo Deveraux's healing skills, the vamp had completely recovered from her ordeal at the hands of Elliot Slater. On the outside, at least.

I knew that Roslyn would always bear the scars on the inside—raw, bloody wounds that would scab over but perhaps never fully heal. My heart still ached for the vampire and everything that she had been through because of me, and I knew that it always would. If I could have, I would have killed Elliot Slater for her all over again. And again. And again.

But Roslyn seemed to be holding her own. And Finn had told me that Sophia, of all people, had talked at length to the vamp about what had happened to her. Finn didn't know any of the details, but he said that whatever Sophia had told Roslyn, it had seemed to help the other woman. The vamp certainly looked more like her old, confident, sophisticated self today than she had the last time I'd seen her—bloody in the back of a police car while everyone gawked at her.

Whether she realized it herself or not, Roslyn Phillips was one of the strongest people that I'd ever had the pleasure to know. And one day, I hoped she would do me the honor of calling me her friend, despite the hell that I was partially responsible for inflicting on her. I hoped Roslyn could forgive me for it someday—even though I knew that I'd never forgive myself.

Roslyn came over to the counter, sat down next to Finn, and smiled at the two of us. "Gin, Finn." The vampire leaned forward and waved her hand at Sophia.

"Hmph." Sophia returned Roslyn's greeting with her usual grunt, but the Goth dwarf flashed the vampire a tiny smile before turning back to the coffeepot.

"Roslyn," I said. "What can I do for you?"

"Nothing. Absolutely nothing. I'm just here to meet Xavier for lunch."

I raised an eyebrow. "Couldn't resist my cooking?"

Another small smile tugged her lips, though it didn't quite banish the dark shadows in her eyes. "Something like that."

We sat and chatted about nothing of consequence. We all knew that it was too soon to talk about anything else, and I didn't want to do or say anything to upset Roslyn.

So Roslyn told us that her sister Lisa and her niece Catherine had finally returned from their beach vacation now that Elliot Slater was dead and the coast was clear, so to speak. She promised to bring them by sometime. I told the vamp that any meal with her family at the Pork Pit was on the house.

About five minutes after Roslyn arrived, the bell over the front door chimed again, and Xavier walked inside. The giant headed straight for Roslyn, and the two of them smiled at each other, their feelings shining in their eyes for everyone to see.

"Excuse us," Roslyn said, following Xavier over to one of the booths by the windows.

I watched the two of them. Xavier was careful with Roslyn, not getting too close to her, putting his hand next to hers on top of the table, but not actually touching her. For her part, Roslyn made an effort, looking straight at the giant, not taking her hand off the table when he edged his a little closer to hers. It was still a work in progress, but somehow I thought they would be okay, despite the last few horrible days the two of them had been through.

Xavier hadn't come to the restaurant by himself. About two minutes later, Detective Bria Coolidge walked through the front door of the Pork Pit. My sister wore her usual long navy coat over a sweater, jeans, and boots. Her gold detective's badge glinted on the waistband of her jeans. Bria waved at Xavier and Roslyn, then sat in a booth by herself in the back of the restaurant to give the couple their privacy. Bria picked up the menu on the tabletop and began to read it.

Finn nudged me with his hand. "Go talk to her," he whispered. "You have to start somewhere with her, Gin. Or else everything we've gone through, everything we're going to do is for nothing."

I stared across the restaurant at my sister. So close, yet so far away. But Finn was right. I had to start somewhere with Bria. There'd been enough antagonism and lies between us already. I wanted to establish some sort of friendly relationship between us, wanted a fresh slate to at least try to get to know my sister. Might as well try to start wiping away the grime today.

I looked at Finn with his bright green eyes. "Have I ever told you how much I hate it when you're right?"

Finn just smirked into his coffee cup.

I rolled my eyes at him, then got to my feet and walked back to her booth.

"Hello, detective," I said in a pleasant voice.

Bria looked up at me and nodded her head. "Ms. Blanco."

"Please, call me Gin," I replied. "Everyone does."

She stared at me a moment longer, then nodded. "All right. Gin. Like the liquor, right?"

I blinked. That was usually my line when I was telling people my name. "Yeah. Where did you hear that?"

She shrugged. "Xavier told me you spell it like that. Seemed like an easy way to remember it."

"Sure." I pulled my pen and pad out of my back pocket. "So what can I get you?"

Bria bit her lip and looked at me. "Actually, I'm here to eat a bit of crow. That's why I tagged along with Xavier today. I was hard on you the last time we talked, and I just wanted to apologize. Roslyn told me that you were just trying to help her, that you really had no idea where she was or what was happening to her. I'm sorry if I upset you."

I waved my hand. "Bygones, detective. Elliot Slater got what he deserved, and Roslyn is safe now, as you can see."

Bria's blue eyes flicked to Roslyn and Xavier, who had their heads close together and were talking softly to each other.

"Any clues as to this person who killed him?" I asked. Finn had his ways of getting information, and I had mine. "What are they calling him again?"

"Her," Bria corrected in an absent tone. "It's a her. The press is calling her the Spider, because of the rune that she left at the crime scene. The one carved into the wood and stone on Elliot Slater's mountain mansion."

For a moment, Bria stared out the window, watching the flow of pedestrians and traffic on the cold street. Then she reached down and slowly turned one of the rings on her left index finger around. The top ring. The one stamped with the spider rune. My ring. I wondered what my baby sister was thinking about, what she was remembering, what she was hoping for.

"Well," I replied, cutting into her thoughts. "I hope you catch her."

A grim smile stretched across Bria's face, tightening her beautiful features. "Oh, I'm going to find her, Gin. Make no mistake about that. What I do with her then, well, I don't know just yet." She murmured the last sentence under her breath.

I smiled at her. "Well, I'm sure you'll have better luck on a full stomach. So what can I get you, detective? Everything's on the house today, in honor of Roslyn's recovery."

Bria ordered a cheeseburger with all the fixings and fries. I helped Sophia cook up her order and also grabbed a piece of blackberry cobbler—today's special dessert. Several minutes later, I carried everything back over to the table and put it down.

Bria eyed the pie. "That looks wonderful. Blackberry's my favorite."

I knew that, even if I couldn't tell her so. "I hope you enjoy it."

I started to turn away from her, to go back and hide behind the cash register like usual, but Finn gave me a small wave of his hand, urging me onward. So I turned back to the table and smiled once more.

"Care if I sit?" I said. "It's a bit slow yet, and since it looks like Xavier's going to be one of my regular customers, I'd like to get to know you a little better, detective."

Bria seemed taken aback by my strange request, but

she waved her hand at the opposite side of the booth. "Sure. I hate to eat alone anyway."

So I slid into the booth and watched Bria take a bite of her blackberry pie. Her eyes rolled back in her head.

"Heaven," she replied. "Simply heaven."

I grinned. "If you think that's good, you should try my chocolate-chip pound cake."

Bria gave me a small smile. "I'll be sure and do that next time I'm in."

I nodded, and we didn't speak for a few moments.

"You know, I finally figured it out, Gin," Bria said. "Why you seem so familiar to me."

I had to work very hard to do nothing but keep blinking steadily at her. "Oh?"

"Yeah," she said, taking another bite of her pie. "You look a lot like my college roommate. Same dark hair, same pale coloring. Her family had a restaurant too. Even your blue apron is the same as hers. I loved that place. I spent as much time there as I could."

She gave me another smile, and I forced out a soft chuckle.

"Imagine that. So tell me, detective. Where are you from?"

I asked the question to change the conversation, of course. To keep Bria from thinking about who else I might look like or remind her of. But I also really wanted to know the answer. I still hadn't looked at the folder of information that Finn had compiled on Bria. For the past few days, I'd been more concerned with how Roslyn was coping and what Mab Monroe was doing to try to find me. And now, with Bria sitting here across from me, I realized that I didn't really want to look at the information. I wanted Bria to tell me herself, the way a friend would.

The way a sister would.

"Please," she said. "Call me Bria. Everyone does."

I nodded again and smiled. "So tell me, Bria. Where are you from?"

As Bria began to talk about her time in Savannah, Georgia, I relaxed against the booth. A small smile pulled up my lips, and my gray eyes flicked to the wall where a bloodstained copy of *Where the Red Fern Grows* was mounted, along with a picture of two young men about to go fishing. Jo-Jo Deveraux was right. Wherever Fletcher Lane was—heaven, hell, or someplace in between—I think he would have been happy with things right now.

With Roslyn's help, I'd struck a major blow against Mab Monroe and her organization. It would take her a while to find someone to replace Elliot Slater, and the other sharks were already sniffing around, sensing weakness in the Fire elemental for the first time ever.

And here I was, Gin Blanco, Genevieve Snow, whatever I was calling myself these days. Sitting here in my favorite place in the world with the baby sister that I'd thought was dead. It was something of a miracle.

Oh, things weren't perfect. Mab Monroe was moving heaven and earth, at least what passed for it in Ashland, to try to find me. And if she did, well, there would be hell to pay. The Fire elemental and I were going to dance one day very soon, and I was going to be ready. I was finally going to kill the bitch who'd taken so much from me with just a wave of her hand.

I had no doubt that Bria had figured out that the Spider was really her long-lost big sister, Genevieve Snow. That Bria was going to do whatever she could to find me. What she did when she discovered the truth, whether baby sister turned me in to the cops or did something else, well, I just didn't know. But Bria was here, safe and warm in my restaurant, eating my food, and telling me about herself in a real, personal way that I wouldn't get from Finnegan Lane's file on her.

It wasn't the relationship that I had in mind with my sister. Wasn't what I had dreamed of ever since I'd learned that she was alive, but it was a place to start. That was all that I could ask for now. And it was much more than I deserved. I knew that. And I knew that I had Fletcher Lane to thank for it all. The old man was the one who'd brought Bria to Ashland. Now it was up to me to do the rest. Somehow I would.

And finally, there was Owen Grayson. That morning at his house in the shower and then afterward in the kitchen; Owen had accepted me—all of me—in a way that Donovan Caine never had. Were Owen and me forever? Could I care about him? Could we build some sort of life together? I didn't know, but I was strangely eager to find out, which is why Owen would be waiting for me at his place later on tonight.

It was enough for now.

Turn the page for an excerpt of the
next thrilling Elemental Assassin novel,

Tangled Threads

Jennifer Estep

Coming soon from Pocket Books

* 1 *

"Are you going to kill this guy? Or are we just going to sit here all night?"

"Patience, Finn," I murmured. "We've only been in the car an hour."

"Longest hour of my life," he muttered.

I arched an eyebrow and looked over at Finnegan Lane, my partner in crime for the night. Most nights, actually. Just after ten o'clock a few days before Christmas, and we were sitting in the darkened front seat of Finn's black Cadillac Escalade. An hour ago, Finn had parked the car in a secluded, out-of-the-way alley that overlooked the docks fronting the Aneirin River. We'd been sitting here, and Finn had been grousing, ever since.

Finn shifted in his seat, and my gray eyes flicked over him. The wool fabric of his thick coat outlined his broad shoulders, although a black watchman's cap covered his walnut-colored hair. His eyes were a bright green even in the semidarkness, and the shadows did little to hide the square handsomeness of his face.

Most women would have been glad to have been in such close quarters with Finnegan Lane. With his easy smile and natural charm, Finn would already have had the majority of them in the backseat, pants off, legs up, steam covering the windows as the car rocked back and forth.

Good thing I wasn't most women.

"Come on, Gin," Finn whined again. "Go stick a couple of your knives in that guy and leave your rune for Mab to find so we can get out of here."

I stared out the car window. Across the street, bathed in the golden glow of a streetlight, the guy in question continued to unload wooden crates from the small tugboat that he'd pulled up to the dock forty-five minutes ago. Even from this distance I could hear the warped, weathered boards creak under his weight as the river rushed on by beneath them.

The man was a dwarf—short, squat, stocky, sturdy—and dressed in black clothes practically identical to the ones that Finn and I were wearing. Jeans, boots, sweater, jacket. The sort of anonymous outfit you'd wear to go skulking about late at night, especially in this rough Southtown neighborhood, and most especially when you didn't want anyone else to see what you were up to.

Or were planning to kill someone, like I was tonight. Most nights, actually.

I rubbed my thumb over the hilt of the silverstone knife that I held in my lap. The metal glinted dully in the darkness of the car, and the weight of the weapon felt cold and comforting, the way it always did to me. The knife rested lightly on the spider rune scar embedded in my palm.

It would be easy enough to give in to Finn's whining; to slip out of the car, cross the street, creep up behind the dwarf, cut his throat, and shove his body off the dock and into the cold river below. I probably wouldn't even get that much blood on my clothes, if I got the angles just right.

Because that's what assassins did. That's what I did. Me. Gin Blanco. The assassin known as the Spider, one of the best around.

But I didn't get out of the car and get on with things like Finn wanted me to. Instead, I sighed. "He hardly seems worth the trouble. He's a flunkie, just like all the others I've killed these past two weeks. Mab will hire someone else to take his place before they even dredge his body out of the river."

"Hey, you were the one who decided to declare war on Mab Monroe," Finn pointed out. "Correct me if I'm wrong, but I believe that you were rather eager to kill your way up to the top of the food chain until you got to her. You said it would be *fun*."

"That was six hits ago. Now I'd just like to kill Mab and give everyone in Ashland an early Christmas present, myself included." My turn to grouse.

But Finn was right. A few weeks ago, a series of events had led me to officially declare war on Mab, and now I was dealing with the fallout—and the tedious boredom of it all.

Mab Monroe was the Fire elemental who ran the southern metropolis of Ashland as if it were her own personal kingdom. To most folks, Mab was a paragon of virtue, a Fire elemental who used her magic, business connections, and money to fund worthwhile charity projects throughout the city. But those of us who strolled through the shady side of life knew Mab for what she really was—the head of a Mob-like empire that included everything from gambling and drugs to prostitution and kidnappings. Murder, extortion, torture, blackmail, beatings. Mab ordered all those and more, practically on a daily basis. But the Fire elemental was so wealthy, so powerful, so strong in her magic that no one dared to stand up to her.

Until me.

I had a special reason to hate Mab—she'd murdered my mother and older sister when I was thirteen. And she'd been planning to do the same thing to me and my baby sister, Bria. But first, Mab had decided to capture and torture me that fateful night so long ago. Which is how I'd ended up with a pair of matching scars on my hands.

I put my knife down long enough to rub first one scar, then the other, with my fingers. A small circle surrounded by eight thin rays was branded into each one of my palms. A spider rune. The symbol for patience. My assassin name.

And one that Mab Monroe was now seeing everywhere she went.

For the past two weeks I'd been stalking Mab's men, getting a feel for her operation, seeing exactly what kind of illegal pies she had her sticky fingers in. And along the way, I'd picked off some of her minions when I caught them doing things that they shouldn't do, hurting people that they shouldn't hurt. A twist of my knife, a slash of my blade, and Mab Monroe had had one less soldier in her little army of terror.

Killing her men hadn't been hard, not for me. I'd spent the last seventeen years being an assassin, being the Spider, until I'd retired a few months ago. Certain skills you just never forgot.

Normally, though, when I killed someone, I left nothing behind. No fingerprints, no weapon, no DNA. But with Mab's men, I'd purposefully drawn the image of my spider rune at every scene, close to every body that I left behind. Taunting her. Letting Mab know exactly who was responsible for messing up her plans and that I was determined to pick her empire apart, one body at a time if I had to.

Which is why Finn and I were now sitting in the dark, down by the docks, in this dangerous Southtown neighborhood. Finn had gotten a tip from one of his sources that Mab had a shipment of drugs or some other illegal paraphernalia coming into Ashland tonight. As the Spider, I'd decided to come down here and see what I could do to foul up Mab's plans once more, thumb my nose at her, and generally piss her off.

"Come on, Gin," Finn said, cutting into my musings. "Make a move already. The guy's alone. We would have seen his partner by now, if he'd had one."

I looked at the dwarf. He'd finished unloading the

boxes from the tugboat and was now busy hauling them over to a van parked at the end of the dock.

"I know," I said. "But something about this just doesn't seem right."

"Yeah," Finn muttered. "The fact that I can't feel my feet anymore and you won't let me turn the heater on."

"Drink your coffee, then. It'll make you feel better. It always does."

For the first time tonight, a grin spread across Finn's face. "Why, I think that's an excellent idea."

Finn reached down and grabbed a large metal thermos from the floorboard in the backseat. He cracked open the top, and the caffeine fumes of his chicory coffee filled the car. The rich smell always reminded me of his father, Fletcher Lane, my mentor, the one who'd taught me everything that I know about being an assassin. The old man had drunk the same foul brew as his son before he'd died earlier this year. I smiled at the memory and the warmth it always stirred in me.

While Finn drank his coffee, I stared out at the scene before me once more. Everything seemed still, quiet, cold, dark. But I couldn't shake the feeling that something was wrong. That something was just slightly off about this whole setup. Fletcher Lane had always told me that nobody ever got dead by waiting just a few more minutes. His advice had kept me alive this long, and I had no intention of disregarding it now.

Once again my eyes scanned the area. Deserted street. A few dilapidated buildings hugging the waterfront. The black ribbon of the Aneirin River in the distance. The pale boards of the dock. A lone light flickering over the dwarf's head—

My eyes narrowed, and I focused on the light; the bright, intact light burning like a beacon in the dark night. Then I looked up and down the street, my gaze flicking from one iron post to the next. Every other light on the block was busted out. Not surprising. This was Southtown, after all, the part of Ashland that was home to gangbangers, vampire prostitutes, and junkie elementals strung out on their own magic and hungry for more. People would just as soon kill you as look at you here. Not a place you wanted to linger, even during daylight hours.

So I wasn't surprised that the streetlights had been broken, probably long ago, by the rocks, beer bottles, and other trash that littered the street. What did surprise me was that there was one still burning—the one right over the van that the dwarf was now packing his boxes into.

How . . . *convenient*.

"You might as well get comfortable," I said, staring at the lone light. "Because we're going to be here a while longer."

Finn just groaned.

We didn't have long to wait. Less than fifteen minutes later, the dwarf finished loading the last of his boxes into the van. Once I started watching him—really watching him—I realized that he'd been taking his sweet time about things; moving slower than a normal person would have, especially considering the bitter cold that frosted Ashland tonight. But then again, this was far from the innocent scene that it appeared to be.

Now the dwarf stood beside the van, smoking a cigarette and staring into the darkness with watchful eyes.

"What's he doing?" Finn asked, taking another sip of coffee. "If the man had any sense, he'd crank up the heater in that van and get out of here."

"Just wait," I murmured. "Just wait."

Finn sighed and drank some more of his chicory brew.

Five more minutes passed before a flash of movement along the dock caught my eye.

"There," I said, and leaned forward. "Right fucking *there*."

A figure stepped out from behind a small, squat shack at the far end of the dock that jutted out into the river.

Finn jerked upright and almost spilled his coffee on the leather seats. "Where the hell did he come from?"

"Not he," I murmured. "She."

The woman strolled down the dock toward the dwarf. Despite the darkness, the single streetlight still burning let me get a good look at her. She was petite and slender, about my age, thirty or so. She had a short bob of glossy black hair, held back with some sort of headband, and her features had an Asian flavor to them—porcelain skin, expressive eyes, delicate cheekbones. She also wore black from head to toe, just like the rest of us.

I frowned. No woman in her right mind would walk through this neighborhood alone at night. Hell, not many would dare to do it during the day—much less wait more than an hour in some run-down shack on a

December night when the temperature hovered in the low twenties.

Unless she had a very, very good reason for being there.

And I was beginning to think that I knew exactly what that reason was—me.

The woman reached the dwarf, who crushed out his cigarette. She said something to the man, who just shrugged his shoulders. The woman turned and scanned the street, much the same way that I'd been doing for the last hour. But I knew she couldn't see us, given where we were parked. The Dumpster sitting at the end of the narrow alley in front of Finn's car screened us from her line of sight.

After another thirty seconds of looking, the woman turned back to the dwarf and advanced on him. For a moment, he looked confused. Then startled. Then his eyes widened, and he turned and started running away from her.

He got maybe five steps before the woman lifted her right hand—and green lightning shot out of her fingertips.

Finn jerked, almost spilling his coffee again. Even I blinked at the sudden, powerful flash of light.

The dwarf arched his back and screamed, his harsh cry echoing down the deserted street, as the lightning slammed into his body. The woman advanced on him, the magical light in her hand intensifying as she stepped closer toward him.

And she was so fucking *strong*. She stood at least a hundred feet away from me, but I could still sense the sharp, static crackle of her power even here in the car. The feel of her elemental magic made the spider rune scars on my palms itch and burn the way they always did whenever I was exposed to so much power, to so much raw magic. And she had plenty to spare.

A second later, the dwarf caught fire. He wobbled back and forth before pitching to the cracked pavement, but the woman didn't stop her magical assault. She stood over his body, sending wave after wave of lightning into his figure, even as the green elemental flames of her power consumed his skin, hair, clothes.

When she was done, the woman curled her hand into a tight fist. The bright lightning flickered, then sparked away into nothingness, like a flare that had been snuffed out. Greenish gray smoke wafted up from her fingertips, and she blew it away into the frosty night air, like an Old West gunfighter cooling down his Colt after some sort of shootout. How dramatic.

"Did you see that?" Finn whispered, his coffee now forgotten, his green eyes wide and round in his face. "She *electrocuted* him."

"Yeah. I saw."

I didn't add that she'd used elemental magic to do it. Finn had seen that for himself as well as I had.

Elementals were people who could create, control, and manipulate one of the four elements—Air, Fire, Ice, and Stone. Those were the areas that most folks were gifted in, the ones that you had to be able to tap into to be considered a true elemental. But magic had many forms, many quirks, and there were some people who could use other areas, offshoots of one of the four elements. Like metal was an offshoot of Stone—and electricity was one of Air.

One that Finn and I had just seen used to deadly efficiency, thanks to our mystery woman.

I was an elemental too. In my case, I had the rare ability of being able to control two elements—Stone and Ice. But I'd never seen someone with electrical power before. And now I wasn't so sure it was a good thing that I had.

The woman stuck the toe of her boot into the man's ribs. A large hunk of his body disintegrated into gray ash at her touch and puffed up like some kind of cold, macabre fog. A sliver of a smile lifted her lips at the sight. Then she reached inside her coat, drew out something white, and tossed it down on his body before heading toward the van and sliding inside.

Thirty seconds later, the woman drove the van down the street, turned the corner, and disappeared from view. But instead of watching the vehicle, I stared at the burned-out body that she'd left behind, wondering what that bit of white was on the dwarf's still-smoking chest.

"You want me to follow her?" Finn asked, his hand hovering over the keys in the ignition.

I shook my head. "No. Stay here and keep an eye out."

I got out of the car and made my way across the street, slithering from shadow to shadow, a silverstone knife in either hand. After about five minutes of careful creeping and lots of pauses to look and listen, I reached the edge of the building closest to the dwarf. I crouched there in the black shadows, out of sight, until I was sure that the mystery woman wasn't going to circle back around the block and see if anyone had come to inspect her shocking handiwork. Then I drew in a breath, stood up, and walked over to the dead dwarf.

Even now, ten minutes after the initial attack, smoke still curled up from his body, like elegant, green-gray ribbons wafting all the way up to the black sky. I breathed in through my mouth, but the stench of charred flesh still filled my nose. The familiar acrid scent triggered all sorts of emotions that were better left dead and buried deep inside me. But they bubbled to the surface, whether I wanted them to or not.

For a moment I was thirteen again, weeping, wailing, and staring down at the ashy, flaky ruined *thing* that had been my mother, Eira, before Mab Monroe had used her elemental Fire to burn her to death, and at the matching husk that had been my older sister, Annabella. Trying not to vomit as I realized the cruel thing that had been done to them. That was going to be done to Bria and me before the night was through. Sweet little Bria—

I ruthlessly shook away the memory. My hands had curled into fists so tight that I could feel the hilts of my silverstone knives digging into the spider rune scars on my palms. I forced myself to relax my grip, then bent down on my knees so I could get a better look at the white blob resting on the dwarf's back.

To my surprise, it was a single white orchid, exquisite, elegant, its petals soft in the dark.

My eyes narrowed, and I regarded the blossom with a thoughtful expression. I knew what the flower meant and exactly who had left it behind to be found. It was her calling card, her name, rank, and trademark, just like my spider rune was. Something that she'd put here to announce her presence, mark her kill, and serve as a warning to anyone who dared to get in her way.

She was taunting me, just as I'd been doing to Mab Monroe these last two weeks.

"LaFleur," I muttered, saying her name out loud.

Because the simple fact was that an assassin had come to Ashland—one who was here to kill me.

Desire is stronger after dark...
Bestselling Urban Fantasy from Pocket Books!

Bad to the Bone
JERI SMITH-READY
Rock 'n' Roll will never die. Just like vampires.

Master of None
SONYA BATEMAN
Nobody ever dreamed of a genie like this...

Spider's Bite
An Elemental Assassin Book
JENNIFER ESTEP.
Her love life is killer.

Necking
CHRIS SALVATORE
Dating a Vampire is going to be the death of her.